# Frail

# JOAN FRANCES TURNER

**BERKLEY UK**
**PENGUIN**

## PENGUIN BOOKS

Published by the Penguin Group
Penguin Books Ltd, 80 Strand, London WC2R ORL, England
Penguin Group (USA) Inc., 375 Hudson Street, New York, New York 10014, USA
Penguin Group (Canada), 90 Eglinton Avenue East, Suite 700, Toronto, Ontario, Canada M4P 2Y3
(a division of Pearson Penguin Canada Inc.)
Penguin Ireland, 25 St Stephen's Green, Dublin 2, Ireland
(a division of Penguin Books Ltd)
Penguin Group (Australia), 707 Collins Street, Melbourne, Victoria 3008, Australia
(a division of Pearson Australia Group Pty Ltd)
Penguin Books India Pvt Ltd, 11 Community Centre,
Panchsheel Park, New Delhi – 110 017, India
Penguin Group (NZ), 67 Apollo Drive, Rosedale, Auckland 0632, New Zealand
(a division of Pearson New Zealand Ltd)
Penguin Books (South Africa) (Pty) Ltd, Block D, Rosebank Office Park, 181 Jan Smuts Avenue,
Parktown North, Gauteng 2193, South Africa

Penguin Books Ltd, Registered Offices: 80 Strand, London WC2R ORL, England

www.penguin.com

First published in the United States of America by The Berkley Publishing Group 2011
Published in Great Britain by Berkley UK 2012
001

Copyright © Hillary Hall, 2012

Map by Claudia Carlson

The moral right of the author has been asserted

Printed in Great Britain by Clays Ltd, St Ives plc

ISBN: 978-0-718-19296-9

www.greenpenguin.co.uk

MIX
Paper from
responsible sources
FSC™ C018179
www.fsc.org

Penguin Books is committed to a sustainable
future for our business, our readers and our planet.
This book is made from Forest Stewardship
Council™ certified paper.

ALWAYS LEARNING                    **PEARSON**

# ACKNOWLEDGMENTS

Once again the greatest thanks to my agent, Michelle Brower, and my editor, Michelle Vega, for their unflagging work on my behalf, and to everyone at The Berkley Publishing Group and Folio Literary Management. To Kenneth V. Iserson, whose *Death to Dust: What Happens to Dead Bodies?* was an invaluable research resource for both *Frail* and its predecessor. To staff and volunteers at the Indiana Dunes National Lakeshore, with thanks for letting me overrun Lake Street Beach, Marquette Park Beach and Kemil Beach with imaginary corpses of all kinds. To Ann Larimer, Betsy Hanes Perry, Liz Barr, Eoghann Renfroe, Merri-Todd Webster and Minette Joseph for their friendship, moral support and reality checks administered whenever necessary. And as always, to my family for always believing in me.

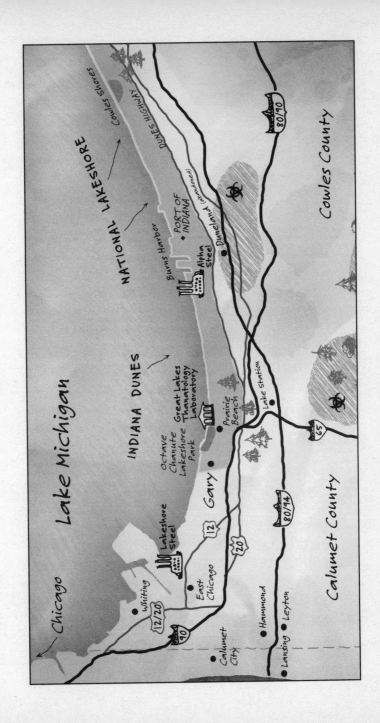

# BOOK ONE

# THE EX

# ONE

When I was fourteen there was a security breach near the intersection of Seventy-Third and Klein and my mother killed her first intruder, and her last. She was on the six-to-three shift and I had guitar lessons a four-toll drive away in Leyton and she was supposed to pick me up straight from school, so we could hit U.S. 30 before the evening checkpoints started. But she didn't show, wasn't answering her cell, so I just sat there in the cafeteria, waiting, inhaling traces of stale crinkle-fry grease and watching the sky fade from drab blue to deep gray. Dave, one of the janitors, was mopping the floor like he wanted to slap its imaginary face and Ms. Acosta slipped and skidded in the wet and almost fell. I was glad to see it after all her clucking to my mother about slacking off and bad attitudes and "twoooo-antsy" (that's how she pronounced it, all bird-whistle fluttery like a comedienne in some old movie). She saw my lips twitching and glared at me, got what my mother called a cough-syrup smile right back, and I was reaching for my phone again when the warning siren kicked to life.

Louder and louder, that singular cadence distinguishing it from tornado and fire alarms: *aieeeow-oooo, woooo-owwwww,* low and moaning like an animal in pain. A very particular animal, creature, inhuman thing, that one-note wail all it had left for a voice. Onomatopoeia, we'd just learned that in English: natural sound encapsulated into speech, like a captured insect buzzing in a new-made bottle. *Onomatopoeia, onomatopoeia,* the word kept winding and tongue-twisting through my head. Remain in your seats. This is only a test.

"Damn," Ms. Acosta said, going pale under her orangey streaks of foundation.

"They're just testing it!" Dave shouted over the noise, supremely bored, nails raking at an angry pink splotch on the side of his neck. "The sun hasn't even set, those things are barely awake—"

The intercom snapped on. *"Code Orange alert,"* said a woman's voice, prerecorded, urgent but serene. *"Code Orange, located at—Klein—and—Seventy-Third—"*

"Halfway across town." Dave shrugged, and kept squeezing out his mop.

*"Please lock all doors and windows and seek basement shelter until the all-clear sounds. If you are outside please seek the nearest safe house or other accessible building. It is a federal crime to deny shelter to any person seeking refuge from an environmental disturbance. Code Orange. Code Orange . . ."*

"Just what I need. Haul it, Amy." Ms. Acosta swept my backpack off the table, grabbed it like it'd burden me too much to run from the crippled hordes. "Dave? Move it! Let's go!"

"They're halfway across town," I said, and folded my arms. No wonder I couldn't reach my mom, there hadn't been a Code Orange in years and never with her on shift. If I could somehow get over there I could watch her toast their asses, maybe flick one with my own lighter if it tried to run away—

"Amy, I swear to God I'm not in the mood—Dave? Dave! Put that mop down and let's go!"

Dave just snorted. "Jesus Christ, Alicia, calm down. They move about two miles an hour and they ain't gonna roller-skate over here—"

"Fine!" She flapped her bony bangled arms at an imaginary audience, the only one that'd applaud her dramatics. "Fine! I'm not your mother, you get a leg torn off like Cris Antczyk did don't bother hopping over to me for sympathy—*Amy!*" The siren kept sounding, Dave nonchalantly fussing with his dirty yellow plastic bucket and CUIDADO: PISO MOJADO sign. "Get up. Follow me. *Now.*"

I got up. Shoved my hands in my pockets, feeling with fingertips for my school ID, town ID, curfew card, access gate e-pass. Followed her a few steps, sizing up her scuffed beige pumps with the one loose wobbly heel, my black flats. Then I ran, sailing over the damp linoleum, Ms. Acosta stumbling and screaming, "Amy, *goddammit!*" and Dave shaking his head laughing but I was already down the hall, out the steel double doors, the approaching sunset tinting Sycamore Street in a lurid orange wash and the sirens making the air tremble and throb.

My chest was a hot hollow husk but I was laughing as I ran, nobody can catch me, everyone else was basement-bound but I was going to see an honest-to-God living dead body get exactly what it deserved. I'd never seen one in the flesh, not even by the roadside, and even on the news all you ever saw was "dramatic re-creations" and shitty movie CGI—I was gunning for the real thing and to see my mother do the deed. She'd get a raise, a promotion, if she faced it down. She could do it without puking or fainting, not like so many of the men. All their big talk. I was proud of her, still one of the only women on the security squads, and this wasn't just to gawk and rubberneck. It wasn't just for me. After everything that happened you have to understand, I'm not lying, this wasn't all just about—

I'm getting ahead of myself. Sorry. You start to ramble, blither, when there's nothing left to talk to but the air. Ms. Acosta, she'd tell you all about that, if she were still alive.

The little white stucco house on the corner of Sycamore and Cypress had gone creamy pink, quivering like a slab as the sun-light went rich and deep; I tunneled through their lilacs and kept on going. Seventy-Third's halfway across town, Dave was right, but Lepingville wasn't that big a town. As I veered off Maple-wood I could already see the police cars and fire engines and Lepingville Civic Security vans blocking the streets, great grape-like clusters of red, blue, bottle-green flashing lights. I picked through backyards and easements looking for the best vantage point and completely by accident I saw her, framed perfectly by the gnarled, curving tree branches around me: my mother, an ambulatory burnt marshmallow in thick padded charcoal-gray fatigues, coppery hair twisted up at the back of her head, wad-dling down Seventy-Third calm as you please as she fitted an-other cartridge to her flamethrower.

Everybody in town joked about intruders but they were still scared shitless. My mother, though, she'd grown up over in Gary with no alarms, no fencing unless you put it up yourself, nothing but a half-defunct PA system, your basement and you. Anything could happen, any time, and you had to keep cool or you'd go crazy. I wanted to be cool, *sanguine*, just like her. I wanted her to get that piece of walking ant bait, the raise, the promotion, she got so much shit from the men she worked with and she deserved this chance, it *wasn't* just all about me—

There it was. All alone, standing there in front of the torn shrubbery and rusted, broken fence point it'd ripped down, arms dangling and limp, perfectly quiet but with its long pearl-gray teeth bared and grimacing. A bloated, brackish, muddy mess, a first-grader's art project shaped with careless palm-slaps into a too-angular skull, a smeared nubbin of a nose and horribly thin fingers; something about those fingers, the way each one was a perfect sticky twig of tacky clay not yet softened to full rot, made a horrible shiver rush up my back, my chest going hot and tight in disgust.

It was a man, had been a man, its penis swung limp and useless from its gaping trouser holes but more indecent than the sight of that ever could be was the smell. You can't imagine the smell, so strong and sharp and porridge-thick that I gagged, gasped as it rolled over me, my lungs squeezing shut under the assault: an overpowering gaseous stink that wasn't even a proper smell of death but of *life*. Nasty, fetid, wriggly life, bursting in horrible exuberance from that thing once a man, fields of mold blooming on fabric and skin, grubs and bluebottles breeding, hatching, crawling from the crevices around eyes, nose, crotch, armpit, elbow crooks, eating and being eaten from the inside out—the police and firemen heaved and retched but not my mother, she didn't even flinch, just pulled on her breath-mask and stood her ground. Kill it, Mom, for God's sake kill that *smell*. All the rest of them just watching. Like me.

They stood aside, the other security guys, they left her to it all alone: The bitch thinks she can handle it? Yeah, we'll just see about that. Cowards. She walked right up to it, there in the middle of the street. The cops raised their guns. Bullets wouldn't kill an intruder, but wounding it might buy some time. My mother took her time. Why shouldn't she? It couldn't run, it could barely walk. Its kind relied on ambush and paralyzing panic.

I stuck a jacket fold to my nose and crept nearer, keeping to the trees. I never even considered how trees, bushes, dark shadowy overgrowths where they could lie in wait were their friends, how I'd never smell others coming over this one's reek. *Sanguine.* That word sounds a lot better than *reckless.*

It made a sound, looking at my mother, and the noise it made sent a strange, prickly disquiet through me because it wasn't like in the movies, it wasn't the right sound. It was a low, full moan that bore an edge of surprise, a living human's dismay and uncertainty turned to stretched-out toffee in that undead mouth. It kept staring at my mother, wide gaping eyes from the collapsed ruin of a face and make it stop, Mom, tell it to knock that off; it's not hungry, I can tell it's not. It's like it thinks it knows you, somehow, from somewhere.

The stench was so awful my throat closed up; I was making little *huhh, huhhh* heaving sounds I couldn't stifle, warm acidy puddles pooling in my mouth. Kill it, Mom. Make it stop.

She took off her mask. The cops, the security squadron muttered in confusion but nobody tried to stop her, they weren't taking a single step closer than they had to. The thing moaned again, an oh-shit, what-now, what-do-I-do noise and some of the squadron snickered. My mother wasn't laughing. Her eyes looked like that thing's voice sounded.

"Get out," she said, her voice shaking. If the smell was getting to her, you'd never guess it. "Go back through that fence and get out."

Why was she talking to it? They didn't understand us. They were beyond speech. She took a step forward, tugging her boot from the soft thick dirt. The thing didn't move.

"You're trespassing on human territory!" she shouted, a strange, strident agitation buoying her voice up over the squadron vans, into the trees, as she rattled off the black-book gobbledygook it couldn't possibly understand. "As a civic security official I am authorized to use all necessary levels of force to address Class A environmental disturbances by Indiana Code Section 17, paragraph 8(d)—"

It made another sound. *Oooooo,* it went. Still looking my mother up and down, like it knew something about her and had no idea what to do with what it knew, and then *oooooooosssss.* Airy, hollow whistling, trying to make sounds a rotten tongue, lips, palate wouldn't allow anymore. *Ooooosssssss.* And it took a step forward.

My mother didn't move. The squadron snapped to attention; you could see it on their faces, fear, and some smirking, because they thought she'd frozen up. It wasn't that, I knew it wasn't, but something was very wrong and even over the horrible stink of living death you could smell, feel, hear the wrongness all concentrated in her voice as she raised the flamethrower and screamed, "Get out! *Get out!*"

It opened its mouth again, making softer, cow-lowing cries like it wanted to wheedle her into something. Coax her. It stumbled forward, slow as they all do, holding out its arms.

I don't know what I was expecting to happen when it caught the flame. Maybe that it'd drop to the pavement and lie there like a proper corpse, a genteelly singed peaceful stinking dead body, or give a little *pop* like marshmallow char in a bonfire and collapse, instantly, into a sighing pile of shitty muddy ash. But instead it stood there with its puppet arms waving, each filthy rag of clothing a tattered fiery flag, and then its mouth opened and jaw came unhinged around a long, hard, sustained scream of agony. Not like the alarm siren, not like in the movies: It sounded human, the sound of those screams was a human being just like me or my mother or Ms. Acosta or anyone else in such awful, unimaginable pain they'd do, give, promise anything to make it stop but there was nowhere to go, no way out. It couldn't run, not like a panicked human on fire. Instead it rotated in a slow tottering circle. It sank to its knees, groaning and sobbing. And it rolled on the ground. And it bubbled, and cooked, and slowly died.

The firefighters moved in to keep the grass from igniting; didn't matter if they doused the flame, the heat would still keep working its way in, sloughing off rotten skin and bone. It was covered in sprayed-on extinguisher frost now, a grotesque Christmas window mannequin with arms curled into useless, foreshortened boxer's fists, and the screaming wouldn't stop.

The smell, as it burned. Kept burning, even without any fire. Mom. I need you to make it stop, now.

She sat down hard on the grass, watching it writhe and sob and burn, and someone grabbed her and dragged her to the vans. It was crying now, full-throated sobs of pain as its bones disintegrated, skin falling off in thick charred pieces like slivers of briquettes from a barbecue. The same sort of dirty gray ash. They'd surrounded my mother now, going Good job, Lucy, you *did* it, you fucking toasted it, just listen to it wail, and I ran from my hiding place because I couldn't stand it anymore. It *had* to stop crying, she had to make all this stop happening and go away, tell me it wasn't really a person and everything would be—and that's when she saw me, and shoved them all aside to get to me.

"What are you doing here!" she shouted, pulling me out of the path, away from the sobbing howling skeleton lying in its own ash. "You're at school, you're in the *shelter*! Why aren't you—goddammit, can't you stay out of trouble longer than five minutes at a time, why are you here! What the hell are you doing here!"

I didn't have any answer and my mother grabbed my arms in a pincer grip and shook me, yelling things I couldn't hear, and Ms. Acosta was suddenly right there puffing and panting in white sneakers like nurse's shoes, and my mother screamed at her to mind her own goddamned business for once in her life, and I wrenched free and ran fast as I could from the smell, the shouting, the cries of pain that just kept growing louder. It all got lower and fainter, faded out entirely around Hollister, and I sat there on the sidewalk like my mother had on the grass, letting my nose and ears fill up with the clean airy quiet. A good hour, maybe more. The color faded and retreated from the sky, everything bathed in the soft formless dark.

I went home and threw up and then sat in the basement, on the cots we had set up in case of tornadoes or what had just happened, and that's where my mother found me. Staggering tired, she looked drained dry, a dried streak of something like blood except sticky and ashen smearing her cheek. She didn't yell at me, we had the leftover baked beans for dinner and went straight to sleep. The next morning and all afternoon she just lay there, quiet, staring at the wall next to her bed. And the day after that. And the day after that.

My aunt Kate said later my mother hadn't been right in the head since my father died, that even before that she'd been strange. Off. A lot of people said that, about my mother. But I knew her, and they didn't, and all I'll say is that after that evening something inside her seemed to bend and twist like that thing's rotten twiggy fingers, tearing in two without making a sound. She never cried. She wasn't the type. She never talked to anyone. She could take care of herself. She went to work. She came home. She asked me about school, how anyone smart as I was (ha) could be barely passing history, asked me about my music, cooked the pancake dinner we ate every Friday she was off-shift. No more lying around in bed. There was no time, and she liked to keep busy.

And then one winter morning a year later, when I was fifteen, I woke up and she was gone. No note.

She used to go out sometimes at night, long after dark, when she thought I was asleep; all she'd ever say was she was taking a walk. Walking for hours, sometimes not coming home until dawn. That was so reckless I got scared, even knowing I couldn't stop her, that her job meant she knew "stranger"-danger better than I ever would, that like everyone else she never went anywhere without her lighter. I'd lie there half-awake, drifting, as the sky lit from iron to pearl, and sometimes I'd fall back into thick heavy sleep and when I woke she'd be lying beside me on the bed, fully dressed, snoring. We never talked about it. Always, no matter what, she came back.

They found her LCS jacket, folded neatly at the edge of a forest preserve a half-mile outside the town gates, her badge and ID in one pocket. The jacket's too big, but it's warm. I like to imagine it's what got me through this past winter.

If you're going to get anywhere in life—this is how I see it—

it's important to always show the truth of things, even when it doesn't make you look good. Even when it makes you angry. You have to be honest, no matter what, or it all just goes to shit. So the truth is that she's not forgiven, my mother, for what she did. I have the power of forgiveness in me and it's the only power I have left; I wave it inside my head like a July sparkler, letting the little line of fiery floating light it traces in the dark mark out the saved, the damned, those forever left behind. She's not forgiven. My father isn't forgiven, for disappearing while coming home from the mill when I was five. Ms. Acosta isn't forgiven, for . . . I'd thought we finally understood each other, when there was nothing else left. But we didn't. That dead thing isn't forgiven, ever, for spreading its filthy contagion of crying, pain, despair—

No, I change my mind. I forgive it because it hurt so much. Only for that. Just like I have to forgive my uncle and aunt, for getting so sick. The way everyone got so sick, the way everyone died—human, zombie, everyone. Everywhere. Except me. I'm one of the only ones left.

Last spring, a year after my mother disappeared, it started. A plague. A famine. Everyone around me got sick, a disease nobody had heard of, no doctor could diagnose. It made people hungry—no. It made them ravenous, insane with hunger and the more they ate, the more the disease ate at them, turning them to great gobbling mouths crammed with meat, drink, garbage, soap, grass, paper, tree bark, dirt, insects, vermin, antifreeze, glue, face cream, Styrofoam, gammon, spinach, anything, anything they could chew or swallow. They attacked and killed their pets, children, each other. For food. Everything they'd ever feared the intruders, the real flesh-eaters, might do to us—

But the undead too. Even them. They got sick too.

But not me. I don't know why. I hid and kept hiding until the sickness burned itself out, hit a peak and a slope and finally the living, the undead, every eating thing couldn't eat anymore, didn't want to. After all that, they starved to death. The disease binged on them, gorged itself sick, and then it purged. And they all died.

No. Not *everyone*.

Some who got this sickness—living, undead, didn't seem to matter—they survived the ceaseless hunger, the self-starvation afterward, and became something else. They look human, some of them used to be, but they're not. Not anymore. As strong as zombies ever were, even stronger, but they don't rot, they don't decay and no matter if you stab, shoot, starve, freeze them, drown them, smother them, torch them with fire, they can't die. They heal right before your eyes, and it's the last thing you see before they kill you. Fast-moving, fast-talking, fast-thinking as humans. Strong as zombies. And no matter what, they can never, ever die. The intruders are dead, but they've left a new generation behind. So many of them. So few of us.

There were only four of us in Lepingville who stayed human, who never got sick, and I'm the only one who got through last winter. And it was a mild winter, this year.

I don't know what I'm going to do. I've got no idea what I'm supposed to do now, and there's nobody to tell me. One foot in front of the other, my mother always said. Step forward, keep going even as your feet sink into the soft lawn mire all around you, the *shuuuck* of your shoe yanked from a pocket of mud making you flinch like a starter pistol just went off by your ear. Keep going. Somewhere. You'll figure it out. You've got no choice.

I think somehow, from all her years working cheek by jowl with death, my mother sensed this was coming, the way animals sniff out impending earthquakes and flee. She was going to take me with her, but it was too dangerous and she knew someone would take me in, they have to because it's a felony otherwise, and once the sickness ceased she'd find me and we'd figure out, together, what to do next. I couldn't die, we had to find each other. I didn't kill myself. I didn't starve. I didn't freeze or get sick or butchered for my flesh, I didn't ever mean to do what I—*I stayed here.* I have a right to be proud of that. I stayed.

That's what they tell you, when you're little. Right? If you're lost, stay right where you are. Somebody will find you. It's inevitable. Someone. Somewhere.

I'm still waiting.

# TWO

Five days, since I left Lepingville. I counted. Six. Maybe seven. Everything was all blurred, that first day or two, like a drawing half-wiped from a chalkboard; my ears buzzed softly and I couldn't quite see straight, didn't really register where I was going. I stopped sometimes, sat down, pushed sticks of jerky or handfuls of nuts down my throat, pissed in ditches, found an empty tollbooth on U.S. 30 and slept in there dreamlessly with my weight against the door. I remembered to bring food. Water. Searched for more. I lost half a day sleeping in that tollbooth so split the difference, call it six.

I can't afford to sleep half the day. I chart and graph all my time now, so much walking, resting, walking, picking through abandoned homes and broken tollbooths and cleared-out underground shelters, eyes before me for thieves and rapists, ears behind me for any soft-footed thing hunting fresh meat, always locating my exits *first*. I have to plan where I'll sleep every night, somewhere small enough to defend or big enough to hide in. Exits first. I never checked like this, before.

There's never anyone. Maybe there's nobody else left.

Movie theaters are good. Sleeping in theaters settles me down for some reason, soft torn-up seats, carpet and concrete flooring lousy with streaks of grease and blood, dried pop puddles, ground-in popcorn kernels, rodent droppings. Signs of life. If everyone else hadn't got to the concessions stand before me and smashed it to get to the popcorn, the glugs of fluorescent buttery grease and nacho cheese, every last Skittle in the candy display, I might've just stayed in that Cineplex out near Morewood. Forever.

I was actually doing okay, sort of, before yesterday. That's the thing.

Warmer now. Good. It felt like it must be March, late March, the wind still slapped me full in the face but its knife-edge was going blunt. Days longer. Snow piles reduced to limp Styrofoam shavings. Relative barometric pressure and humidity of—I could figure out what month it was, counting back to September using Kristin's pregnancy, except I think the baby came early anyway. All of a sudden, she was in labor. No warning.

Every night, before I sleep, I take inventory, the few things I brought with me that I really don't want to lose. My sewing kit, not those useless store miniatures but my own bag with needles, *big* thread spools, scissors. Sunglasses. Aspirin. Hunting knife. Lighters, a whole collection: metal, plastic, monogrammed, filigreed, engraved, embossed, painted with pinup girls and cartoon characters and company logos and skulls and rainbows and pot plants and flowers. Kristin's, this one, purple with forsythia sprays. She gave it to me before she died. Mine had a picture on it, a girl playing guitar with long red hair streaming over the strings. I lost it last fall when they broke into our house, all the sick folks looking for food. Sewing kit. Already mentioned that. I forgot.

Pocket atlas. This one has all my scribbled notes, places Dave went hunting and said later to avoid, landmarks to look out for. My cell phone. My last birthday present ever, from my mother, before she left. Defunct, of course, but they weren't getting it, not after they got my lighter. I keep it in my front jeans pocket with her old LCS ID, her driver's license, security clearance card, everything with her name and photograph. A record she really was here.

I think I'm going crazy. Taking inventory, reminding myself where I've been and what I have, it doesn't help because last night I saw something that wasn't really there. I was on Caldwell Road, that long stretch snaking through the industrial park outside Briceland, and I stopped to rest, squeezing my eyes shut against the fading afternoon sun; I opened them again, and I saw staring back at me a pair of disembodied eyes. Rheumy, sickly yellow pinpoints, smudged and faded like gaslights coated in soap, gazing steadily from the air, the sky, from nowhere. Dog's eyes.

I slid to my feet, ready to run, but there was no dog there. Except there was. There in the air, a ghost, a chimera. I turned my back on it and the eyes were there again, following me past the little steel mill, the auto body shop, over the harmonica-cluster of railroad tracks. Afternoon became evening and when I lay down in the remains of an antique shop the deep gray night took shape around the eyes floating in it, scrabbling into outlines of a single cocked ear, a thick solid neck, a ridge of hair bristle-straight all down a phantom spine. Hard, sharp teeth, bared against me. Swift strong legs, ready to spring.

There aren't as many stray dogs out there as you'd think: They were some of the first casualties, when everyone was going hungry. I'm not afraid. I can't walk around afraid of everything. But this was different. It was like how when I was young I was afraid to look in the bathroom mirror at night, scared the face staring back wouldn't be mine at all but something distorted, grinning, a melting predatory mouth about to swallow up the room's darkness, and me. I turned my head to the shop wall, I closed my eyes and halfway toward sleep I *felt* it, there beneath my hand, the fleeting sensation of hunched-up muscle beneath rough, ungroomed fur. It's not guarding me. It's not guarding anything. It's lying in wait, so I can't get away.

It's not there. I *know* it's not. And I thought it'd go away, I thought my brain was just worn out and inventing its own cheap thrills, but today those eyes are still watching, waiting, melting right into the sunlight, magnifying to make a Panopticon of the air. Judging. Waiting. There's nowhere for me to go where they're not.

Then I blink, and shake my head, and they vanish.

Somebody needs to tell me I'm not crazy. But it's like I said, there's nobody left.

Taking inventory, that's not helping. Or looking at my mother's badges and cards. The only thing distracting me from that damned dog is my tribunals, when I think hard on everyone dead or lost and organize their fates as I see fit. I need to keep my mind occupied, and if I can pretend sorting out the whole endless mess of living and dying is my job, I feel calmer and I can sleep. So court's always in session, day and night.

This is what I remember, the evidence the tribunal considers:

My uncle John, at my aunt's funeral. Kate died in less than a week, breathing in guttural gasps until her throat swelled permanently shut, and at the reception John stood hunched over the funeral buffet, glassy-eyed, bloated with illness, and ate so fast that the egg salad oozed from one side of his mouth even as the teeth on the other side tore at chunks of ham. Stares of shock. Then others, fingers twitching, shoved the gapers aside to get at more ham, potato salad, handfuls of tortellini dripping sauce scooped straight from the steam tray into waiting, scalded palms.

Jenny Waldman from my English class, sitting at her desk blue-tinged and shivering, unable to keep her hands from the full grocery bag of lunch at her feet. Drippings of peanut butter smearing her copy of *The Sound and the Fury*. Cheese slices piled in teetering, gelatinous wedges on a half-loaf's worth of bread. She gorged and shivered right in front of us and nobody knew what to do and then, still chewing, she started to cry, got sick everywhere. When Mr. Lowry dragged her to the nurse three other kids fought over the vomit-smeared bag, cramming what they could get in their mouths and then rocking back and forth, trembling, hands clutched into greasy fists.

Grocery store riots. An ashen-faced man lying in a pile of shattered display glass, blood welling up from beneath him like rainwater permeating a basement. The sick with puffy, softened skin and loosening nails sitting in the aisles, emptying cereal boxes and diving into the sugary sawdust piles, wrenching out teeth trying to gnaw frozen meat. We the supposed healthy ones shoving, pushing, screaming for a spare can of green beans, a crushed coffee cake, anything, anything at all. One of them grabbed me and I kicked him in the head so hard something crunched and gave way, I didn't look down, I was hungry too. There was something dried on my shoe, I saw later, blood and something else. He was dying anyway. It's not my fault.

The woman in the street, gnawing on something charred in the shape of a hand. Cats, dogs, anything small and snareable, disappearing. That last day, just before I left for good, when I—

Enough. Tonight's verdict: innocent, forgiven, all of you. No matter what. You were sick, and hungry. Innocent. Except the pet killers, you can go to hell. Now let *me* go to sleep. I need to sleep.

I'll reach Leyton tomorrow. A rich town, a lucky town, they got the plague early and died quick. The shelters will have food. That'll distract me. You see things when you're hungry. Everything will be better, in Leyton.

My first bona fide first-stage town! Let's have a party. Most folks here died in the initial phases like my aunt, suffocating in a bruising diphtheria before the monstrous hunger hit them and emptied every last shelf of food. The beautiful turn-of-last-century brick homes were hardly touched, only a few gas-explosion craters here and there, and all those pretty parks, and a *forest* smack in the center of town. Vanderhoek Woods. A tiny Franciscan monastery right next door, signs advertising TRIDENTINE and POLISH MASSES. Pilgrims welcomed. Fancy. I wonder if they got into fights with the Ukrainian Catholic Church across the street, like rival high schools at homecoming. There were still infirmary cots set up in both of them, long rows. The smell hit you coming and going.

Lepingville, we were second-stage. Very secondary.

The things that took the zombies' places don't like it here, they like the beach. The shoreline. Which makes sense because the shoreline was always dangerous, off limits to everyone but the thanatological scientists; Dave, he used to insist the sickness, the exes—ex-humans, ex-zombies—it all had to do with the shoreline itself, with the sands. Fairy tales, if you ask me, just like the old stories about how a meteor hitting the Great Lakes basin started waking the dead in the first place. But listening to him rant helped pass the time.

Pale, hard blue sky this morning. I'd slept in a grotto in the monastery yard and woke up sweating, and to peel off all the malodorous layers of fleece and flannel was a luxury you can't imagine; just airing out my feet, letting them soak up a warm, steady breeze, made me close my eyes with how good it felt. They stank, of course, just like every other part of me, and itched and burned incessantly between the toes but I let myself imagine sunlight really was the best disinfectant before I pulled my socks back on—turned inside out for the illusion of changing them—and grabbed for my mother's charcoal jacket. Time to get what I came for.

If she were here now, my mother, she'd be ashamed of how bad I smelled, from a yard away, like a homeless person. I *was* a homeless person. But that'd been my choice. I kept going, following the grimy yellow signs with the DESIGNATED SHELTER logo. I didn't need a home when I had safe houses.

They call them safe *houses* but they were actually built underground, like big tornado cellars; every town above a certain size had to have at least one, government-subsidized. Lots of private ones too, in a town this rich, but they were a dodgier bet: Builders cut corners and the walls cracked, seepage got in, ventilation systems didn't work right and you went to sleep feeling all cozy inhaling pure carbon monoxide. A family of six, once, over in Taltree. You'd hear stories. The manhole-cover entrance was rusty and hard to turn but that was a promising sign, other hands hadn't touched it in a good while. After an eternity of sweating and swearing I got it moving, felt the hinge creak and give way, climbed down the metal ladder, sawed my socked toes furiously back and forth against the ladder railing; scratching made it worse but sometimes I couldn't stand it.

I don't like basements. I don't like windowless spaces underground. They scare me. Making this quick. If I could find enough bottled water I'd have a sponge bath, outside.

Almost no clothing. Disappointingly thin blankets. Very little bottled water. A whole lot of vodka. Vodka and buckets of pancake mix. Whoever supply-stocked this place was insane.

Dave wouldn't like it, that I'm still foraging instead of hunting. While he was still strong enough he tried to show me how to build snares, use a rifle, field dress a carcass into meat. A new dawn, a new day. No whining. Adapt or die, Dave said.

Dave died. Diabetes. We foraged everywhere, Ms. Acosta and I, houses, safe houses, drugstores, pharmacies, hospitals but insulin doesn't work right if it's too cold, too old, and there were all these different types, fast-acting, slow-acting, we couldn't measure it right, and we had Kristin to worry about too with her pregnancy and banging her head bloody on the floor for her dead husband, her dead daughter, her missing son. So Dave lay there gasping for breath, vomiting, heart thudding beneath our hands; he slipped away with breath stinking of fruit gone bad, apples and pears soft and brown and nauseously poison-sweet. We pretended he was sleeping.

Dave Myszak, janitor. Alicia Acosta, school administrator. Kristin Wilson, medical transcriptionist. Baby Boy or Girl Wilson, not yet born. Amy Holliday, nothing. The entire surviving human population of Lepingville, Indiana. And now, just me. Be proud of me, Dave, wherever you are. I'm adapting.

Canned pears, a whole shelf full. I took the can opener. Those are like gold.

Portable lighters. Very good. More D batteries. Excellent. Bandage scissors. Band-Aids. Q-Tips. Dental floss. Tissues. Tampons. Athlete's foot powder. Aspirin. My backpack bulged, it was a supermarket sweep. I was about to strip my shoes right back off and powder my itching feet when I heard a scratching sound from the long, angular corridor connecting the safe house rooms, then rustling like something scuttling to a nest. Rodents. A stray cat, gone feral. But how could it get down here? Maybe it got trapped. Maybe it needed help.

A soft, slumping crash, like boxes full of fabric tipping over. I had Dave's old hunting knife, a big drop point blade. It'd do me no good against a gun. But then guns did no good against one of *them*. I pulled the knife out, switched off the flashlight, kept it like a bludgeon in my other hand. A cat. A disoriented rabbit, wandering the wrong warren.

A hollow *click, click* of toenails against concrete, rounding the corridor, so loud but nowhere nearby. Not a rabbit. Not a cat.

Two rheumy pinpoints suffusing the room in dim, sickly light, like a candle about to gutter. No. Not again. This isn't *fair*.

"What do you want?" I shouted. "You hungry? I don't care! Get your own fucking food!"

The nail-clicking stopped, the pinpoint lights sputtered and faded out. Then something that wasn't there growled low and ravenous straight into my ear and I threw the backpack down, scuttled up the ladder and ran.

You're not there, I thought, my too-big boots slapping the ground as I ran through someone's front yard, found the sidewalk bordering the preserve, headed counterclockwise toward the monastery. You're not there, hurts to run, acid sickness all in me, could vomit up everything since last fall but what I did eight days ago maybe nine will sit inside me like a gravel sack until I die, and afterward, through all of eternity—

The sky was a cake of blue ice, clusters of thin tree trunks cutting across its surface like skate tracks as the dog emerged not from the manhole but from the woods, big and coffee-colored and baring long yellowed teeth, running toward me. Not my phantom but a genuine, living dog gone feral, the collar and tags still jingling round its neck. I skidded to a stop, dropped my eyes. If you looked them in the face it was a challenge. It braced its paws on the sidewalk and growled low in its throat, a great walking stomach gurgling at the sight of more food.

I couldn't breathe. I don't like dogs, never did, not after that Great Dane bit me when I was five. This was a boxer, mastiff, I don't know what the hell the breeds are, something bullet-headed and muscular and huge. I took a step backward and it growled louder, drawing out victory as long as it could, and I was running again knowing it was the worst thing I could do but I couldn't stop, it flew after me in a blur of deep brown with silvery sunlight glinting on those useless tags, so much faster, I couldn't run any faster—

My boot caught on a torn-up crust of concrete and I pitched face-first onto my own skidding palms, the breath knocked out of me. It growled straight in my ear and I felt a stinking heat on my neck, my back, and I couldn't lie still for my punishment. I thrashed and screamed, torn-up hands trying to shield my eyes, my face. Teeth sliced at my jacket, my mother's jacket. My arm, searing, wrenched away, any second now it'd snap—

Feet thudded toward me and the hot murderous weight on my back suddenly lifted, a stone dragged from the mouth of a cave; I turned on my side and saw a woman, skinny, lank-haired, wrestling with the dog, rolling from the sidewalk to the dirt at the edge of the spindly inky trees. It tore at her in a frustrated frenzy and she was beneath it now, pinned and kicking as it ripped at her breast, arm, side of her face and there was blood everywhere, her blood, oozing onto the sidewalk like juice from an overripe fruit.

I was crying and grabbing for something to throw, shoe not heavy enough, hurt to hold anything in my hand—but if I did it'd run back at me and I was such a horrible coward, lying there bawling while they rolled and tussled on the fouled sidewalk. She clutched the dog in a bear hug, almost sliding along the pavement. It tore her open from shoulder to elbow, she lost her grip howling in pain, it got teeth hard and deep into her throat and I bawled harder, watching it savage her, watching her die—

But she didn't go down. Her own blood sprayed thick over her face but she closed her eyes, arched up with a great roaring burst of strength and she pinned it, her broken bleeding hands gripping sticky brown fur so hard that I waited for, dreaded the crunch of snapping bones. But she pulled away like she didn't want to hurt it, like screaming in its face to scare it was enough, and it whined and bawled in her grasp knowing it'd lost and then it was running, frantic, tail down, past the woods and the monastery and into the remains of a neighborhood that might once have been its home. Gone.

And she was still there, kneeling breathless in the thick tacky puddle of her own blood. The long gaping rips in her jacket and shirt were still there too but the awful lacerations in the flesh beneath, the arterial ground-chuck mess of her cheek and throat, it was all knitting up smooth and whole before my eyes like nothing had touched her, like she'd gone out for a walk with a song in her heart and tap-danced into a bucket of red paint. All washes out. For them. For one of *them*.

She pulled herself to her feet, ran fingers through the blood tarring her hair. I wanted to stand up to run but my hands hurt, my arm hurt, my back, my legs, I couldn't move. It's a sign of aggression, to meet someone's eyes. Asserted dominance. The ex stared straight at me, just daring me to raise my head.

"Are you all right?" she said.

They don't speak like us, the ex-zombies, or the ex-humans, whatever she is. They went from mush-mouthed moaning, palates reduced to rancid syrup, to hard glassy rat-a-tat-tat, each syllable a cap gun cartridge exploding between their teeth: *Are! YOUUU! allriiigh-TAH!* Onomatopoeia inside out, twisting English into noise; everyone would forget what humans were supposed to speak like, sound like, all conversation warped into sleet clattering on a thousand metal roofs. They're even taking away our talk. She can't have anything else. Go eat the dog, you're so fucking hungry like all your kind.

"You're hurt." She was coming at me. "Let me—"

"Stay away from me." I put my hand to my belt, reaching for my knife—and I'd lost it. My knife, Dave's knife. No good against her but now I couldn't even try to fight her, I didn't want to die, my arm hurt so much I just wanted to crawl away like that dog and wail. "Stay away."

"It's all right. Are you the only one here? My name's Lisa, I just—I won't hurt you—"

Bullshit, Lee-SSSaa-AAAHHH. "Don't you touch me."

"I won't hurt you." Hands outstretched like that meant she wasn't armed, like those fingers alone couldn't snap me to pieces. "You're bleeding, your hands are torn up, let me help you. I don't want to feed off you, I'm human, I was human before—"

"You're not now. I'm getting up, I'm leaving, if you try to stop me—"

"You're hurt. Can you stand up? Let me get a look at your arm—"

"No!" I don't want to die. It's dripping down my elbow now. I'm bleeding to death. "Go away!"

"I'm Lisa. Lisa Porter. Could you just tell me—"

"I don't give a shit what your name is! Leave me alone!"

"I'm not going to hurt you!" Her voice cracked like thin porcelain, going high with frustration. "Goddammit, I just saved your life, you could be grateful for one damned second, if I were after your ass like you think I am I could've just let that dog tear you to shreds—"

"The hell you're not! Think you look like such a good Samaritan—you'd just rather do it yourself! Fuck off, freak! Fuck off and let me—"

I bit down hard on my lip. My arm was killing me. How dirty were dog bites, were they as bad as cat or human teeth? What if it had rabies? I wouldn't know for weeks. I cradled the arm in my other hand and saw the raw mess of my palm, tiny pebble-shreds embedded. There were new shredded tears in my jacket, my mother's charcoal LCS jacket she left behind for me, bullshit it could withstand zombie jaw pressure if one starving dog could do this, I would not cry anymore in front of this bitch. The sidewalk blurred and distorted and she was squatting down beside me, tugging at her own ripped-up sleeve, putting a hand to my arm. Go on, then. Do it. Your teeth are just as sharp. She glanced behind her, down the street where the dog had run.

"Poor thing," she said. "It still had its tags. The owners must've died, or couldn't feed it, last winter—it went feral. Maybe it still thinks about them, sometimes." She let out a hollow little laugh. "Maybe sometimes it still misses its mommy."

That used to drive me up a tree, people acting like their pets were really children and going on about being "dog mommies" and little Sergeant Blueberry Muffin's poopy-poos until it made you sick, but I'd seen hurt and starving dogs since then. Crying, like kids. Cats too. They had the brains of toddlers, dogs and cats both, I read somewhere; maybe even in the fever of new-found wildness they wondered sometimes, late at night, what the hell happened, how everything they knew could be gone, why nobody who loved them was there to take them home. Maybe this one was just scared, it thought I'd hurt it and attacked first. I could've fed it. She looked so sad, that ex, like she was thinking what I was thinking, that it confused me, made me want to shout at her more. They didn't have any feelings, exes, they were just hunting and eating machines like all the zombies gone extinct.

"Stay here," she said. "Okay?"

She trudged back down the sidewalk, a pencil smudge over-powered by splashes of cobalt paint overhead, scarlet underfoot.

Disappeared into the trees, came back with a battered nylon backpack groaning at the seams. She rifled inside it frowning, muttering, then pulled out a plastic jar of handwipes, a water bottle, a clean towel, a handful of alcohol swabs in little paper packages. She tore one open neatly across the top and gave it to me, not touching me anymore with those gripping hurtful hands, those horrible undead-strong teeth.

"You have any grit stuck in your hands?" she said. "I have a tweezers."

That's something I hadn't thought to bring. I did have more swabs than I needed, though, Dave's diabetic leftovers. I cleaned my palms, gritting my teeth, nothing staying stuck in the flesh, took new swabs as she opened them, let her run a soothing stream of water over my hands when I'd finished. Made myself sit up. Nothing felt broken. She wet part of the towel, handed it over.

"Amy," I said, mopping my face. "Amy Holliday."

"How old are you?"

"Seventeen."

"My sister's fifteen. Well, was." She scraped at the blood on her boot, pulled at the sticky candy-apple latticework of her hair. "I'd been living with her and her friends, this winter, but I thought—I don't know what I thought. I left, to see what things were like outside."

"They're crap," I said. "And you're an idiot if you left a half-way decent shelter for—"

"Are you alone?"

"I was with some people. I mean, actual people, not like you." I s tretched o ut m y b itten a rm i n s low i ncrements. " They're dead now."

"Can I see your arm?"

Maybe she really wanted my jacket. It was too big on me, the hem dipped close to my knees, but she was tall like my mother and the sleeves weren't all that torn. She'd fit in my jacket. She wasn't getting my jacket.

"It's fine," I said. "Just give me more of those—"

"You've got pretty hair," she said.

That surprised me enough I didn't know what to say.

"I always wanted to be a redhead." She scrubbed her boot against the sidewalk, scuffing the leather without scrubbing off the blood. She talked when she was nervous, you could tell, though what one of her kind had to be nervous about I couldn't fathom. "Something distinctive, anyway, when I looked in the mirror—Jessie, my sister, she dyed her hair blue once, that bright robin's-egg blue. It looked great on her, actually, you wouldn't have guessed. Is your arm still bleeding? Just let me look, for God's sake, if it needs stitches you can't do that yourself."

"If it needs stitches, I'm screwed anyway—"

"Will you just *let me look at it* and then I'll go away forever! All right? Just humor me and let me think I didn't leave you to bleed to death and then I'll be out of your life forever! And good goddamned luck to you, if that dog comes back!"

You want a *pet*, because you walked out on folks and now you're lonely? Here, girl, I've got butterfly bandages and a can of Desenex! Sit, stay, *good* girl! I'd rather die. No, seriously, I really would rather die. "Are you threatening me?"

"Take it any damn way you want. I can't stop you."

A thin ribbon of blood was stiffening and drying on my jacket sleeve, like a varsity stripe. My whole arm burned. I wouldn't know if it were rabies for weeks.

"What if it's rabies?" I said.

She shook her head. "I've seen rabid dogs, along the road. This one wasn't."

We kept looking at each other. Her eyes were large and brown and sad in a sharp, thin, completely undistinguished face. Pass her on the street, never even register you'd seen her. I slid off my jacket and sweatshirt and cotton sweaters down to an old Army T-shirt, arm aching deep in every muscle, and let her roll up the T-shirt sleeve, wet the towel and run it over the wound.

"Not very deep," she said. Her voice kicked up lightly, it sounded like sincere relief. "Mostly got a mouthful of jacket cloth—let it bleed. That helps clean it out. I have a needle and thread—"

"I've got a whole sewing kit." I folded the jacket up, clutching it in my lap; it wasn't just her, I didn't like anyone else touching it. I put my hand to my jeans pocket, making sure ID cards, license, dead cell phone hadn't fallen out. She dug in her backpack again, pulled out what looked like a pair of old gardening gloves.

"For later," she said. "If your hands still hurt. They're clean on the inside."

I took them from her and stood up, the jacket tucked under my arm. "Thanks."

No answer. Wobbly on my feet, but my knee could take my weight; I rocked side to side, felt pain shoot up my back, down my arm, through my hands, I had to go get my knife and my own backpack but all I wanted to do was lie in the grass and take another nap. Couldn't do that. Especially not now.

She looked so sad, about the dog.

"There's a shelter over the ridge," I said. "I have some stuff there. More supplies than I can use."

She just kept looking at me so I nodded, feeling almost embarrassed, and limped away. A wind gust spat a clot of dead leaves over my shoes, and behind me I heard footsteps, boots squeaking with that gassy little squelch they make when the soles are starting to loosen and split off. If I turned around right now, yelled at her to leave me alone, she would. I was sure of it. She wouldn't bother me anymore.

But if I had somebody to talk to then the black dog, the ghost dog, would go away.

"So we were all living at the beach," Lisa said, as we sat in the grass near the safe house entry. "My sister, Jessie, two of her friends and me. Out by Cowles Shores, over the county line. They'd been undead, all three of them, before they got sick." She frowned. "It's not like we didn't get along, just, they didn't *understand*. They don't think like humans, even now. Jessie loved to remind me of that, that humans and undeads literally don't have the same brains at all—"

Her voice was giving me a headache, that ceaseless jackhammer of hard spitting t's and d's and popping p's hitting my ears like ball bearings on a saw blade. She couldn't help it, I could see her twisting her mouth into slow low shapes to try to soften the blow of her words, but it didn't work with that palate like hard-formed plastic, her tongue a rubber band snap-snap-snapping against it. "You're taking all the chips," I said.

"Sorry. I used to crave sour cream and onion. It's been a while." Chastened, she took one last big handful and handed over the party-sized bag, already half empty. "You have the rest."

Chips, beef jerky, honey roasted nuts, a jar of raspberry preserves. Her teeth ripping at huge chunks of dried beef looked like mine but just the smallest bit longer, a fateful bit sharper; she could tear straight through flesh and bone, reduce anything living to shreds and pieces just like an undead. A whole stick of jerky in two bites. Bits of dried potato sprayed all over her like plaster from a collapsing ceiling. I must've looked disgusted because she ducked her head, shrugged.

"I can't help eating like this now," she said. "Or talking like this. It's from the sickness. I mean, you're not hungry like—like before, thank God, but still when you see food sometimes you forget everything else. Sorry."

She shoved that handful of chips in her mouth, gulped it down with the barest hint of chewing. I still had no proof she wouldn't decide to do that to me. The sickness. Always the excuse. Dave got attacked out in the woods, while he was setting snares for rabbits, he was lucky to get away. I think that's how the trouble really started, for Dave: (In)human teeth are horribly septic, I read that somewhere, only cats' mouths are worse, and diabetics don't heal well.

"So that's why you left?" I asked, around a handful of chips. I was shoving them in too but I still felt downright dainty, hearing her crunches and lip-smacks and belchy gulps. "I don't get it. You're the *same*, you all died of the plague, you all came back—"

"We're not the same," Lisa said, an edge to her voice. "I know I'm not human anymore, believe me I know it, but I still have the mind of a living human being. The same thoughts, emotions, perceptions, personality . . . but the undeads, something happened to their minds, when they died originally and then came back—"

"Yeah, I know." I spooned up more jam. "Their minds turn to mush. Everyone knows that."

"Everyone knows shit." She sucked more salt off her fingers, wiped them on the tarp we'd brought up for a blanket. "They felt, reasoned, communicated with each other. They had a language, mostly thoughts and hands. I mean, you know, no tongues, most of them. But they remembered." Chomp. Gulp. "They knew us, when they saw us. We were the stupid ones. Who forgot them, because we couldn't deal with how they looked. Or smelled."

That thing my mother killed looking at her like it knew her, like it remembered. No way to talk to her, beg for mercy, plead to die again, the words were all stoppered up in its rotten mouth like a wad of putty it couldn't spit out, couldn't swallow. All it could do was scream.

"They didn't think like us," I said. I took the jar of nuts, sat it in my lap. "They didn't think at all."

Something like a little streak of lightning flashed through her eyes, all righteous sparking, then subsided. "So where were you from?" she asked.

"Lepingville."

"Me too." Her fingers twitched, wanting to grab the nut jar, and even as the salt burned my raw fingertips I kept eating slowly, steadily, delicately just for the pleasure of seeing her try to hold back. Go rip off a squirrel's head, if you're that hard up. "Over on Meredith Street, near the old Baptist church."

Where the rich people lived, though not half as rich as here. "We lived on Cypress. So what'd you do, before?"

"Had a lot of nervous breakdowns."

She shrugged, matter-of-fact, like it hardly mattered anymore, and of course it didn't. I put the nut jar back between us, but she didn't touch it.

"I wasn't much good at taking care of myself," she said, scratching hard at her scalp. "This has all been quite the education. I lived with my brother." She cracked open a cream soda. "He was a researcher at the big thano lab in Gary, over on the Prairie Beach side of town. Still no idea just what he did. You certainly couldn't go there to look. They'd shoot you, no joke. I wasn't supposed to know about that. Hell of a lot I was never supposed to know about. But I learned it."

A thano? No wonder they had a house on Meredith. My mother hated lab types, said they'd say absolutely anything to keep their jobs and special privileges, access to any restricted area, all those closed-off beachfronts, no curfews, no road tolls—but then she got slivers of that cake too, working security. *My hands are filthy too,* she was the first to say that. I still didn't believe zombies had any thoughts besides *food, eat, meat, kill.* They made all that up to get more research grants.

"Do you want those nuts?" Lisa asked. "If you come with me we can pack some more, if you want, they're not heavy."

"Come where?"

She pried the jar away from me, gently, kept staring at me until I looked her in the eye. Her bloody hair looked like rain-soaked cotton candy; only a pounding storm would get it clean.

"We were at Prairie Beach for a while, before," she said. "My sister and her friends, but—things didn't work out. They all wanted to leave, so I left with them. But . . . like I said. We're not like each other. They're all wrapped up in each other, they have years together Jessie and I never had—"

"You grew up with her. They don't have that."

"And she's not the person I knew. She never can be again. It's not her fault." She shrugged, laughed. "I want to see what things are like again, back at Prairie Beach. There's supposed to be a lot of us there now, there'll be others like me who remember being human, who think like—I want to see it for myself. Stop just being tolerated, put up with."

Her big dark eyes were full of something soft and pleading you wanted to poke, prod just to watch it burst and leak. Maybe that was the real problem, that this Jessie always poked and prodded right back. I lived my whole life a human amongst humans and I was only just tolerated too, me and my mother. "So what's this got to do with me?"

"There's human settlements forming. There's one right outside Gary, over in Elbertsville. They need anyone they can get, anyone young, strong, they'd take you in a second." She munched down a handful of nuts, a faint scrim of oil clinging to her fingers. "You can't wander alone forever, food deserts, wild animals, gangs of—why am I telling you what you know? Come with me as far as Elbertsville, I'll keep you company. Keep you safe."

"Why do *you* care about keeping me safe? You don't know me. You don't know where I've been."

You don't know what I've done. You and your big soft kindly eyes, your own blood smeared everywhere, powder-ground into your skin neck to knees, making stiff corrugated paper of your clothes. At least you can say that much, that it's your own. This time. At least.

"There's a little creek, a mile or so north," she said. "It'll be freezing, but we could both have a bath, slap some laundry on a rock—"

"How do I know you're telling the truth?" I tilted the jam jar and watched the little streams of raspberry juice flow from the bottom, serous bits of stained glass sliding up toward the lid. "That there's anything in Elbertsville? That I might not as well just stay here?"

"You don't. You've got no proof at all, none."

Fair enough. "And why me? You already got this far without—"

"Because I'm selfish." Her mouth curled up suddenly at the edges and there was a fleeting, self-mocking light in her eyes. It animated her whole face, made her almost attractive. "I don't do well without someone to talk to. I never have. Talking to myself doesn't work, you see, even I don't think I'm much in the way of company, and I'm heading north anyway, and you can't last here by yourself, and—Christ. You remind me a lot of my sister. Okay? You do. I mean, the way I remembered her before. Not like now." Nails sawed at her scalp, back and forth, down and back. "I *hear* there's a human settlement in Elbertsville. They need anyone young, anyone strong. If it's not so, or you don't like it, we'll turn right around—"

"And if I don't like it there, *you'll* already be long gone. In Prairie Beach." I poked my fingers through a slit in the tarp, rubbing at the short damp spring grass. "And I can't ever go there. Not with your kind."

Lisa stretched out her legs, curled her arms over her head. Sharp shoulders, pointed elbows, jutting hips, a stick-figure drawing scratched in haste by an angry hand. Not a trace on her of anything she'd eaten; it all melted away inside her, just like with the famished sick.

She folded up the empty, greasy potato chip bag, smaller and smaller in a neat little square, then changed her mind and shook it out again, dropped the empty cream soda can and jerky wrappers inside it. I took more jerky sticks from the pile she'd left on the tarp, stuffed them in my jacket pockets. She didn't stop me.

"What month is it?" I asked.

"April," she said. "April fourth. I've been keeping track. You want a bath?"

"First I want my knife."

It was on the concrete safe house floor; I must've let it go without thinking, to grab the ladder railing two-handed. Lisa went down to look for it, my leg hurt too much for the ladder, and gave it right back, then headed creekward with her soap and little detergent bottle. Of course it didn't bother her at all, me right behind her at the perfect vantage point to stab her in the back—Dave's knife wouldn't do a damned thing to her. I knew that. It was still mine. She wasn't getting it.

The wind had died down, the air thick with increasing heat. Behind me I heard a harsh heavy noise like breath and boot soles, like someone pounding at panicked speed against the asphalt, sobbing for air, finally losing all direction and staggering around and around in a bewildered, foot-thudding circle before falling down to die. There was no one behind me, nothing corporeal that could be making that noise. The trees sprouting pale lacy green rustled furiously and bent double in a sudden wind gust that I couldn't feel, that didn't touch my hair or Lisa's clothes at all, and as the boot soles faded away another soft sound filled my ears, steady and insistent. Not quite barking. But close enough.

Lisa didn't turn around for that. I knew she couldn't hear it. Barking mad. This is how it starts.

I just need someone to talk to. That's all. To keep distracting me. Then I won't be crazy anymore.

# THREE

Grocery carts crammed with junk and roads ripped to ribbons from frost heaves are an unholy combination. Less than five miles of maneuvering around the potholes, heaving onto back wheels, slamming back down on the front pair to jump the gaps, and my bitten arm felt like raffia tugged into frayed little threads. How septic were dog's teeth, anyway? We'd found antibiotic scrub but maybe it wouldn't work. Lisa kept offering to push both carts, take my backpack, but I wasn't giving my sewing kit and lighters to an ex, not for anything. She looked worn out, actually, wrestling past another pothole, the skin under each eye an uneven smeary bruise like unblended shadow, but that was her lookout; she fussed over *me*, I never made any promises. A screwdriver and flashlight flew from her cart and she swore in frustration, squatted on the curb, ran an anxious finger over the flashlight lens seeking out cracks.

"I don't know why you didn't pack that on the bottom," I said. My own cart had some of our creek-laundered clothes draped across the top, dirty again from falling damp into the road a half dozen times but at least the worst of the sweat stink was gone. "It could—"

"Break, yes! I know that!" She shook it, heard something loose rattle inside, crammed it deep inside a pile of towels in frustration. "I wasn't thinking. It happens. A lot. Just ask anyone."

She yanked her cart sideways, trying to angle it toward the curb. Creek-dampened hair stuck to her cheeks in thick ribbons, like dead leaves on a car windshield; her arms pushing the cart, her ankles in an old pair of canvas sneakers were long twisted strips of sinew, perpetually flexed and poised to burst straight from her shoes and run. I checked my pockets again, feeling for my cell phone, my mother's licenses and badges and cards, they were all there and she hadn't stolen them while I was bathing. Yet.

"Do you even need flashlights?" I jammed my cart wheels through a little jigsaw puzzle of broken asphalt. Not a pothole, it looked like someone took something sharp to the tarmac and tried cutting it up, bits of a thick-peeled fruit mired in tarry, frozen syrup. "I thought your kind could see in the dark. Like cats."

"That and X-ray vision, and we control the international banking system—no, our night vision's no better than yours. Or any human's." She dug into the pile of dingy towels again as we trudged down Van Dijk Street. "So can I fly too? Walk through doorways? Heal scrofula?"

A lot more signs of human life, this side of town. Cars abandoned in the middle of long-gone traffic. The trees fronting the Catholic school and the library missing long strips of bark, torn away by famished hands. The grocery store's parking lot glinting with so much broken glass it was a great gleaming dead river-bed, the shining shore-sands of a lake drained dry. Van Dijk was the main artery feeding into I-80/94, second-stagers from every-where might've passed through. The stripped trees looked like upended loaves of bread with fistfuls of crust torn away; I was amazed so many were still budding and alive.

Near where the grocery parking lot ended and the town se-curity gates began were skeletons, piles of them dressed in bird-torn rags, ripped parkas oozing cotton batting from dozens of little wounds. Gnawed to the bone, no more maggoty stink and mess, but right there against the fencing was a little bag of bones with a larger one cradled round it; the big one was crouched down, the little one in its winter coat and hat and mittens and knitted snowflake scarf and tiny puffy red boots tucked up un-safe in its lap. So graceful how they fell, or someone posed them that way, or the bigger bone-bag took something, fed some of it to the little boy or girl, sat them both down to die.

Something in me wanted those miniature red boots, wanted to pull them off and hold them because surely they'd still carry the last ghostly traces of clean, sweet childish sweat, the blood-warmth of fat little feet seeping into the soles and lining—something else. Think about anything else. I *wanted* those boots. Something touched my shoulder and I jumped, jerked my head away and saw a miniature CD player in Lisa's upraised hand.

"You want some music?" she asked. "Might be nice."

Trying to distract me, like another little kid. "You can eat anything," I said, pushing my cart curbside by a squat, grimy gray brick building marked HISTORIC LEYTON TOWN HALL. "Liv-ing, dead, raw, cooked, you're real genuine omnivores. That's what they say. You don't need sleep. You don't age, don't decay— I just saw you can't get hurt or die. Maybe you can grow fingers back like a starfish if they get chopped off, how would I know? Compared to us, to humans, nobody can touch you."

The front yard of Historic Leyton Town Hall had big bare patches of dry gray dirt, grass pulled out in raw clumps for waiting mouths, but there were scattered threads of green already starting to come up. That made me feel a little better. The bark was growing back, some of the flowers ripped from the garden boxes dotting the periphery. Tulips, in commemoration of the town's first European settlers being Dutch, I read that on the Historic Leyton Town Plaque in one of the Historic Leyton Town Parks. All those skeletons by the fence, they can commemorate the Indians. Another one lay beside a flower box, a dead, dried-out tulip bulb cradled egglike in its palm. Lisa stood beside me staring down at the body, her cart forgotten in the street.

"We need rest," she said. "I'll need it soon enough. I've been walking for days."

"Can't die, though. Just stay like you are forever."

"It hasn't even been a year." She tugged at another clump of hair. It was uneven, thinner in some spots, like she'd chopped bits of it off and it was regrowing in fits and starts, or like she kept ripping it out at the roots. "I don't know if we age. I don't know if we die. Just because certain things can't kill us, doesn't mean *something* won't. Jessie thinks that . . . that we'll all die in the end, one way or another—"

"You eat like you're starving. Are you?"

She angled her head, studying the tulip box skeleton up and down like she'd never seen such a singular thing before. It was wearing a thick, tweedy-looking brown coat, not all that torn up.

"That might fit you," she said. "Squeamish about taking it?"

"How the hell do you think I got these boots?"

She knelt and started undoing the scuffed brown buttons, full and curved like little dinner plates.

"Do you have sex?" I asked. "I know zombies never did." I really did want to know. But I also suddenly felt like being incredibly rude.

"The phenomenon exists, yes," Lisa said dryly. The corpse's unbuttoned coat gaped open, revealing a filthy pink blouse, the remains of a gray skirt. "I'm not sure we can get pregnant. I don't get periods anymore. Neither did Jessie, or her friend Renee, or—"

"I wish I didn't." The safe house tampons would last five, maybe six months, then I'd be back to folded-up washrags. "You'd have to be crazy to want that now. To want to risk having a baby. Absolutely crazy."

Lisa eased one skeletal arm out of the coat, going slow and careful like she might injure the dead thing inside. "My little girl had a pair of boots just like those," she said.

She slid those dirty bones from the sleeve so careful and slow. "I didn't know you had a little girl," I said. What a monument to stupidity, those words: Of course I didn't know. I hadn't been told. So she told me.

"I don't know what happened to them." She eased the skeleton's clutching hand from the tulip box, holding it in hers so its finger bones still cradled the bulb. "After Karen, my daughter, after she died. Those boots, or her pink coat I bought her for Easter, or the little busy-box toy she liked in the crib—I hate this thing where they want you to box up everything a dead person ever owned and give it away, God forbid you—" Her hands shook, her eyes were shiny-wet. "God forbid." An anaerobic stink seeped from the coat's satiny beige lining, the rotten pink blouse's armpits. "We sure learned."

Lisa was right, it would probably fit, the skeleton was small like me. No way in hell you could pay me to wear it. If her baby got a funeral, family boxing up all her clothes and toys and whisking them away, it must have been long before all this.

"One of the people I was with, she was pregnant," I told her. "She lost her baby. I mean, she had it, but she lost it. It was stillborn."

Lisa scrubbed the coat lining with a bandanna, like that could clean it. "I want those boots," she said. "Tell me I shouldn't take them. It's ridiculous."

Why shouldn't she? Plenty of room. Especially since we both knew we weren't taking the coat.

"Tell me I shouldn't," she repeated. Louder. Harder. In a way that scared me.

"They look like someone posed them that way," I said. "Like, they couldn't bury them, but that's close as they could get. You'd be desecrating a grave."

Lisa thought that over, for a moment, and nodded. I stopped holding my breath.

"She didn't starve, did she?" Lisa asked. I shook my head in confusion. "That woman you were with." She picked at the tulip box's splintering wood, pulling off robin's-egg paint in little chips.

"Not exactly. There was food, but she couldn't eat." I glanced back at our carts, making sure they were still there. "She had an infection, I think, I mean, she was bleeding when she shouldn't have been. And some of the blood smelled strange." Kristin was sweating hot near the end, feverish. That wasn't my fault. That part.

"Was it a girl or a boy?"

Even a heavy cart could take off, in a good gust of wind. It was picking up again. I walked back to the curb, making sure the wheels were tilted against sudden flight.

"The baby," Lisa kept saying. "What was it?"

I'd grabbed some books from the remains of the library; I pulled up blankets, toilet paper rolls, making sure they were still there. *The Wind in the Willows*. My mother gave me that, one Christmas. Lisa stood by the curb, watching me, scratching at her scalp.

"Were you able to bury it?"

I put the books back in the cart, tucked salted almond cans more comfortably against my old folded-up Yale sweatshirt. Uncle John got that for me, we didn't know anyone who went to Yale. That was him all over.

"The ground was still frozen," I said.

Lisa turned back to the tulip box, unhooking the skeleton's fingers like she was prising open a clam shell. She took the moldy, dirt-caked tulip bulb and perched it on the clothes in her cart's kiddy seat, like she might need to keep staring at it to make sure it was still there.

"I guess we should leave," she said. "No point putting it off."

The sun was so hard and clean it was starting to hurt. As I slipped my sunglasses back on there it was, again, the faintest outline of a black dog with watery amber eyes staring at us from the fencing, from the town hall yard, from around every corner and inside every breath. But she couldn't see it. I had no advantage in a fight so I had to keep her thinking she was the crazy one, not me, that she might need my clear sober skull when her nerves got jangly again. Don't say a word. Not when she keeps asking so many questions.

"That's a pretty paint," I said, nodding at the tulip box. "That color."

"That's what my sister's hair looked like. That time she dyed it."

She walked back to the box and I thought she might take a little peel of paint, as a reminder. But she stopped just long enough to redress the skeleton in its rotten old coat, button it back up to the neck, and we took up our carts and headed for the expressway.

It's sort of comforting, when nothing's what it used to be and never will be again, how all the dull shitty soul-killing things keep right on being dull and shitty and soul-killing right up to the end of time. Get past the bodies by the roadside, jackknifed semis stuck in ditches, cars already rusting out and I-80/94 looked exactly like it always had, cracked chunks of tarmac, sad spindly trees, wispy grasses in a thousand tints of drab. Carpets of loosestrife, which they said was choking out all the native plants, but it was a relief how its clumps of tiny purple flowers blotted out the endless eaten-up grayish brown, the bare patches of dead dry dirt.

I'd stopped seeing the dog too the minute we left town. It must've been Leyton, must've been all the death clustered all on the edge of town where I hadn't seen it. Does things to your head, makes you remember—

Tollbooths, with the old signs still on the side. DESIGNATED ABOVE-GROUND ENVIRONMENTAL SHELTER. ATTACKED? PURSUED?

CALL *999 FOR ASSISTANCE. FUNDING ROAD SAFETY. TEN CENTS A MILE TO RIDE IN STYLE. (But take the wrong exit and you're on your own, no protection for rural roads or poorer neighborhoods and private funding was a joke, my dad's mill had to strike before the company hired mill yard sentries and the zombies got him anyway—but the lettering was too big for all that to fit.) Inside one of them, a thick pair of canvas and leather work gloves that actually fit my hands, hers were way too big. Lisa looked thrilled to death.

"Keep those on," she said, as we pushed along. "Your hands look bad enough, even without the scrapes—did you have a decent pair of gloves, this winter?"

My hands had been scaly white and cracked bright pink for so long I barely noticed anymore; lotion vanished into them like a stream of water in a drain, half a bottle's worth couldn't get them smooth. "Sick folks got into my uncle's house," I said, "stole all our stuff. Tore it up trying to eat it. I didn't have much left."

"I was gone. By the time the plague really got going."

"They kicked you out?" They started doing that, folks who were still well, when the sickness spread. Sometimes just shooting anyone they thought was walking funny. You had to hide.

Lisa shook her head. The wind was sharper along the expressway and she'd taken an old wool cap from her cart, dust-matted pink and gray yarn pulled low over her forehead and ears. "I said, I was gone," she corrected me. "They wanted to kick me out, yeah, but Jim, my brother, he hid me. Then I got away."

"They found out he was hiding you?"

"I got away," she said softly. "Don't ask me from what. Or whom."

A coyote lay by the shoulder, its fur dancing and leaping with flies; Lisa stopped for a second, staring, then pushed forward. "You said you were with some people. I was all alone, until I found Jessie and her friends. I might've liked some human company—"

"They're dead," I reminded her. "All of them. So they weren't much company, were they."

"What were they like?"

She wasn't going to just shut up about it, not ever. Push and push until she heard what she wanted.

Ms. Acosta looked so different with her face scrubbed clean of that streaky orange foundation, gray hair all crowding out the "auburn" because she couldn't do a Bozo henna rinse anymore. Furzy silvery hair and clammy white skin and pale eyes, a washed-out watercolor woman, but they were big clear eyes, almost pretty; when she shut out everything else around her, dismissing the stink and mess and waste to concentrate on finding more bottled water or canned peaches or insulin or antibiotic cream, it's like they almost shone from the inside. Shining with a sort of other-ness, that everyone has in them but you never actually see: the person inside the "person." The flesh in the breath, though every-one mistakenly thinks you should say that the other way around.

"Ms. Acosta pretty much told us all what to do." I yanked my cart over another pothole. "She worked in the principal's office at my high school. Dave was one of the janitors. When I got out of my house, my uncle's house, when I got out of the basement, I couldn't think where to go so I ran to the school, they were both there—"

"Out of the basement?" Weirdly interested now, like a detective whose murder suspect just let everything slip without knowing it. "Was this when they broke into your house? What happened?"

I woke up and my uncle was standing over me with a knife.

That's what happened. Everything had disintegrated by then so there was no school, no 911 or 999, no LCS patrols, it was either wander the streets watching everyone die or stay home, hide what food was left, try to keep him away from it. I'd started keeping it under my bed, anything I could salvage; I had to eat too and there was no hope for him, none at all, I didn't starve him. The disease did that. So I closed my eyes for just a second and next thing I knew, there he was. He was sick enough by then that his grasp was weak, his fingers unnaturally pliant like toothpicks gone damp, and that plus the headboard of my bed being in the center of the wall so I could slide out the other side, that's why I lived. I was going to go out the window. Then the window broke. Other sick ones were coming in.

"Ms. Acosta told us all what to do. How to organize ourselves, how to—concentrate on stuff. She was good at that." A crashed car, an ashy gray shell with burnt bread crusts of bones in the driver's seat, sat cheek by jowl with the warped, bent guardrail in a little pool of melted glass. I'd seen a sculpture like that once, at a museum in Chicago. "Dave, the janitor at our school, he used to hunt and fish a lot, zombies never scared him so he'd go wherever he wanted. He had a woodstove in his house. They broke in there too, sick ones, but he shot a lot of them. That made it better, this winter. His woodstove."

Dave died. But before that, before his woodstove and hunting and mud-smeared fishing-line snares that saved us all, I ran to the school, that night my uncle woke me up. Dave and Ms. Acosta were already there and he almost shot me before he realized, I couldn't be sick, the sick couldn't run, and I was doubled over gasping and my feet felt like someone took a knife, Dave's big hunting knife, and stripped all the skin off the soles. When he realized what he'd almost done he came running out to me, shoved me through the school doors so hard I smacked into Ms. Acosta and we clutched each other not to fall, and there were more sick people coming out of the lilacs near the schoolyard gate. One of them staggered in a circle, fell to his hands and knees with a thud and a cry and sprays of cascading gravel, but sick as they were they'd still grab anyone they could, kill them, eat them, if you let them close. Dave stood there in the doorway, still pushing us back with one arm, huge expanse of shoulders hunching up the cloth of his shirt like a drawstring pulling shut on a sack.

"I don't wanna do this!" he shouted, at the ones approaching the yard. "I don't wanna do it! Go away!"

He'd have done them a favor, if he shot them. Dying so drawn-out, starving, screaming in pain. Dave knew that. Even then he must've suspected how drawn out it'd be for him, diabetes, no insulin. The set of his shoulders, as I stood behind him, was rigid and unyielding but the slackness of his fingers on the rifle told me he still just couldn't do it.

"I used to hate the idea of hunting," I told Lisa. "Not vegetarian or anything. Just squeamish. But he taught me how to make snares."

"How to look out for yourself," she said. Reaching out a hand to the melted-glass car, like a little kid in a museum needing to touch the smudgy haystacks. "Not just rely on his own hunting, fishing. That was smart of him."

"I was squeamish. But the first time I got a rabbit, from one of my own snares, I was really proud."

Dave stood there in the doorway, that night, and the sick people kept coming. "Don't make me do this!" he shouted.

"We're hungry," one of them shouted back, and it was nothing but truth, the only truth left for him and for all of us, but the rasping, gulping ruin of his voice gave me a revolted shiver. "We just need food, all we need is—"

"You're always hungry." Dave's fingers tightened. He didn't want to. But he would. "And you're dying. And we're not. There's not enough food in the world for you. And we're not dying—"

"Help us!" another one screamed. A woman, her face one huge, skin-sloughing bruise, nails dangling crazily loose from her fingertips and her teeth already tarnished and far too long. "You have to! You have to! Jesus Christ, help us—"

Dave fired a shot, then another, over their heads. They crawled off, sobbing, still human enough that there was hurt and loneliness in that sound along with the agony of famine. Dave grabbed us both and we were running again and when I almost fell he tossed the rifle to Ms. Acosta, grabbed me, hauled me like the light inconsequential thing I was into the school basement. There might be healthier ones on their heels, guns of their own, mouths to feed. You had to hide.

"He acted like I was his daughter," I said to Lisa. "Like it was his responsibility to look after me. He didn't have to. But he did."

When they got into Dave's house, the night before my uncle and the others came for me, they'd grabbed his daughter. Starving mouths, famished hands. He got a lot of them then, no warning shots that time, but he never got her back. His wife was already dead. I don't have anything to whine about, knowing that.

"And the one with the baby?" Lisa asked.

She wouldn't let up—fine, hear it. Hear everything, it might surprise you. "Kristin. Kristin was sick. She couldn't help much." Soft pale hair like the feathers of some helpless little bird. Dried blood on her scalp where she'd deliberately knocked it on the floor and a raw rictus of grieving, vindictive fury for a mouth, that was the beginning and end of Kristin in my mind. I slept two feet away from her for months on end, and that's honestly all I remember. "She couldn't do anything. She was useless. She knew she wouldn't live. She kept saying so, over and over. And she was right."

"She didn't kill herself, though," Lisa said softly.

"What if she did? Why would you care?" I clutched my cart harder, pain shooting up to my wrists. "She's gone. Dave's gone. My uncle's gone. He tried to kill me, there were a whole lot of sick ones with him wanting to kill me, but he died." My voice was shaky and skittering, a shopping cart hurtling down an empty road in a blast of freezing wind. "I promised Kristin over and over I'd keep her baby with me and it didn't make any difference, baby's gone, Ms. Acosta's gone, my aunt's gone, my uncle, my mother—"

"Music!"

She stuck a foot right under my cart wheels, trying to block my path, and I shoved the cart over it without thinking and she let out a shout of pain. She grabbed my cart two-handed, watched impassively as the wheels spun in place on the asphalt; when I gave up and let go she reached into her own cart, pulled out the CD player, skipped several tracks ahead and pressed play.

I blinked in surprise. I couldn't help it. "You like The Good Terrorist?"

"I guess so." She turned it up. "I never heard of them before, I just grabbed a bunch of CDs from someone's house. I like this song, though. Are they popular?"

"No." Whose house? Nobody in Lepingville would know about a band like The Good Terrorist, or care. "They're good. That's what they are."

She shut up and we stood there, listening. "One Door Closes." Track five from *Songs for Children Behind Chicken Wire*, my favorite. I practiced the chords from this one until my fingers went raw. Lisa glanced at me, quick little eye dart like she feared I might try to break her foot in earnest, then listened until the last embittered little crash of drums at the end.

"Play it again?" I asked.

She pressed the repeat button and rested the player in the folds of her torn-up jacket, down in the cart, and we got going. Nick Hawley's voice was thin and anemic against the wind, spiraling up lost into the air around us from cheap tinny speakers, but there it was, for as long as there were batteries. Things would get so much worse once the batteries ran out, the canned chili and chocolate and cool ranch chips were all eaten up, the last aspirin bottle went empty, the last bar of soap—"The Last Transit," track six. The live version could make you cry. "Over and Out." Track seven. The weakest on the album, Stefanie Scholl phoning in the bass line, but it was them and that was enough.

"I could play it from the start," Lisa said.

I nodded and she cycled back to "Screams from Somewhere Else." The cars were thinning out again, the clusters of phantom traffic jams fewer with every mile.

"So who else do you like?" she asked. "I don't know anything about music, I never did, Jessie used to make fun of me for it—"

"Dirty Little Whirlwind. Do you know them?" She shook her head. She'd probably heard their one sort-of hit, the one that became a margarine commercial, two hundred times and didn't even know it. "Tortoise D. Hare? The Medium Soft?" I'd have been amazed if she'd heard of the Medium Soft, nobody had. "Anyway. That's who I liked."

Sometimes when I was practicing my guitar or blasting The Good Terrorist or Tortoise D. or Pleasure To Serve my mother would come in and sit on my bed, just listening; it never felt intrusive or like she was trying to prove something by liking what I liked, she just plain wanted to hear it and I didn't mind sharing. Nobody at school gave a shit about real music.

"My mom didn't know anything about it either," I said. "She said once you turn thirty it's like a switch gets thrown in your brain and you don't even know where to begin? Like you're condemned to listen to whatever you liked when you were fifteen over and over again, forever? That's bullshit. It's never too late. I mean, look at Stefanie Scholl, right? She never even picked up a bass guitar until she was twenty-three."

It was actually getting hotter as the sunlight weakened; the wind had died, the air felt thick and heavy. I stripped off the gloves and blew on my sore, sweaty hands. Lisa rooted around in her cart, tossed me another tube of Neosporin. I'd slather my dog bite in it once we stopped for the night.

"Don't talk to me about your friends and family unless you really want to," she said. "It's just I haven't had human company in so long, I like hearing about them and I forget—I'm sorry." She pulled her cap off, combing fingers through her ponytail. "But I'd like it if you talked about music some more. Just, any time. Whenever you want."

I thought I'd already been pushing it, wanting to hear the whole CD. Even though she did ask. "What for?"

"It's never too late, right? Didn't you just say that? So I can learn something about it now, even if I'm thirty-four. I like this band, I learned that." She folded her hat into a puffy, furzy square, shoved it in her pocket. "And because your face, when you heard them? I think that's the first time I've seen *you* since we met. Your eyes lit up. Your whole face. I liked seeing it." She shrugged. "I told you I was selfish."

The first time she saw me. Like the first I saw her, standing there by the town hall, letting me see how badly she wanted those red boots. A fair trade.

"Nobody's ever heard of the Medium Soft," I said. "Outside Germany, anyway." I wished more than anything I could've been to Berlin, before everything happened. All those clubs. "But without them there wouldn't be any Good Terrorist. I don't see the point of talking about music, seriously, when the batteries run out on that thing then—"

"Batteries? That's seriously what you're worried about? I've got batteries to burn. The great thing is you can't eat batteries, can't even get a good bite in. Break your teeth. There'll be plenty left." She gave me a sidelong look. "Also, there's this thing called live music? They used to play it at something called 'concerts'? Last I checked, guitars don't need batteries at all."

"*Electric* guitars," I explained, all slow and patient, "need to be plugged in. That's why they call them—"

"I told you I don't know shit about music," she said, ramming the wheels right through the remains of a squirrel. "Don't get all technical on me."

I craned my neck away and pretended to contemplate the treetops, so she couldn't see me smile.

We passed clusters of houses every few miles, long-abandoned half-built subdivisions, office parks and industrial parks yawning and empty, but we wheeled straight past them in favor of an open scrubby field, a shallow bowl of gray dirt circled by a little windbreak of birches. The bark was nearly intact, no bare patches from grabbing starving hands stripping it clean, and something superstitious in me decided that augured well and I sat straight down in the dirt without waiting for Lisa to agree. I ignored the expressway signs and pulled out my road atlas instead: about ten miles from Lake Station. Decent mileage, for one day.

Decent mileage, and no more unwanted company. It'd be all right now, as long as I didn't talk too much about the wrong things. I could even risk sleeping outside, maybe. A tollbooth on a night like this would feel suffocating.

"You want me to sit up and keep watch?" Lisa asked.

"You said you've been going for days without a break. You're not gonna sleep?"

"I'll be fine. I don't need as much sleep as I did, before."

That was a lie, I could tell just by looking at the shadowy mess of her face, the way her arms shook with exhaustion as she tossed me a blanket from her cart. I folded up my LCS jacket for a pillow and rested my hurt arm on my backpack, wrapping the other one around the straps; if she tried to take it from me as I slept I'd wake up, she'd have to fight me for it. Even though we both knew how that'd go, even with my knife. She sat down beside me, arms wrapped tight around her knees. Somewhere down the road her talk had all dried up.

"It's amazing how big the sky looks," I said, "without any other lights." I was still used to a close little sky glowing like sulfur, the harsh sterile yellow of the roadside safety lamps making everything look jaundiced, but now there were no lights, almost no clouds, nothing but a deep wash of darkness with pale splatters of stars. "Just don't ask me about constellations, okay? I hated science."

No answer. She rested her cheek on a kneecap, rubbed it vigorously against the dirty cloth of her jeans.

"Karen would've been ten, yesterday." She picked at a loose thread, yanking with the fixed look of a cat stalking a moth. "April third. Way too big for those boots."

In June I'd be eighteen. My mother would've been, would be . . . thirty-eight? Thirty-nine? She had me young. We shared a birthday. I used to get such a charge out of that when I was little. Of course when you're little enough you get a charge out of managing not to piss yourself, so it hardly matters.

"I'm sorry," I said. The thing is, for a second I wasn't even sure I was sorry, who'd want their child to live through—I couldn't think that way. I knew how that went. That was the last thing I should be thinking.

"There's nothing for you to be sorry about." She pulled hard on the thread, letting it snag on her fingernails. "You didn't fuck up her leukocyte count, you didn't try to deny her insurance claim when—"

"I used to write songs sometimes too. Did I tell you that? Before?"

She shook her head. Her eyes looked dull.

"I didn't have a band or anything, I just—I had a notebook full of them. I lost it last fall, it got all torn up. Someone tried to eat it." Any sort of paper, cardboard, tissue, the sick shoved it in their mouths and goat-chewed it to shreds; I went back to my uncle's house just once, to look, but I couldn't stand to touch the wads of it littered everywhere, I was afraid I might catch the disease from their spit. "I had a lot of songs."

Don't ask me to sing them, I thought, whatever you do. Things between us were already awkward enough.

Her fingers faltered on the loose thread, the fabric starting to gape and rip. "What were they about?"

"Just stuff I was thinking about that day, or, whatever." I

rested my chin on my backpack. "Greek myths, some of them. I liked mythology." That was my favorite part of English class, freshman year. I didn't know why everyone whined about how haaaaaaard Sophocles and Euripides were to understand; it all sounded clean and sharp and like things moving forward, not just characters standing around spouting poetry, and Euripides especially never wasted a word. I'd read ten Euripides plays any day, over *Julius Caesar*. My mom found me a secondhand copy of Ovid, two dollars, with illustrations that made me wish I knew how to draw.

"I never knew much about Greek myths, either," Lisa said. "It's one of those things you know you're supposed to know at least something about, but you don't?"

"Like Shakespeare." I felt my pockets again. Cell phone, ID cards. Good. "My favorite I wrote was about Callisto."

Lisa shook her head. Nobody ever knew that one, or they confused her with Calypso. "Callisto was a beautiful nymph," I explained, "a follower of Artemis. One day, Zeus saw her wandering over the mountaintops. He raped her. Once he was done with her Artemis banished her, as punishment for no longer being a virgin." That part confused me no end, the first time I read it; I thought Artemis was meant to be a lesbian, you'd think she'd understand. "Then, because she just wasn't punished enough, Zeus's wife, Hera, turned her into a bear—but the worst part was she still had her old mind, trapped in a bear's body. She tried to beg the other gods for help, tell her family what Zeus had done to her, but she'd been robbed of speech forever. And she didn't know her own strength. I mean, she literally didn't know her own strength, in her head she was still a young girl. She fled over the mountaintops because she was terrified of the other animals, she couldn't see herself for what she was. She hid in a cave, away from everyone, crying for everything she'd lost, but all that came out was the sound of an animal that'd crawled away to die."

My mom cried when I played it for her, that song. I hoped it wasn't just because I got nervous and fucked up all the chord progressions. I stared up at the slope of the sky, the little pizza slice of the quarter moon.

"So what happened to her in your song?" Lisa asked.

"She got captured by a circus. She became a dancing bear. Then one day, right in the middle of her act, she suddenly understood that she had teeth. And claws. And enough strength to decapitate an animal trainer, with one swipe of her paw."

Something too high-pitched to be an owl called out a few times from the birch trees, lapsed back into silence. There was a faint rustling sound in the trees, the grasses, some small furry thing scuttling toward its hole. Nothing had changed, for them. Nothing at all.

"Would you mind if I closed my eyes for a while?" Lisa asked. "Just a few minutes. It's been a hell of a day."

"You're the one who kept saying you didn't need it. Not me." I clutched my backpack tighter. "Good night."

"I'm just taking a nap. Get some rest. Good night."

She stretched out on her side and in seconds was sleeping like an animal sleeps, flinching limbs and piteous snoring cries giving way to deep sighing breaths and a sort of graceful weightiness; her whole body sank straight into the blanket with the heaviness of fatigue. I'd never slept that soundly, my mother once told me, even as a toddler. It'd be her thirty-ninth birthday, in two and a half months.

What would I be doing, in two and a half months? In Elbertsville? Weeding a vegetable garden. It was too early to grow anything now, weird hot weather or not, the last frosts didn't end until after Memorial Day. Mending clothing pulled off dead people, after slapping it clean on a rock. Laying snares for rabbits. If this arm didn't get me first. If Lisa were wrong about the rabies, it'd definitely have happened by then.

I fell asleep dreaming I snared a little skeleton wearing a zipped-up parka and tiny red boots and a soft rabbit-fur hat, the rabbit ears still attached and flopping over smelling of death. *Promise me you'll take care of it,* Kristin begged me of the skeleton, pleading low and soft and desperate like she had last winter, *I know what I'm putting on your back but please promise,* and I did, because I had no choice, because otherwise the circus bears would break loose and kill us all. But the thing is, their cage doors were all open already, someone unlatched them while we weren't looking. I tried to tell Kristin that, in the dream, but she just wouldn't listen.

I told Ms. Acosta too. In the dream. She laughed, and said she'd unlatched them herself. As a joke. *Run, Amy,* she said. *Run very fast.*

# FOUR

The next day was even hotter, a little bit of July in April; the air felt liquid and huge shaving-foam banks of clouds drifted slowly through the sky, growing taller as they wandered, with trailing underbellies like columns of dark blue smoke. That was something neither of us had, a raincoat or umbrella. I let her pick the music, some eighties New Wave compilation—those synth keyboards were twice as grating as her laughter, but I owed her. I'd slipped the Good Terrorist CD into a zipped jacket pocket, that and a Victims of the Dance CD still sealed in plastic. Souvenirs of old times until all the batteries ran out.

"I don't like that sky at all," Lisa said. I could see the clouds changing too, the white candy tufts dissolving into a sticky mass of dark sugary gray rolling over the sun. "It'll soak everything in the carts."

"What about the tarp?" I asked, knotting my jacket sleeves

tighter around my waist. Lisa had an extra pair of sneakers that as good as fit me, and I'd sprayed so much athlete's foot powder inside my socks that every step was cool and squishy like I was walking in fresh mud. It still hurt like hell to grip the cart handle, but the sweat bath from those gloves was worse. "If we move the paper stuff into one cart, and cover it—"

"Let's pull over here. You look ready to drop anyway."

In a sickly patch of field, a WARNING! KNOWN ENVIRONMENTAL HAZARDS, ENTER AT YOUR OWN RISK! sign still sticking out of the ground, we pulled all the Kleenex and toilet paper and Triscuit boxes and winter coats from one cart, stuffed all the canned goods and anything that could take a soaking rain into another, threw the tarp over the first cart and tucked in the edges and sat down on the grass, me shoving cold canned ravioli in my mouth as hard and fast as Lisa. Midmorning, maybe ten or eleven o'clock; another thing neither of us had was a watch. The sky had gone the color of slate, the backlit clouds thicker and darker every passing minute.

"The tarp's not long enough," Lisa said, as she demolished a snack cake. Stale flaked coconut stuck like dandruff to her jacket, her sweater. "The rain'll get in the sides, but it's better than nothing. Whatever's left is yours, when we get to Elbertsville. It'll make it easier, I bet, if you have stuff to give everyone."

I scraped the spoon along the bottom of the can, trying to dislodge a last ravioli—raviolo?—stuck in bright red glue. "I need to stop," I said. "Everything hurts."

The CD player kicked back to "Digging Your Scene" and Lisa snapped it off. "There's some houses down past the trees. I don't want to wake up soaked."

We trudged through dead grass full of pull tabs and depleted lighters and cigarette filters devolved back to soft pussy willow tufts. It wasn't a whole subdivision, just nine or ten dilapidated houses, some still with the Tyvek sheeting nailed to their plywood sides, plunked down in the middle of a field with a half-finished road stopping dead in the grass before them. This used to happen all the time: Developers went and built outside the designated safe zones, there'd be an "environmental incident," the thing would sit there half-finished forever while the developer settled all the lawsuits. Steak houses, kids at school called them, when the homeless people moved in.

There was a faint, full rumble in the distance, like a sluggish winter car engine finally kicking to life. The storm, a huge one, was moving in fast from the west. I followed Lisa, letting her fight with both sets of cart wheels leading down the embankment, and went straight for the first house: huge, hollow, that pasteboard look of a crappy town house masquerading as a mansion. The front hallway had a neck-craning ceiling, two stories high, a light fixture studded with pink glass protuberances like tumors. Every fixture, every outside window broken, and in the next, the next. The fourth house had the jackpot: sleeping bags tossed around the enormous front room, a battery-operated space heater—dead, of course—in the center. Ridiculous thinking that little thing could warm a room this big, this many windows, at least the walls of my movie theaters were good and thick against the cold.

"How do you know it's really empty?" I said. "These things all have eighty thousand rooms, they could be hiding upstairs—"

Lisa pointed silently to the staircase's broken remains. We shook the mouse droppings from two of the sleeping bags and hauled them out.

There was a cracking sound from far away, then another low rumble, something metallic being dragged across the surface of a vast tin tub. The bottom of the tub split open and rain spattered against the windows, a sudden wet cool breeze dancing around our clothes and hair, spraying stray droplets through the open doorway.

"I'll drag everything in," Lisa said, as she ducked outside. "We need to sleep."

The softness of a sleeping bag, after a blanket or two laid flat on concrete floors, industrial carpets, hard-packed soil, was such heaven I was floating. My whole head felt floaty and insubstantial, actually, I wasn't sure I could get up again on short notice. I burrowed in deeper and Lisa curled up next to me. The light was dim and dark gray, choked with chalky clouds; so much rain was coming down, like someone was pouring it off the eaves from a vast pitcher. The wind picked up, sliding through gaps in the windows, the door frame, the fake-brick siding and I pulled my jacket back on, suddenly cold.

"It's too early in the spring for this kind of weather," Lisa said. She was lying back now with her eyes closed, hands tucked under her head. "Little bit of late May out there."

"More like July." I rested my cheek on my good arm. "August. But cold as March—"

"Go on and sleep. If the thunder won't keep you up."

"I like it," I said, closing my eyes. Not a lie. The close-by storms scared me when I was small, the ones where a great overhead rumbling shakes the roof, the walls, the bed frame, and then the lightning flash, the *crash!* a half-second later, makes you flinch and crouch in your bed gazing vigilant at the window, watching for the angry thing outside to come crashing in. But the gentler thunderstorms, a steady but sedate pounding of water and some pot-and-pan banging from far away, those were just white noise that made you happier to be inside, dry, nesting in the dark.

I'm inside, I'm dry, it's as dark as the daytime can get. Nothing's really changed that much, then, has it? I should be grateful. Lisa was already snoring next to me, the sorts of soft little sounds she couldn't make anymore while she was conscious. Like sleeping in Dave's living room, all huddled together, all winter.

*Promise me,* Kristin said, lying there on the floor by the woodstove, dazed and sick, *that you'll take care of my baby. That you won't let anything happen to it. I trust you, Amy. I know I can trust you—*

I promised. Over and over. And I meant it, I always did. It wasn't a lie. Ms. Acosta heard her sometimes, saw her clutching my hands, and she shook her head. *Amy, we'll all have enough to do keeping ourselves alive—never mind a baby, if it lives. Don't make promises you can't keep.*

I could have. I could have kept it. That wasn't a lie. That's what nobody, nothing, seems to understand.

If I'd just stayed in Lepingville, that ghostly black dog wouldn't have found me on the road, wouldn't have sniffed out exactly what had happened and—too late for that. I should've stayed. That's what you're supposed to do, sit, wait, and somebody will find you. That's how it works. My mother, what if she'd already found her way back, and I wasn't there?

What if she were there all along, all through the winter, but on the wrong side of town too afraid of exes or feral dogs or nobody knowing her to go any farther to find me? What if I'd had her, I'd *had* her, and then—

But that's just what happened anyway, isn't it, years ago. I had her. Then, because I wasn't paying attention, because I couldn't see how far she'd fallen, I let her slip away. If I'd stayed awake that night, that one night, if I'd *stayed* for her, she would never have left.

And none of this would have happened. None of it.

*Oh, my dear,* Ms. Acosta said once, last winter, when I told her this. *My poor Amy.* Her arms around me felt papery and fragile and so weirdly soft, that crumpled-paper softness of bones and muscles growing old, and she pulled away quickly as if scared I'd push her off. Would that have been what it felt like, a grandmother's touching you? But Ms. Acosta wasn't old enough for that, fifty at the most. And I never knew my grandparents. They died before I was born.

Lightning flickered through the room, a match blown out the moment it caught flame, and only many seconds later came the thunder. The rain was coming in sporadic bursts now, the storm already passing.

I thought I was still awake, lying there in wonderful padded softness with the thunder and Lisa's snoring and the dim smoke-colored afternoon light, but things began fading in and out and I had to go answer the phone that was ringing, somewhere up those broken rotten stairs. No, it was my own phone, the opening guitars from "The Last Transit" I'd set as my ringtone, playing right here in my pocket loud as—

Dead battery. Dead people, who used to live here. Who used to live there, everywhere. Dead everything. That's how it is, from now on, for the rest of your life. All your life. And you're only seventeen.

As I drifted deeper into sleep I kept right on hearing it, in my dreams. Those first opening bars retreating and repeating in an endless loop like an evaded promise, soft, insistent, impossible.

## FIVE

Something heavy and furious and swollen with blinding, meteoric light flew from the sky, hitting the roof with a crash that rattled every wall and window frame and made the air shudder, ravenous, growling. Thunder straight on top of lightning, jolting me wide awake with a shout, another storm passing through and the windows were still shaking, the sky even darker—I ran for the door. When I pushed it open against cascading streams of rain and the winds trying to seal it shut I saw everything overhead tinted a deep algae green, green bisected by a smokestack column of blackness growing bigger, wider, closer with every passing second. I knew it, I *knew* it—the winds slammed the door shut for me and I ran back to Lisa, already on her feet.

"Tornado," I said; my voice was high-pitched and taut with the need to burst out laughing: I take us all the best places, don't I, Lisa! "It's coming this way, look out the window—"

Lisa gave the carts a frantic glance and then we were both heading down the hallway, out of that ridiculous egg carton front room, looking for a way downstairs. The front door, I thought, as I went from kitchen to family room to living room to bathroom, weren't you supposed to open all the doors and windows if a tornado was coming, less air pressure, where the hell was the—Lisa was yanking up strips of the filthy hallway carpeting, tearing away glue and nails easy as pieces of papier-mâché and she looked just like I felt, on the verge of laughter turning to screams.

"There's no basement," she said, almost giggling as she hurled the carpet pieces into the kitchen. "No fucking basement, no safe house, a half-million each and they're all built on slabs—"

The bathroom, you were supposed to take shelter there if there was no place else, curl up with your head in the southwest corner of your bathtub and pray the roof somehow stayed where it was. I ran for the front room, my backpack, my lighters, my atlas with all the notes, and I was reaching down to grab it when the windows exploded. The palm of a huge, suffocating hand propelled me backward, eyes squeezed shut and arms wrapped around my face, and Lisa had me, shouting, dragging me back down the hall; we tripped over each others' feet hurtling into the bathroom, half-falling into the bathtub together like a pair of drunks. She was whispering something beneath her breath, over and over, her words lost beneath the shattering roar outside.

"Blessed art thou among women," she repeated, hard unforgiving tongue and teeth snapping every soft petitioning syllable in two, "and blessed is the fruit of thy womb Jesus—"

Everybody talks about freight trains when they try to describe a tornado's sound but it's nothing like that, nothing like it at all. A freight train sounds just like what it is, a rattling, groaning Lego-piece mechanism always this close to flying apart—but it stays right where it's meant to, follows those straight solid double lines so obedient with eyes for nothing else, shouts to warn you it's coming, leaves nothing but quiet behind when it's gone. A tornado starts off with the same distant inchoate roar but then keeps getting bigger, louder, a great jaw unhinging around a long deranged scream; it jumps its tracks, cuts its own path over everything it sees, opens wide as it can to swallow up the greenish-black skies, the biggest and deepest-rooted of trees, the miserable ticktack slapdash nowhere houses. And us. The screaming sky was all around us and inside us and I screamed too, loud as I could against the devouring thing smashing through the living room, coming to find and kill us, and my voice was lost to the dirty whirlwind but I could still hear Lisa, her lips to my ear. Shouting into the void. Almost crying with fear.

"Holy Mary, mother of—"

Something banged and crashed above us and the roaring hit a crescendo: The roof had gone, the outer framework, maybe everything but our own four walls. The bathroom was an egg-shell and when the winds broke through the soft oozing contents of our skulls, guts, blood vessels would spill out unstopping—no, not ours. Mine. Mine only. I put my forehead to the plastic masquerading as porcelain, beseeching nothing.

"—pray for us sinners, now and at the hour of our death."

You don't need prayers, Lisa. Not like me. Sins mean nothing, when you can't die.

A hard thump against the bathroom walls, once, twice, and the noises of the wind dropped and diminished but that meant nothing: Tornadoes l iked t o c ircle b ack, finish what they'd started before they spun out exhausted and dead.

I stayed curled up in the bathtub, a sprouting thing cowering in the shell of the seed. Lisa had an arm curled around my chest and little threads of blood were trickling down the sides of the tub, wet like tears against my face, the tiny wounds from hundreds or thousands of flying shards of glass. Hers, mine, I couldn't tell. Inside, outside, we both still looked the same. But it's s he w ho's p raying, c rying, b eseeching t he a ir, w hen s he needs no shelter and can't die and nothing can ever touch her, nothing at all. The wind was softer now but it still wouldn't stop. I made an angry lowing noise like a scared cat, scaredy-cat, and her arms held me tighter.

"Oh my God," she whispered, "I am heartily sorry for having offended thee . . ."

Too late.


The roof above our heads got ripped away, I'd been right about that, but the bathroom held, the rooms above it held. The back half of the house just collapsed, our hallway reduced to a teetering mountain of plywood, plaster chunks and cottony pink puffs of insulation. The front room where we'd slept, foyer, faux-atrium all sheared clean away, like a chunk of cake torn off by a toddler's grasping fingers. I saw a dented can of pineapple peering from the wreckage, a torn bit of red nylon with a backpack strap still attached, but otherwise nothing but broken roof tiles and splintered wood scattered over grass illuminated, as if from within each blade, by soft, powdery fistfuls of glass. Four of the other houses were just gone, leaving only ribbons of rain-soaked Tyvek like wet toilet tissue; one of our shopping carts lying there upside down and empty. The second cart was stuck up in a tree, back wheels poking out almost abashed like it was trying to pull free and fly off to some new adventure.

I had some glass cuts on the backs of my hands, shallow little wounds that kept opening up, and a huge bruise on my shoulder where I'd banged it on the faucet. The air was cool, wet, fresh, and everything felt oddly drained and subdued; the sun lit the edges of the pearly cloud wash still masking it from view, the rain hadn't quite stopped. Lisa poked at one of the rubbish piles, then stepped back shaking her head.

"All buried," she said. "Or blown miles off." She gazed up at our shopping cart. "So much for those damned flashlights. And all my batteries."

Most of the blood in the bathtub was hers, she'd taken a forearm full of glass when she grabbed me, but of course she was already good as healed and pulling the shards right out of her skin, pick, pick, tug, yank, until I winced and looked away. Little dragons' teeth like in the legends of Thebes, sowed in her flesh to spring out as brand-new exes, a progeny of monsters. I had a song about that too in my old notebook. Suddenly the loss of all my songs I wrote down and kept right on writing after my mother left, so I could show them to her when she came back, hit me like the winds had just carried them off and I felt something flattening inside me, my whole chest a torn, deflating balloon.

My jacket, I still had that. Her torn-up jacket. Her ID cards, the CDs Lisa said I could keep with me, my broken cell phone. It didn't help.

"I can't go to Elbertsville," I said, and turned my back on Lisa.

Lisa tossed aside a fistful of wood and slipped an arm around my shoulders, ignoring how I twitched and tried to shy away. "I didn't mean you needed to bribe anyone," she said, her voice thick with remorse. "Just that it might've made things a little— people, that's what they need. Manpower. They'll take you. We're only a few days away, I can get my own food . . ." She glanced at my knife, Dave's knife, that I hadn't dropped or lost this time. "I've got a lighter in my pocket. With that, and your knife, I can fix it so you can—"

"No." It irritated me, the way she kept dancing around the subject—she could hunt just fine for herself in the woods, I got it, and she never needed to bother with cooking but she'd roast me a few leftovers. Did she think I didn't *know* she was only living on fruit slices and Bronson's Best Chili because she thought otherwise she'd scare me? "You go hunt without me, I don't care. There's still some stuff left here, I'll dig it out and—"

"Amy, see sense. Even if you could find any of it, we don't have a can opener anymore."

Stop r eminding m e I s hould've k ept o ne i n m y p ocket, a lighter, batteries, aspirin, that the *first* t hing I s hould've d one when I saw that dark green splotch of a sky was grab my backpack and— "I'll smash them open on a rock or something, okay? Just, go eat something, I know you're hungry. You're always hungry."

"I'll do it all where you don't have to watch. All right?" She was facing me now, a hand resting on my shoulder but even her lightest, most cautious touch felt like she was trying to force me to my knees. "I'll just, I'll take care of all that, so we both have something to eat, you won't have to see it."

"No!" I shoved her arm away, the cuts on my hand opening again like weeping mouths. "I know it was fucking stupid not to keep a can opener with me, okay? I know I should've kept it in my jacket, just in case, I—"

"That's not what I said!" She forked fingers through her hair, seized hold of a few scraggly ends and tugged. "That's not what I said and it—"

"You just want my knife. I'm not giving you my knife."

"Amy, *listen to me*. We're a good three days from Gary and the safe houses up north are all depleted, you can't keep walking with no—"

"I can't go there!" I was crying now, hard, I'd sworn I wouldn't do that in front of her or anyone else but it was like my skin got torn away in that storm, just like the rooftops, every nerve exposed to the agony of the air. "Why don't you listen to me, I can't go to Elbertsville and I can't be around other people, I don't want anyone else to die! I can't stand it! And you're not killing anything walking around the woods minding its own business— you're not doing it, just so I can stuff my stupid face!"

I kicked at a small white stone stuck in the damp ground, slammed it harder with my toe, again and again. Lisa stroked my arm, the barest brush of fingertips against cloth, and her softest touch had the tension of muscles aching to clench and grab and her voice could never be tempered, never be soft, but she couldn't help that. Any more than I could help standing here, wailing over squirrels and bunnies like an infant fool.

"Don't cry," she muttered. She sounded embarrassed, at me, at herself, I didn't know. "Is this all about my killing something to—"

"Yes!"

A lie, all a lie, I'd been so proud I could hunt my own food. Before. I ducked my head, folded my arms tight and protective against my chest. Raindrops hit dispiritedly here and there, making black spots on my charcoal sleeves.

"That ravioli you had for breakfast," Lisa said, not unkindly. "There was beef in it. Dead cow, last I checked."

I know I'm being stupid, for God's sake, Lisa, I know that. Too much blood, a different kind of blood, and now I wasn't proud of anything anymore. That's all. You don't understand and I can't explain it to you, I can't ever tell anyone. I wiped my eyes, my nose on my sleeve.

"God." Lisa was laughing now, helpless, the blood from another tugged-out glass shard trickling down her arm. "You and Jessie, when she was still alive—did I tell you about that? All her animal rights stuff? One day when she was thirteen, it's like she woke up and decided she was PETA's new pinup girl. Never mind meat, she'd give us all hell for eating eggs, milk, butter, threw out half her shoes because they were leather—stop crying, Amy, just, three more days, maybe four. That's all. We'll both get somewhere better. All right?"

The mighty bunny hunter and crazy tree hugger, a real pair of Wonder Twins. Was this supposed to distract me or something? I needed a tissue and, of course, we didn't have them anymore. I snorted it all back, scrubbed at my nose, made myself look her in the face.

"That tulip bulb," I said, "from when we left Leyton. Why did you take it? We couldn't plant it. It'd gone rotten."

Lisa looked startled, like she'd completely forgotten. Then her face actually flushed. "I thought, maybe you could peel the outside skin off, where it'd gone soft, and the inside would still be good? Good for planting. Something pretty to look at, for later on. But I don't know anything about gardening." Her mouth twisted in a mirthless little smile. "Or music, or Greek myths, or anything else. Hunting, eating, eating, hunting. That's pretty much it, kid. That's all." She shrugged, tugged again at the sagging ponytail flopping over one shoulder. "That's what you've got."

There was such sadness in her eyes, flooding them like a sudden tide overwhelming the sands. I tensed up, my skin almost itching from a sudden uncomfortable, crawly curiosity: What was it like, what was it really like, to lose yourself to this disease? To lose yourself entirely, for real, to sicken yourself eating and cry in disgust at what you must look like in the cafeteria, classroom, funeral home, to go down in starvation-wracked delirium and come back to yourself lying in a rigid, unyielding carapace that looked like you, but would never be you, ever. No way to smash through the shell, no way out. Did it actually hurt? How could she stand it? But that wasn't the kind of thing you could ask someone, at least not someone who could snap your neck as an afterthought.

"If I go to Elbertsville," I tried to explain, "something bad will happen."

"Amy, it won't always be as bad as this. It won't. I swear."

No, I believe you. It won't. It'll be worse.

"You didn't get through the whole winter on peaches and ravioli," Lisa said. "I know you didn't. You told me you didn't."

I shook my head.

"I'll find u s s omething. D ress it, m ake a fire. God knows we've got enough wood. But you keep the knife for now. It's your knife." She hesitated. "You should still come with me. Safer."

"I'm fine here. I can see any more coming a mile away." I nodded toward the ruin of the houses. "Especially now."

She wanted badly to hunt by herself, just to be alone with herself and her hunger. I could feel it. She was twitching in her shoes, the spasmy jolt of muscles aching to stretch out and move. "Those trees over there, down past the—"

"I see them."

"Don't go anywhere." She gave me a suspicious look. "And don't go digging in this crap, if you hurt yourself I haven't got any first-aid kit left."

"You're the one who looks like a walking mirror ball. I'll be here. Go."

She went.

Dave wouldn't be pleased with me right now. Not at all. *Leave her alone,* Ms. Acosta used to snap at him when he'd nag me about helping set the snares, her bird-fluttery voice trilling even higher with anger in a way that made me want to stifle laughter even as my stomach twisted watching them fight. *We spent six hours today foraging for more insulin for you, six goddamned hours, if that's not "pulling her weight" in your fantasy kingdom then you can just go to—*

They shouted, and Kristin screamed, and Dave screamed right back and slammed fists against his own living room wall so hard he drew blood. Diabetics don't heal. Ms. Acosta drew me aside later and said, Amy, you have to understand. His wife, his daughter. And I thought, there's nothing I can do about that, nothing at all, but I just nodded. *Six hours,* she kept saying. *Does he understand anything? And Kristin, she's got to pull herself together, I know she's sick but she can't just lie there waiting to die, Amy, talk to her, try to, she listens to you—*

What did she want from me? There was nothing I could do about Kristin, nothing at all. And the one thing I promised her, the thing that kept her going, I went and—stillborn. Dead at its first breath. There was nothing I could do for it. Nothing at all.

My skin was damp with sweat though it kept getting colder; I raised my arms up in the too large, floppy-sleeved jacket, letting the air whoosh through the fabric of my T-shirt, and then I heard it: a small, muffled, insistent sound, inside my front jeans pocket. "The Last Transit." Those opening guitars, sprightly and melancholy and tentative all at once. My cell phone.

My dead cell phone. I hadn't imagined it. It rang again and I scrabbled frantically to pull it from my pocket, maybe I'd been wrong all this time, the battery was just dormant from the cold or—lighting up, it was all lit up but no number came up, just ringing, it didn't stop—

"Hello!" I shouted. My voice was heated and shaky. "Hello!"

No answer. Not even the sound of breathing. Just flat, airy silence and no one could have called me, there was no way but it was all still lit up, I heard it ring, I imagined nothing. "Is anyone there? Can you hear me? Is anyone—"

The screen light sputtered and faded out. I cradled it in my hands, pushed every button on and off; it just lay there, warm and stone-smooth in my palm, a useless chunk of sparkly purple plastic.

I shook the phone, pressed star-six-nine. So what if it were crazy? Who's watching but some squirrels? Nothing. No noise, no light.

I'd be ready. Next time, I'd answer it quicker, on the very first ring, I'd be ready and they wouldn't hang up. There'd be a next time. I knew there would be. Because this couldn't be me, huddled up mud-soaked in the remains of another destroyed subdivision in the dozenth destroyed town, waiting for a monster to feed me like a baby bird and then abandon me to strangers who'd die all around me when the winter came, all over again. They'd find me, the stranger on the phone line, wherever they were. They'd help me. I knew, without having to call any tribunals in my head, that they were on my side. They'd know what to do about the dog too. I was sure of it. All I had to do now was wait.

Lisa was walking back with something limp and furry and dead dangling from each hand, and I slipped my secret back into my pocket. I was surprised somehow that she wasn't lolloping along on all fours with the dead things gripped in her bloody mouth and I was ashamed of myself for those thoughts, after Lisa fed me and prayed over my body and saved my life outright twice in two days. But she'd understand, I knew she'd understand. Why'd she ever have left them behind, her own family, if she didn't?

We had rabbit for dinner that night, roasted. I don't know what else Lisa ate in the woods, by herself.

"How's your arm?" Lisa asked. The rain was coming down again in long thin streams, trickles of pure cold damp making me shiver and twitch as they rolled from my jacket collar down my back, but neither of us wanted to stop walking. Clearly no good ever came of rest or sleep.

"It's all right," I said. It still ached, all the way down to the wrist like something was sinking in dozens of fingernails. My palms felt less raw but were starting to itch, which my mom always said meant the skin was healing. "You were right. Let it bleed."

She glanced at me, then the sky, as our strip of expressway wound past a used-car lot shiny with smashed metal and glass. Nighttime was closing in again and Lisa looked pinched with exhaustion, head bowed and sodden withes of hair plastered over her face, but I had that dangerous sleep-deprived second wind where everything's louder, sharper, more colorful: I could walk forever, march right past Elbertsville until I found another empty movie theater, all cool and dark with a concession counter still half intact. Wish Lisa luck at Prairie Beach, sleep on more thin flowered utility carpet until the popcorn was down to the last half-exploded kernel and the rats, the black dog, closed in. Until my secret caller found me, and helped me. I kept taking the phone out to check, I couldn't help it, but the call screen looked just like the sky, dull dim gray that wouldn't light up for trying.

"I bet it rains all night," I said, grabbing a handful of hair and squeezing more water all over my sleeve. "We could stop in one of those cars, or a tollbooth. If you're tired."

"Just another mile or two," she promised. A squirrel snake-danced across the road and something in her started for a moment, drawing up all tight and eager, then subsided. "Then we'll wring ourselves out."

"Whatever you say."

It wasn't sarcastic but she whipped her head round, glaring at me like I was trying to start a fight, and I just squeegeed more rain from my hair and pretended not to notice. The sky was a deep slate diminishing to black, the soft rushing sounds of the downpour nothing but an amplified silence all around us. My tangerine canvas sneakers had gone blood orange from the puddles, my feet would never stop itching once they were dry again, if they ever were dry again—

A sound at my back, a soft *clomp, clomp* noise like someone stumbling slowly along in shoes far too large. It teased my ear, an itch of noise growing louder and more persistent beneath the wash of water, and I grabbed for Lisa's hand; she stopped in her tracks like she already knew why.

"Behind us," I said. Softly as I could, like something might overhear. "Do you hear it?"

She shook her head. "Count of three," she said, just as softly.

One, two—we both turned around, quick, sharp. Nothing. We kept walking. No more noises.

"Another squirrel," I said, under my breath to myself, brushing streams of water from my face. A deer. A possum. They're heavy-footed things, possums, besides being ugly as hell. Lisa kept hold of my fingers, gently as she could manage, swinging her arm idly like we were having a happy little romp through the puddles.

*Clomp. Clomp.*

I whipped my head over my shoulder ever so casual, just checking the perimeter, and there following in our footsteps was a tiny, upright skeleton in winter coat and hat and mittens and knitted snowflake scarf and miniature bright red boots. It stumbled as it walked, clomping in the boots, like a living toddler just learning how to find its feet; empty sockets like black-tarnished coins stared up at me, a flesh-stripped little jaw grinned at me, when my eyes met the remnants of its face and couldn't stop staring it stumbled faster, nearly fell, held out its puffy chrysalis arms for me to pick it up. Its bit of a jaw opened wide, and it made a sound. A sound like a whimpering, wounded dog.

My fingers closed around Lisa's and I jerked us both to a stop; she spun on her heel looking where I looked and then shook her head. She saw nothing. It opened its jaws again and whined louder, a stray's furious *arrouuuu* of uncomprehending, starving loneliness. Louder, yelping piteously like an animal in pain. Like the dog Lisa hurt to save me.

I was so tired that every cry, every noise was magnified and it was like being in a dream, like when I was asleep before the tornado hit and didn't even realize what my brain was inventing right before me. No dream, though, not now. No dream. I stretched out my arms.

"Amy?" Lisa was frowning in confusion, the beginnings of fear but she sounded so calm, contained, like she could will us both not to fly apart. "What are you looking at?"

Stumbling toward me now, slowly. Crying harder, like a living baby.

"Amy!" She grabbed my arm, forgetting to be gentle. "I'm not joking! What are you looking at!"

Go away now, Lisa. It doesn't concern you, what I'm seeing. It never did.

The baby, the dead thing, took another step, inside its rotting stuffed-cloth shell, and then finger bones became claws and something in the shape of a huge black dog flew at me, its yellow lamplight eyes and filthy white teeth gleaming in malice, starvation, murder. It knocked me to the pavement, out of Lisa's grasp, and no mere ghost had that weight, that power; it growled deep and low against my face like the rumbling of another storm and I kicked, furious, screaming.

Lisa struck out shouting at what I knew she couldn't see or hear and her hands passed right through the dog's body, all that solid muscle and skin-soaked fur was nothing to her but an armful of dead air. She grabbed my forearms to haul me up, grabbed me too hard and I screamed again, it was agony, her fingers were vises twisting down to break my bones; the black dog howled in frustrated fury, sank teeth into her arm that never even pricked the skin, and I was up again running in blind panic down the road, back where we'd come from, down and down all the way back to Lepingville where I'd die, where I should long since have died—

"*Amy!*" Lisa was screaming. "Oh, Christ! Stop!"

Blinding sulfur-yellow light flooded the sky, the ground from nowhere and there was a hard screeching noise that went on forever, searing the asphalt, a stench of burnt rubber and gasoline—my palms hit smooth, rain-slicked metal and I crumpled to the pavement, o ut o f b reath, c urled u p u nhurt a nd d isbelieving against the hard, thick prune skin of a car tire. Headlights, that searing yellow glow. Squealing brakes. An actual working car, barreling the wrong way up the exit ramp and down the middle of an empty expressway and now someone was climbing out of the backseat, coming toward me as I edged away. Tall, thin-faced, a neatly clipped head of thick gray hair, wrapped in a capacious oilskin raincoat with a faded yellow logo splotching one arm.

"Well, hey there!" he said, stretching out a hand, all bouncy, brisk footsteps and crocodile smiles even as his eyes looked me up and down, down and up, like something too distasteful for words. Like some little rodent from the woods, that runs in front of your car. "You need to be more careful than that, Janey almost hit you!"

JUH-uhhhh-aaannEEEEE! all*must* HIIT-T-TCHAA! I knew it. Your people, Lisa, your lost tribe, you handle this. Lisa had come up behind me, circling and protective, rubbing through my jacket sleeves like an apology at the bruises she'd left on my arms.

"I'm Don, by the way," the man said. Smiling, still smiling, in a way I didn't like. "What's your name?"

I shook my head, trying to look stern, disdainful; let Lisa talk for b oth of u s, m aybe h e'd t hink I w as o ne of t hem t oo. No chance of that, my hand was bleeding from where it scraped the asphalt and I'd seen his eyes flicker to it and then back to my face, he saw how it didn't heal. At least his car scared my dog away, it was nowhere in sound or sight. The woman behind the wheel had a tidy blonde pageboy and bright red lipstick, like an actress from some old fifties movie, scarlet mouth curved up pondering some private joke I knew I didn't want to hear.

"I asked you a question," Don said, and stopped smiling. Raindrops rolled down his oilskin like little waterbugs sailing the surface of a river. "Didn't I."

"Leave it," Lisa said. "We're both tired. We've been walking all day."

"Wonderful exercise," he said. "Can't beat it. You going somewhere?"

"No."

"Yes, you are," he said, and there was a gun from inside the folds of his black raincoat and it was pointing at me.

My head felt all floaty and dreamy, like I really had fallen asleep standing there. Maybe I had, because that black dog growling nose to nose had felt so much more real than this. Lisa drew in a sharp, angry breath and he shrugged, actual apology in his eyes.

"Get in," he said, talking over my head to Lisa. "You want Prairie Beach, right? Like everyone else? Well, they're full up now, no room at the inn, but I can take you to the next closest—"

"We're not going with you," Lisa said. "We're not going."

He shrugged again. "That's all right with me," he said. "But you seem fond of your little pet frail, I know how easy it is to get attached, and she's a stain on the road shoulder if you don't come so just think it over, 'kay? Think hard. And hurry up."

He had a hand on my arm now, closing tight on the spot where Lisa nearly broke it, and the barrel was right up against my cheek as he cocked the trigger. Just like in a movie. The woman behind the wheel kept sitting there, dreaming her own little dreams as she waited, and Lisa said something to Don I couldn't seem to hear, and he laughed, and then Lisa was in the car's front passenger seat and I was in the back with the gun and Don. Don had my knife too, Dave's knife. I wasn't sure how he got it, all that was another blur. The seats were so soft, a dried sticky streak on the leather like some kid had spilled a can of pop ages back, and the heater was turned up so high I felt cool steam evaporating from my soaked skin. I shivered, folding my arms in my sopping wet jacket they hadn't yet taken from me, and looked from the side of Lisa's anxious, knotted face to the dark paper-scroll of the interstate to Don, who tilted his gray head and gave me a grin.

"Am I dreaming?" I asked, as we headed right down the middle of I-80/94 at forty, fifty, sixty miles an hour.

Don laughed. The same sort of laughing sound Lisa made, a deep, barking cough that shot the air from his throat like he was angry at it.

"You were all daydreaming," he said. "All humanity, everywhere. Now you've had your wake-up call. So how d'you like it?"

He looked suddenly almost warm and wistful like the very thought of that made him happy, like some great iron band binding him tight had just loosened and his whole being was shifting, stretching in relief. The rain clattered against the car windows, the headlights illuminating the deserted expressway, defunct service stations, signs counting down the miles to cities now inaccessible if they still existed at all; I drew my fingertips across the condensation on the glass, three thick, clear, foreshortened lines in the fog, and waited to see how long it would take my last little traces to be erased.

# BOOK TWO

# TOPSY-TURVY

# SIX

"Well, my God, you don't need to look like *that*."

Janey, the woman behind the wheel, stared at me in the rearview mirror, big gray-green eyes narrow with amusement; up close her hair looked disheveled and glassine, like she'd coated it thick with hairspray without bothering to comb it first, and her lipstick was a haphazard greasy smear. "Nobody's driving you to your funeral, now are they?"

Human. Her voice. I don't know why that surprised me so much, but I sat up straighter against the padded leather and scrutinized that little rectangle of her eyes, nose, mouth like it were a rebus full of clues. "I don't know what you're taking me to," I said.

"Of course you don't," said Don, who'd put the gun away and was cleaning his nails with a little paring knife, bored as you please. He was sitting passenger side, right behind Lisa. "You're a human. You don't know anything, you don't understand anything, it's like expecting a muskrat to stand up and recite Racine—"

"*Don,*" said Janey, her greasy mouth screwing up in a reproving pout. "Be nice."

"The truth isn't nice or not nice, dearest Jeanette," he said, not looking up from his pinky finger. "It just is."

"I want to know where you're taking us." Lisa kept twisting around to look at me, then back at the road signs. If it weren't for me I bet she'd just throw herself right out of the car, any broken bones a mere fleeting inconvenience. "If you won't tell her, you can damned well lower yourself to telling—"

"I told you already, didn't I?" Don put the paring knife away, stretched out his long blocky legs so his knees pressed into the back of Lisa's seat. "You said you'd been walking all day, and you were heading north. That makes your destination fairly obvious, if you have any clue what's left standing—and I assume you do, you may be ignorant but you're not fools. You—" He pointed a finger at Lisa. "You want Prairie Beach. You're a bit late in the day, they're not taking anyone new and they wouldn't want your frail anyway—"

"What about Elbertsville?" Lisa demanded. "There's a human settlement there. That's what everyone told me."

Don pulled a matchbook from his pocket, digging under his nails again. Janey squinted at the road.

"You ran into one of those twisters, didn't you?" he said, his mouth pursed with concentration as he sawed the matchbook's thin paper edge back and forth. "A couple touched down in Hammond too and one right outside Lake Station. Bad, bad weather. You don't look like the sort who'd travel with a pet but no supplies, you must've lost them all along the way. You might as well come with us." The matchbook edge frayed, bent, and he turned it over for a fresh plane of attack. "Janey and I patrol the roads sometimes looking for folks just like you, who've lost your way—you're lucky we stumbled over you. We're open to everybody. We don't discriminate."

"They don't discriminate," Janey repeated, veering such a sharp left to avoid a fear-frozen deer that I grabbed for the door handle, nearly bashed my head on the window. "Everyone's welcome. You'll be happy there."

"Where is there?" I asked. "If it's not Elbertsville or Prairie Beach, then where are we going?"

Janey sped up to seventy-five and clunked right over and through a pothole, a yawning frost heave, so roughly I winced for the car's transmission. North, obviously, still north, to Gary. But not Elbertsville. Lisa fumbled in her pockets and stretched her arm back, handing me something: a little half-crushed foil packet of peanuts, like the kind you get on airplanes. Spicy Red Hot flavor. Don chuckled when I tore it open.

"You'll be earning your food from now on," he said. "No more handouts. But it won't be bad. You'll see. Plenty for everyone."

"Plenty for everyone," Janey crooned, her smile filling up the rearview mirror. Her tongue swept over her large, square front teeth, mopping away a lipstick streak. "And nobody will take you away from—what's your name, anyway?" She turned to Lisa, who glared silently back. "Nobody will take you away from each other, we respect family ties. It's all about family, one way or another." She sailed through a standing puddle, a soft swishing sound of water as the wheels sank inward, and onto the U.S. 12 exit ramp. She rubbed a hand over her eyes and I saw violet-gray circles beneath them, soft crushed-looking skin like flower petals in a mud puddle, and something in her sagged wearily against the seat cushions before she straightened up, clutched the wheel tighter, gave the mirror a resolute smear-free smile. "All about family," she repeated.

Nobody'd asked my name. Maybe I don't have one anymore, as far as they're concerned. I guess they can have the knife, it was Dave's anyway, but they're not taking my cell phone. My cards. The CDs Lisa gave me. I licked my fingers and rubbed them over the oily foil, picking up the last peanut crumbs and salt.

I want to go home.

The padded car seat felt good. The heater. Heat that came out of a machine whenever you wanted, the touch of a button, drying your clothes without leaving any damp or mildew behind. Already that felt singular, seductive. It was dangerous to let comfort suck you in, heat, soft chairs, the promise of gasoline and food and lipstick. Be like Lisa. Sleep anywhere, eat anything that comes your way. Don't give a shit. But I've *been* doing that, I've been, and nothing's worked out right.

The car clunked and skidded into the outskirts of Gary, a silent teeth-rattling ride over empty railroad tracks past steel mills and coil makers and warehouses gone to hollow caverns. Maybe it was Janey who called me, or Don, warning us they'd be right along. But it couldn't be. Don would've smashed my phone right on the pavement, crushed it under his shoe, just for fun. He wasn't getting my phone.

Stick with Lisa. She'll help me. She's got to.

We clattered down a residential side street, all overgrown forest patches and neat little houses with worn siding and tiny piebald lawns. The protective fences were torn down, or simply never there: Property taxes paid for all that, zombie fencing and warning sirens and sulfur lights up and down the roads, and you could tell these houses had never been worth much. Bodies by the roadside, flesh-picked or clean rotted away, skeletons curled up in the grass. Janey slowed the car to a near crawl, staring wide-eyed at each house in turn like a thief casing the neighborhood, and Don looked up from the shredded remains of his matchbook.

"There's no point in foot-dragging, Jeanette Isabella." He returned the matchbook to his pocket. "We're almost there."

"I'm not *foot-dragging*, I'm just enjoying the view." Janey leaned back in her seat, let the speed drop from twenty-five, to twenty, to ten as she smiled beatifically at the dead grass, limp shrubbery, wan dilapidated little sardine-tin houses. "I love cities at night—they're just so big and spread out, so full of people and life and activity. So many possibilities. Don't you love the lights, Don? Look at all the lights."

Other than her headlights, the street was completely dark. Lisa swiveled around in her seat to face me, eyes silently warning me to keep quiet—what the hell did she think I could say, anyway, to that?—and gave Janey a calm attempt at a smile. "My name is Lisa," she said. "My friend, the human girl, her name is Amy—"

"Janey," Don interrupted, calm and unruffled, "start the fucking car up again before I hurt you."

Janey flinched, like some random noise had just jostled her from a daydream, and sped up. Still smiling. The rain had slowed, nearly stopped. Lisa squinted at the street signs. "Ogden," she said. "This *is* near Prairie Beach then, I can tell just by all the trees—"

"An invigorating hike away," Don agreed. "So close, and yet so far."

Ogden, Illinois, Buell, Indiana, Pennsylvania. Janey pulled up at the curb right off Massachusetts Avenue and I saw the metallic glint of a restored fence, curving over and across the street, people with flashlights leaning bored against it like sentries. One of them had a gun in a holster, like Don. Another one, a hunting knife like Dave's. Lisa reached back and took my hand and held it as firmly as she could without breaking it, to stop the trembling.

"This is my 'pet,'" Lisa said, glancing from Don to Janey in turn. "Not anyone else's."

"You're worrying about nothing," Don said, squinting out the window. "We have nothing to worry about anymore, our kind. Nothing can touch us. Leave the fruitless hand-wringing to the weak and frail."

A man was coming through the gate, tall, stout, white-haired, in a dark gray suit inches short at the wrists and ankles. He flapped an impatient flashlight beam at us and Janey leapt like a happy little puppy from behind the wheel, stumbling over to Don as he unfolded himself from the back seat and slipping her arm through his. She was in high heels, a good size too large, sliding precariously up and down inside them as she tugged the stiletto tips from the soft wet dirt at every step. I waited until Lisa came over to my side of the car, opening the door for me and taking my hand again as I made myself climb out.

"I'll handle it," she whispered, even as her wary glances from ex to ex—I didn't need to hear them to know what they were—told me she had no more clue what she was handling than I did. "He said nobody would separate us. Let's call his bluff. Just let me talk."

"Why are we here?" The night was soft and hazy, the smallest bit of moonlight filtering through the clouds and making the budding tree branches look anemic, sickly; no lamplight eyes peering at me through the bushes, no black dog. I almost wished it were there. It wanted only me, if they tried taking its prey away it'd make them all shit themselves. Even smug, smirking Don. "What do they want?"

"Just let me talk."

The short-suited man banged his flashlight on the car hood, like we didn't already have his attention, shone the beam fast in our faces. Up close his hair wasn't white but a pale golden blond, soft fluffy locks like feather tufts, his eyes narrow and ice-colored and as sour as his thick pink twisted-up mouth. He marched up to me and Lisa and his pale exposed ankles, his broad bare feet looked incongruously shapely and fragile, like wax sculptures threatened by a match.

"So whaddaya got for me, Don?" he asked, in a voice gravelly and thin all at once like a rain of tiny pebbles. "Because you never bring me shit no matter how far you drive, and this don't look like any exception—"

Don laughed, a wispy stream of mirth like tobacco smoke. Janey clutched his shoulders from behind, massaging with her fingertips. "One of us, and a frail. Since when can't you use more work crews, Billy? The frail's young, strong—well, strong as her kind ever get, anyway." He pulled out a packet of cigarettes, a lighter. "She'll do. As for the other, well, ask her if she wants to stay. The frail's her little pet goldfish, she probably will."

Billy leaned forward, squinting at us like he had bad eyes. His breath had the same faint traces of brine and decay as Don's had, and Lisa's didn't. I backed away without meaning to, as he looked me over, but he seemed pleased with that.

"That's mine, what you're nosing around," Lisa said, cold and steady, moving in front of me. Almost nose to nose with Billy, staring him right down. "I'm Lisa."

Billy didn't seem put off at all. Normal meet and greet, maybe, for an ex. "That's yours, huh?" He glanced over at Don, who'd shaken off Janey's clinging fingers like someone flicking away an ant and was sucking deep on his cigarette, eyes squeezed shut in pleasure; Don held the packet out to Janey, who took her own cigarette with a delighted squeak, and Billy's narrow eyes went narrower with distaste. Disgust, even. "Like we don't have enough of that shit round here already—"

"She's my sister." Lisa spat the word, all shortcut sibilance like Don blowing out a match. "So just leave it. If you want her so bad, and I don't know why you do, you'd better take me too."

"Don't lookit *me*." Billy snorted, all lit up now like he and Lisa were just sharing a friendly joke. "The trash Don likes to collect from the side of the road, I ain't got nothing to say about it, but she looks young enough to work and if you stick around you won't have all the burden of feeding her, you should be fucking grateful—*Phoebe!*" He turned and shouted at the gate guards, so bored they hadn't moved an inch from their haphazard posts. "Where the hell's that Phoebe, I know she's on night crew this week! Get the dumb bitch over here now!"

He hadn't been looking at her but Janey jumped and twitched, taking a last guilty draw on her cigarette, before she dropped it in the dirt and pulled off her shoes to run; she scuttled at double speed through the gates, Don strolling leisurely behind her, and after a few moments another woman came running out. Curly black hair cropped close to the scalp, blue T-shirt, sensible red sneakers, an angular rail of a body vibrating with so much nervous energy everyone else looked half-asleep in comparison. She skidded to a stop in front of Billy, one narrow hand shooting up to her temple in a playful little salute.

"Chieftain?" She grinned, and actually clapped her feet together like some soldier on dress parade. Human. I was starting to get a little feel for who was who, even before anyone talked.

Billy stood there looking at her, nostrils flaring like she stank. Phoebe just kept grinning, a wide-eyed toothy cheekiness that made you tense up inside waiting for someone to slap it right off her face. "New meat," he said, nodding at me. "Show it around. That's Lisa, she owns it. Do what she says like you'd do what I say, or I'll beat the living shit out of you. Go get them beds."

He turned and stalked off, the bare bits of his nearly hairless shins gleaming like wax, like bleached bone. It should've been ridiculous, him striding away barefoot in his little short pants, but the edges of his heels looked sharp enough to slice skin. The moonlight bisected Phoebe's thin ferrety face and she gave me this strange eyeblink of a look, like she thought she knew me from somewhere but couldn't quite place the face, then she slipped between me and Lisa and locked arms with us like we'd all three been jolly pals all our lives.

"You must both be *worn out!*" she shouted, grinning at me like that was the best and jolliest thing she could imagine. Up close she looked older, faint webbing all around her eyes, patches of old acne surrounded by flaking skin; her teeth were uneven, unhealthy nubs, like crumbling tea-stained sugar cubes. "We all sleep in the women's dorm, plenty of room for everyone. Couples and families, they have their own space—but they don't like to *encourage* that, you know, the big bosses, not if they can help it, don't want any more *really* little mouths to feed, know what I mean?" Her laugh was a soft low titter. "You'll get your work assignment tomorrow, after you sleep—see, you can get a little shut-eye first, they're not running Parchman North up here no matter what anyone's been telling ya!" She squeezed my arm, hard. "Welcome aboard. You'll be glad you came!"

Lisa? Make her stop talking. I'll pay you. Lisa just studied the gate guards, glaring at them while they glared back but none of it seemed hostile; one of them nodded courteously and handed her an extra flashlight as we passed through the gate, into another emptied-out subdivision of plain lawns and sad shrubs and slightly bigger houses. A little group was gathered on one of the lawns, scooping something into a tall brown leaf bag. Phoebe was humming all high and sprightly under her breath, my theme-song welcome to Don and Billy's Home for Wayward Batshit Crazy Humans. "Where are we?" I demanded, pulling my arm from Phoebe's. "What is this place?"

The guard nearest us, the one with the hunting knife, turned and grinned at me. Her eyes weren't unkind. "Some of you frails started calling it Paradise City. Why not. Compared to what things are like outside? That's no lie."

"We're staying long enough for Amy to rest," Lisa said. "Then we're leaving again."

One of the lawn folks, watching us as he kept the leaf bag's edges standing upright, shook his head and laughed. "You're leaving when Billy and them say you can leave," he said, as another of his fellow humans dropped something into the bag: an armload of filthy old bones, mixed with clumps of last autumn's wet dead leaves. Cleanup crew. "She is, anyway."

"She's with me. She's my sister." Lisa was glaring down the guards again, whipping round to spit rebuke at the bone gatherers. "I say when we leave and when we—"

"Lady, just let it go." The second cleanup crew guy, big and sturdy as a linebacker but with a gentle, patient face, big blue eyes, straightened up and wiped his leaf-mucky palms against his jeans. Careful not to get his Bears jersey any dirtier than it already was. "You've been out there, haven't you? You know what it's like. It's shit. It's hell. Especially for a girl. If you care about your sister you should be glad you both got here, one way or another."

"Let's *go*." Phoebe grabbed my arm again, right where Lisa had bruised it up. "The women's dorms are over on Elbert Street. I'm on shift, y'know, I have to get back to the kitchens or old Mags'll have kittens."

She led us through a weed-choked backyard and a knot of elm trees onto the next street: Elbert, the fourth house down, a defeated-looking white clapboard pile with peeling black trim. There in what used to be the living room were cheek by jowl rows of beds, futons, cots, sleeping bags, more in the next room, maybe two dozen in all; some empty, some with shoes lined up before them and exhausted barefoot heaps lying fast asleep. Phoebe made a needless little keep-it-down hand gesture and motioned to an unoccupied cot in the corner.

"You can't stay here," she whispered to Lisa. "The bosses have their own housing; this is a human dorm—"

"I'm not leaving Amy." Lisa's ex voice turned down low was a seething hiss, like a pressure cooker threatening to blow. "You can't just grab people off the streets, sweep them up like those leaves and—"

"You can't stay here." Phoebe had dropped all her nudges and nods and grins and stood staring up at Lisa, mouth in a grim line and feet planted wide apart like she was scared of being pushed. "This is ours, the sleeping quarters are ours. Bosses don't get to come inside. That's the rule. We get our own space, and you can't just drop in and out whenever you want to. It upsets everyone."

"I'm not anyone's boss, and I'm not trying to do anything but—"

"Don't make me get Mags." Phoebe was hissing like Lisa now. "These here, they're on day shift, they can't sleep in, it's not fair, it'll wake them up and be all your fault but *I'll* still get blamed for—"

"It's all right," I muttered to Lisa. My whole head was wrapped in cotton batting, my eyes stinging and pricking with exhaustion; just looking at the little cot made me dizzy needing to lie down. "It's okay."

Phoebe smiled at me again, a quick spasm of thin lips and bad teeth like someone had tugged puppet strings hidden in her hair, and gave me that same funny, penetrating look as she had back at the gate, as if I were telling her some unsavory secret without even knowing I was doing it. I sat down on the edge of the cot, fumbling with my LCS jacket zipper.

"We'll figure all this out tomorrow," Lisa told me, squatting down and pulling my T-shirt cloth free of the zipper teeth like she really was my mother. I got the message, as she zipped it to my neck: *Keep this on. The rest of your stuff could disappear.* She rifled through her own pockets, passing me another foil peanut packet, as Phoebe pursed her lips and shook her head in delighted reproof.

"Can't do that," she whispered. "Can't do that, no special treats or favors if you don't prove you can work—"

"I decide what my frail gets," Lisa hissed back, rising slow and easy to her feet. "Not you, human."

A little eyeblink pause, as some of the sleepers murmured and stirred, then Phoebe shrugged.

"No offense, memsahib," she said. "No offense. Nighty-night, Amy."

They went out, the door creaking behind them. I curled up on the cot, patting my pockets, and ate my peanuts with as little foil-rustling as I could. All these people made me want to slip under the cot and hide. Tomorrow. Sort all this out tomorrow.

*I decide what my frail gets. Not you, human.* It came out of her mouth so cold and hard, so easy. Frail. Mine. Like she'd been waiting her chance to say it, all along.

The second I closed my eyes I slid down a long, smooth chute, cool like metal and with the contained darkness of a womb. Somewhere far away, minutes or hours later, there were sounds of people getting up and leaving and others dropping into the beds, futons, cots they'd left behind; sunlight came hard and clean through the grimy windows, turning the womb-space behind my eyelids from soft black to a cloudy illuminated amber.

"Is she new?" someone whispered, right overhead. People standing over me, looking down at me. Maybe wanting something. Still couldn't open my eyes. "Or did they change her shift?"

"How would I know?" someone else whispered back. "Who fucking cares. Welcome to Shit Town. Next nine exits."

Their footsteps receded and a door slammed and I slept and slept.

# SEVEN

The next thing I knew the sun was rich and fading like late afternoon and someone was wrenching my arm, my bitten arm, making me shout as I bolted awake.

"Night shift's up," she said, a barrel-built woman in her fifties, maybe older, deep lines in her face and a hard, unforgiving look in her eyes. "Get the hell out of my bed."

"Rise and *shine*, night shift!" Phoebe's voice came sailing from the porch steps, through the open door like a baseball whizzing toward window glass. "Don't give me all that five-more-minutes-Mom, some of us have been out and about for *hours* already, you don't see us complaining!"

She had my arm and we were out the door again before I could say two words.

"I am *exhausted*," Phoebe shouted, half-dragging me down Elbert Street. "I mean, I couldn't sleep half the day, tossing and turning, all this excitement! New people! It's all too much! Don hasn't found anyone alive in the longest time, you know, the last one cut her foot on something before he got there and the gangrene had already set in by the time they—here we are!" Half a street down, a canary yellow bungalow at the corner of Elbert and Massachusetts. "Welcome to our humble commissary as I like to call it, have to get you fed and dressed and pressed before your first assignment, we don't want the bosses thinking I'm cutting you any slack . . ."

There were piles of clothing stacked against the front room wall, clean and filthy alike all neatly folded; little hand-lettered MEN'S, WOMEN'S, CHILDREN'S signs with pointing arrows divvying up the piles. Cardboard boxes everywhere, less organized, overflowing with all the same safe house stuff Lisa and I had crammed in our carts and then watched blow away. "C'mon, kid. Down this way, bathroom. Chop chop, said the executioner."

"Where's Lisa? You told me that—"

"All in due time, kid—she's sleeping right now, she's plumb tuckered out. Lotta work, looking after *you!*" Phoebe's eyes got big and bright and she was laughing again, soft chuckles and indulgent head-shakes like she just couldn't get over me. "Hell of a job, convincing her you were just sleeping like the dead and not roasting over a spit for the bosses' dinner, plug up that bathtub drain like a good girl. *I'll* be back in two shakes, once I get the water going."

Breakfast—brunch, late lunch, early dinner—was canned peaches and tuna fish and then a bath in *hot* water, buckets of Lake Michigan water heated on a fireplace woodstove and hauled into the bathtub. There were new socks, new underwear, sneakers that fit, antibiotic salve for my bitten arm and hydrocortisone for my scraped-up itching palms and athlete's foot spray for my toes and I was trying hard not to care about comfort, to become someone who could march all the way to the Volga on bare blistered soles, but my hair felt clean for the first time in months and there was hot coffee, instant stirred right into the cup but I even drank down the sludge.

"Well, you must have questions," Phoebe finally said, as I sat dressed and pressed on the toilet seat sipping my second cup. "So fire away. Now or never."

"Paradise City," I said, shivering with the early spring chill and pressing my palms tighter against the warm cup. The words felt thin and sour against my tongue like drops of ink. "What about Elbertsville? There was a human settlement there, just humans, Lisa said."

Phoebe pulled her clothes off, trailed fingers in the luke-warm tub; she hadn't had to tell me not to drain the water. "I wouldn't know anything about that," she said. "Maybe there was one, could've died off last winter, could've been raided. There's gangs all over the north county, y'know, human, extra-human, some of those folks could be over here now, all I know. If your Lisa didn't just get the whole story wrong to start with."

Naked, Phoebe was all jutting bones and splotchy skin, angry eczematous patches interspersed with gleaming grease: mois-turizer slopped on too thick, or maybe corn or olive oil, like Ms. Acosta and I used when we couldn't stand the winter scali-ness. Bits of her skin shone with it like the elbows of a worn-out suit. She jumped into the tub, dug fingertips into the thick wet scum of the soapdish. "Anyway," she said, "what the hell does it matter? Trust me, kid, we humans are a hell of a lot better off here than on our own. We've got protection, guards—"

"They're not here to keep us in?"

She shrugged, scrubbed at an armpit. "Sorry to disappoint

you, but they're a lot more worried about keeping gangs *out*. And away from us. We're valuable to them, we clean, we cook, we keep everything up and running while they're off sleeping and hunting and fighting with each other—"

"And what you said about being roasted, on a spit. You were joking, right?"

My voice was high and wavering and I didn't realize how hard I'd been thinking about that, wondering, as Phoebe let me stuff and fatten myself with as much fish and fruit as I wanted. They ate anything, exes. Anything. Phoebe put the soap down, shook another low soft volley of laughter from her throat like someone rattling a pair of dice in the cup.

"Rabbits, deer, squirrels, possum," she said. "All over the woods. Lots of woods around here, you've seen, don't forget this whole side of the city's *inside* national parkland. And they don't give a shit what they eat as long as there's a lot of it, they don't fight us for the canned stuff—I mean, you don't want to know why the streets around here are mostly clean of bodies. Long-dead bodies. Little girls don't need to ask." She plucked a dry towel from the bathroom floor, wrapped it around her tight. "Cattle, they had plenty of those before we ever came along. What they really need are mules."

I could see the bottom of my cup now. I sipped slower. But still, Phoebe, still they *can* eat anything.

"What's a skip?" I asked. "I heard someone talk about cleaning up—"

"Dead body," Phoebe explained. She shook her jeans, layers of thin T-shirts, thick cotton sweaters out, threw them back on. "Buggy skips, bony skips, like I said there aren't that many, but the cleanup crew handles what we've got. That and the hunting remains, the bosses leave that shit lying everywhere. Everyone rotates through the different work crews, cooking, cleanup, construction, you'll get your turn, *no fear*." She chortled at the thought. "I don't suppose you were a little math whiz or anything, were you? Tops in your school science fair, building A-bombs in your bathtub for fun?"

"I hated science."

"Pity." Phoebe took the cup as I held it out to her, gulped down the last muddy mouthfuls. "Every now and then we get someone who was an engineer, doctor, sewage and sanitation—they get the plum assignments, working on getting the electricity and the water and all of that up and running again."

"How are they going to do that?" I didn't know anything about how all that worked, less than nothing, but I was pretty sure you needed oil or natural gas or something and there was that Amoco refinery, up in Whiting, but Whiting might as well be on the moon. "I mean, without any oil or—"

"The kid's a little technician now! Don't ask *me*, that was never my area. I just know there's blueprints and plans and all kinds of fuss about it, maybe they can get the generators up and running or something." She dipped the coffee cup in our abandoned bathwater, scrubbing it out with soap-scummy fingertips. "Or, that giant lake, right over yonder, hydroelectricity or—hell, I don't know. Above, my, pay grade." She shook out the cup, her face easing from its rictus of friendly fervor into weary, sagging resentment. "I'm a scientist, you know. I'm a biologist, I worked at the lab in Prairie Beach before the plague hit. Me and Kevin, my husband. We're not allowed back there, it's bosses-only now. Except under 'special circumstances,' and don't ask me what those are, they're not talking. So where are you from, anyway?"

"Lepingville." I reached over and worked the sink faucet, like I had the tub's; nothing came out, of course, but something in me still wanted to test it, make sure. "But I was in Leyton for a while too."

"Yeah, we've all wandered all over the place. Step ahead of the microbes, right?" She flashed me a grin, kept swooping the cup through the grimy water gone a faint gray. "So you lived in Lepingville all your life? Or did you move there from somewhere else, you and your mom and dad?"

"My mom and dad and I," I said, jiggling the toilet handle and hearing only hollow rattling metal, "and my older sister and brother, we all lived in Leyton. My mom and dad were both lawyers." Lawyer, that was rich enough for a Leyton house. I liked this, kind of, inventing my own little false family history; I'd have to tell Lisa about it, so she didn't give me away. "But I was born in Lepingville, they lived there before that, when Lisa was just—"

"Kid, we all know Lisa's not really your sister, give it up." Phoebe pressed her lips together in a prim little pout, shook the cup out again. "It's okay. So did you really have a brother and sister and all that? Or was it just you and your mom? In Lepingville, or maybe Leyton?"

She was staring at me now. Staring hard. That fading afternoon light spilling soft from the bathroom window, it was no bare police station bulb. I stared right back. "Do you really have a husband, named Kevin, and all that?" I replied, smiling that same wide-eyed way she smiled. "Are you really a biologist? In Prairie Beach, or maybe Burns Harbor?"

Something in her face twitched, subsided. "You don't need to get all sensitive, kid, seriously. I mean—" She was winding herself up again, I could see it, every bit of her down to the ends of her wispy cropped hair bristling like her thrilled-up nerves. "—I mean, I'm just curious, I was just wondering, we're all in the same boat, we're *all human beings here*! 'Cept, of course, for those who aren't."

She smiled at me again. "Your mom's not with you. That's too bad. I'm sorry. Did she get through the winter okay, or did—"

"What work crew am I on?" I asked.

"So was it just you and Lisa, then? Last winter?"

"Kevin, your husband, has he stopped beating you?"

Phoebe's eyebrows shot up, two feathery black gulls rising from the sands, and she gave the coffee cup one last swish and jumped to her feet.

"You're a gofer, to start off," she said, frowning at herself in the mirror and picking strands of my hair off the brush before dragging it over her scalp. "Go from group to group, do what anyone needs, you'll get your own crew eventually. Don't get lazy and wander off, you'll get reported." She chuckled, scratched hard at a dry patch. "Billy and Mags, they're in charge of everything around here, but you don't bug them with questions, ask the crew supervisors instead. Your shift's sundown to sunup, breakfast when you get up, dinner at three A.M., you just had your weekly bath. There's a few latrines dug over by Olney Avenue, two blocks west, we're working on more. You need supplies, tampons, tissues, aspirin, whatever, you run it by me or Jenny from the day shift and you never just come in here and grab shit, there's an inventory. We'll find out."

She turned from the mirror, the patch she'd scratched bright pink and oozing, like that thing on Dave's neck that never healed up. "You're a good kid," she said. "I can tell. And you'll get used to it. You're a lot better off here than on the outside. Give it time. Okay?"

"Okay," I said.

"*Okay!*" She scampered past me onto the hallway's flattened, filthy beige carpeting, sweeping an arm furiously behind her for me to follow. "That's the attitude I like to hear! I'll give you to Kevin's crew first, sure I'm prejudiced but trust me, he never bites . . ."

I trailed behind her, watching the living room windows catch fire in soft flickering golds and roses. Sunset. They'd better not be lying about Lisa. If I don't see her again by sunrise, I'm not letting anyone shut me up about it. Not Phoebe, or that Billy.

Maybe Don will shoot me, if I ask about Lisa. I need to teach myself not to be scared of that. I saw someone shooting people in the street once at the height of the plague, I think his wife and then himself, and as long as it's in the head it's quick. Messy, I screamed watching it, but quick. I need to remember that.

# EIGHT

Kevin, Phoebe's husband, turned out to be the genial over-sized linebacker guy from the cleanup crew; he was easy to be around, big and steady, one of those people whose inner calm is like the warmth from an invisible furnace that seeps right into your own bones. Keeps you steady too. I couldn't imagine what the hell he'd ever seen in Phoebe, but my mom once said that that was more marriages than you'd think. I helped him and his crew clear more clumps of dead leaves from the gutters, no skips buggy or otherwise this time, and then he sent me to help another crew dig holes for trash burial, and then to help a gardening crew sort out salvaged hoes, rakes, gardening gloves. No serious planting yet, not until the middle of May.

The others, they weren't friendly or unfriendly: mostly quiet and contained within themselves, that way folks have of holding their eyes down, shoulders drawn in, elbows close to their bodies to show they need to grab a bit of space any way they can. They didn't care if I were new or not, didn't care I was clumsy with a shovel and almost sliced my wrist open trying to hack dried dirt from a trowel. A lot of them, their shuffling feet, hollow eyes, greasy lank hair never mind the weekly bath, you could tell they'd stopped caring about much of anything. Kristin, all over again. I turned my back on it and kept working.

No exes, not in charge of the crews, not anywhere. If you stayed away from the guard perimeter you might never see them, never know about all the invisible hands divvying up our labors. I wanted to ask about that, but all those dead faces stopped me cold.

A few dozen humans on night shift, a few dozen on day, no more, all clustered in four or five Elbert houses that hadn't flooded. Men's dorm, women's, family dorm. The "commissary" building and other houses, here and there, held the supplies foraged from dozens of safe houses; there were scouting teams that still went out, looking for more, but those were ex-only. A huge falling-apart manse on Illinois, with another woodstove in it, that was our dining hall. The old zombie fencing we'd passed through on Mass Avenue, the bits of forest ringing the whole neighborhood, those were our borderlands. Five or six blocks in each direction, our whole world. Prairie Beach, Lake Michigan, no more than a few miles removed but still, on another planet.

The exes, a few dozen of them, had the bigger houses on Indiana Avenue, but folks said some of them never got over their zombie habits and still liked to sleep in the woods. "You could stumble over 'em," a garden crewwoman named Corinne warned me. "Just lying there, sleeping the meat off like a wino on a park bench. If you do? Step right around 'em, then run like hell." She poked at the dead leaf piles, clustering them together so the day shift could lay them down for mulch. "Or you might not come back at all."

"Quit scaring her," someone muttered.

"It's true." Corinne looked up from her mulch pile, bulgy blue rabbit eyes daring them to deny it. "Isn't it?"

The other crew members snorted, smirked, went back to scrubbing the rust off rake tines. Maybe I was being hazed. I didn't care. I got the real message: Even when you don't see the "bosses," they're always around. And they'll get what's theirs. One way, or another.

So really, when you think about it, nothing much has changed at all.

Dinner. I followed Kevin's crew across the backyards toward Illinois Avenue, all except him ignoring me entirely and talking among themselves, and then I jumped when someone slipped from between the houses and stopped me in my tracks. Lisa. I grabbed her hand and she hugged me, carefully, just draping her arms around me and not squeezing.

"I was worried," she said, almost abashed like she thought I'd laugh at her. "You can't get any straight answers from anyone—"

"Neither can I," I said, and rubbed at my arm, bitten, bruised, aching down to the fingertips from helping dig the trash holes. Lisa frowned when she saw that, scoured a dirt streak from my face with her knuckles. "Where've you been? Kevin said you were all hunting? We never see any exes when we're working, outside the guard perimeter—"

"Hunting. Sleeping. Like you. There's a big house on Indiana, mint green siding, where they graciously let me bunk."

I took her arm and we wandered into the yard of a big gray house with holes all through the roof and a back porch half clinging to the house wall, half-collapsed into a pile of rotten wood; the front porch was intact but with boards missing here and there, dark rectangular gaps like the black keys on a piano. Inside it was hot and stuffy, even with the faint nighttime chill and all the windows open. Flashlights were propped in every corner, the big industrial kind, turning the room into a constellation of rushing shadows and melting spotlights; people threaded their way toward tables crammed with a profusion of mismatched chairs.

"You, Red," someone growled. Right by my ear. "In here, you and your owner. I want a better look at what Don's dragged in."

Billy. I swallowed, pushed back into the front room with Lisa, grabbed a chair. Kevin was already there, sitting hunched up and awkward on a too-small chair and looking about as happy as I felt. The rest of his crew were in a long line snaking toward the kitchen, or maneuvering past with plates full of food; they went back out the door, to eat on the porch steps or the lawn. Billy sat right across from us, towheaded and lounging easy in his chair and even though it was so stuffy, he wasn't sweating a drop. Sitting next to him was a woman with big gray eyes and curly, deep auburn hair spilling over her shoulders; she had soft pale skin, a soft fleshy body spilling out of a wine-colored summer dress, a fat little cupid's mouth pert and prim and painted Janey-red. A worn-down torch singer from some really old movie, she looked like, any moment now she'd jump up on the table and start caterwauling about how her man done her wrong. Billy noticed me looking, and gave her a nudge.

"You got an admirer, Mags," he said, half-sneering and half-proud. "Lookit it, even meat on two legs knows a good thing when they see it—*Naomi!* Get your ass in here *now!*"

Something came swift and panting through the forest of legs, like a rabbit fleeing across a lawn, and a little girl of six, maybe seven, dark brown hair chopped off raggedy short around her ears, came skidding to a wide-eyed stop in front of Billy. He grabbed her by the collar, baring his teeth.

"What're you doing in there?" he demanded, voice all sweet and his mouth frozen in a smile like a clean, exposed blade. "Sitting i n t he k itchen w ith y our t humb u p y our a ss h oping someone throws you a few more bites? You ain't no pet dog. Get the table set *now.*"

Lisa had half-risen from her chair but the little girl was gone again, shoving through the crowd back into the kitchen like her life was at stake and it probably was. The auburn-haired woman, Mags, she just smirked and lolled her head backward so we all got a better look at her cleavage, damp and dimpled like a bruised fruit from the back of the fridge. Naomi came rushing back, silently setting out stained paper and cloth napkins, china and plastic plates, and in Lisa's eyes watching her there was this full, quiet hunger, like a rain droplet on a leaf tip growing rounder and fatter until you almost held your breath for it to fall. You just didn't see many small children, not anymore, just like you almost never saw anyone truly old: They got sick first, they had less to get them through the first winter. The smallest babies, good as wiped out. Some of the humans, waiting for their rations, they had the same look in their eyes too.

When she was done Naomi stood behind Mags's chair, dead quiet; Lisa gave her a friendly little glance but Naomi just ducked her head. The table was filling up: Don and Janey next to Billy and Mags, Phoebe next to Kevin, because this wouldn't have been a shitty enough meal already. The seat on my other side was empty until a thin tall boy—a little older, maybe twenty— came in hauling a huge tray steaming with food, his arms almost buckling under the weight; he slammed it down before Billy so hard that m eat juices slopped everywhere, running over the table in rivulets like dirty puddle water, then threw himself into the last empty chair with a loud sigh. Phoebe squirmed on her cushion and rubbed her hands together, working herself into a paroxysm of put-on delight.

"Well!" she cried, beaming at us all like Bob Cratchit over the Christmas goose. "Isn't *this* another legendary spread, Stephen, you kids in the kitchen have outdone yourself yet ag—"

"Shut up, you stupid little frail hoocow bitch," Mags said, her voice rich and rolling like a cool spring fog, and flung her shoulders back in another burst of sweat. "For what you are about to receive, you should all be goddamned fucking grateful. Everyone eat."

She dug her bare hands into the bowls and platters, Billy eagerly following suit, and us handful of humans waited our turn; Don doled out a plateful for Janey, Lisa did the same for me. "Naomi," she called out, quite deliberately. "Aren't you going to sit with us and eat?"

Naomi shook her head, still staring at her shoes. What had happened to her parents? Had Billy, this Mags, been part of it? Mags gave Lisa a tilted little smile, then made a show of passing Naomi a huge slice of meat; Naomi gobbled it down so fast I wondered about her for a moment, but no, she was human, you just knew it. Human, and kept constantly hungry.

"There's corn too, Naomi." The boy next to me, presumably

Stephen, held out a ladle overflowing with neat, toothlike kernels. Human too. "You like corn, don't you?"

"It's none of your damned business," Billy spat, the other side of his jaw still frantically working at his meat, "what she—"

"I bet you do," Kevin said, and took the ladle from Stephen. "Have some."

Billy stared at Kevin, at Stephen in hard, glassy-eyed malice. Naomi dipped her small head right into the ladle, pecking like a scared, starving bird. Canned corn, canned green beans, white rice, venison, rabbit. Glasses and cups of water to wash it down. All around me rose a chorus of raggedy sighs and smacking lips and wet air-sucking gulps as the exes shoved it all in, fistfuls of rice, whole slices of venison, spilling cornucopia-spoonfuls of corn; I concentrated on my plate, on taking calm, reasoned, slow mouthfuls.

"This is *wonderful*, Stephen," Phoebe sighed, giving him a wide, happy smile studded with stuck kernel skins. "Every time it just amazes me, how—"

"So what trash heap'd she pluck you from, frail?" Billy said, leaning forward with eyes dancing like he was about to laugh. Laugh at me, hard and mean. "Lepingville crest on that jacket, that's right down the road from where Mags and I used to like to hunt. Looks like we were neighbors, don't it."

My jacket sleeve. Which is how Phoebe knew I was lying, about Leyton, because I'm just that much of an idiot—Lisa was quiet, waiting to take her cues. Kevin glanced from Billy to me, big round blue eyes tense and wary like he'd seen this before, like it'd been him on the hot seat before. "So what if she's got a jacket?" he said, glancing down at his Bears jersey. "I never played football. I found this in someone's closet, last winter."

"I got it off someone dead," I agreed. Following his cue. "I don't come from—"

"Uh-*uh*," Phoebe singsonged, with the dancing, gleeful expression of a kid getting a bigger sister in trouble.

"Phoebe," Kevin closed his eyes in exasperation. "Don't."

"Well, she said she did," said Phoebe, sulky and put-upon, as she stabbed hard at an errant bean. "I heard her, Kevin, you didn't. Lepingville, by way of Leyton, or was it the other way around—"

"And only a human would care," Don interrupted, serene and half-sated, putting thin little bits of rabbit on Janey's plate. "Human towns, human cities—all dead, all gone." He gave a tight half-smile to me, to Stephen, the convulsive mouth of a salesman forcing himself to grin at the boss's awful jokes. "Our undead turf too, all the old forests, nature preserves, little hived-off bits of prairie, abandoned farmland, dead subdivisions—remember how we used to think that made us something, Billy, decades spent stumbling aimlessly from tree to bush, marinating in our own squalor and rot, and if we managed to jump a careless human every other month or so it made us queens and kings? Here lurks Ozymandias, right behind the dung pile! Look on, ye frail-fleshed and shallow-boned, and pretend you saw nothing!"

He laughed, thrust his fork into another slice of meat. "A nasty, brutish, vermin-riddled farce disguised as living. Stray dogs had more dignity. And then, suddenly, by utter accident—life! Actual, inexhaustible life!" His eyes narrowed as he studied Janey, Stephen, me, and he grinned in earnest. "The only true life there ever was, the only life that isn't slow nonstop rot. And we have it. And I mean to make the most of it. Doesn't it make you want to dance, Billy? I mean, really dance, not just that pathetic fall-over psychic two-step we used to think was cutting a rug?"

Billy frowned and chewed his beans with a funny, lost look on his face, like a senile old man at his own birthday party who'd couldn't fathom why total strangers were handing him cake. Janey sat looking at her meat, nonplussed, like it was some strange art display, and then Don waved a hand and she let out a murmur of surprise, shook her head, quickly ate the slices all up and looked to him for a nod of approval. She only ate when he said she could, then, just like with Naomi. Maybe he punished her if she disobeyed him, no driving privileges. No lipstick.

Don was gazing at me now, with the same grimace of distaste he'd given me on the roadside. "You never answered Billy's question," he noted. "Did you."

"She doesn't have to answer anything," Lisa said, her voice tight. "Or was that all just more crap you fed me, about 'respecting family ties—'"

"You've been fed half the day and your frail don't stink anymore, you can let her pony up when she's asked." Mags's voice was drawling and singsong like she was beyond bored. "You have any more family here, kid? Mother, brother, other—"

"You already know she doesn't," said Kevin. Gripping his plastic picnic spoon like a weapon. "They'd be here. Just—"

"They're not here," I said, just so Mags would stop talking. My mother wasn't dead. They kept telling me that, saying it for years now and they were wrong, but I didn't say "my mother" and I didn't say "dead." You don't confirm lies out loud, that's dangerous. My stomach twisted up and I wanted to shove my plate away, but I was afraid they'd punish me if I didn't eat. Pick up your fork. Eat it like medicine. Then something struck hard at my hand and the fork flew right out of it, and I was rigid in my chair as Mags loomed over the table, arm still raised.

"When one of us talks," she snarled, "you listen, and answer. You understand?"

Her t's, k's, d's jabbed and stabbed at my ears even as her voice went hissing soft, like fireplace pokers wrapped in moldy velvet. Lisa was on her feet, Kevin too but I could feel them both holding back, gauging how far they could go before I got punished for what they did; Lisa put a hand on my shoulder, careful, just the palm.

"She's right, Amy," Lisa said, voice soft, a stroke of the hand in silent apology as we all sat back down. "Go on. Don't act too good for the room."

*Or you'll get your head kicked in and I can't stop them.* Just like with Don. "We lived in Lepingville," I said. I looked Mags straight in the eye, her big dolly-eye fringed with the longest lashes I'd ever seen. When did women stop having round-cheeked doll faces like that? She must've died decades ago like Don, longer. "Me and my mom. That was it. Lisa's not my sister. We met on the road. She thought saying that would make it easier here. My dad died when I was little. My mom . . ." You do not affirm lies out loud. ". . . is gone."

Janey held my fork out to me, timid, confused, and I didn't take it because I couldn't pretend to eat anymore. Don gave her a little nudge. "Your food, Jeanette Isabella," he muttered. "It's only half-gone."

Janey looked flummoxed for a moment, then smiled like she'd just worked out an impossible math problem and dug in, with my fork. I'd been wrong, she wasn't waiting for permission. She needed Don to remind her to eat at all. Stephen, who'd sat picking at his green beans and glowering in silence, pushed his chair aside and stood up.

"New platter," he muttered, and dumped what was left on Don's, Billy's, Mags's plates, carelessly as a farmer slopping pigs. He took off for the kitchen, all long skinny shambling legs; as he came marching back with another meat-piled platter Naomi suddenly darted into his path, reaching for a napkin that had dropped to the floor. He tripped right over her, fresh utensils and meat and gravy and gloppy rice splattering over the dirty wooden boards like some great invisible creature sicked it all up.

Stephen shouted in surprise, sprawled on hands and knees in the mess, and Naomi let out this breathless little scream of terror like a rabbit seized by a cat. Billy was out of his chair, thick pale fingers in her scalp clenching her chopped-off hair and nobody was doing anything, we were all sitting there, standing there, holding our breaths, waiting. Even knowing it'd take him only seconds, a second, to snap her neck.

"It was my fault," Stephen said, almost slipping again in a juice puddle as he dragged himself to his feet. "I wasn't looking where I was going, she was picking up—"

"You little shit," Billy whispered, nose to nose with Naomi. His hard ex's voice had gone soft and molten like wax under a match, as if the rest of us were squawking receding dots he couldn't see, couldn't hear through the fog of his own rage. "Do I keep you around so you can starve me? Do I do that? Do I keep you so you can *fuck with my food* and get your miserable scrawny meat-stick ass in the way of—"

"It was my fault!" Stephen shouted. "I wasn't looking!"

"Leave her alone," Lisa whispered, and she was out of her chair again like someone had pulled her by the collar, like slow strangulating strings were forcing her to rise. "Get your hands off her, and leave her alone."

"You fucked with my food." Billy shook Naomi until I felt my own teeth rattling. His face was a smooth, bloodless mask, eyes the thinnest of paper slits. "You *fucked* with—"

"I didn't mean it!" Naomi's voice came out in a warbling little croak, like she hadn't spoken in hours or days, and then she was sobbing hard knowing it wouldn't do her any good. "I was picking up Janey's napkin, I didn't see, I'm sorry—"

"This how you want to behave, Naomi?" Mags was perfectly calm, sitting there popping another chunk of venison in her mouth as Naomi went scarlet from crying. "You want the Scissor Men to take you away? Because if you don't wanna be a good girl, if you don't even wanna look where you're going, they can come take you someplace bad—"

"I don't." Naomi was gasping, snuffling back tears, Lisa was standing there vibrating with rage trying to judge her moment, couldn't just jump in case he hurt Naomi, and Don was smiling at Stephen daring him to try. "I don't want to go with them, I'm sorry, I'm sorry, I want to stay here with you—"

"Come on," Kevin whispered, pushing back his chair, taking my arm ready to haul us both out the door. "Come with me and Phoebe. They're too angry to care who they hurt. Come on quick."

I stayed where I was because I couldn't move. Phoebe sat there too, her eyes dark with unfeigned fear.

"You wanna go to the bad place?" Billy was singsonging now, a sneering lullaby from behind gleaming grinning teeth. "They'll take you there, you little bitch, the Scissor Men'll take you there *right now* and they'll snip your hands clean off, snip your feet off, you'll never run and trip people ever again, snip *snip*—"

Naomi made another sobbing screaming sound and Lisa was grappling with Don, who'd thrown himself feet-first in her path. Don's chair went flying, Phoebe leapt out of the way before it could hit her and Kevin shoved her protectively behind him; Janey sat there smiling at nothing while Don and Lisa feverishly punched and kicked, scrabbling in the fallen meat scraps and drying smears of rice. Mags just laughed and kept stuffing her round pretty face and my skin felt swollen hot, my arm was raised with my water cup ready to fly at Mags's head and then Janey, spacey oblivious Janey had my arm in a death grip, forcing it and the cup down with both hands. Stephen was brandishing something long and tarnished in Billy's face, the big carving knife he'd dropped tripping over Naomi, and even though that was nothing to Billy but a rusty scrape, a papercut, we were all watching, the whole room was suddenly still and quiet. Stephen's teeth were clenched tight and his face looked as flushed as Naomi's, hot as mine felt, not with fear but rage.

"You had your fun," he told Billy, his knuckles pale and taut around the knife handle. His face was as thin and angular as Billy's was smooth and full. Naomi just stood there between them, crying. "It's not enough you make that new girl turn her life inside out for you, now you have to beat up on a little kid, again, because you're such a pathetic fucking freak you can't handle looking at—"

Billy hit him in the jaw and Stephen went sailing, face-first to the floor. Don wrenched himself from Lisa's grasp and kicked Stephen in the side, hard, again, and Stephen made retching sounds and stretched an arm out, shielding his face. His fingers uncurled slowly, he let the knife drop, and Billy motioned Don back.

"Don't fuck him up too much," he muttered to Don. "He's our best cook."

Don kicked him a few more times, the ribs, the back of a knee, and Stephen made a choking noise, retched in earnest; he curled up, knees to chin, rocking where he lay. Janey still had my arm and when she stared at me it was like a cloth suddenly swept cobwebs from a smudged window, she was alert and urgent and every part of her signaled *Be quiet, be still and quiet—* and then she blinked and her eyes filled with formless, benign shadows once again. She sat down and smiled at the air until Don returned to her, patting her hand reassuringly like someone else had caused all the fuss.

Phoebe, standing back against the wall, let out a high-pitched, seesawing giggle; Kevin gave her a sharp nudge to silence her. Billy still had Naomi clenched in his hands, beneath the panic in her face I could see how much it hurt, and Lisa was reaching for the carving knife when Mags polished off the last of her rabbit, let out a huge rumbling belch, stood and slid her fingers up and down Billy's arm, down and up. His mouth curled up, slowly, into a sulky pucker; he let Naomi go, and Mags smiled.

"I think we got the point across, William," she said, and even with all those poker thrusts of the tongue it was the softest ex-voice I'd ever heard. "The whole point. One of these days, you'll go and kill her without meaning it."

She shook her hair back, every part of her rippling and shuddering beneath the wine-colored dress, and bent her head to Naomi, crouched in a huddled heap of misery by Don's chair. "We were just angry, pet." Naomi was crying again, tiny little sniffing sounds as she mopped a small hand across her cheek, and Mags murmured and cooed. "We didn't mean it. We're sorry. You're a good girl. There's no such thing as Scissor Men—"

"There are!" Naomi shrieked, her hands balling into fists by her sides; coughing up snot, big brown eyes pinned in terror, but the words flew from her in a paroxysm of frustration. "You're lying, you're lying to everyone, I've *seen* Scissor Men, they're all over the beach, there are, there are, there are—"

Billy flew at her, and Janey and Phoebe both screamed; Mags grabbed and wrestled him backward, forcing him back into his chair like he was the little kid misbehaving, and shoved him back against the cushions while Lisa held tight to Naomi, teeth bared, febrile and vibrating to hurt something like she never was with that feral dog. Stephen tried to get up and Don kicked him again. Billy made a horrible sound, a squeezing strangling noise as if his own body were throttling him, and then caught his breath. Inhaled like some agitated horse, with a loud, whinnying whistle.

"Okay," he said, staring up at Mags, not resisting her anymore, breath slowing as she rubbed the back of his neck. "Okay. Okay."

Mags twined fingers in his hair, pale blond and cornsilk-fine so it slipped away as she touched it. She gave Lisa a rueful little smile. "You better take her," she said, glancing at Naomi. "Mood he's in, he really will snap her neck. You want the run of her so bad? Go on, then. Play saint for a few days. You'll get sick of her soon enough. Trust me."

Billy got up from his chair, sliding an arm around Mags's waist; they turned and headed for the back porch, side by side. Naomi, who'd been staring from ex to ex wide-eyed and fearful, pushed hard against Lisa's arms.

"Daddy!" she shouted at Billy's retreating back. Neither of them even slowed their steps. "Daddy! Mommy! Don't leave me again!" Lisa bent close to her, trying to soothe, and Naomi beat fists against Lisa's body as her face distorted, crumpled. "Mommy, *Daddy*, come back, I'm sorry! *I'm sorry!*"

"Later," Lisa told her quietly. She couldn't see us, the whole rest of the room had vanished. Only Naomi. "They'll come back later, when things are better, not—"

"*Mommy!*" Naomi screamed.

I ran for the front door as fast as I could go.

Illinois Avenue was empty again and I kept running, away and away from the back porch and that whole house, until I was winded and dizzy and had to sit down hard on the curb at Buell. I pulled out my cell phone, I was going to call whoever called me, find them, ask them to come get me out of here, but it was dead a nd w ouldn't l ight u p n o m atter h ow m any b uttons I pressed and I choked back all my shouting, shoved it back in my jeans. Closed my eyes. Still dizzy.

I had my head hunched down and my jacket open to let in cool air, trying not to remember that boy Stephen puking sick because I already felt nauseous enough, and then I heard footsteps and jolted my head up. Phoebe. She gave me a big hearty grin, like we were old friends meeting in a bar, but the whole rest of her face sagged in exhaustion.

"They're not actually her mom and dad, you know," she told me, sitting down next to me. "If that's what got you all upset—"

"So tell her that," I said. I took my jacket off, folding it up on my lap. Maybe I'd sleep somewhere around here tonight, use this as a pillow. Eating, that'd be a problem, but I'd think of something. Berries. Nuts. Spring was coming.

I want to go home.

"They hate each other, you know," Phoebe said, her voice sprightly with the chance to pass on gossip. "They can't stand each other."

"I can tell," I said. "I was there—"

"No, I mean, the bosses like Billy, Mags, Don, who really were dead? Undead, however you want it? Can't deal with the ones like your Lisa, the plain old living humans who got sick and passed over. It's like the Serbs versus the Albanians, or whoever the fuck they were fighting." Her toes raked against the knife-scarred asphalt. "I mean, makes sense, no? The undead ones, some of them kicked maybe a few years ago and some of them like Don, his time stopped in the *forties*, for God's sake, I think Mr. and Mrs. Mae West are even older than that. Imagine your great-great-grandmother trying to make a clue of this world, for God's sake they didn't even have antibiotics." Her face knotted up, imagining it, and she laughed. "Of course, neither do we, anymore, for now. But yeah. You and I only think Lisa's the same species as all of them, but she's as different from them as from Naomi. Or me."

Don's smell, Billy's, that pungency of decay steeped in salt-water. Pickled. When I was five or six there was some sort of environmental security conference in Boston, discounted group rates for everything, and my mother got to go and so we flew on a plane for the first and only time in my life; there was a day trip to one of the protected Cape Cod beaches out by West Dennis, and for the first and only time in my life we saw the ocean. I grabbed a huge chunk of bright green seaweed and started chewing it and it was rubbery, sticky, oozing this salty sap that was like sweat solidified but brinier and I spat it out, Mom laughing at me. Then she chewed some herself just to see what it was like. Don and Billy, Mags, that's what they smelled like. That seaweed, sitting on a dry shoreline oxygenating and going rotten. Lisa, her skin, it just smells like skin.

"Fine, so they can barely stand each other," I said. "What's that to me? They hate all of *us*. They hate Lisa because she doesn't hate me—"

"Don doesn't hate Janey either, or maybe you didn't notice." Phoebe beamed, lay back on her elbows on the grass. "Doesn't hate her *at all*. Billy, I think it sickens him. Oh, well. My point is, kid, never make the mistake of thinking they're all some sort of tight little tribe, they'd kill and eat each other if they could and I'd bet that's actually happened, once or twice. They don't like each other. They're not each other, period. I mean, at least *we* can all say we're one and the same."

Phoebe one and the same with me, after she called me a liar right in front of Billy? Who the hell did she think she was kidding? She just wanted to get me out of Lisa's corner, use that for her own leverage. Like my mom used to say, subtle as the Black Death. I hate people who think I'm stupid.

"Poor Naomi," I said. I hadn't even tried to help her. Too scared what'd happen, if I weren't still and quiet.

A faint little line popped up between Phoebe's brows, then subsided again. Up this close her skin was equal parts oil slick and iguana hide.

"That 'bad place' of hers?" she said, making little spinning-fingertip quote marks against the sky. "The one they keep her hopping with, boohoo Mommy Daddy don't send me away? It's not half so bad. Honest. Sooner or later, folks will understand that—"

"It must be bad enough, if she got that scared." I patted my pockets again, making sure nothing had fallen out of them when

I ran from the house. "Or maybe you thought that was all a big laugh, like Mags did—"

"Oh, kid, for Christ's sake don't start with the *melodrama*, you saw what happened when Good Sir Stevie tried jumping in. Coulda told him. Have told him. But nobody ever listens to ol' Pheebs! Not even her own damned husband!" She shouted that last part loud enough that I looked all around me, worried a gate patrol might find us. "There's no 'bad place' and no Scissor Men and no whatever else that kid's got mucked up in her head, she's probably seen enough shit since last winter that she's scared of everything that moves." She shrugged, scratched hard at her scalp. "What're you always looking for in those pockets of yours, anyway? Every time I see you, you're patting yourself down like a cop."

"Nothing." I forced my fingers still. "Just habit."

"The b ad p lace," s he r epeated. " So-called b ad. I t's n ot s o bad." She tilted her chin, glanced at me. "You, kid, end of the day I think you'd actually understand that. Better than anyone."

No trumpet blasts, no shouting. Just this concentrated look in her eyes and such quiet, intense purpose in her voice that something prickly and unpleasant began working its way along my skin, like a caterpillar undulating its way across droughty grass.

"I don't know what *place* anyone's talking about," I told her, trying to talk in razor slices of rancor like an ex. Pretending I was singing it, up on stage, my own band. I couldn't make the consonants punch and bleed like exes could. "There's no such place, there's a place but it's not a bad place—make up your mind, is this a riddle?"

Phoebe pursed her thin colorless lips, like she really was thinking that over. "Kind of," she said. "Kind of."

She pulled herself upright in exaggerated fits and starts, like an actress imitating an arthritic old woman. "Go back to the ladies' dorm and get some rest," she said, curling her arms over her head, arching her back with a show of gritted teeth. She headed down Buell in a brisk little jog, and vanished from sight.

The sky was going soft and striated around the edges, the weakest bit of dawn sun showing like lamplight through a thick paper shade. Tomorrow. I will figure this all out tomorrow. I'll tell Lisa. Right now she's just got her hands full.

The few thin streaks of gray morning light were getting fuller, yet softer as I reached Elbert and the front porch steps, swung my hand to the wooden railing, and then I jumped and almost shouted as someone darted from the bushes right by the front door. A girl thirteen, maybe fourteen, long straight dark hair and a bottom lip chewed raw, holding something rolled up in a cloth napkin. I remembered her, vaguely, from the line of crew workers snaking into the kitchen.

"Are you Amy?" she whispered. "He said red hair—"

Wonderful, total strangers *everywhere* know me on sight. Can we trade scalps? "Yeah. So what?"

"Supposed to give you this." She shoved the napkin into my hand. "Don't show it to anyone. I gotta go."

She ran off across the lawn and into the trees. I stood there holding the avocado green napkin, smeared stiff with gravy and wrapped around something hard, almost afraid what I'd find. I unrolled it—

A fork. Like the one I'd lost at dinner. Wrapped around the handle was a note.

*This isn't much of a gift, but after what happened at dinner you looked like you needed a token of . . . something. Ignore Billy, he likes to torture people. Your friend Lisa is burning up the place angry about what they did to you. And to Naomi. It's good here to have Lisa's kind on your side, get what you can out of it. Ignore Phoebe. As you probably figured out, she's nuts. Speaking of how Billy likes to torture people.*

*Things aren't usually as bad as this.*

No signature. Janey? She wouldn't be anywhere near this lucid. I read it again, turned it over but the other side of the paper was blank.

Ignore Billy. Laugh in the flying-glass face of a tornado.

I wrapped it all up again, fork and note and napkin, zipped them into my empty jacket pocket. The day shift was still sleeping but there was an empty futon in the far corner and I lay there curled on my side, waiting for tomorrow, waiting to see just how bad things usually got.

# NINE

Commissary breakfast, this time, was honey-roasted nuts, sardines, stale onion crackers like plaster slices with little poppyseeds that burrowed into the gums. I was looking for Kevin's crew again, like Phoebe told me to, when the girl who'd passed me the note ran up, still biting her lip, big brown eyes perpetually anxious and her dark hair a sleek shiny curve like the back of a seal.

"You're supposed to go in the kitchens," she said, whispering even though nobody was there to overhear. "Billy said, he decided it, ask anyone if you don't believe me. It's only Stephen there now, but the rest of the cooking crew comes in later—"

"What's your name, anyway?" I demanded. Stephen. I didn't want to see him again, it was embarrassing thinking what he'd look like after trying to stand up to Billy while I just sat there, like Phoebe, doing nothing to help. Up close every part of Seal

Girl was in constant movement, eyes blinking and fingers twitching and body shifting from foot to foot like she needed to run to the latrines. Maybe she did.

"Natalie," she said, and as I caught her eye she ducked her head and her soft-shoeing doubled. "I'm on gofer duty, I have to leave."

"Where's Lisa?" I grabbed her arm.

"I don't know, out hunting with them or . . . why do I care? I'm not her slavey. I don't want to know."

She yanked free and ran, skittering into the bushes just like last night, before I could ask about Naomi. Kitchen duty. One of the best jobs, the most prestigious, all that food in easy reach—why in God's name would Billy want me there, after last night? This couldn't be right. Maybe it was all some horrible trick. Steeling myself, I walked down to Illinois, pushed open the dining hall door and went inside.

The front room was dim, just a few standing flashlights, remains of yesterday's fight still all over the floor. The kitchen smelled of old grease and was crammed with canned goods, boxes of instant cereal and potatoes and rice, cartons of pop and bottled water, an aboveground safe house with an apple green wooden table in the corner. Stephen was sitting at it, with a notebook and pen and a pile of soft, sprouted onions, hacking at the tops and wrinkled skins with a knife. I cleared my throat. He kept on slicing.

"So where do we cook, exactly?" I asked. The stove was piled with boxes and cans nearly to the ceiling, but then it was dead anyway. Electric dials.

"Didn't you see the grills, out in the backyard?" He didn't look up. "We have a decent supply of briquettes and propane. There's a couple more houses with wood ovens, the foraging team dragged back a bunch of camp stoves—the 'kitchen's' out back and all up and down the street, this is just the dining hall."

He put the onion down and gazed at me. In the beam of the big screwtop lantern on the table he had a lot of short dark hair and a washed-out face, homely in that mismatched way where nose, cheekbones, chin were like the wrong jigsaw pieces forcibly pressed together. One cheek was a faint purple, swollen so your fingertips twitched at how painfully tender the skin would feel, but nothing as awful as I'd imagined. His eyes were big and dark and impenetrable, so much like Natalie's I wondered if they were brother and sister.

"Pity we're not closer beachside," he said, motioning for me to sit down. The chairs were hard, straightbacked, the same austere pale green. "The really rich parts of Prairie Beach, those houses some of the lab types had right on the shore? Backup off-grid stoves, gas-powered generators, unbelievable safe houses—"

"Lab types get everything," I said. My mother used to complain about that, over and over again. Security people were all bitter, they got the actual work of dealing with zombies on the ground but maybe a tenth of the scientist perks. "Even now."

"I wouldn't say that." Stephen handed me a knife of my own, a soft slumping oversprouted onion. "Those gas generators, those safe houses? You have to be alive to enjoy them and the plague ripped through here like a forest fire. Half of Prairie Beach dead or dying in the first two weeks. Well, it would've, wouldn't it?" His face, hunched over the onion, looked grim. "I mean, everyone says they created it, the labs, one of their experiments—"

"Nobody knows where it came from," I said. The *labs* that spent all their time on "pest eradication"—you weren't supposed to know that, but everyone heard stories—they created a disease to make zombies stronger? Invulnerable? That was the craziest idea yet, that one. "The labs, the Saudis, the Chinese, illegal immigrants, bioterrorists, I've heard all that too but nobody knows where it really came from—"

"I do."

I put down the knife—so sharp I had to watch my sore fingers—and stared at him. I was sick of all that, rants and fulminations about What Really Happened. Bad enough, last winter, hearing Dave go on about how it was all Mexican illegals spreading disease—good luck to them or anyone getting past the Rio Grande, who needed a border patrol when that dry heat mummified zombies so they lived for centuries. So you heard. He and Ms. Acosta would scream at each other for hours when he got going about Mexicans: *For shit's sake, Alicia, I don't mean you!*

"You do," I said.

"Of course not," Stephen said. He sliced into the heart of the onion—rotten, just like the skin—grimaced and shoved it aside. "It's just that everyone here's got the inside story, and I don't want to feel left out—whose fault do *you* think it should be? How about Freemasons? I've heard Jews but not Freemasons, and you'd think, wouldn't you? Or the Vatican? Is there a Vatican anymore? Nobody knows how far this has spread, or if it's just us, or what the hell we're gonna do but by God, they all know exactly who did it. Help me sort through these."

He hauled a dirty cloth bag from under the table, spilling over with potatoes. They all looked greenish and squishy, lousy with eyes. "Anyway," he said, "gangs raided that whole bit of Prairie Beach, after the homeowners died. Used up all the gas running the generators, ate themselves sick in the safe houses, had a grand old time until the irregulars found them—"

"Irregulars?"

"Our overlords." He nicked the eyes off a slightly less green potato, hand moving neat and fast like he was shuffling cards. "My name for them, they don't call themselves anything. At least not that I've heard. We feed about sixty people on the dinner shift, thirty-two of their kind and the rest are humans. A lot of them kill and eat in the woods instead, but we still have to be on standby. For the ones who like to sit with a knife and fork and pretend, remember the old times." He glanced up from his pile of potatoes, discolored and collapsed like shriveled, deflated tennis balls. "Or just use it as an excuse to play with people, like Billy does. The rest of the kitchen crew's out right now hauling water—"

"Why did he want me here, anyway?"

"You're new and he's a sadist. Who cares why? You didn't bust out crying, that's the big thing." He shook the bag, a few more salvageable potatoes clattering over the tabletop. "And you didn't jump in to play superhero and get yourself hurt. Let them do the fighting. That and eating's all they live for."

"You mean like *you* just let them fight it out?" I winced, remembering him almost screaming in pain as Don's foot slammed into his side. An ex on a tear could've torn him right open, easy as stomping Bubble Wrap with a stiletto heel. "And didn't say a word?"

He shrugged. "You heard Billy, the poor bastard actually thinks I know how to cook. So I can risk it. You, though, what can you do for anybody?"

He tossed the empty potato bag on the table and stared at me with eyes gone hard and suspicious, demanding I prove myself. *What can you do for anybody?* A good question. I faltered in the face of it, bent my head back down.

Green potato, yellow potato. Green potato—it was hard to tell in the lamplight, some of them had that translucent golden skin that takes on a natural, copper-roof tinge if you squint. I held them up near the bulb for inspection. Stephen swept the rejects back into the bag, all tumbling and knocking against each other like a lot of kittens set to be drowned.

That'd been a test, before, that talk about how he knew-he-just-knew the labs made the plague. To see if I bit, what bait I offered in turn. Jew-baiting, Mexican-baiting, whatever else. This was another one. I can't stand it when people do that, play those games. There's no easier way to get on my bad side.

"Thank you for the fork," I said. "Thank you so, so much."

I pitched my words sickly-sweet and sugary like it'd been roses, a ruby ring, and something in me felt better to see him scowl. He tossed another cankered potato in the bag with a dull, soft thunk. "Watch out for Mags," he said. "She's smarter than Billy, doesn't fly off the handle like he does. Makes her more dangerous. Don, you don't need to worry about him."

"You're kidding, right? He kidnapped us right off the high-way. And then keeping that Janey like a slave or something—"

Stephen shook his head. "It's not like that with them, it's . . . I don't know. It's not sex, I don't think, even though everyone assumes it is. He found her crying by the side of the road. I know something terrible happened to her, before, but I don't want to know what." He picked up the potatoes I'd dropped, shoved them into a little pile. "Don brings her presents and doesn't ask her for much of anything. You saw how Billy likes that, to him it's like one of us keeping a rack of lamb as a house pet—if you're waiting for me to shut up just say so, for Christ's sake, I was trying to help you out."

"I never said you weren't." I picked up a potato covered in scaly gray patches, the skin dirt-dry, but it split and oozed a watery porridge the second my fingers touched it; the nauseating contrast of it made me shiver and I tossed it in the bag, scrubbed my palm on my jeans.

"Don't run away next time," he said. "There's nowhere to run." He dragged his paring knife over the tabletop, chips of apple paint flaking off the blade, his fingers twitching like they wanted to stab hard at the wood. "There's nothing. Nowhere, and nobody, and nothing left."

His teeth were clenched and he kept staring down at the short little blade like he dreamed it was last night's carving knife, the table Billy's flesh, like he could plunge it in and steal away blood and bubbling life and maybe that would give him somewhere to go, let him salvage something from all this. No chance. Nowhere. Not for anyone. His forehead furrowed beneath the tangled clumps of dark hair and I thought, looking at him, how sorrow is the twin face of rage.

"Thank you for the note," I said. No sugar, this time. Because I really had been thankful. "I wasn't sure who sent it, just it probably wasn't Janey."

The furrows eased, for a moment, his whole face striving toward good humor. "Be nice to Janey, and Don'll leave you be. They hate each other." He swept nicked potato eyes into the discard bag, using the side of his hand like a scraper. "Don and Billy, I mean. But not just them—the ones who were human, before, hate the ones who were undead. The ones who hate humans, who want to use us for what they can get, they hate the likes of Don and Lisa, as traitors . . . so, you know, it's like it's always been, since forever. It's National Brotherhood Week around here every week, and everyone's got an agenda."

Just like Phoebe said. This wasn't like talking to her, though, how she kept trying to decide if I were whole, firm and clean to bite into, or rotten all inside; Stephen's face was calm like he had no suspicions of me, no expectations, as if he expected nothing—*what are you good for, anyway?*—but that meant I owed him nothing. I was a free agent, here in this kitchen, nobody's and nothing and going nowhere, exactly like everyone else. Exactly like him. Just the thought of that, the quiet relief of telling no lies because finally someone didn't care to ask me any questions, despite his tense eye-lopping hands and sullen face it made me start relaxing, a little bit, for the first time since Don hustled us into his car.

"Exes," I said. "That's what I call them." I pushed the rotten onion bits into the bag. "The ones who changed, I mean."

He thought that over and then, to my surprise, he smiled. It didn't magically transform him to handsome but it did give his plain piecemeal face a split-second, illusory semblance of harmony; his eyes, animated and intelligent, leapt up right along with his mouth. Gone, that little moment, as swiftly as it came. "Short and to the point," he said. "I like it. We're all pretty ex, though, these days. No idea what we are."

"I still know what I am," I said. My voice was sharper than I'd meant it to be. "Maybe other humans started acting different, but I haven't. I got through things, I got through the winter without—"

To say a lie aloud is to confirm it. To be complicit. No. My tongue felt dry and thick, refusing to be party to any of that; how I acted, let's never talk about how I acted. Ever. I was scrutinizing every little scratch and paint bubble in the tabletop, then I couldn't stand it anymore and raised my head, looked into his eyes. None of Phoebe's devouring curiosity, there; instead a flicker of something quick and unquantifiable, as if I were looking into a window and saw a hand twitching at a heavy curtain, exposing just the faintest, swiftest glimpse of what lay inside.

Pale silvery wedge of wallpaper, flash of bright blue from flowers in a vase, a sliver of a hesitant, hidden face already retreating from view. A room I knew, from somewhere. A face I knew, someone I remembered arranging those flowers. Then, quicker than his smile, it vanished.

"Our assignment," he said, "is dinner for sixty. Every human gets rationed so many calories based on male, female, old, young, type of work crew—" He reached for the spiral-bound notebook, flipped it open. "Sometimes the exes bring us extra meat to cook, like last night, that makes it easier. You can help me plan the cooking for the week. I hope you're good at arithmetic. Assume the average ex eats about quadruple their human equivalent, when you add it up. Bottomless pits, all of them. Assume if there's any left for us, ever, that we're lucky."

His voice was quiet and steady in its bitterness, a thread unwinding at its leisure from the spool, and despite it all it felt like just another day, just another thing, nobody here wanting anything of me but work. That suited me. His face wasn't so ugly, actually, close up. Some of that had just been the distortion of flashlight shadows.

"Those lights," I said, nodding toward the industrial lamp. "They must take a lot of batteries."

"We've got more of those than we know what to do with." He pulled the bag's drawstring shut. "Batteries, I mean. And cheap plastic flashlights, and lighters. Every safe house, every gas station, every convenience store—"

Lisa had been right, then. I smiled, thinking about it, I couldn't help it. I hadn't believed her. "So it'd be okay to waste some, sometimes. Maybe."

Stephen's brows crooked in polite puzzlement. "Waste them on what?"

I unzipped one of my LCS jacket pockets, pulled out the CDs I'd rescued from our supply carts: The Good Terrorist, Victims of the Dance. "If anyone's got a CD player," I said. "I thought . . ."

He was silent for a minute, probably reflecting on how he could possibly have ended up sitting here listening to me whine for something so frivolous, and I was about to shove the CDs back in my pockets when he picked them both up, examining them, and shrugged.

"Good luck competing with Al," he said. "He's all Charlie Parker and Coltrane, all the time. And he's about six foot seven, so ask nice and be ready to run."

"Jazz is okay. I guess." Stefanie Scholl, from The Good Terrorist, she talked about jazz in interviews all the time. Some of my magazines with her were in German so I couldn't read them, but there'd be an *ich bin blah blah Django Reinhardt achtung das ist Bill Evans und so weiter* every now and then; I always wrote the names down. "I don't know much about jazz."

"I don't know anything about music at all." He slid the CDs back to me. "But I never knew how to cook before, either."

He flipped the notebook to another page. Dinner for sixty. We'd worked it all out for about thirty-eight when the back door slammed open: the rest of the kitchen crew with rabbit carcasses, half-wild asparagus, buckets of lake and well water. Working until the sun came up, chopping, cooking, cleaning, writing it all down. Too busy to miss Lisa or anyone else.

Too busy to think about what came before, what would come after, what might be waiting for me out there in the trees. Just another day, not talking about what happened.

# TEN

People actually talked to me on the kitchen crew that night, not like with Kevin's cleanup squad, and I learned everybody's names. Al, he really was about six-seven—Stephen wasn't kidding—shaved head, arms solid vein-blue from all the faded tattoos, had been in prison and I sure as hell wasn't asking for what. He was one of the exes' favorites, and they let him carry a gun; whenever he talked to Stephen his voice got cool, distant, exquisitely polite with dislike. Watching how Al looked at Stephen, the way Bonnie and Dan slid so carefully past him in the kitchens like they couldn't stand any part of their bodies even fleetingly touching him, it was clear they just wanted to leave him behind. Let me, the new low woman, deal with him up close, if anybody had to.

"You need to be a little careful around Stephen," Bonnie warned me, that same night, taking me aside while Stephen and

Emily snapped asparagus, peeled garlic dug up from someone's defunct backyard garden, Al roasting rabbit out back. Already my mouth was watering. "He's a decent enough kid, he's just . . . he's got some problems. That's all."

"What do you mean, problems?"

"Look, he's a good kid. Like you. It's just . . . hard to explain." She tugged at her sweater, a thick pea-colored tangle of yarn. "So just don't get too chummy, okay?"

A good kid. I'm always a good kid, apparently, no matter what. That's my job here. Like it's Phoebe's job to make everyone crazy.

"Okay," I said. She smiled, and grabbed for another box of instant mashed potatoes.

So Stephen's a good kid, I thought, as I sat by one of the camp stoves waiting, waiting for the potato water to boil. A good kid, with some problems, that you need to be a little careful around, except we can't explain why but, boy, if you *knew*? I can't say it out loud, I just can't, I won't, but if you just knew?

I think we'll get along just fine. He and I. Maybe.

It was two-thirty A.M. and I was alone in the kitchen with Bonnie, stacking up piles of plates while she wrestled with a tray loaded with cups. The back door swung open and there was Natalie, the girl who'd brought me my fork, my note, my new plum position; I smiled at her because she looked even more like she needed it and she shuffled her feet, twitched her mouth like she wanted to smile back but couldn't work out just how. Bonnie put her tray down, strode toward Natalie in three quick steps and slapped her so hard she went staggering backward, clutching her face in both hands.

"What the hell!" I shouted, and grabbed Bonnie's arm, still clutching a plate in my other hand—I'd been trying to be careful, Al with his gun, Alice's notebook full of our citations and demerits reported back to Billy, but neither of them were here and I couldn't believe it. "What'd she ever do to—"

"You're an hour late," Bonnie threw at Natalie from behind clenched teeth, shaking off my fingers like bits of lint and stepping closer so they were both nose to nose. "You were assigned *here* tonight, I told the goddamned gardening crew I needed you, where the hell've you been?"

"I forgot," Natalie said, in a still small voice, eyes full of the knowledge she'd never be allowed to make it right. Her whole face, not just the slapped cheek, had flared up in striations of angry pink. "I was helping cut back some dead plants and—"

"And what, it was everyone else's job to remind you, is that it?" Bonnie yanked at Natalie's arm, rattled the wrist with a man's salvaged wristwatch dangling from it like a bangle. "What the fuck are you even good for if you can't *turn your goddamned head* and read the—"

"Knock it off!" I grabbed Natalie's shoulders and pulled her away, so fast Natalie let out a squeak of surprise and stumbled against me. "Fine, she forgot, she's here now. Just leave it."

Bonnie shook her head in disgust. Her own face, as she swiveled round to glare at me, was flushed the same deep pink as Natalie's. "You give the orders here now, huh? Is that it?"

Another fight, just like at that dinner. I'm not having another goddamned fight. I can't take it tonight. "She's here to help with dinner," I pointed out, calm as I could. Let her try to slap me, I've had worse. "Not to stand around doing nothing but get yelled at. Right? You want Billy to find out we're *all* standing around right now? Doing nothing? When he's hungry?"

Silence. Bonnie looked from me to Natalie and back again, still whistling useless anger from between her teeth. Then she glanced down, at Natalie's big square-faced gunmetal watch with its lit-up second hand ticking a tinny pulse, and let out a long breath.

"Potatoes," she said to Natalie, pointing at a box of instant flakes sitting open on the kitchen table. "Get some water boiling."

She turned her back on both of us, started stacking cups again like nothing had happened. As she turned her gaze away Natalie's whole face contorted into a sudden, silent rictus of misery, her shoulders shuddering holding back the need to break down and cry; then she swallowed hard, tucked the potato box like a baby into her arms and headed out.

"You shouldn't have done that," she whispered in my ear as she passed me. "You'll get everything I get, for that. You shouldn't."

Fine, I get what she gets. I didn't care. She glanced back at me as she slipped through the door and her eyes, tears or no, were full of surprise and gratitude.

Bonnie and I kept working side by side, not looking at each other, the air heavy with our dislike. Then the door swung open again and Lisa was there, smiling, Naomi trailing behind her like a little thundercloud after the sunlight. I smiled at Naomi and she hid her face behind her hand. Lisa barely seemed to notice, stroking Naomi's hair as she motioned me out the door. Bonnie, wrestling with a tray loaded with cups, actually looked impatient when I hesitated.

"Well, go on then!" she said, and gave Lisa this respectful little head-duck like some English servant bobbing a curtsey. "Go with her. Crew or no crew, you don't forget who you belong to."

Lisa's smile faded a little, hearing that, but she led me and Naomi down the back steps and past the array of camp stoves, into a quiet front yard halfway down Illinois. Naomi kept her head lowered as we walked, shuffling through the violet-studded grass clutching her fists together and mumbling to herself like she was saying grace. A big, heavy-footed possum suddenly shot across our path and under a rusting Pontiac, its skittering toes like long, unkempt anemic fingernails, and she didn't even flinch.

"I told Billy to leave you the hell alone," Lisa said. She paced up and down in front of another cluster of barbecue grills, her ponytail flopping back and forth across her shoulder. "You could say we had words. And fists. And teeth. Dear Christ, I needed that." She shook her hair back and actually laughed, a gruff little bark of satisfaction, livid moonlit ghosts of bruises fading from her throat even as we spoke like quickly drying water stains. "I needed it so badly and I didn't even know it—I shouldn't tell you that, you'll think I wanted to hurt *you*, but I didn't. I just, you're all right now, in the kitchens? They're treating you okay?"

"I'm fine," I said, my voice receding and backing away. I could tell she heard it because she wilted almost instantly, all her fight-triumph spoiled, and gazed down at the dandelions like Naomi.

"I can't help it," she muttered. She put a gentle hand to Naomi's head; Naomi pulled away and squatted down, yanking viciously at the weeds. "I really can't. I needed it. All right?"

"I didn't ask you to apologize for anything." I wanted to plunk down next to Naomi, go to work on them myself. The old game we used to play in elementary school, clutching a plucked dandelion in one hand and then decapitating it with a casual thumb: *Soldier got a zombie and the head popped off!* That's me, now, and Naomi. Shaggy-headed, thin-necked weeds. "Aren't you in trouble now? For fighting him? And does that mean I'm in trouble?"

Lisa hesitated.

"That's the thing, Amy," she said. She glanced at Naomi, bent over a half-denuded patch of earth and still pulling, and then back at me. "The kitchen crew, he says it right out, 'Those are the ones I don't want touched.' And now you're on it. That was his idea, not mine." She lowered her voice, even though Naomi was oblivious. "I don't have any idea why, and nobody's talking."

I shook my head in confusion. Stephen, a favorite? Billy loathed him. He loathed all of us. "Do you think we're, you know—food? Maybe?"

My hands clutched up tense, asking that, like they were ripping the blossoms from flowers. All of Phoebe's hollow Plasticine reassurances, they didn't amount to shit. Lisa took my fingers in hers, gently straightening them.

"If I thought that," she said, with a quiet ferocity, "we wouldn't be standing here right now. All right?"

"All right," I said. Though it still wasn't.

"I'd know by now, believe me. Fights or no fights they run in gangs, like the zombies all used to do, they're gang animals, pack animals, and Billy's the head of the pack. Him and Mags. And they don't eat your kind, so nobody else does either. They're a lot more hipped on stray dogs."

I imagined Billy, Don, the rest of them sniffing out that lamp-eyed, fetid thing following me, tearing it limb from limb. They couldn't, it wasn't a real dog. Not like the one in Leyton.

"It's okay in the kitchens," I told her. "They let us listen to music."

Stray dogs. I couldn't stop picturing it, the horrible thing that had trailed and tracked me two weeks running curled up quiet and dead like a car-struck badger, torn apart by famished ex-hands and ex-mouths. *You can't have that,* I thought, a flash of feeling coming out of nowhere and connected to nothing. *It's mine.*

What the hell was wrong with me?

"What does Billy want with us?" I asked. "With me?"

"I don't know. I don't know." Lisa reached out again, tucked a lock of hair behind my ear. "Do we stay and try to find out?"

"Does she have anything to say to you?" I nodded toward Naomi. "Or anyone?"

Lisa shrugged. "She'll get there."

Ye of great faith. Naomi had abandoned her weeds and was rocking back and forth where she sat, humming at the sky, her fingers streaked with fresh wet smears of green and dandelion yellow. Sticky crayon colors. She got up on her feet and came toward us.

"I think we stay," I said.

"I think so too."

Naomi looked from Lisa to me, and back, and frowned.

"Can I stay?" she asked.

Her voice was hoarse, like she hadn't spoken in days. Still worn out from all that crying.

"Of course," Lisa said, and put an arm around her. She shied from the touch, ducking neatly down and away, but stayed by Lisa's side with a cheek pressed to her thigh.

"I should get back to work," I told Lisa. "It doesn't look right otherwise. If everyone's listening to you, you should put in a word for Natalie. That gofer girl with the dark hair and the striped shirt. Everyone hates her, and I don't know why—"

"Natalie's dead," said Naomi.

Lisa turned toward her, gazing down at her so intently that Naomi ducked her head again.

"Who's been saying that?" Lisa asked, quietly. "She's not one of my kind, Naomi, she's human just like you." Silence. "Has someone been saying they'll hurt her? Is that what—"

"Nobody's going to *hurt* her," Naomi muttered, that singsong impatience of kids who can't fathom you don't speak their home planet's language. "I told you, they can't hurt her. She's already dead. The Scissor Men got her. They snipped her all in pieces."

"Naomi—"

She grabbed at Lisa, clutching her leg hard enough that her small thin fingers went splotchy pale. Lisa was frowning in confusion and dismay but pitched her voice light and easy as she told me, "You were right, Amy. You'd better go back."

"Tomorrow?"

"Yes."

I left them standing there with Naomi hiding her face, gripping Lisa's shins for dear life, Lisa whispering soothing useless words.

"All right, then?" Bonnie asked me, nearly as bright-eyed as Phoebe, when I came back into the kitchens. She had another armload of asparagus, the stuff had gone weed-wild in patches everywhere we looked.

"All right," I said, and sat down to help her snap stems. All that night while I worked I kept my eyes down and my mouth shut, like Naomi, not letting anybody in. It was safer that way, but then, it really always had been.

That strange feeling that had gone all through me at the thought of my black dog, my ghost dog lying there hunted and dead: It was guilt. Guilt at having wanted it dead. That tight, shivering feeling you get in the pit of your stomach imagining every familiar hallmark gone, every edifice crumbled away. Everyone you ever knew, who ever loved you, dead.

Except my mother isn't dead. She never has been, whatever

anyone says. So I'm not like anyone else around here, all mourning and wailing inside. There was nobody but her for me to lose, not ever. My father, I suppose, but I barely remembered him at all.

This is not all about to vanish right beneath my hands, dying like everyone died, fading and melting into nothingness the harder I try to pull it to me. I have not fabricated anything. Everything around me right at this moment, Lisa, Naomi, Don, Janey, Billy, the mournful lowing bird sounds and small fearful animals rushing unwitting into our snare and the cool supremely indifferent night sky—this whole city is not all just a dream. It can't be. It can't be because if it is I will lose what's left of my senses long before I ever wake up.

# ELEVEN

Sunset, again. Work. Again. I was wandering down to the cook-houses on Illinois, staring at grass blades sliding up through the sidewalk cracks wondering how long it would take them to eat up all the concrete, when Phoebe came slithering from behind a willow tree and slid her skinny arm around my shoulder. I kept trying to pull away and she kept gripping tighter, her longer legs setting the pace.

"So how're you *doing* lately, kid?" Grinning right in my face, her eyelids still puffy and dropping with sleep but her jaw clenched and twisted tight with the tension that never left her; she was a tooth-grinder, you could tell just looking at her. I'd hear my mother doing that sometimes as she slept, a soft little *squeak, squeak* from the next room like a blunt knife sawing at Styrofoam. "It's been *days*! Settling in okay? Rest of the kitchen kids treating you all right—"

"Don't you have any work to do?" I asked, shoving hands in my pockets. I was tired of being polite to her. "The commissary must be busy, this time of day."

"Don't ask me, kid—not my bailiwick this time!" She tilted her chin back, staring up into the darkening sky beaming and beatific like she expected starlight to shoot up her nostrils. "Not today, not me—I'm heading over to the engineering crew, see what they want me to fetch and carry. Bosses rise with the setting sun, a human's work is never done."

She was a gofer, then, nothing more than that; no better than Natalie, or me before Billy intervened. All that fussing and take-charge, all for nothing. "Everything's fine," I said, and started tugging free in earnest. "I have to go to work now."

"So nobody's giving you a hard time?"

Her arm around mine was trembling, nonstop, not with any sort of fear but like she might burst out of her skin and start screaming any second with all the pent-up, frustrated energy. I should have felt sorry for her, I know I should've, but she wasn't wasting any pity on me. "So how're you getting along with that Stephen kid? Because not to tale-tell outta school but that boy's got an attitude, he hasn't made too many friends around here, y'know, not many friends at all—"

"Not like you."

Her mouth twitched, subsided, hearing that, then she smiled even broader than before. "So you're getting along, you and he? I heard you were getting along." She had my arm again. "See, 'cos it's like I told Billy, I just had this feeling? When he moved you to the crew? I told him, I said, if *anyone* would hit it off with Stephen, I just bet it'd be you."

Something like a hot little needle poked at my insides, leaping up at her words to jab and sting. "What do you care how I get along with anyone?" I yanked my arm away from hers, checked for CDs and cards and fork and dead cell phone in the sudden certainty she'd slid up so close to pickpocket. "What the hell business is it of yours? You didn't even know me three days ago and now—"

"Calm *down*, kid! For the love of Pistol Pete!" Phoebe had pulled back in earnest, hands midair and waving like I was a swarm of gnats she had to fight off. "I didn't mean anything, don't know why you're always so *suspicious* of anyone who looks at you slanty-eyed! I'm just saying, same age or thereabouts, he doesn't have any family, you don't . . . or at least none you'll talk about, either of you." She halted in her tracks, fixed smile suddenly wavering. "And you both had a hard time, right before you ended up here. I mean, you know, maybe even harder than usual. For a lot of reasons."

The needle jabs inside became a slow, steady pain, like someone was easing a knife blade down my sternum, patiently slicing the flesh open layer by layer. "We all had a time," I said. "We all had a time, this winter."

"Well, there's a time . . . and then there's a time." She smiled at me again, with the faintest little glint in her eyes. "Isn't there. Must've been especially bad for you, right? I mean, not having your mother or your dad around at all, for all those—"

"Amy!"

Lisa was coming out of the trees, wiping something from her mouth; Mags was right behind her, barefoot in a flowery blood-spattered green dress, all cascading auburn hair and soft pale folds of flesh. Mags blinked at me, like she'd already forgotten who I was, and gave Phoebe a look that would've made anyone in their right mind take off running. Phoebe, though, she bounced right in her shoes like an excited child, nearly split her face in two with welcoming smiles.

"Where's Naomi?" I asked, before Phoebe could ooze rancid honey all over them both.

"Sleeping," Lisa said, and gave me a touch on the arm. Like she was actually glad to see me, not totally wrapped up in something younger, littler, nicer. "Amy has to go to work now, Phoebe, you're holding her up. Go to the cleanup crew, Kevin needs you."

"I was just telling Amy," Phoebe kept right on going, like she was one of them and they couldn't wait to hear her reports from the field, "I'm not one tiny bit surprised she and Stephen get along so well. I mean, they've got so much in common, they're both so *quiet* about how they got here in the first place, making up all those silly stories about sisters and mothers as if anyone would believe—"

"And what the hell business is it of yours?" Lisa stepped forward, inches from Phoebe's wide, glinty grin. "You don't run this place, you don't get to interrogate anyone on how or where they—"

"I bet you and Stephen would get along great too," Phoebe said. She wasn't backing down at all, she was crazy enough or reckless enough to thrust her face right at Lisa's like an eager sniffing dog. Mags just stood there, arms folded, watching it all happen. "I mean, you've both got the lab in common and everything—" Her smile was suddenly reserved, calculating. "You know what I mean."

Lisa's face went pale. But why? She hadn't made any secret of having lab rats in her family, when she met me, unless all that was somehow different among the exes—but Mags looked as confused as I felt. "Be quiet," Lisa told Phoebe, and something in her hard, blunt voice was so much harder and heavier than

I'd ever heard before that I wanted to back away. "Be quiet, and stop talking."

"Do you know what I mean, Amy?" Phoebe had turned back my way and had her hands clasped behind her, rocking from foot to foot, swaying with a triumphant ease to some music only she could hear. "What's she been telling you, anyway, about *her* plague year? Because she was right at the heart of the action, belly of the beast, God forbid they ever let me who had more fucking brains than all of them combined near any of the half-way relevant research but *now*, oh frabjous day, here's Jim Porter's so-called rhesus girl, here's Patient Zero right in the flesh—"

Lisa's hand shot out and grabbed Phoebe's arm, the fingertips squeezing deep and hard so I saw instant dark bruises welling up and Phoebe let out a harsh little scream. Mags laughed in appreciation, rocking back on her heels watching, and Lisa kept squeezing and squeezing, her eyes swallowed up by the pupils and fixed like a cat's on her target. Phoebe hissed between her teeth with pain, started screaming even louder—my hands were on Lisa's arm, no power except persuasion to pull her away, but she flinched like I'd hit her and made herself let go, I could see the effort it took to uncurl her fingers and step back. Her arm was shaking, under my touch. Phoebe was trembling and sweating, cradling her arm and moaning a little bit like the sound could soothe it better.

"Broken?" Mags grunted, looking bored again.

Phoebe shook her head, scrunch-shouldered and miserable. Mags threw her curly head back, let out a long trumpeting belch.

"Then get your ass to work," she told Phoebe.

Phoebe stumbled into the trees, nearly falling over a thick dead branch before vanishing from sight. Mags snorted, shaking her head, then turned to Lisa.

"So what's all this 'Patient Zero' bullshit?" she asked. No particular avidity in the asking, that I could sniff out, just plain postprandial curiosity.

Lisa didn't answer, just stood there breathing hard and stomping her feet like she could shake her flared-up temper out through the soles. Her fingers slid to her head but instead of yanking at the hair, wrenching it ragged like she always did, she scratched back and forth at her scalp like she could dig something out, yank it loose, toss it back into the overgrown shrubbery so it'd scuttle away and cease all its torments.

"Crazy bitch," Lisa finally said. Her head still down. "That's what it is."

Mags thought that one over. "Jim Porter," she mused. "Who works in a lab. So . . ." She wrestled with the neckline of her dress, stuck and slid down on one shoulder so I could see the crease between arm and torso, the sidelong bump of a breast. "So you must be Jessie's Lisa."

She actually swallowed, staring at Lisa, like she was quite scared of being wrong. Lisa's chin rose up slowly and she stared at Mags, her mouth open.

"Jesus Christ," she said. "So you're—" Lisa started laughing, shaking her head, looking at Mags with sudden gratitude like she'd just dropped something sweet and nourishing in her lap. "I'm an idiot, I'm such an idiot not to—she talked about someone named Maggie or something like that, a couple of times. I never knew—"

"Where is she?" Mags too looked unmoored all of a sudden, knocked off her pins by the eagerness for something she couldn't beat or threaten out of anyone. "What happened to her? Did she get sick like us? She musta got sick, she was one of the first of all of us to—"

"She got sick." As she spoke, something in Lisa's face suddenly closed up, the little burst of gratitude and hunger retreating and sliding away. "Very sick. Then she got better. She's like us now."

I was waiting for Mags to sneer, Not like *us*, dear, not at all like us but like *me*—ex-undeads sticking up for each other, but Mags just nodded, let out this ragged breath and smiled like people d o w hen t hey're t rying t o c ontrol t hemselves. " Well, Jesus Christ," she said, a soft almost sweet little chortle weaving through her ground-glass words, "William is just about gonna shit himself when he hears that, we were sure she was dead and gone just like the rest of 'em. Isn't that a pretty picture? All of us dead, from the old gang, all the undead gangs everywhere around here. All of us except me, and Billy, and her."

Lisa opened her mouth to say something, and then closed it again. Her sister's friends, that she'd told me about, that Lisa had been living with on the beach until she left. She wasn't going to tell Mags about them, wouldn't tell her where they all were, if they were alive or dead—still angry about Naomi, or she had her own reasons I didn't want to know about. Ex-politics. Mags kept yanking at the neck of her dress, a soft coppery green thing with rivulets of something's blood dried on it like rust, and finally wrenched the fussy little bib of pearl buttons properly in front.

"You human types," she told Lisa, "you don't know what the hell you were all missing, behind all your gates and locked doors and your little safety booths popping up everywhere. Your 'storm' cellars. You never had any idea what freedom felt like." She'd plain forgotten I was standing there listening, she couldn't even properly see her own surroundings; she was too wrapped up in another place, another time, the exact same longing I saw from the humans around me every minute of the day. "Everything around us, the woods, the animals, the empty roads and buildings, all ours while you all huddled up in your little houses scared of your own shadows. I hated that, when I was alive—don't do this, don't do that, nod smile act right sit down shut up if you don't want your ass beat, you could have all of it. I woke up in that potter's field with all those real dead bodies all around me and I was laughing, laughing like crazy, nothing could keep me back anymore. Nobody would ever fucking tell me what to do."

Her head pivoted around and then she was staring at me, big shiny gray clear-water eyes so pale you could see right down to their bottoms but it was me who was transparent, pinned down and shot through, as sure as Phoebe when Lisa had her arm. Mags looked me up and down, and her lip curled. "You never liked it either, did you, frail? Being told what to do. I can smell it all over you. Never, ever."

I was afraid not to respond so I shook my head. Confirmation, denial. Let her decide.

"Smell it all over your nasty human skin like a stench. I always could, you know. The humans who should've been us. Who, when they died, if they came back, really *would've* been one of us." Her mouth became a straight prim line, the haughty contempt of a teacher faced with a willfully worthless student. Then she chuckled. "Ate 'em anyway. But I always felt bad about it. Jessie, that's what she's like, she was another one who could never stand the hoo-life, something in her always screaming to get out of that meat-body like a corpse outta the coffin—she was born to be dead. So angry. So hungry. One of the best." She turned back to Lisa. "You got no idea what it's like, do you? That hunger. That heat to hunt all coursing through everything. That *being*ness. You so-called living. I heard about you." She laughed, a rough little bark devoid of triumph. "I heard what you're like. Sister or no sister, you were never her family."

Lisa just stood there, pondering this still and quiet. Something small and high-voiced called out from one of the trees, *oooh-ahhh-wooo, woooo, wooooo*, then the leaves rustled and it flew away.

"My sister's a good person," Lisa replied. Fingertips shoved in her jeans pockets, idly rocking back and forth on the side of a sneakered foot. "A good human being. Living and dead. Though she wouldn't ever believe it herself, no matter what anyone said to her. She just wants to be left alone, live whatever sort of life this is we've all got now—she's not out threatening unchanged humans, enslaving them, making them run and fetch for her and feed her like some overgrown screaming infant. She's out in the woods, hunting for herself. You're her family?" Lisa took a step forward, the quick, strutting step of someone ready and aching to fight. "Go on and tell her that. You *find* her, if you can, and tell her that. Because family or no family, she wouldn't want anything to do with you, the way you are now."

I held my breath, waiting for Mags to rear up, snarl, jump on her striking and biting like a cat teased past its limit. Instead Mags just stood there sagging in her own skin, a big soft deflated balloon with all her bravado a lost exhaled breath.

"No," she said to Lisa. Completely calm. "She probably wouldn't. The way we are now. She's not the only one."

Completely calm. So sad. Those eyes so pale and clear that you'd never see tears coming until they spilled over and rushed down her face, but she wasn't anywhere near the brink. It wasn't grief that I saw, but regret. She glanced at me again, and frowned.

"Fuck off to work," she said.

I fucked off to work. Only nodding quick at Lisa as I left without trying to catch a glance, both because lingering might really set Mags off and because that face of Lisa's that I'd seen, the hungry angry thing huddled up behind her eyes like a bear in a cave, it scared me and that wasn't fair after Lisa had kept me safe over and over again. It was my own fear I didn't want her seeing. She wouldn't have done that to me, what she did to Phoebe, even if I pushed her.

Unless she forgot, like sometimes tamed animals forget themselves, or decide they've had enough. Except she'd never been close to tame in the first place. She just kept trying to tame herself. I wasn't jealous of Naomi anymore, didn't feel like she was taking anything from me. I just hoped she was safe, in Lisa's care, the gazelle on whom the lioness took pity.

What they didn't understand was that the person folks should really be afraid of was me.

# TWELVE

Al, Bonnie, Alice were on water duty. They were the only humans on the kitchen crew authorized to go past the gates, down to the Prairie Beach neighborhood where they could access Lake Michigan water: hard, heavy, grueling work, filling all those containers and hauling them into the back of an ex guard's pickup truck and then unloading and going back for another. I was glad I wasn't allowed. The second they left, Stephen steered us out the door on a garden scavenge, leading me into a tiny white bungalow at the corner of Milstead and Braeburn.

"What about the onions?" I asked, as he shone his flashlight all through the living room. Stephen kicked idly at the carpet, bringing up a cloud of dust.

"In a minute," he said, and motioned with his flashlight, glancing out an uncurtained window as if he thought someone were watching. "Over here."

We surprised a little nest of mice, darting away from our feet swift as big sleek silverfish, and then we were in what must've been the dining room, a dollhouse-tiny chandelier and one of those god-awful vista murals painted on the wall and a big wooden table with one wonky leg. Piled up on the tabletop, sliding from their moorings thanks to the short leg, were dozens of CDs. Stephen stood back, still aiming the flashlight at the table, a museum curator showing off some new exhibit.

"I collected them," he said, "from some of the other houses. And this one. I wouldn't know what's good, you pick."

His voice was impatient, almost brusque, like I'd nagged him into foraging for me, but it hardly mattered. Music. I started sifting through them, wiping the grimy plastic covers clean with my fingers, my own private garage sale: Dirty Little Whirlwind— that one CD of theirs that everyone had—and Kelp's first album, and Bellepheron's first album, and a Nina Simone best-of my mom had had. I loved how deep and furious she sounded, like a righteous tide coming in sweeping every dirty thing off shore. I was glad she'd died before all of this happened. Sins of Our Fathers' third CD, crap for the dustbin. Some hip-hop I vaguely knew, a string quartet—I liked violins—I made myself stop, we needed room for the onions. Stephen watched, unsmiling, his hands curled around the tabletop; his fingers were long and thin, knobbly and bulging around the knuckles like they were swollen up from overwork. And probably were. I opened the CD cases, one by one, just to make sure they weren't empty.

"Al won't let me play half of these," I reminded him. "You were right, if it's not Ornette Coleman or whoever, he doesn't want to know—are you allowed to hoard these?"

He shrugged. I loaded up the bag, let him sling it over his shoulder, and we went back outside to nose around deserted neighborhood gardens, seeking out promising bits and pieces of edible green like any actual four-legged rabbit. I remembered my Safety and Crisis Management classes from high school, Ms. MacAllister's fat rump in clingy pink polyester making us giggle every time she turned around and her thickened, clammy fingers like moist potato slices pointing to the old 1930s USDA poster: IF THE TOWN GATES CLOSE, CAN YOU STILL FEED YOUR FAMILY? START A "HAZARD GARDEN" TODAY. I never paid attention, during the gardening parts. I hated crouching down in the sun, sweating, grabbing stray handfuls of poison ivy weeding, driving soil so far under my nails that it hurt trying to dig it out.

Everybody living here had been good, while they were alive; they nearly all had dedicated hazard patches to root through. I found a clump of what looked like dandelion greens, tugged it up. The night air was perfect, that cool half-wet freshness that smelled and felt like being enveloped in a single new soft spring leaf.

"Phoebe came by the kitchens," Stephen said. His fingers hovered over a clump of mushrooms, tiny little deep orange tabletops at the base of an oak. Of course Billy or Mags wouldn't lose a beat if he slipped them a toadstool. "Jabbering, like—"

"She keeps acting like she knows stuff about me," I said. Dandelion greens were bitter as hell anyway, why was I scrounging for them? Rather have the instant rice. "Like a couple days ago at dinner, you saw it."

Stephen sat down next to me. In the moonlight the bruising on the side of his face looked like a great smudge of dirt, charcoal ash smeared on his skin; it was almost reassuring, a mark of mutual humanity. Our defanged voices, our fragile skin, our frail little bodies that won't just up and heal. A whole race of turtles who've forever lost their shells.

"I shut her up," he said. "She started talking, and talking, like she does, like there's a damned windup key all in her back, and I shut her the hell up. It was my pleasure."

Something fierce crossed his face, heat flaring suddenly from the dead ashen debris of a fire pit, and he laughed, dry and rasping, like a cigarette cough. The sound of it made me hope he never found anything funny again.

"She can't help it," I said. Phoebe running hunched over and tripping over her own feet, half-crying, still cradling the arm Lisa had hurt. "I hate her too but she can't help it, she's crazy—"

"Oh, you're right about that," he said, and laughed again. Just sucking in that smoke. "Everything she does is crazy, says, thinks—"

"What did you do?" Sharp, verging on angry, because I wouldn't be made to feel sorry for her, but his eyes, his laugh, I didn't like them right now at all. "One of the exes almost broke her arm tonight, I hope you didn't decide to finish the—"

"I scared her," he said. So calm. He tugged the orange mushrooms out by the roots. "I just told you that. Scared her enough to shut up and go away. I didn't need to hurt her." He turned, looked me square in the face. "I'm good like that. When I want to be."

I looked him right back. Eyes so dark you couldn't see to the bottom of them, thick smears of paint that never quite dried. We had gray eyes, my mother and I, like Mags did. I'd always wanted eyes like his, that deep opaque brown that's nearly black; light eyes illuminated too much inside you, glass instead of paint. Left you too exposed.

"Is that supposed to scare me?" I said.

"No." No more smiling. "There isn't much scares you, really. I don't think. So why would I try?"

He held up a mushroom, waxen and caked in dirt, already

bruising like his face from the light touch of his fingertips; he bit off half the cap, chewing methodically, swallowing. I waited. Nothing happened. Maybe it wouldn't until tomorrow. I'd seen wild mushrooms in the woods near Dave's house a lot of times, foraging in the fall when our food was already running thin, but I never dared touch them.

"The thing is," Stephen said, "Phoebe thinks you remind her of someone." He ran his free hand through his hair, standing it up on thick bristly ends and then letting it collapse. "I guess someone from her precious lab. She thinks you're holding back something big, something you'll use to get things you want. Things she wants, like getting back to Prairie Beach. To whatever she thinks is still going on t here." He snorted, t ook a nother b ite o f m ushroom. "She's welcome to it, what went on there was—anyway. That's what she thinks." Another bite and he made a face at the mushroom's aftertaste, licked at his lips like a cat. "I mean, you never were there, right? Even just sneaking in, like kids used to try to do sometimes?"

Too casual, that question, and he knew I knew it. I waited until he looked up again, then deliberately bit a mushroom in half. A little rubbery, a bit earthy, a faint bland sourness like soil slowly transmuting to wax. I waited. Nothing happened.

"I don't know what the hell she's talking about," I said, and licked dirt from my fingertips like sugar. There was something oddly comforting about the tangerine color of the cap. "My dad was a steelworker. My mom—nobody I know worked for the labs. I've never been halfway near the beaches in my life. So I guess she really is just crazy, and I get to be her crazy fixation. Lucky me."

Weirdly that was almost a letdown, a slumping feeling inside, like I'd been on the verge of some horrible but truly interesting revelation about . . . something or other, and it all came to naught. It was the boredom of this place, the boredom of every place now, the utter tedium of putting one foot in front of the other, in front of the other, every day, hour, minute . . . for what? My cell phone was stone dead now, nobody ever called me back. Farther from my mother than I'd ever been. Lisa had Naomi now, I didn't hate either of them for it but it was still true. Me, I was treading water. Sliding backward, like a moving glacier. I finished off the mushroom.

"Phoebe thinks she knows Lisa too," I told him. "And so does Mags." *Jessie's Lisa.* Whoever this Jessie was, Lisa's lost sister. I didn't think much of them both together, to be honest, if they'd had each other's company and then just decided one day to throw it away. I wouldn't have behaved like that. I knew what I had before I ever lost it.

"Maybe she does," Stephen said, pulling himself to his feet, offering me a hand up. He didn't seem particularly interested now. "Bully for them. Time for an onion hunt."

I was expecting more stumbles through knee-high weeds but the patch of ex-garden was right there, big patches of dirt still untouched by grass and with the telltale long, slender spring onion shoots poking from the depths; some thinner ones too, that might be garlic. I dug carefully around the edges of a bulb. "Anyway," I said, "Phoebe was jabbering at me and then Lisa and Mags showed up, thank God, never thought I'd say thank God for Mags, and then Mags got really weird—"

"She hurt you?" Stephen glanced up from where he knelt, an onion bulb in each hand.

"God, no—she was going on and on about her old gang, I mean, her gang back when she was really dead. And then she was talking about her childhood or something, I guess, when she was human and alive. Alive for the first time. It's just . . . weird, isn't it? I mean, I always thought they were just sort of bags of flesh, walking around. Bags of rotten flesh with nothing inside."

That seething, swollen thing that looked at my mother like he knew her. Like he was trying to tell her something. I pushed him from my mind, even though it'd been him who took away everything I had, before any of this ever started. "But they think and feel like we do—I mean, they've got whole histories inside them, everything that happened before they died. They remember everything. Everything a human remembers, about their own past. Isn't that weird? They're actual people. I'm sorry, I guess that sounds stupid but I'll never get over it—"

"So that's your yardstick," Stephen said. He was just kneeling there now, the trowel idle. "How good someone's memory is."

His voice was distant, and far too brittle. I stopped digging and slid one fingernail under another, sawing at the ground-down dirt. "My yardstick of what?"

"Whether they get to be human or not." Staring back at me now, detached and cold. "Whether you, yourself, deign to think of them as a person."

What the hell had I said? "I didn't—"

"So the more you remember, the more human you are. And if you can't remember it, you can't *think*, for any reason? That's that for that. Good to know. Takes care of anyone with Alzheimer's, or who got hit on the head, or just has trouble stringing their thoughts together for any—"

"That isn't what I said." I threw the onion bag onto the grass. "That's not what I said at all, and you know it."

"I do, huh?" His eyes were sparking. "Yeah. I do. I'm not fucking deaf, and you just said—"

"I said I was surprised that *Mags*, you know, the *zombie* as was, I'm surprised whenever she sounds halfway human! And I am! All right? I'm surprised when any of them sound halfway human! It's not like they think of themselves as human and I'm taking that away, now is it? They hate us! Work until you die, that's us, then they feed off what's left! Just like before! I'm not fucking talking about *humans* with Alzheimer's!"

I turned away to stare into the depths of the garden. Weeds everywhere, predictably, clumps of shiny reddish leaves and patches of soft spring-green furze and a tiny vine with purple flowers I could see winding slowly, mercilessly around far bigger plants. Alzheimer's. What if you were human before, with Alzheimer's, a nd t hen y ou g ot p lague s ick a nd r ecovered a nd were s tuck l ike t hat, f orever? W ho w ould t ake c are o f y ou, knowing you'd never die and let them catch a break? From the corner of my eye I saw Stephen, back on his feet, fingers curled vine-tight around the trowel and glowering at the peonies like he wanted to tear them in fistfuls out of the ground.

"Everything that's happened," he said, "and that's what surprises you."

I kept my eyes on the garden: a bush with huge, top-heavy creamy-lacey blooms already a mess of petals on the ground. Bright orange poppies, a vibrant deep orange with the petals blushing all over like skin. I used to think they only came in red.

You were right, I thought. You don't scare me. Though I guess you got me to shut up anyway, just like Phoebe. Enjoy it.

"They surprise me too, Amy," he said, something tangled in his voice like a snarl of hair too painful to comb out. "All the time, they do. But that doesn't get me anywhere."

I turned back to him, slowly. He'd stolen those CDs for me, and that fork. He could get in trouble. He was probably remembering someone old he'd seen die and he got upset.

"Are you and Natalie related?" I asked.

He blinked in surprise. "If we are," he said, "it's news to me. She came here without any family, just like me. Why did you think that?"

"I don't know, I just did. Making up more stupid things to be surprised about." I dug under my nails again, ignoring the raw-skin feeling making me wince. "Why does everyone here act like she's contagious?" And you too. Diseased. Though we don't talk about that, we pretend not to see it even as it happens right in front of us. Nothing's changed. Nothing's changed anywhere.

"Amy—"

"Why are we even doing this?" I flung a hand at him, bent over the dirt again and scrabbling hard, a dog set on digging but all grimness instead of animal bliss. "I hate dandelion greens. Everyone hates them. It's like when everyone was sick and eating the grass like goats."

Stephen looked up at me, our faces inches apart. This close his bruised side had a yellowing tinge, greenish-yellow like those potato skins. The jaundiced ugliness of healing.

"I don't know why we're doing this," he said. "I don't know how the hell we ended up here at all."

Fate. Ms. Czapla, my eighth-grade English teacher, she loved that I liked Greek myths, she said it was especially hard for an American to wrap their head around the Greek idea of Fate since our big myth was that anyone could do anything. *Hubris is in our national DNA,* she said, *we think every good thing we have we did all by ourselves,* and then told the story of Niobe. There was no Fate or destiny or grand plan, she said; life had no point at all, in the end, but to perpetuate itself. She got in trouble sometimes, talking like that to us kids. I don't know what happened to her when the sickness came.

"Maybe we only find that out when we die," I said.

He looked down at our hands, grime-caked and digging side by side. About to tell me just how full of it I really was.

"Have we met before?" he asked.

I frowned in surprise. "I'm serious," he said. "There's all sorts of holes all through my memory, things just keep dropping out and reappearing and I don't know why. Maybe Natalie really is my sister. I don't know." He shrugged. "But, you say things that'd be crazy out of Phoebe's mouth but right off I know what you mean, so—it just seems like we've talked before. Enough that we both know what to talk about and what to keep—"

He shut up quick, and got back to digging.

"I can't remember stuff either," I said. "There's spaces where there shouldn't be, like my mind's this big mouth, biting down on reality, and there's gaps all in the teeth." I reached over and yanked out a clump of weeds, greens, something I couldn't identify. "And things I do remember, it's like they're—pulsing, inside, but my head keeps shoving them away. Forgetting while I remember."

He didn't answer. Angry still, a taut vein of it pulsing through him with a soft, persistent beat like blood. So what? Jabber-jaw crazy or smoke-sucking angry, those were the only two choices left, and maybe he was only now coming out of a long stretch of crazy. That notebook of his, writing everything down because otherwise it might all vanish. My atlas, that I lost in the tornado.

"Only four of us lived," I said. I sat back cross-legged on the grass. "Me and Kristin, and Dave, and Ms. Acosta. She kept saying to call her Alicia but I can't think of her by her first name. She worked for my school. Her and Dave. I hid, we hid, in the school basement, when our town fell apart. A couple days later we found Kristin, in this little white stucco house near the school. She was holding her daughter who was dead from the disease. Suffocated. Her whole face, the little girl's, it was so swollen and blue-black that her eyes just disappeared inside it. Swallowed up. Dave's house had a wood-burning stove, and he knew how to hunt, so that's where we went. That was us, the whole town."

I hadn't talked for months on end, not truly, not since I fled my uncle's house, and now it poured from me like the rain in last week's storm. "I should've maybe written things down, or something, but I couldn't think straight enough, it's like pieces of my brain got shoved around like blocks inside my head and—see, this is why I didn't bother writing it down, I'm shit at describing things. It's easier with songs, songs don't have to make sense, they just have to sound *right*—"

"You write music?" he said. He was sitting next to me now, arms wrapped around his knees, the garden's remains forgotten. His head, a shoulder would angle forward when he was really listening to you, I'd noticed that before.

"I used to. Stupid shit. I thought I was going to have my own band and live in Europe, and—it doesn't matter what I thought. There's no point." My fingers curled around a shin, the denim rough and worn enough I could feel the fraying cords of the cloth like tiny wires losing their insulation. "Everybody thought they were going places, didn't they? But we got shown up, shown up good. Me and Dave, and—and Kristin."

Mourning doves. Those birds I kept hearing, when Lisa and Mags were with me, all over the place: *oooh-ahhh-wooo, woooo, wooooo*. And again, when I woke. I liked the sound of mourning doves, I always had before too; you would hear them calling from the grayness as the afternoon faded and you felt like something was saying it like it was, like their song was the perfect low, subdued sound to encapsulate the disappearance of the light. Onomatopoeia.

"Kristin was pregnant," I told him. "And crazy from losing her other kids, or maybe just from being sick—she couldn't stop throwing up for months, nothing went right." That time Ms. Acosta found her lying on the floor with something wrapped around her neck, too weak to stand up and hang herself but trying to tug on it and strangle out her own life. Her hands were freezing, Kristin's were, when we got that scarf or extension cord or whatever it was, I couldn't remember, off her, her fingers never got properly warm again after that. "I promised her over and over again I'd take care of her baby, sometimes she'd make me say it dozens of times in a row and it didn't work, none of it, Kristin died and it was—"

Skip to the next part. The part that came just afterward, the aftermath that mattered, it wasn't sayable.

"It was stillborn," I said.

I stared down at my jeans, the little coronas of worn threads turning to fuzz. Stephen turned the onion bag over in his hands, cradling our few finds through the cloth.

"I wrote a lot of music," I said. "That's what I was going to do with my life. My mom, she was never all over me to go to college instead." Something inside me was thin and delicate like a shell, mentioning her to Stephen, and I couldn't let it break, what spilled out of that particular crack inside me would never stop. "She always said, *when* you have a band. Not if. She said I could do it, that—I wrote a lot of songs. But I've lost them all."

"You must remember some of them." He actually almost smiled. "I mean, I wouldn't be able to, but—"

I laughed and then felt rotten about laughing, but he didn't seem to mind. "Of course I remember some of them."

"Then could I hear them sometime?"

He asked that with respect, a respect I could feel. Like he understood you don't just casually ask someone to share that huge part of themselves, scoop out bits of their insides and offer up the tasty pulp any time they want the flavor. Respect, and the near certainty of being refused.

"Not now," I said. There was something stuck in my throat like bits of that hard thin dry shell all inside me, the idea of singing around that felt impossible. "Maybe later. Like, maybe later for real, I'm not just saying that to—I can't, right now. But when I can."

The bushes rustled and all sorts of things I couldn't quite see hurried through it. I hoped none of them ended up in the kitchen traps and snares, it wasn't fair, but then neither was any of this. Stephen wouldn't stop looking at me and I kept my eyes on my folded-up shins, the muddy rubber of my shoe toes.

"There's a huge old community garden, over at Fisher and Elbert Gary Place," he said. "There's bits still fallow where we might find stuff. I'll head over and you finish up here, meet me when you're ready."

"Okay."

He put out a hand and we helped each other up; one of my feet buzzed and stung, tucked under my leg too tightly, and I rocked back and forth on it until it stopped.

"I could've saved her baby," I said. "Kristin's. But it just—things didn't go my way. I would've done it." My foot worked the dirt like a sewing pedal, tingling toes pushing down, then back. "Fed it. Done everything. I would've done anything, to keep it alive."

Stephen didn't answer. Just looked so sad, just for that split second, it was like he might decide to forget to breathe.

His fingers around mine were gritty and knobbly and scraping-dry, like ancient parsnips pulled from drought-dry soil, and I felt a pang inside when he slid them slowly away and let go. He picked up the full onion bag, the one with all our music in it, and left me the lighter one.

"Fisher," he said. As if I'd suddenly forget. Maybe that was what it was like for him. His papers, carried place to place because without one reminder after another he'd be lost. I nodded.

"Fisher," I said.

He walked off. The garden looked so picked over and dug up the more I trudged through it, those pretty poppies to stare at but all the edible parts reduced to scraggly little tufts, that I shook my head and thought, Fuck it, I'm leaving now. Can't dig up all the onions anyway, the gardening crew needed those as reserves. I tilted my chin to the sky, the darkness overhead thin and clear to the eye as a cup of plain tea.

"Kristin's baby was stillborn," I told it. Because sometimes there were certain things I needed to say out loud, when no one else could hear me. "My mother is alive. Kristin's baby never was."

There was a sudden little tremor in my pocket, and my cell phone, my stone-cold doornail of a birthday phone, let out a squawky, urgent beep: the text message sound. They found me. They found me again, whoever first somehow made it ring and somehow left no traces behind found me again and—my stomach dropped and I paced around for a few moments there in the soft soil, trying to calm down, more nervous the more I put it off, and then slid my hand in. 1 NEW MESSAGE—

LIAR, it said, flat and quiet. ALL LIES.

Then the screen went dead.

# THIRTEEN

Back in March, just a few weeks ago, there was a storm that came in fast and thin, that winter thinness of cold sharp air sweeping through a gray sky and bare tree branches and over depleted ground because there wasn't anything growing there to stop it, and then it turned thick with wetness and mushy snow that dissolved into clumps of sleet. Drippings and snifflings. I shivered and pulled on two more sweaters and made myself stay away from the woodpile Dave had left us, we were rationing it now thinking no point wasting it on late winter, but Ms. Acosta stood by the window smiling, almost her old pompous fluttery self again. Kristin lay on the sofa like always, face pressed to the arm.

"See that, Amy?" Ms. Acosta said, sharp beaky chin angling to motion me toward the window. She'd given up even trying to talk to Kristin, barely seemed to notice she was in the same room. "That's a spring sleet, right there, all wet and loose and . . .

disjointed, and a lot of it's not sticking. Spring really is coming. We've started getting through it." She smiled, wider and so much happier than her careful cautious words, and put an arm around my shoulders as I approached. "We're really almost through the winter—"

"Snow is wet and loose," I pointed out. "And that's not *spring sleet*, it's another ice storm." There'd been one three weeks back that took down a whole row of power lines, which at least didn't factor when you hadn't had electricity in ages. "I know you have to take what you can get when it's barely March, but—"

"It's not an ice storm. See? It's subsiding already, it's not washing over everything. Winter's running out of steam." There was a sour smell to her, this close up, not only from armpit and mouth but her anemically faded hair, the folds of her own jackets and sweaters; it didn't bother me, I'd already become so quickly used to the aroma of unwashed body. "Things'll be better now. We can go out there, plan a garden, clean up a few things—maybe look for some more people. We're almost through the worst of it, Amy."

She smiled at me, so washed out and depleted from the winter but her eyes were sparky and bright, like a bird who'd just found a lovely seedy tree-cone in the snow. She glanced over at the couch, Kristin now half-asleep, and her voice slid lower. "And whether she wants to be or not she's through the worst of it too. She has to help us out, Amy, she has to start contributing something and actually hauling ass and—we'd all like to lie on a couch all day crying, okay, Amy? But we don't. We can't. Dave was sick all the time and he didn't behave like that, and pregnancy's not a disease. She listens to you, Amy." Apologetic now, embarrassed at the task she asked of me. "Talk to her about that. Work up to it, but . . . she needs to rejoin the living."

There was only one thing Kristin ever listened to, from my mouth or anyone else's, and that was the word *yes*. Said after, *Will you take care of my baby once I'm dead swear to me Amy I mean it you've got to promise me*, over and over and over again. Nothing else ever got through. Ms. Acosta looked from me to Kristin and as she did her face went from nervous contrition to pitying contempt, mouth pursing up in that way where you know someone's thinking, Oh, poor *you*. Poor burdensome, worthless you. I turned back to the window.

"There's no point in talking about all that yet," I said, running a fingertip along the glass near the sill. Little designs on the dirty pane. "She hasn't even had the baby yet, and then she'll be—won't she need extra food? To nurse it?" I swore I'd read somewhere that if you breast-fed you had to eat for a whole football team to do it right. Nutrients for the milk and things. "We should be getting all that ready. Baby clothes. Anything we can use as a diaper." I turned to Ms. Acosta again. "She's big as this room, we haven't got much time left."

Ms. Acosta gazed out the window, and didn't say anything.

"I asked Kristin about a name," I said. "She won't think of one. What could we call it? David, for a boy." For Dave. "What about a girl?"

Ms. Acosta didn't say anything. "What," I said, deliberately louder, "about a girl?"

The wet pale-gray clumps of stuff broke up falling as we watched and turned into actual rain, rain that washed away some of the ground's old snow. Kristin had her baby two weeks later. It was a girl. There's no point in saying anything about that.

And nobody can make me.

.   .   .

When I got to the kitchens there was a little crowd gathered, other shift workers milling and shoving around the back steps like it was already dinnertime; I saw Phoebe there wriggling with anticipated trouble, beaming like Christmas when she saw me, Kevin taking her arm and pulling her back stern-faced from barreling into my path. Stephen drew me aside.

"Natalie's missing," he said. "Since this morning. Her and Maria, another girl from the cleanup crew. They're gone."

My stomach dropped. "I don't think anyone took her," he continued. "Natalie, I mean. Someone on the gardening crew yelled at her for something and she started crying and shouting, I think she'd just had it, and she ran off into the woods and—"

"And good riddance!" someone shouted from the steps, a man with a potbelly and scraggly gray ponytail and T-shirt crust-spotted with garden dirt. "You think people don't know she was just like you? Another freak? And they let you cook our food, it'd better not be contagious—"

"You stop that." Janey, fragile, crimson-mouthed, stern and gentle like a nursery school teacher. Janey with no Don in sight, all made up like always and nowhere to go. "Nobody here's a freak, we're all family and when a family fights it—"

"Shut up, you fucking whore," said the ponytailed man. "Go spread for dead some more and keep your mouth shut."

"Little necro," someone else added, and giggled. "Nympho-necro."

Janey ducked her head and sat down on the porch steps, shoulders curled up and hands in her lap. I waited for Al, Alice, to pull out their notebooks, their infraction notebooks they kept to show to Billy and Mags, and write that up. They didn't.

Stephen turned back to me. "They don't give a damn about Natalie," he said, his eyes and voice hard, "like you can tell, but they think she talked Maria into going with her, they were starting to be friends—"

"You were trying to make nice with her—that Natalie." The ponytailed man, who seemed to think he was in charge, was trying to stare me down and pin me to the wall. There was a glassy, feverish look in his eyes, a woman right behind him crying quietly. "We've seen you. Did you put it into that freak's head, letting her think she could run off and take my little girl with her and—"

"Pete," Kevin called out. "Leave it. Just leave it. She doesn't know what the hell you're—"

"Don't give me that bullshit!" He rounded on Kevin, snarling. "We're all sick to fucking death of your fucking Uncle Tom act, I wanna know what she has to do with this and I want my kid back!"

"I've never seen your daughter in my life." I tried to be just as hard and glassy in return, ignoring the crying woman. Just like she'd turn her back on me. "I don't know anything about her and Natalie. I don't know anything about this."

"*You* were making friends with her." He was coming at me now, that Pete was, Kevin and Stephen hastily stepping into his path but no one else even trying to hold him back. "Just like you're all friendly with *that* now"—he jerked his chin at Stephen—"all you little freaks together, plotting against us and getting us sent off to Paradise when it should be you that—"

"I don't know what you're talking about!" I pushed past Stephen to get right in Pete's face, if he wanted it that bad, fuck his daughter and fuck his crying wife what one of them gave a shit if I disappeared, if Natalie they all spat on was gone. *Natalie's dead,* Naomi told me. This is what she meant. "I don't have a clue what happened to Natalie and I never met *Maria* in my life—"

He shoved something at me, a folded-up, crumpled piece of notebook paper. *I can't stay here anymore,* it said, when I smoothed it out, *I have to leave. Amy and Stephen from the kitchens understand why. They're just like I am and people like me don't have anywhere to go. I won't bother anyone anymore.* Signature, a scrawled letter *N.*

I shook my head in confusion. "I don't know what this means."

He gave me a look that made me take a step backward, Stephen darting between us, Kevin right behind him, the little gathered crowd ready to descend. Al and Alice, they just stood there. Didn't try to stop it. "You planned all this, didn't you? You and him and that little freak, you figured you'd bribe your way into never having to go back by giving them a normal human girl for—"

"Go back *where*? Plan what?" I was shouting now too, feet planted wide and solid in the grass like that could keep me from getting hit in the face. "I don't know what you're talking about!"

"The fuck you don't!" He shoved Stephen aside, grabbing my shoulders and yanking me close as if for a kiss. "Give me my daughter back!"

Stephen knocked Pete aside so fast it sent me stumbling, punched him again, again so he grunted with the blows and gasped as he punched back. Scrabbling in the dirt now, just like Don and Lisa back at that first dinner, and Stephen's bad eye caught a fist and he did something that made Pete almost howl in pain, and then Kevin was between them both, his arms around Pete, pulling him off so quick and easy that Stephen's arm swung at empty air.

"Pete!" Kevin gripped Pete hard as he struggled, dragging

him back as Stephen, breathless, came at them both for more. "She's not lying! For Christ's sake stop it!"

"I'm not stopping anything! I want my fucking kid back, or I swear to God I'll break her—"

"Try it," Stephen spat, and he was laughing again, that horrible dry-stick laughter, corner of his mouth bleeding like my dog-bitten arm. "Try it! You gonna fucking try—"

"What's going on here?"

Lisa. Standing there on the sidewalk with Mags and Billy and a couple of other exes I couldn't place, gripping Naomi's hand and poised on the balls of her feet like a dog ready for the attack. She glowered at Pete, just waiting for him to get in her face like he had mine. He stared back, a sort of sweetly perfect hate in his eyes, and slowly went limp in Kevin's grasp. Stephen, breath rasping, blood from his lip trickling down the side of his neck, looked from me to Lisa to Billy and lowered his arms, turned from Pete, rocked back and forth and back on his heels like that could exorcise the seizing need to hit, kick, break.

"Come here, Amy," Lisa said quietly.

I stayed where I was. I'm not your fucking dog, I'm glad you're here, Lisa, but I'm not your pet dog. She nodded like she'd heard and understood that, turned to Billy. "You see what crap everyone pulls," she said. "With *your* kitchen crew."

"I want my daughter back." Kevin had let Pete loose and Pete was standing before Billy now, actually wringing his hands, drained and weary and all the fire gone out of him. All the jeers about other humans playing Uncle Tom. "That's what the bargain's supposed to be here, *protection*, we work for you and this kind of shit doesn't happen, you make sure we . . ."

He trailed off when he saw two guards come up the sidewalk toward us, a little girl between them with her head down and crying. Pete stared at them, and then actually sat down right there on the grass. The smaller girl, I guessed it was Maria, ran toward him, sobbing harder, and he stumbled to his feet and wrapped her up in his arms. Maria's mother, the crying woman, she ran to them both. Billy just shook his head and smirked.

"You're welcome," he said. "Now fuck off back to work, all you little happy family, before I pound your skulls into the pavement right in front of each other—and you can all forget about dinner tonight and tomorrow, for that little stunt." He glanced down at Maria, now mopping her eyes, like he wanted to hit her. Like the idea of hitting her consumed him. "And that's getting off easy. Get out of my sight."

"Where's Natalie?" I shouted. The little girl didn't answer. "What happened to her? Your *friend*, what happened?"

They ran, the three of them. Actually scuttled with their heads down. The rest of the crowd started breaking up too, still buzzing with all the truncated excitement. I bet they were disappointed it all ended so soon, that they couldn't excite themselves more imagining two little girls wandering around alone, hungry, even better grabbed by someone else and dragged off, hurt, raped—not that they cared when it happened to Natalie right here, not that anyone gave a damn if it were the freak. The "dead" freak. All except me and Stephen and Janey, the corpse-whore, sitting there so curled up and sad. Another freak. Without Don she'd be like Natalie, she'd have no one and nothing. Like me without Lisa. My chest felt hollow and thin like an eggshell, a dry shell going to powder with what was meant to be curled up inside it long since rotted away.

"Where's Natalie?" I repeated.

"They haven't found her yet," Lisa said softly. "They've been searching. For hours."

Something damp was on my cheek and Stephen had my hand, hanging on with a hard awkward grasp, and then Phoebe in my face again, always Phoebe in my face no matter where I went or what I did, patting my arm with a palm I half-expected to leave a sticky syrup stain on my skin.

"They'll get her back too, kid," she said, all jocular like this was a fucking scavenger hunt, her lips little rubber bands tugging and snapping around the words. "Can't *not* get her back, I mean, she's *kind of important* to this whole enterprise! Right, Janey?" Janey whipped her head around, sweeping Phoebe with the searchlights of her eyes in a way even she wouldn't have dared if Don were around. "Isn't that right?"

"Phoebe?" Kevin was tugging at her arm, trying to get her away from me. "Not now. Seriously. Not fucking now."

"Nah, why not now?" Billy was leaning against the porch now, arms folded, like this was all a play being put on for his amusement and God knew, maybe it was. Mags just stood there, silent as Janey, unreadable. "Ain't never any time like *now*. Is there, Feebs?"

"Phoebe," Kevin said, with that pained steadiness you get when someone you love is mortifying you publicly, "you have to stop this, all right? Just, leave the kid alone and let's go back to work."

Phoebe shook her head. No more crazy smile, no trying to kiss up, we both knew she wanted something from me and now everyone else knew it too. "Get out," Stephen told her, disdainful and cold. "We've got work to do."

"No," Phoebe said softly, shaking her head. "Why should I?"

"Because I'll hurt you again," Stephen said, still holding my hand, and the thin, flat quiet of his words told me he meant it, he'd do it. "That's why. So get out."

"Phoebe? We've talked about this. You know we have." Kevin kept trying to pull her back, she kept resisting like there were tree roots anchoring her feet. "Leave her alone. Leave them both alone."

"Don't be an idiot, Kevin." Sharp and impatient, like he was nothing worth getting fussed about. "You know the lab needs to know about—"

"You're not getting back to the fucking lab!" Scarlet-faced, Kevin slammed a fist against the porch; Janey flinched and shuddered at the sound, like she hadn't at all the yelling. "Do you get it yet, Phoebe? It doesn't matter what you do or what you know, there's no more lab, there's no more Prairie Beach, there's no more of any of that shit for human beings so just be happy we've got a place to stay and we're not starving to death! You have to stop this, Phoebe! You're gonna make that kid crazy—" He broke off and I could hear *as you are* floating in the air, unsaid b ut h eard b y e veryone, b efore h e g athered h imself u p with a hard, shaky sigh. "Phoebe," he said, pleading, his hands open and reaching out in entreaty, "honey, just let it go. Okay? Let it go."

"There's so much you *think* p eople d on't k now a bout y ou, isn't there, Amy?" Phoebe was smiling now, crazy again but also calculating and triumphant and so happy to be shouting it out in front of all the bosses, the elect, the exalted ones who died but hadn't died. "I mean, you poor kid, you think you can just pass for anyone else—but I figured it out."

"Go fuck yourself," I said, soft and almost breathy now because otherwise I'd scream it. Because she was scaring me. "Just go fuck yourself."

"I know where you come from now. And you're one of the only ones left, you must've had to hit the road in a big damn hurry after you—"

My hand wrenched itself away from Stephen's and my arms flew out and I hit her, fast and hard. I caught her off guard and she nearly fell, staggering sideways under the impact, and then something was rushing at me and she had a handful of my hair, a skin-scratching hair-pulling worthless fighter but I knew how to throw real fists. Dave had taught me. He knew I'd need it someday, he was smart like that. I thanked him inside as I hit hard bone with real fists, the right sort of fists, and my fingers shook and throbbed with the impact but it felt good, better than good, when Phoebe let out a scream.

Phoebe got me in the mouth, pain all through my jaw and the taste of a new wet warmth, and then Kevin had Phoebe and Billy had me, barely even gripping me by the fingertips but it hurt, it hurt bad, Lisa was trying to yank me away but Billy had me. Like he had us all.

"Crazy little bitch!" Billy was roaring with laughter, wiping his eyes with his free hand. "Jesus fucking Christ, get them crazy enough and they start thinking they're us, trying to fight like they—basement, kid. You started it. You can sit in there for the rest of the damned night, that's enough of a show—"

"You're the fucking bitch!" I screamed at Phoebe, as Al and one of Billy's gate guards took me from his grasp. "I'll kill you, I'll sic my fucking dog on you—"

"Give her back!" Lisa was shouting. Naomi was wrapped around her leg, her forehead pressed to Lisa's thigh and eyes squeezed hard shut. "You give her back, she's *my* goddamned—"

"You want her neck broke?" Billy snarled, giving Lisa a shove. "Huh? You want her neck broke, you want your big pet and your little pet lying in the dirt all twisted up like a car crash? You want it?"

Lisa peeled Naomi off her leg and she and Billy were going at it, kicking and pounding like I never could've without breaking in two, scrabbling on the sidewalk in smears of quick-drying blood. Naomi ran to Stephen, sobbing now like Maria; Stephen was shouting something I couldn't hear, couldn't hear anything over the roar in my own ears. Janey closed her eyes to the fight and turned her head away, humming some tuneless, sickly melody like fever turned to song. Kevin frog-marched Phoebe into the trees, no more sweet reason. Mags just stood there, watching all of us, taffy-apple hair spilling into her eyes and broad-beamed body solid like something sculpted, a chunk of granite surrounded by cracking beams of plywood. There was no expression on her face at all.

I went limp and let my feet drag on the ground, like those funeral-home protesters you used to see on television, but they just hauled me off my feet and into one of the empty homes on Connecticut Street, shoved me into the basement, locked the door. One dim little light, as I quit pounding the door screaming about dogs and groped my way dizzy and hurting down the stairs, a small flashlight lying forgotten on the floor that let out a dying battery glow as I switched it on. Filthy old mattress in the corner, ripped open and oozing batting that gave off a mushroom-stink of must; a workbench opposite me, stripped of all its tools, a dark stain painting the top and soaking into the wood. Emergency supply shelves, all empty, long since raided or gone to the commissary.

I marched around the workbench, like it could tell me something, and then sank down in a corner away from that disgusting mattress and wrapped my arms around my knees, twitching with the feverish exhilaration of needing to hurt something, hurt Phoebe. My hands were puffy and sore and my throat scratchy from shouting and my lip swelling up where she got me, the skin raised and tender like my own mouth was some foreign growth attacking my face. Every part of me felt not mine, turned inside out, I knew this feeling from the last time and Phoebe knew about that time, she knew everything, so *what* if she knew everything? With the way she planned and schemed, she and Kevin never got here just by accident—

"So where are you?" I yelled into the dim light, at the near-solidified stench coming up from that mattress. "I could've used some teeth in that fight! Some claws!"

Well? Here, boy! You know where to find me!

How about you, phantom caller? Anybody? Dead phone, no battery, that's nothing to you! Talk!

Nothing. All alone in the dark. Lisa wouldn't come, I was sure of that. She was too afraid of pushing Billy into really hurting me, or Naomi. All that strength, invulnerable flesh and just like with Don, on the road, it doesn't help. Helps nothing.

I curled up against the wall and cried some, and slept, and then someone was at the top of the stairs, rattling the door handle. Key sliding into a lock. Maybe this right here was "Prairie Beach," the place where anyone who acted up ended up, the tide sweeping their dirty unfit selves off their feet and into the crawl space—I stood up, waiting. Darkness in the doorway, and then a pair of eyes, piercing sulfurous lamp-eyes—

Stephen. He had a flashlight, one of the big industrial ones from the kitchens that he didn't switch on until he'd closed the door behind him, and a bulging black tote bag on one arm. He glanced behind him, and with the bag lying across his back trudged down the stairs.

"How did you get in here?" I asked. Half-whispering, because maybe someone really was outside. My voice was scratchy and hoarse.

"Through the door," he said dryly. "Just like you. I brought you some stuff, it's not much but it's what I could take without being missed."

He emptied it all out on the workbench, not noticing or caring about the stain too dark to be water. Another small flashlight. A box of wheat crackers. A jar of peanut butter and a little knife. Some apricot jam. I'd never liked the taste of apricots but that didn't seem relevant just now. A tightly folded blanket. Some books, random paperbacks he'd obviously grabbed in a hurry. "Your notes will be off now," I said. "The supply inventory."

"This is the commissary's food." He laughed. "Their books. Their shit. Phoebe's problem, not mine."

There was a reckless little glint in his eye that reminded me far too much of Phoebe. "Billy will miss you, serving dinner—"

"He went off hunting with Mags."

"Al, then. Alice."

"They're both afraid of me, in case you haven't figured it out. Guns or no guns. They think—fuck it, never mind what they think. They can think what they want. They're not here."

He passed me a handful of half-flattened Tootsie Rolls. I shoved them in my pocket.

"I want to know what they think," I said. I sat back down on the floor, the folded-up blanket beneath me. My stomach was a peach pit, I couldn't eat. "Why they're afraid of you, and why everyone hates the kitchen crew but Billy won't have us touched.

And all that stuff about Prairie Beach, and Natalie, and us three being alike." I tugged at strands of my hair, like Lisa would. "And why everyone avoids you—"

"Your mouth's swollen," he said, sitting down next to me. "Like mine. I can't steal first-aid stuff, they guard it—"

"It doesn't hurt."

"There's rumors," he said, slowly, like he'd lose the whole unspooling thread of his story if he rushed it. With what he'd said about his head, maybe he would. "That the lab at Prairie Beach, the big one doing all the thanatological research before the plague, that it's started up again—"

"Researching *what*? And how? There's no more undead, everyone keeps saying they're extinct, and even if there were there's no computers left. No electricity, or, anything."

"Hippocrates didn't need computers," Stephen said, brusque and impatient. "Galen didn't need electricity. All either of them needed was a test subject, and a knife."

Something flashed in his eyes, and was gone again before I could take the measure of it.

"So something really is going on there," I said.

"I don't *know*. I just hear. I hope I hear wrong."

I yanked harder on my hair and Stephen put out a hand as if to grab mine again, stop me, but it hovered midair and descended, rubbing against his jeans leg. I made myself quit pulling even though I could see why Lisa kept on: Those tiny flashes of pain were a perfect distraction. I found a loose thread on my sleeve, ripped at that instead. "So how long have you been here, anyway?"

"Since last December." He felt gingerly at the bruise on his face, faded pale yellow now springing back to darker life. "Long enough."

*Natalie's dead.* Scissor Men. *Amy and Stephen are just like I am.* Don't lay hands on the kitchen crew. It all meant something, it had to, though probably what it meant was Natalie was lonely and Billy was hungry and Mags found a good way to scare the shit out of a little kid.

"I hope Natalie didn't do something to herself," I said. There wasn't any point in not saying it, we were both thinking it. "You don't think Maria would've kept it to herself, if she saw—"

"Are you kidding? They'd be throwing a fucking party to celebrate right now."

His voice cracked on the words, harsh and bitter. I took his hand, my fingers t ense l ike a ny s econd h e'd w rench a way from their touch. He shifted closer and put an arm around my shoulders.

"I wish I knew what Naomi meant," I said. "When she said Natalie was already dead."

"There's still rumors flying around that zombies aren't really extinct." He shrugged. "I don't believe it. Everyone just wants things back like they were, after all that—"

"Because, see, it's just like how for years they kept telling me my mother's dead, when I knew that wasn't true." It was like heat all of a sudden inside me, an itchy prickly sweat that wouldn't break out but just escalated into fever, a furious sickness. "I knew it wasn't true but they just kept saying it and saying it like, Oh, we're doing you *so much good* to stand here and keep telling you lies, and I used to think, they're all gonna look so stupid when she comes back, when she walks through the door, they'll think she fell dead without a fly on her but she'll be alive as any of—"

So angry now I couldn't talk, congested up inside me stopping my throat. My mother. Kristin's baby. Natalie. Lisa's baby. Naomi. S tephen. A ll d ead o r w ished d ead. L ike t here h adn't been enough of that. They got up, walked, the fallen-dead people. They thought, felt, remembered things. Apparently. They could understand us. *Talitha cumi,* Jesus said to that dead girl in the Bible, and she got up again. A few streets down from us there'd been one of those weird little storefront churches, the kind that said that and the Lazarus story meant zombies weren't abominations, that Jesus created them for a reason. Talitha Cumi First Bible Church. They got a lot of death threats. We were agnostics so it was all the same to us.

Stephen turned to me. Our faces were inches removed and the look on mine, twisted up as I could feel it was, it didn't faze him.

"If you say your mother's still alive," he said, "then I believe you."

Believe me? I don't need you to *believe*, like a favor you grant me. I *know*. But someone who believes me. Someone who knows I'm right. And says so, out loud.

"I don't know why you talk to me sometimes," he said. No self-pity, no fishing for swoony praise, just so dry and matter-of-fact. "A million questions, just like me, and I haven't got any answers."

I took a few crackers, forced myself to munch them dry. They stuck inside my mouth like soaked tissue paper. "I wish I'd brought a toothbrush," I said. "Would've already lost it anyway, in the storm, but—"

"I can get you a toothbrush."

"I wasn't asking for one—"

"I know. But you should have stuff." There was faint color in his face when he said that but he pushed forward anyway, a defiant set to his mouth. "You're . . . very pretty."

That word slumped and fell as he said it, like a cake collapsing right out of the oven, and he turned away in embarrassment, touched gingerly at his bruised mouth. Pretty. There wasn't much I could do with that now, but then there hadn't been before either. "Janey's prettier," I pointed out. "So's Mags."

He didn't answer that, just snorted.

"Phoebe knows things about me," I said, and the thought of that made me scared, no, it reminded me I was scared, that that hadn't stopped since Lepingville ended and the dog found me. Being around people, that hadn't stopped it. "She—what happens here if you've done something bad? I mean, before you got here, if maybe things were, they got mixed up in your head, and then you did something that was—"

Stephen put a hand over mine. Steadying it. "None of what happened before," he said, "is anyone here's fucking business."

His eyes were hard, his words, like he'd had to remind someone else somewhere of this. Phoebe, probably. "I mean it, Amy. Nobody gives a shit. Because if they did, they'd find out there's always someone who knows what *they* did, and they'll wish they hadn't reminded them."

"I don't want to think about before," I said.

"Then don't."

"Everybody acts like things only started falling apart last year. But they've been falling apart for—my mother, she worked security, for our town, did I tell you that already? She got a kill, it messed up her head and she—she left. She walked off one night and never came back, just like that, everything had *already* fallen apart, okay?" And now I was half-yelling, voice like a damp sponge threatening to squeeze out tears. Crazy as Phoebe, as anybody. "Don't they get that?"

"No," Stephen said, and shook his head. "And they never will."

He wasn't humoring me. He was listening, every word, his

face as he looked at me full of feverish vindication like he'd felt just this way too, like things had long since gone sour for him too so none of this was a surprise. The whole world outside, losing itself like the way it'd collapsed inside me, wasn't a surprise at all: It's always been this empty, always been this lost. Everything you thought you had was a shell, a disguise, tap a finger on it and it all cracks open, there's only nothingness outside. Always was.

I put a hand to his face. I don't know why I did it, except, I could see he knew exactly what I was talking about. My fingers touched a cheekbone, the puffy yellow side of his jaw, and he swallowed and was silent.

"I saw a sick man in the street," I said, "during the plague. I still dream about him at night. He was . . . you know how they got when they were so hungry but nothing stayed down, when they'd eat anything? When they tried chewing Styrofoam, cloth, bits of wood, swallowing glue?" My throat closed up saying that, something lethally sticky congealing inside it. "He was squatting in the road shoving pebbles in his mouth, trying to scratch up bits of asphalt, to swallow, like it'd melt back to tar. Like molasses. His fingers were bloody, the nails were almost gone. And then," I was laughing now, and then just as quickly not laughing at all, "then he looked down at his own fingers, at all that meat waving around in front of his face, and he slid a couple of them into his mouth and—"

And. I'd screamed out loud when I saw that, louder than I ever did when I saw that other man shoot his family and himself, but I didn't faint or get sick. And that made me think there was something wrong with me, something not quite human in me, but then maybe that's what things had always been like, in their own way. Inside everyone. Stephen looked somber, sorrowful, hearing me talk. But not surprised. I was so thankful he wasn't surprised.

"I don't want to think about before," I said.

He leaned closer to me, eyes crackling. "Then *don't*."

"Kristin's baby." The sticky congealing thing was back. It would never leave me. "Kristin's baby . . . wasn't stillborn."

Stephen put a hand to my shoulder, so cautious and careful like my arm might shatter beneath his touch.

"I'm going to hell," I said. "I can't tell you why, but I am."

"You already told me why," he said. No contempt. No hate. "Because Kristin's baby wasn't stillborn. It's nothing to what I've done. I can tell you that much and it's true."

"I haven't even told you what—"

He had both my shoulders clasped in his palms, trying to stare me down. Trying to win this fight that wasn't one. "It's nothing," he repeated, "to what I've done. At all."

"Is that why they're afraid of you?"

"I can't explain it." His fingers curled tighter. "I'm sorry. I just can't."

"Are you an ex, underneath?"

I had to ask. I'd wondered ever since I saw Billy hit him like that, and not kill him. "I know. You can't be. You talk like a human. You don't heal as soon as you're hit. But they all act like you're not really . . . here."

His face contorted, his eyes hardened in a way that made my stomach twist. Then he forced himself to smile, and it passed.

"No," he said. "I'm not one of them."

He didn't let go of me. I was glad of that.

"I keep telling myself how different I am from them," I said. "From the exes. But sometimes I think I'm just kidding myself, and they know it. Like, all the human parts of me were always just this thin thing, pasted on, an eggshell, and the glue's drying up and it's all flaking and the real parts coming out. Like wallpaper, when it's peeling off a wall, and then underneath the plaster's all eaten away and inside, there's all these cobwebs. A nest of rats. And that's what's really me. Since before. Since, forever. Inside, I don't feel human at all."

This is the thing I'd been afraid to say all along, the first thing. The second I can't ever say out loud, not to him, not to anyone. Stephen stared back at me. Listening. Not surprised.

"Then it's not just me," he said, and kissed me.

Kissing him back was easy, like I'd done it all my life. Like I already knew from long years of kissing him what it should be like between us, like putting hands on him for the first time was really an old familiar habit. My skin twitched like his own hands might go all the way through me, like my body would collapse into its natural hollow nest of crumbling thin plaster, but the shell stayed intact. He had a good thick solid shell, over his own emptiness, I couldn't feel the hollowness at all.

"I can't get pregnant," I said, the words slipping out in a quaver because I was embarrassed but it was true. It wasn't just I can't *afford* to get pregnant, in this world, as things are. It was how the mere thought of being pregnant, like Kristin, it filled me with horror and he didn't need to know why. Nobody can make me say it. I put hands in his hair. Stephen nodded.

He had his face turned away. I looked at him and I saw too much to take in at once, no matter how close or long I stared; when people would say you could love someone and still never really know them, that must have been the feeling they were talking about. Overwhelming, the most mundane things like the way one lock of hair would crook and cowlick away from the rest of the scalp, the contrast between coarse tissue-paper fingers ruined by freezing dishwater and the smooth soft skin along the back of a wrist. The hunch of shoulders under a shirt that still smelled faintly of some stranger long dead.

"Hang on," he said. Reaching toward the flashlights.

"I wish you wouldn't—"

"Please, Amy."

His face looked urgent in a way I didn't understand; he couldn't possibly be that shy. But I nodded anyway. He switched them off and we lay there in the dark.

"Can I stay here?" he asked. A question thick with actual fear.

"Yes," I said. So he did.

I didn't suddenly just forget about everything else, like they talk about in books. You'd have to be psychotic, to forget everything but yourselves that easy. Honestly most people in books seemed a little psychotic, acting that way. But things still changed around us. For a while.

# FOURTEEN

In the morning I woke up alone, like I'd expected I would, and Lisa came to let me out, her face full of a tight, contained urgency as she slipped an arm in mine, silently escorted me up the stairs and through the remains of the house. Distracted, she looked, the hair over one temple pulled and tugged into a scraggly snarl of tension, and the sun was already high overhead like she'd forgotten I was here. She didn't let go of me as we approached the front door.

"This way," she said, pulling us leftward, toward a cluster of magnolias whose rotting petals had the color and smell of apples going brown. "I took Naomi down to Carlisle Street, a house there, she'll be waking up."

"Carlisle's the other way," I said, remembering the street signs from my onion hunt. We can shortcut across here and—"

"No. This way—Amy!"

She was tugging hard at my arm to haul me left but Carlisle was on the right, I remembered that from the onion hunt, and as I crossed over Connecticut, reached a Dogwood Avenue backyard, I saw something lying sprawled on the grass before me. Navy sneakers with bright red stripes, big wide sneakers for big wide feet, and blue-jeaned legs with one thighbone's jagged, broken whiteness torn clean through the bloodsoaked cloth.

The other leg, there was spongy scarlet where the knee should've been and the whole thing crooked backward at a crazy angle, impossible angle, bent entirely the wrong way. The outstretched hands, their fingers, had no proper form anymore, pulpy sponge-cakes soaking in their own dark syrup. Concave chest, a stretch of Styrofoam stomped down by heavy shoes, and something spilling lividly rich and exuberant from where his stomach had—his face was gone. His eyes. A slab of rawness, like something hung up skinned, with a few teeth still clinging to it. But Kevin's eyes, those were gone.

I squatted down sick right there but nothing would come up, just teeth-clenching cold rippling through my stomach and over my skin, and Lisa was pulling me away, putting her palm against my turned head like a horse-blinder so I mightn't see what I'd just seen, that slabby rawness dressed in Kevin's Bears T-shirt lying forgotten by the curb. She walked me back to Connecticut and the magnolias and I sat right down in slimy-soft heaps of falling petals, shivering. Lisa sat down next to me.

"Billy," she said.

I threaded hands into my jacket sleeves, trying to get warm. "Billy did that," Lisa repeated, flat and distant like she was reporting some disaster halfway across the world. "Last night."

Kevin. Phoebe's Kevin, who tried to step in for me when he could. Right after my fight with Phoebe. He had no eyes left.

"I did this," I said, and I laughed without meaning. "I fought with—"

"It was nothing to do with you and Phoebe. Kevin got him angry, somehow, I don't know how. And so Billy hurt him. He was screaming, Kevin was. They told me. I was blocks away, with Naomi. Billy beat him to death." Lisa's face was chalk-colored but she looked terribly calm, that grim peace that comes over you when every troubling option gets closed off at once. "We're getting out of here, Amy. We're—"

"I have to talk to Phoebe," I said. I don't believe you, Lisa, that Billy forgot us fighting, forgot Kevin trying to keep her away from me before it even started. It's freezing cold here in the sun and I don't believe you.

"It happened on Johnson Avenue." Her voice was still so dry and distant, arm's length from me and everyone else. "When I went to where he lay Phoebe was screaming about burying him. Billy would never allow that so some of us carried him to Dogwood, it's out of the way enough to dig without Billy seeing—she's not well, Amy." Lisa folded her arms around herself, around her shirt streaked and stained with Kevin's blood. "She was barely functioning with Kevin around and now—"

"I'm going," I said. "I have to talk to her."

She didn't try to stop me. Everywhere I went were little clusters of folks from the garden, cleanup, engineering crews standing around murmuring distorted and high, like the distress calls of stranded birds; one turned to stare at me, an old man with a seamed old face and mouth tugged sharply down like a drawing of Tragic Grief, and he shook his head like we'd known each other ages, were mourning together. Then he looked away.

Phoebe was huddled on the commissary steps, a tight little ball yet also loose-limbed and rattling and broken. All alone. I looked at her and kept on feeling that same old overpowering dislike, that prickling tightness of my skin prematurely shying away from her, but she was a broken thing and I made myself approach her. My mother, Lisa, Stephen—three people I had and she had nobody now, she was poor and I was rich. I owed her, somehow.

"Phoebe," I said.

"Oh, Jesus, kid. Oh Christ, oh Jesus Christ." She kept on rocking back and forth where she sat, rigid with grief but also something in the muscles of her arms and shoulders weirdly relaxed now that her crazy had a target, a reason anyone could understand, now that none of us could have contempt for it anymore. Her eyes were brimming and spilling over with tears that never quite fell, there were strips of skin torn from the back of one hand with the cuts she'd made oozing blood.

"What happened," I whispered and instantly thought I should never have asked, never ever, but she grabbed my arm with two hands and held on with a pleading look like yes, finally someone wants to hear it. She opened her mouth around the word, "He . . ." and then her lips twisted up and puckered, like a section of orange peel drying up in seconds before my eyes, and then she was rocking harder, sobbing, like Kristin with her little daughter, and I grabbed for her, though she was sitting down, like she might fall.

"Oh, kid," she moaned, with a horrible laughter. "Oh, kid— Kevin was, he, last night he took some fucking garden tool without asking first, a hoe, rake, or—what the *fuck*, kid, stuff disappears around here all the time, *he* never cared before, Billy never cared, he's dead!" She was sobbing in loud, spasmodic bursts, the shock of it breaking over her with cruel freshness every time. "He's—that Mags tried to stop him." Laughing, suddenly, not bothering to wipe away tears, futile, they would never stop. "She said, 'Billy, Jesus Christ he's a frail, you'll kill—'"

She rested her forehead in her fingertips, as if she could barely stand to touch her own self, and sobbed so hard she coughed and choked. I couldn't touch her, put arms around her, it'd be horrible hypocrisy after what had happened between us. I sat down next to her, waiting.

"We'll leave," I said finally, when she had to stop to catch her breath. "We'll get out. You and I and—"

"Oh, kid, Jesus, you must've seen what's left of things, when you two came here, *there's nowhere we can go!*" She let out a shrill, hooting laugh. "Run away like Natalie? Run away to *nothing*? Nowhere to go and nowhere to hide and nothing but this for the rest of—"

"You, and me, Lisa, and Naomi, and Stephen—we can't take it here anymore. We're leaving. Come with us."

"His body." Her face was scarlet and the corners of her mouth drawn back rigid with bottomless grief, a Glasgow smile of anguish. "Like garbage, like all the stuff he'd clean up for them, working for *them*, they left it in the street like—"

She grabbed at the splintering porch railings and made a noise like a scream. The sight and sound of that made a coward of me and I left.


The kitchen houses on Illinois Avenue were desultory chaos: people wandering in and out at random, Alice sitting subdued on the porch steps four doors down, Al nowhere to be found. Stephen was waiting for me near the mini-forest of barbecue grills, everyone else milling out front, and we slid arms around each other and held on. My skin had twitched in a weird, self-conscious embarrassment, seeing him again, but that passed as soon as both our skins touched. We sat together on the edge of an old chaise longue someone had stuck next to the grills, rusting metal covered with dirt-caked tangerine cushions. Rough, knobbly fabric, like an actual orange peel.

"I don't believe this," I said. I did, but I didn't.

"Why not?" Stephen pressed his face to my shoulder and then pulled back, calm and grim. "Billy's been itching for this forever, he was bound to snap."

"What the hell does he want with us, Stephen? Is it just food, or—"

"I thought I was figuring it out." Stephen's chin rested on my head, he rocked us absently back and forth like he didn't realize he was doing it. His voice was low and shot through with quiet frustration. "This place, the kitchen crew, I thought I was putting together—never mind what I thought, I strung together A and Q and eleven and thought I had an alphabet. Gibberish. I've got nothing."

But it wasn't just me, trying to make alphabets, new words from all this. That was something. I glanced around, nobody in earshot. "Lisa and Naomi and I," I said, "we're leaving. The night guard-crews switch off every other day, Lisa said the head guard gets careless. We'll just go into the woods, not come back." Like Natalie. "We're going to try to take Phoebe. You're coming too."

I'd said that as an imperative, an assumed thing, but as soon as it was out of my mouth I shrank away from it. "You are, right?" I asked.

Stephen ran a palm over the dirty orange-skin cushions. "So we should leave in the middle of all this," he said. Trying to sound casual, like it was just some thought exercise, and failing. "Leave and cause even more disruption—"

"They're distracted, for God's sake, aren't they? Stephen, we have to get out of here."

His obstinate silence, the stubborn set to his mouth I couldn't understand. I reached into one of the cold barbecue grills, fingering the remains of a briquette: Strangely satisfying, to watch the dark gray lumps of ash give up the pretense of solid form, crumble and disintegrate in my palm. "You don't want to leave," I said. "Do you." Nothing. "Stephen, I saw Kevin's body, what was left of—for what? A garden rake? That's what Phoebe told me—"

Stephen glanced behind us, the thick furze of overgrown trees, the impenetrable clumps of weeds. "Not toward the lakeshore," he said. His face was open now, quietly urgent, refusing to plead but also refusing to back down. "I won't go there. I can't."

My palm was covered in fine gray ash, chalky, like what I imagined nuclear fallout must look like. I brushed it clean against the filthy seat-cloth. "Not near the lakeshore," I repeated, turning the words over in my mouth. "Where the old lab was. Is."

Stephen gazed back like he was trying to gauge something about me, like there was something I was supposed to know and didn't. Patient Zero. Belly of the action. "What happened," I said.

Silence, a yawning, echoing space full of things he wouldn't ever say out loud. Not to me, not to anyone. Fair enough.

"Please come with me," I said. "South, back toward Leyton. There was food there, places to—I got scared. I shouldn't have left. Food and water, the Little Calumet River runs through there. Then we'll, just, figure things out from there."

Stephen nodded, slowly. Looked away from me, fingers tugging at the ash-smeared chaise fabric. "You're sure you want to bring Phoebe along," he said.

"I have to."

That night Billy and Mags and Don and Janey came to dinner again, we had to serve them, and Billy looked smug and happy, lolling in his seat like some mob boss from an old movie flush with cigars and wads of cash; he sucked down instant mashed potatoes and fried squirrel and rabbit like he might actually die if he didn't eat. Mags wouldn't look at him, just made absent placating sounds whenever he chucked her chin, and picked at her food like exes never do. Don watched them both, cold and calm, sardonic lines creasing his forehead in lieu of a smile. Janey ate nothing at all.

# FIFTEEN

Lisa's and my idea was to commandeer a car, but there wasn't any chance of that; humans might sometimes slip in and out but supplies like vehicles, gasoline, the ammunition that couldn't kill them, those the exes guarded with our lives. In the end I just got up at sunset the next night like always, took an onion bag to gather greens, headed toward Milstead and kept on going. We met just outside Washburn Street, Stephen, Lisa, Naomi and me; Phoebe showed up late and dragging, eyes down and mouth twisting convulsively around words she couldn't spit out, but there was grim determination lurking inside the crazy all the same.

"So how hard is it," I asked Lisa, "to skip this place?"

"A lot less hard than if Don were on," Phoebe said, before Lisa could answer. "There's not enough of them to make a fuck-ing *building* security team, never mind surround a whole town. Kid, let's just go, can we just go now?"

Don was out, driving the abandoned roads with Janey looking for more human conscripts. Or just getting away from us all for a while. Billy and Mags and a whole pack of exes were hunting on the other side of town, where the deer were too stupid to stop congregating. Time to move.

Stephen, who hadn't said a word since we started out, he took Naomi's hand and helped lead the way. We humans zigzagged through the gardens like we were foraging and Lisa walked ahead, an ex going where she felt like going, ignoring us at her leisure. Leading us out. A cleanup crew, not Kevin's, came by dragging a fleet of empty wheeled garbage cans; we wandered around a yard digging for onions, not looking up, until they passed. (Naomi actually found one, a tiny shriveled thing like Lisa's Leyton tulip bulb, and insisted on keeping it.)

Milstead. Clyburn. The soil was getting sandier now, the vegetation scrubbier and giving way to piebald vacant lots, a strip of empty fast-food places, a rusted metal bench with John 3:16 emblazoning the wooden seatback in defiantly huge black on white.

Kentucky Avenue. The enclosed little neighborhoods of Paradise City—Richmond Park in better days—opened up here to more lots and shops and a straight shot to Lake Street, the beaches, but we turned our backs on it and slipped like dead things after the hunt into the overgrowth consuming the yards and back alleyways, the stretches of woods reverting back to actual forest. People who'd never been here, my mother said once, who never lived here, they heard about the steel mills and oil refineries around Gary, saw from the interstate the city-sized spreads of smokestacks and thought the whole county looked like that, thought Gary wasn't just too poor and too black and too flyover but also looked like the surface of a sulfur-stench moon.

The beaches and the nature preserves were my mother's own secret, growing up. She wasn't afraid of the labs, the undeads, she'd slip in and out, she'd go anywhere. The cast-iron nerves you needed for security work. I tried to pretend I was her daughter, that way, as we walked.

Phoebe walked beside me, twitching, jumping at the sound of a calling bird like it was going to fly off and warn Billy we'd vanished. "Where're we going, anyway," she muttered.

"The long way around," Lisa replied, her neck craned and eyes scanning the trees. "We'll circle through here and back into the preserves near the beaches, and pick up U.S. 12 from—"

"Oh, Christ, you can't do that." Phoebe seized my arm and Lisa's, her grip somehow tight and limp all at once, and though Lisa flinched she didn't pull away. "There's actual no-shit patrols on Route 12 ever since the spring started, those crazies who think they run the lab now are all—"

"Just what's going on over there?" Lisa demanded. "And don't tell me nothing. You've known all along it's not nothing, poking at my past to see what you could dig up and use. Little scavenger, just like all of them. Worse than any zombie." Nearly nose to nose with Phoebe. "Right?"

There was a hate in Lisa's eyes that I'd never seen before, that made m y o wn fist-swinging animosity a paltry petty thing. Phoebe twitched, wriggling a little under Lisa's gaze, and studied the ground as she laughed.

"I told you," Phoebe muttered, spilling her heart out to the underbrush and a clump of marrowy mushrooms, "they won't let me back in. Supervisory head, my own research division, and I try to go back, I get nothing. But *what I hear* is they're picking up people, humans, taking them over there, and I don't know what the fuck happens now when they arrive. Hell, maybe what happened to you." Looking Lisa in the eye now, no more smirky coyness, they both knew what they were talking about even if the rest of us were shut out. "Yeah, Billy knows about it, Don too, think they've got a little exchange student program going on. What for, I don't know. Them and the lab. So we gotta go another way—"

"I don't believe you," Stephen said. As matter-of-fact as when he'd warned Phoebe he'd hurt her, again. "There is no way to get out of here without picking up Route 12. Unless you want to wander s traight i nto t he l ab's b ackyard a nyway, r ight a cross Lake Street, because we're way too close already—"

"Are we *going*?" Naomi pleaded. Not whiny, but afraid. Like me. "We have to go. You said we could go."

"Look, I know some shortcuts, okay?" Phoebe paced impatiently in front of an oak tree, picking up sock-cuffs of last fall's leaves caked in tarry mud. "You should know them too, I mean, *considering*, you go straight through and loop around the back end of the trees and—oh, fuck standing here arguing all night, follow me! Or don't!"

Phoebe barreled over the leaf clumps and I could feel it in all the rest of us, even Naomi, that collective desire to let her wander off, go wherever she was headed all alone, turn our backs and head for U.S. 12 without her grinning, gesticulating crazy as our gyroscope. She'd stopped now, waiting, twisted and tense where she stood.

Lisa glanced at me, and her, and then just shrugged. "I can find our way back out again," she said. "And she might be right. We don't need to go through all this just to run back into Don."

A penny for the widows and orphans. The four of us trailed after Phoebe, Lisa holding tight to Naomi's hand, Stephen silent again. He hadn't wanted this. He was a grownup, for Christ's sake, he didn't have to say yes. Phoebe led us deeper into the trees, like she'd promised, the ground a bendy lattice of dead branches over a pie-filling of sticky mud and the leaves overhead still n ew, a lmost s parse o utlined a gainst t he d arkness. L isa stepped lightly over the underbrush, almost dainty on the balls of her feet.

"Over this way," she told Phoebe, drawing us closer to the edge of the woods, the empty roads near the holy park bench and the shell of a McDonald's, a dry cleaner's. "If we follow the perimeter of the roads—"

"Then they *find* us, for Christ's sake," Phoebe almost growled. "C'mon. This way."

"Hunters know the trees," Stephen said, not moving from where he stood. "Lisa's the hunter here, not you. Do you have a clue where you're going?"

"Better than you do!" Phoebe was almost shouting again, her natural volume bursting out of the box. "I know, batshit crazy Phoebe couldn't find her way out of—you think I don't know what people say? If Kevin were still here, if he could still—"

"Phoebe." Lisa's voice was quiet, weighty, a stone dropped into a field of rustling, agitated grasses. "Don't think about that now. We just need to get out of here, then we can fight all you want. Okay? So just tell us what this path is and where it leads."

Stephen shook his head. "I'm not going anywhere she leads. We follow the perimeter, right, *Lisa*?"

"You don't give the orders," Phoebe said, whipping her head toward him like she'd been slapped. "I'm done with that, you understand? I'm the scientist here, the educated one, I supervised my own fucking research group, I'm done listening to the freaks, the workups, the *experiments* who think they can shove me around now just because—"

"The only good thing," Stephen hissed back, a soft snarl, letting go of me and stepping forward so ready to hit her. "The only good thing about any of this, was watching all of you *educated ones* fall apart and fucking die—"

"Stephen." Lisa moved between them, swift, pleading. "For Christ's sake not now—"

"For Christ's sake *right now*!" Stephen turned on Lisa, his face contorted with a fury I'd never seen in him before, not with Billy, not with anyone. "Right now, right here, if she wants to try to fucking pull rank like it's still—"

"She's trying to distract you," I said, another smooth stone in the wind-whipped field. "You and all of us."

"Oh, you smart kid." Phoebe was laughing again, laughing in all our faces. "We coulda been friends, you know, Amy, I coulda helped you, but you weren't having it, the second you could you threw your lot in with the freaks. Guess you can't help it, with your family tree you just can't help it, but—"

"What are you waiting for?" Leave her here, to rot or starve. Leave now. "Seriously, just come out and say what you're waiting for—"

"Here!" she screamed, her eyes full of urgency and fear and horror at herself, at everything that had become of us all, and the triumph of following my unwitting cue. "Here! They're over here!"

They spilled from the trees, from the path Phoebe tried to lead us down, from everywhere and nowhere all at once because she distracted all of us, so easy, so easy to take us all in. Tall and muscular and full of febrile eagerness, the faces of exes in a hunting pack, except they bristled with guns and knives and they shone yellowish in the moonlight, like the sulfurous lights that used to flood every highway, the watery eyes of a vengeful ghost dog. Lisa grabbed at Naomi, flung an arm toward me like she could somehow pick us all up and run, and then there were guns on me and Stephen just like when Don found us, there were knife blades like open scissors prodding the base of my throat. Not Phoebe. They didn't touch Phoebe. Phoebe stood aside, watching it all.

"Keep clear," one of them said to Lisa, in the hard dragging consonants of an ex: *KAH-ee-puh! KUHLEARRR*. "Keep clear and go away."

"The fuck I'll 'keep clear,'" Lisa whispered, and I could see all the strength gathering in her, making her tense and flushed and ready to spring on them all. "Get away from them or I'll—"

One of them, thin and redheaded and with eyes like granite, pointed a casual gun barrel at Naomi, cocked the trigger. "Keep clear," he repeated. Almost laughing at how easy it all was.

Two others had a death grip on Stephen and even as he tried to wrench free his eyes were fixed with fear, like he knew what was coming, like he'd seen it all before. "Let her go," he said, so calm, like he already knew begging would do no good at all. "I don't know what you want with her but you made a mistake, Amy's not like me, she—"

The redheaded man reached up, slammed a pistol butt in his bruised face. Stephen shouted with pain and I shouted, hauling at the hands holding me like a barge balloon against its ropes, and then the gripping fingers wrenched so tightly I went limp and light-headed, sagging without meaning to against a plaid flannel shoulder. It laughed, the thing hurting me, and

Stephen thrashed and struggled but he was like I was, pinned and helpless.

"It's been a while, Stephen, hasn't it." Another one, stepping forward, with a sleek dark ponytail bouncing against her shoulder blades and a smile like bits of putty pressed into a curve. "You've had your time off, we all have. It's time you came home."

"You don't want Amy." His voice was twisting in terror, a futile hatred he wasn't even trying to hide. "You don't want Amy!"

Her putty smile stretched, widened, then she was all solemnity. "We need her, Stephen," she said. "We need her very much, just like we need you. Someday you'll understand what an honor that is."

"You're wrong!" Lisa was thronged by gun barrels now, all pointing a t N aomi, s he'd p ulled h er j acket o ff a nd w rapped Naomi in it like that somehow made her bulletproof. "You're wrong! I don't know what you want but you made a mistake, it's not them!"

"Okay, y ou b elieve m e n ow? You finally believe me now I showed you? I gave you what you need." Phoebe was trying to push her way back from the periphery, elbow into the center of attention, but it was like they didn't even see her and so she kept getting louder, shoving harder at their backs. "I gave you this, Jesus Christ, they're the real thing, the new flesh, *look* at her, you can see in her face who her mother is—"

"You don't want them!" Lisa shouted, clutching the sobbing coat bundle that was Naomi. "You want me! You want experiments? I'm the *first* experiment! I started all this without even knowing—it's my fault!" Her voice cracked and broke and something human-sounding slid out of it: fear, pain, panic, guilt, sorrow, all we frail ones had left to offer. "It's my fault! Take me!"

"You have to bring him back now." Phoebe found the ex

who'd struck Stephen, clung hard to his arm. "I've done anything you could ask, reported back to you every fucking night, I've kept eyes and ears out all along for you and you promised me, if anything ever happened to me, happened to Kevin, you'd bring us back—"

"Get the fuck off me." The man she held on to, redheaded and thin-faced just like my mother, like me, he shoved her aside and she hit the ground hard, gasping. She pulled herself upright and dug fingers into his chest, wild-eyed, vibrating not in fear but thwarted rage.

"You promised me!" she screamed. "Last night, just last night you stood here and promised me Kevin, you'll bring him back to me, you fucking promised, you know how to bring people back—"

The man, the Scissor Man she clutched in entreaty, he shoved her away and stuck his gun barrel to her temple. Her head popped into pieces and sprayed into mist, like that man I'd seen shooting his family in the street, and she fell. Naomi moaned long and low and Lisa let out a sob, clapped a palm to Naomi's eyes too late, and the man kicked Phoebe's body aside like a crushed soda can, pressed the gun under Naomi's chin. Naomi just stood there, a garden statue, and Lisa made a sound like something dying.

"Please," she whispered, her arms wrapped around Naomi. "Don't—"

"You two," he said to Lisa, "get out of here. We don't need you."

"What do you want?" Lisa screamed. *"What do you want?"*

I was screaming then too because one of them was grabbing Stephen's legs, pulling him off the ground, and Stephen was thrashing and horse-kicking and the dark-haired woman raised her gun, slammed him in the temple. He went limp with blood streaming down his face and they hauled him over their shoulders like he weighed nothing, just another bendy twig on the forest floor; they carried him away and the others already had my arms, my legs, I was going airborne as they kept guns pointed at Naomi and Lisa cried out, *I'll get you back, I'll get both of you back*, but she lied. They all lied.

The exes with Stephen were already yards ahead and I was still screaming, screaming up at the sky as they carried me and then a hand came around my throat, gripping and crushing until all the air left me and I fish-flopped for more. The hand went away and I gasped and gagged.

"Careful," one of them muttered. "Need them both alive. Don't break her neck."

I tried to shout out, *Leave us alone* or *Lisa* or *Fuck you*, but my throat was closed up and no air got in, no sound got out, and we were deeper into the trees and I couldn't see Stephen's captors anymore. I was flung over someone's shoulder now, face toward the ground, the sky shut out. They were moving faster, on the march, their footsteps everywhere, loud and crushing, rising up to blot out any other sound—

A tobacco brown dog, a real dog gone savage, was bounding toward us bullet-headed and muscular and huge. Its long dripping teeth were bared and hungry and it couldn't kill them, the exes, nothing could ever kill them but it came at them over the twigs and leaves like it was happy to die trying. One of them raised a rifle as it approached us, took a calm steady shot—

—and he got that dog between the eyes, a neat little pop of

red bursting forth right on target, but the dog didn't fall. Its dark slitted eyes narrowed with hungry hate and it was running like bullets and blood were nothing, it leapt, it was on the ex who'd throttled me tearing furious at his legs, his hands, any bit of flesh within reach. The redheaded ex had a knife, like my big hunting knife Don took away, and he came running at the tobacco dog to slice its throat—and then there were more dogs, a pack, a gang, rushing in cacophony from behind every tree. Ghost dogs, phantoms, materializing from nowhere, I saw it happen, five, six, seven dogs baring teeth, jumping quick and high, savaging the exes who held me. Shouting, bewildered yells, and their damp, sticky inhuman blood oozed over my own skin as they lost their hold on me, let me fall hard and breathless to the leaves.

I couldn't get up, not right away, so I curled in a defensive ball but the dogs didn't want me, they had all the meat they needed. A couple of exes were on the ground now too, their wounds might heal right up tight and quick but it still looked like it meant something to lose all that blood. You get them good, Fido, Rover, Champ, King, Cujo, hurt them horribly before you turn on me and I die. A pack of dozens now, big, small, every color of fur, every breed, every pitch from low rumbling growl to high piercing cry. Eyes squeezed shut, his own blood thick over his face, the redheaded man started shooting again, all for nothing. And then he was aiming at me with hate twisting his face into a monstrous thing and the bullet went wild, ricocheted off a tree, I was somehow back on my feet and I ran.

"Stop her!" someone screamed, her voice lost in the sea of howls. "Stop—"

I was running, stumbling and I couldn't hear anything but

the dogs, the sound of them kept getting louder even as I got farther away, and then it was right there in front of me. The tobacco brown dog. The same dog, exactly the same that had rushed me back in Leyton, no more collar and tags from bygone days, that red smear on his forehead that didn't matter because he was dead, he died long before they shot him. A famished ghost, vengeful chimera—and the sulfur-eyed black dog padded out of nowhere, so soft and soundless against the night sky, stood side by side with the brown dog. Ready, at long last, to have his tribunal, pronounce his sentence, execute.

I ran.

My feet were raw in their shoes, my chest closed up and heaving, no sound in the world but growling, howling, the deafening thud of ghost-dog feet in pursuit. I clapped my hands to my ears but it was everywhere, I ran one direction into brown and another into black and they were trying to flush me out like a fox, just kill me now, just kill me. The night had gone watery sulfurous yellow and my whole head was full of their barking, agonized whining, and beneath that something high and shrilly insistent, like bells, like musical notes, like the ringtone of a phone—

I was doubled over nauseous for breath at the very edge of the trees, in a neighborhood of houses and giant scrubby yards I didn't know. My chest burned and I let out coughing heaves and the cell phone in my pocket rang over and over again, the same musical loop, fifteen times, sixteen—I wrenched it out of my pocket ready to throw it against a tree and it wouldn't stop, the screen all lit up but no number showing, someone was trying to torture me and I didn't know how they were doing it. Someone calling me a liar. Someone who knew everything, knew how to find me, and wouldn't come get me. My hands were shaking as I punched the receiver button.

"Leave me alone!" I screamed, not waiting to hear even the sound of breath. "You won't help me! You won't show me where you are! Leave me alone, you fucking—*leave me alone!*"

Airless silence, on the other end. Then the sudden raspy clearing of a throat.

"Just keep going," the voice said. "And I'll find you."

The roiling, burning-jelly thing in my chest spread through my whole body, so thick that my nerves stuck together not letting me perceive, react. Psychic honey, sugary and crawling with hungry flies. My whole body was shaking now.

"Mom?" I said.

Her voice. *Her* voice, at the other end. All this time. Every day. "Mom, where are you. Where did you go. Come and get me. I'm in—"

"Just keep going." Her voice was so calm, too calm, as if everything were just that easy and fretless wherever she was. "Just keep going."

"Mom, you need to come and get me." Tears were rolling down my face and my brain was racing sticky-wild with thoughts, plans, we could go back to our old house, I'd explain what had happened and she'd forgive me— "Mom, I had to leave, I'm in Gary now, I don't—I didn't want to come here but I can get out, you have to come and get me. You have to say where you are."

"I'll find you." Too calm. Too measured. Just short of mechanical. Mom! We don't talk to each other this way! "I'll find you."

"Do you know where I am?" Silence, and then I was shouting hoarse and unsteady. "Do you *know where I am?*"

"Just keep going, and I'll find you."

"Mom. Where are you? Are you okay? How can I find you?"

Silence.

"Mom," I said. "Come on." Silence. "Where are you? What's happened to you? Where are you?"

Silence.

*"Mommy!"*

The phone went dead.

# SIXTEEN

I threw the phone as hard as I could and it hit a tree, a big tree, and then I picked it up again and threw it again and tried to smash it under my shoe before I kicked it through the underbrush, ran from it like it might explode. Fuck you, fuck everyone who ever lived—I'd throw the thing in the lake but I wasn't anywhere near the fucking lake. Another residential neighborhood like Paradise City, small deserted houses fringed by ankle-deep lawns soon to be up to the knees. Rusted cars in the driveways, curbside. I stumbled down the middle of the street, trying to work out which direction Lisa and Naomi had gone. Where my mother had gone.

I was crying out loud but nobody was there to hear me, Lisa, Stephen, my mother—it was a trick. A prank, some ex's horrible prank! Isn't this just the sort of thing Billy would do, how, how the hell could he possibly do it!

Streaks of dark gray, in the soft black sky. It was past midnight, it couldn't possibly be that late, we'd started out at nine or ten. I couldn't have been running around those woods for hours, black dog to the left of me, brown dog to the right, it wasn't—my feet were on fire, every muscle sore like I'd just finished a race. There must be some mistake. I'd know, if it were that long.

My idea. My fucking idea to bring Phoebe along because I felt sorry for her, because—Stephen. He never wanted to leave because he knew this was out there all along, he didn't tell me— maybe they'd found Natalie too, maybe that's where she was. Farther north, the lake, the lab, where he never wanted to go. They might be there right now. Keep going and I'll find you.

"Fuck you!" I screamed at the sky, and coughed until tears came to my eyes. My throat was stuck-together dry, my clothes full of sweat. Like I'd been running for hours.

Phoebe, all her little smiles, all her crazy lies. *You can see in her face who her mother is.* What the fuck would you know about my mother, Phoebe? What would you know? I'm glad you're dead. I'm glad you're dead. I'm glad.

Keep going. Keep going where? North, toward the lake. Which way is north? Down . . . Colfax Street. Okay. Follow it and see if it ends in sand. I have time. Unless they find me again, those Scissor Men, unless—

As I crossed a thin little sidewalk there was the click of a rifle, from the adjoining yard, and then I was looking into a dozen avid, smiling faces, the barrels of a dozen scavenged, loaded guns.

"Hi there," said the one with the rifle.

Human. Maybe my age, no older than twenty. There were

more of them coming from the yard now, all armed, all men and boys, the youngest looking only thirteen or fourteen. I started to run and one of them laughed, grabbed my arm where the exes had wrenched it and twisted it until I shouted, and then he had fingers in my hair, horrible dirt-caked fingers and the others were snickering, whistling, gathering in a tight little circle. The one with the rifle shoved them aside, looked me up and down.

"Prettier than the one we got now," he said. "Whaddaya think, Jason?"

"No tits," said the one with fingers in my hair. Then he grinned. "Guess we can't be fussy, though, right?"

"Like you even want any, you faggot." Another of them, calling in a singsong jeer from the corner of the yard. He had a woman with him, I suddenly saw, his arm gripping hers as she stood there with her head hanging down, a filthy torn-up yellow nightgown her only clothes. "Day Mike finally plows your sad ass'll be the happiest in your whole—"

"Shut it," said the one with the rifle. Mike, surely. He had pale blond hair in a bristle-thick crop, bristly brows, a face made of hard straight planes that overlapped and sawed against each other like they might split apart fighting any second. He reached out and felt at me and that seemed to happen so fast that I couldn't do anything, just make this sort of shouting noise that roiled in my throat and didn't go anywhere, and even without the thought of Phoebe's skull popping and leaking open I couldn't move. Then he pulled his hand back.

"I'm Mike," he said. "You're coming with us." As an afterthought, "We've got food."

I nodded like that all was perfectly sensible, like I had any choice, and then that woman and I were standing face-to-face, looking at each other. She had long dark hair and for a horrible moment I thought it was Natalie but she was too old. Too tall. I'd never seen her before. I wished I could stop seeing her now.

Jason, the filthy-fingered one, he laughed. "You girls make friends," he commanded.

I could tell she couldn't even hear him. This is a mirror. It's a mirror of the future, my future, it's what I'm going to look like after they've finished with me. Her eyes stared straight into mine and they registered nothing, empty scooped-out cups of dazed disorientation like they'd blinded her too, like she'd die in earnest if she ever let herself see. Janey without a Don. This is what he found, by the side of the road. This is why he had to remind her to eat.

"Where are we going?" I asked. My voice was a harsh croak.

Instead of answering, Mike circled fingers around my arm and we all started walking into the dark and the streets of empty houses. A bird called low and sweet from the trees and I was trying inside to fly up into the branches but I couldn't do it, the ground and the half-broken sidewalk kept me down, they'd shoot me anyway if I flew. My throat pulsed in little shallow swallows as I tried to keep from throwing up and that Mike, I knew he could see it, he loved it, it would make it even better for him when they got started. I could see him smiling wide and fast, from the corner of my eye.

The woman next to me was too broken to need restraint anymore, they just kept shoving her forward as we passed a deep, tilting bend in the street. I could see her neck pulsing, throbbing like a panicked bird's, and suddenly she barreled forward and shoved through the sea of arms and ran. Her limbs flapped like pennants, her body so small and thin in the translucent, blood-streaked nightgown as she ran across the street, toward the yards, if she could, I could—

"Oh, fuck you, you smelly used-up bitch," Mike whispered, like an incantation, a prayer, and he raised his rifle and aimed but he missed. She kept running. It was Jason, on my other side, who pushed forward and aimed and then the greasy lemony nightgown cloth was fresh thick bright red, he'd got her in the chest, she tottered where she stood and she fell to the grass.

"Bull's-eye!" Jason shouted, his voice thick and congested like it was gathering into a sob, a tearful wail of victory over nobody and nothing. She twitched where she lay, once and violently like a dead thing hooked up to electrodes, and he let off more rounds, slamming into her arm, stomach, chest like a fist into a pillow except where it tore open there was blood instead of feathers, blood spraying everywhere. Pieces of her insides bursting and falling out of her and soaking the sidewalk, the grass. Then she stayed still.

Then one of them nudged the small of my back with a gun barrel and we continued down Colfax.

Still walking. Need to keep walking forever. It was when we stopped that everything would start. I want Lisa. I want my mother. I want Billy, fucking Billy, who said I wasn't to be messed with. Except when he snapped his fingers, his nasty fingers that should still be properly rotted away and said it was time to carry us off, take us to the lab. If Phoebe were even telling the truth. Home. Time to go home, Stephen. Help me, Stephen, Lisa, Mommy. Please—

Another abandoned house, white clapboard with a satellite TV dish still clamped to the side like a big gray shelf fungus on a tree trunk; armchairs in the front yard, junk strewn everywhere, a big wooden picnic table sitting right next to the chairs. They were pulling me toward the picnic table. My feet pressed hard against the grass and tried to root themselves down, all those stories from that book my mother gave me of nymphs and girls picking flowers and god-rapists and escaping the god-rapists by turning to trees, and Jason giggled again, Mike grinned and gave a hard shove between my shoulder blades and I stumbled and fell, facedown, cheek hitting hard enough to bruise. Someone had my wrist, holding it to the splintering wood so careful and precise like anchoring pins through a dead insect wing. Someone else—

Their hands pulled free like they'd suddenly forgot, like some sudden distraction grabbed them by the scruff, and as I raised my head I saw her, saw them all staring at her in unabashed shock. Her hair was still limp and lank, that girl they'd shot until she'd run with blood, her skin still soaked in bruises fresh and fading, but her eyes that had been little hollow teacups now brimmed over big and dark and sparking bright with happiness. She smiled, a wide triangular smile like a television newscaster, except instead of a newcaster's false dolly-cheer she was all joy, all peace, not a single bullet rip in her flesh or tear in her clothes. She looked them up and down, without a trace of fear.

"Step aside," she said.

Soft-voiced, human-voiced. She couldn't be an ex. An ex could've fought them all off, an ex would've healed on the spot. Mike just kept staring at her, gaping, and Jason let out another demented volley of giggles. "You fucked a *zombie*, dude," he gasped, in between wheezing seizures of mirth. "I don't fucking believe it, all the girls over in that hog pen you could've grabbed and you went and boned a fucking corpse—"

"You shut up," Mike whispered and then he slammed the butt of his gun into Jason's face. "You shut your fucking—bitch, you want more of it?" He brandished the gun at her, the woman I'd sworn I saw die, kicking Jason as he huddled moaning on the sidewalk. "You want some more? I'm gonna blast your fucking head off, you piece of—"

"Step aside," she repeated. Like no one had spoken.

Mike jerked his head toward his gang and they all raised rifles, they all aimed, they all fired at close range. And she just stood there. I don't know where the bullets went but nowhere near her, all the blood stiffening up that sunshiny nightgown was old blood and they couldn't possibly have missed but they had. She rocked casually from bare foot to foot, a nightgown strap sliding down her arm so one breast was nearly bared, a twisty-turny little smile playing over her face.

"Try again?" she offered. So cheerful. So calm.

She was staring at me now, smiling even broader, sister to sister. Mike was breathing hard from between his teeth and then something exploded inside him, like a shook-up soda bottle bursting under froth and pressure, he was scarlet-faced screaming and they all were screaming as they rushed her, a panicked mob of gazelle thinking they could tear a lioness apart. She stood there, watching, and she lifted her arm with thumb and finger poised like an imaginary pistol. Mike wasn't more than a yard away when she pushed down her thumb, the imaginary bullet found its mark—

And he fell. She hadn't even touched him and he fell to the sidewalk, face and limbs flopping and slack, and then he was quiet and still on the ground. Jason, there next to him, eyes closed and arms flung out like he was beseeching the sky. A half dozen more in a pile of limbs and winter-stinking clothes and guns clattering from limp fingers, and then all around me, all the men and boys, every one, still and dead in the weedy spring grass.

The trees, I thought as I clattered past a half dozen houses waiting for the ghost bullet to find my skull, if I went back into the trees she might corner and kill me there but better than running in open air like the flushed-out deer, rabbit, field mouse that I was—

She was standing right in front of me, blocking my path and I had no idea how, she just *became* from one place to another. My feet skidded, my arms airplaned for balance and she watched dispassionately, as if from very far away.

"You see how things are now, Amy," she said. "I do think you finally start to understand."

"Don't kill me," I said, in a thin crumpled-paper voice. It was time. It'd all caught up with me. I'd thought I was ready but I didn't want to die, don't kill me, don't let me die. I don't want to die.

"I'm not armed," she said. "Not against you. Come with me now."

"I'm not coming." I shook my head, and then backed away shouting, as if my hysterics could defend and wound. "I'm not coming with you!"

"There's nothing to be afraid of. I'm on your side." She, it just stood where she was but that meant nothing, she could reappear right beside me or maybe even inside me whenever she chose. "No matter what. You're one of mine."

"You're my dog, aren't you." My whole mouth was sticking dry. "You're the black dog, you're what's been following me since—"

"He's a good boy." She shrugged her bared shoulders. "He was a good boy alive. So was his little brother, the brown one.

Good, and deserved more than they got." She looked down at her body like it were a curiosity, something she'd thrown on from the depths of the closet while dressing in the dark. "So was this poor, wretched woman. And that Stefanie Scholl whose bass playing you loved so much. And your friend, Ms. Acosta." A step forward. "And Dave, and Kristin. And her small one, not still-born. And your mother."

That smile again, that beaming gleaming dark-polished smile. "And you."

Don't kill me. No matter what I've done, how much I deserve—I was running again and there was nowhere to go because that thing looking like a dead woman was everywhere, part of the air, the night, watching and waiting to spring from the corners of my own mind I'd thought dark and safe and alone. I veered up the curb, into the tall grass, and where the dead woman had been Kevin, Phoebe's Kevin, was now waiting for me.

"I know what you've done," he said. "I've seen everything, eyewitness, in the flesh. Even if you didn't see me."

I stumbled toward an oak tree in the backyard, a cluster of wild half-dead lilacs, and there Phoebe *became*. "I'm tellin' ya, kid," she shouted, loud and brittle-bright just like always, like the handful of days I'd known her, "you don't need to run like this, I'm on *your* side! Christ! Your side!"

And nothing changed about her, her features didn't bubble or shift before me but just suddenly, somehow, she was Kristin. Lank blonde hair, vacant eyes, a too-thin arm draped over a belly swollen like a tumor.

"Your side," Kristin, the thing that took Kristin away, whispered. "Even after everything you've done."

A block, two blocks down and I could feel it behind me even though I couldn't hear it, my feet would split open at the soles,

I was gasping sick. I crouched over a parked car with my palms pressed against the hood, fighting for breath. Dave strolled casually up to meet me, in the old Marines T-shirt he wore under everything, soaked in rotten-apple diabetic's sweat as he died.

"I know what you've done," he repeated. "I've always known. When you're ready to say it out loud, I'll be here for—"

"Leave me alone!" I screamed, let it laugh at my panic, mock my useless flight like it had the dead boys, dying with dignity was a myth like all the others. "I hate you! I won't go!"

"Amy," it said in a new voice, older and female and almost sorrowfully pleading, "you still don't understand."

Ms. Acosta. Standing there with her pale eyes full of reproof, harbingers all in her face and her wild, flying-away hair gone wholly gray—I was shaking and I couldn't stop. And she, it, looked at me with pity, with *love*, and that made me want to scream all over again.

"Stop," I said, and there were tears leaking over now, trickling down my face. "Please stop."

"I can't." The thing that stole her body wasn't smiling anymore. "This is what I am. This is all that will ever be."

"I'll hurt you." I tasted salt now, all through my mouth, and the crying wouldn't stop. "You know I can do it. I won't let you hurt me—"

"I hurt no one." It had been on the other side of the car but now it was next to me, there in the street, close enough to reach out an arm and take me away. "I take away hurt. I'm the one the tortured and tormented scream for, everywhere, the one they beg to help them. And I do. Because it's what I am." It slipped broad, thick-knuckled hands into its cardigan pockets. "I'm the stopping point of pain, Amy—and you've stumbled right into my backyard."

"I won't go with you," I said, and my fingers curled into a fist like I could actually fight it off, like I had any chance at all. "I won't go."

"You don't have to." That strong, unwavering timbre, the line of swaying-branch grace in her high-held shoulders and back: just like the real person, just like she was up until the end. "There's the ones I have to take with me, by force—but then there's the ones who invite me in. Like your friend, Billy. Beating a grown man to death because he was in a bad mood." A smile, curling its tendrils up around her cheeks, like no smile I ever saw on the real woman's face. "Like that fellow you saw shoot his family in the street. That Don you're so afraid of, your dear pal Phoebe's killer, your Lisa, your new rapist friends, so many people you'd never guess . . . and you." The smile faded, dissolved, like the whorl of some elaborate sand painting brushed away by an invisible hand. "And now you."

This is how rabbits feel when the fox or cat or sadistic child's on them, the hot shaking *inside* every limb that won't translate to movement, lungs and throat alike tamping down so you can't gather air to scream. Those phone calls. Playing with me, all this time, while I walked straight into the trap. "Are you my dog? Are you my black dog, that—"

"I'm nobody's dog," it said softly. "I don't come when I'm called. I do the calling. But you came running to me of your own accord, Amy. All on your own. That makes you one of my special ones. Long as you live—" Another twist of a smile. "—however long that is, you'll never be rid of me. Ever."

Sweat pooled under my arms and trickled, tickling, down my sides, my bladder tightened and twitched. I'd pissed myself with fear, before. I knew the feeling.

"Show me my mother," I said.

It *laughed*. It stood there and laughed and fury forced my windpipe open, gave me air enough to yell. "Show me my mother! If you can look like anyone, anyone who's dead? Be *her*! I want her back! Give her back to me!"

It shook its furzy gray halo-head, a mocking imitation of real regret, and my eyes were leaking and my hatred, for myself, it was bottomless. *"Give her back!"*

Nothing.

"Then give me—" I tried to say "Stephen" but the word, it got choked off by snot and saltwater. The angel, demon, whatever it was, it watched me, hands in its sweater pockets, immovable and indifferent.

"I'm not punishing you, you know," it said. "It's just things are . . . complicated with your mother, that little girl Natalie, that wretched boy they're cutting open right now. More complicated than plain old life and death—but! You'll have to figure that out for yourself." A dancing, derisive little smile. "I sent you guides, harbingers, they brought you to my backyard—but the rest, you're on your own."

The smile got broader and wider and ripped open that guise of a human face, splitting it like a tomato rotting on the vine. From beneath the mask something came spilling out that was like midnight darkness and blinding sunrise all at once, endless night, endless light, and it swallowed the moon and the hidden sun and all the sky and I was in the throbbing, suffocating heart of it, a womb where all humanity were infants crushed and drowned. I choked, gasped with fear and the certainty of my horrible punishment, nothing but this sensation and this void for all the rest of eternity—

And then it was plain soft nighttime again and I was in an empty street in a deserted lakeshore city where everyone was dead, dying, unnaturally resurrected. The Angel of Death's backyard, and only now did I feel what that meant, did I start to understand this mausoleum emptiness was all human life now, everywhere forever. And I did what I always do. I turned, and I ran.

"Now, that's a good girl!" it shouted. "You go, and you find her!"

Laughing, taunting, its voice coming from everywhere at once. Dozens of bits of voices strung together as one, echoes of a thousand dead people kaleidoscoping together into one gathered cry. I kept going. Colfax Street. Benedict. Oak.

"If you find her?" it said. No farther away than if I'd stood still, everywhere at once, inside my head and part of me for the whole rest of my life. "If you find that Stephen? Be good to them! Be good to all of them, just like you were to me!"

The street went quiet, and I stood all alone.

# SEVENTEEN

I threw up from fear and exhaustion, crouching next to another parked car pitted all over with winter rust, and it was a horrible relief like I was heaving out the last ragged remains of that . . . something, that vast blinding-white darkness, that had tried to swallow me up. Nothing to be done, absolutely nothing. I bent down, back groaning like an old woman's in protest, double-knotted my laces so they wouldn't slip loose.

"Oak Street," I said aloud, just to try to ground myself. I was at the corner of Oak and Harvey, another unknown part of town; I went through a backyard, a series of backyards, found a thin twist of trees and I was back where we had all started out hours, lifetimes ago, in the woods. What am I doing? Where am I going? I don't know. Maybe that's my punishment. I'll never know.

I should've taken one of their guns with me, those men who tried to grab me. All that ammunition. What would I do with it? What was in charge now had nothing to fear from bullets—

It saved me, from those boys. That thing, that death angel. It came back as that poor girl whose name I never knew and it killed them all, swept them aside, because of me. Because I belonged to it now. That thought made me cry again. I dodged a bullet. And fell into a furnace.

The trees were getting thicker now, closer together, sticky furbelows of grayish-white fungi and green oatmeal-clumps of moss smeared over every trunk. The sight of it made my skin twitch in revulsion and I wanted to tear them all off, the wads of leaf and rot, make the bark and all the woods clean and smooth. The sky, filtering in, had gone from black to gray.

I broke my own rule, when I demanded her back. I told the universe my mother was dead. I lied. You little fucking liar. I tribunaled myself, right there in the woods as I walked, and it was plain and clear I required execution. Of course I did. It was why I'd become a fugitive, my last day in Lepingville.

But not yet. Not now. I was going to find out everything, everything I could, before I died.

*That boy they're cutting open.* The lab. Stephen was scared of the lab, of nothing but the lab. Naomi's Scissor Men, who were all real. He wouldn't talk about anything past, he wouldn't—

The trees opened up on me and I stumbled in surprise, grabbing at a branch slippery with green muck for balance. Right up ahead was a little lavender-painted house that must've been a restaurant, tables in the front yard and on a wooden balcony; on the wide, paved street fronting it was a clapboard church, a couple of shops with their smashed front-window glass still a powdery sheen on the sidewalk. A tiny movie theater, last showing some arty documentary I'd just vaguely heard of. I could go live in there, close the doors and settle in relaxed beneath the empty screen and wait for the inevitable, but beyond the theater and shops and the PRAIRIE BEACH: SAFETY IN THE SANDS SINCE 1905 merchants' billboard was a long, sinuous line where the ground should've been, blue-black against the steel sky: Lake Michigan, the end point of Lake Street. Naturally. Where there was the lake, there was the lab. Where there was the lab, there was—

There's no point in expecting anything. None. My mother is—gone, whatever else became of her. Stephen is dead. Natalie is dead. Soon I'll be. That creature didn't save me just to save me, I was sure of it, there was something he wanted me to do and he'd given me directions, instructions. *You've stumbled into my backyard.* Of course, he'd be at the lab. Nobody of any importance, around these parts, ever was anywhere else.

I walked in fits and starts down the middle of the street, toward that soft thick blue crayon line. All alone. Maybe Johnny Angel cleared the whole area for me, sweep of the hand. When you got to the end of Lake Street, the road veered off to the left and became a narrow, winding thing leading you straight to the source, the lab and all the associated buildings: My mother, she'd told me about it once. She'd seen pictures. Keep walking. There's no point in crying anymore. The only question is, how much more can I find out before the Angel of Death, the Fall-Dead Thing, comes back? There's nothing I can do with that knowledge but it's the one thing I can offer, the devotion of trying. You can't just let yourself die, knowing you didn't even try to accomplish anything. Work first.

I hope my mother was wrong and there is a heaven, after all, one that looks like the movies. Movie theaters. But it hardly matters. Either way, I won't be there.

I knotted my laces one more time and walked toward the blue, no looking back.

# BOOK THREE

# UNDERWORLD

# EIGHTEEN

There's rules, for going into the places where dead people are. I learned them years ago, when they were all supposedly just stories. Don't eat or drink anything they offer, not so much as a pomegranate seed. The ferryman wants payment, to take you across the Styx. There's a dog at the gate, three-headed, who wants food. Something sweet, sticky, made with honey.

I still had them in my pocket, bent and flattened, those Tootsie Rolls Stephen gave me. They'd do.

The road to the lab was short but it swung and bent in this easy way that made me think of graceful things, happy things, like a tipsy person staggering home from a wonderful party left, right, the wide loops of their feet drawing the lines of the pathway. Nothing bad could ever lie at the end of that sand-white gravel road, crushed lake stones with the same sharp grit as ground glass. I stood on it, and closed my eyes tight.

I was about to make a bet, that I wasn't actually alone. I hadn't been, even when I thought I was, ever since Lepingville.

I let out a low, soft whistle. A warm blast of wind rustled the trees and sent my hair streaming over my face, bringing scents of full-blooming lilac and the last dying magnolias; then I heard it, the snap of twigs and soft crunch of gravel as something came out of the trees, trotted steadily toward me and paused at my feet. It made a little snuffling sound, not quite a bark.

A big fellow, coming up past my waist, bigger than he'd looked when he'd been tracking me from town to city to beach shore. Large as he was, he wasn't threatening me, no bristling or bared teeth. I could turn my back on him right now. Send him back to his real master.

"Good boy," I said.

He just stared back. His pale yellow eyes looked dull and colorless, windowpanes smeared with dusty grime so the light couldn't filter in, but there was intelligence there, alertness, that wary poised canine calm. His breath was a sharp wet odor of dog slobber and gamey meat and an unmistakable, faint waft of decay. I reached down to pet him, my fingers shaking. He wagged his tail.

His fur was there and yet not quite there beneath my hand, like touching the froth of soap lather in the bathtub just as the bubbles were all melting away. So fleshly solid and still a chimera beneath the skin, a hollow wineskin carapace holding a ghost, and I wasn't his master but he was still mine. He'd saved me, him and that poor dead dog from Leyton, making my kidnappers drop me, chasing me by fits and starts onto the path toward the lab. My good boy.

My guardian? In earnest? Let's find out. He sat there looking up at me, waiting. Play today?

"Lab," I said. When I started walking he followed, trotting with soft crunches behind. The road bent more sharply, a little statue of Jacques Marquette lurking in the brush to greet us; the sand dunes arched up and up toward the hillside, toward the tuftlike clusters of beach grass with a few lone, scrubby trees up near the top. Something in me wanted to run down that long easy sand-slope toward the deep blue line of the water, keep going until I finally found the place where lake and sky meet and become one great consuming sea, but I had work to do.

A little white building up ahead, surely not the lab, all Greek columns and an empty, open-air second floor: GARY AQUATO-RIUM, said the sign. Skeletons down in the sand, below and beyond the little white building; you could see the bones sticking up like listing, half-buried signposts. Bones, those are nothing. Everyone's seen so much worse.

The road twisted off to the left, the ground rising again and trees all around me, and then gave way to a long swath of grass, a choppy green lake-wave of clover and dandelions crawling up to a tall, sprawling structure of sandy pink brick. Not exactly a castle, even with the towers and sharp-angled rooftops: too small, like a short little man trying to puff himself up with pride but having to stand on tiptoe to do it. Several of the windows were covered in cardboard, nailed-up wood. No sign of life.

How do you go inside a place, knowing you'll never come back out? Even dumb animals, I'd heard, cows and pigs, they sense what's coming when they get herded from the transport truck to the intake tunnel and they try to run, to buck and kick but there's nowhere to go. I had the sky, anyway, I had as close as anyone around here gets to the sea. Not so dumb animals, actually—pigs are smarter than dogs, and this dog, here, he'd always been smarter than me. He just waited, watching me dither in silence. He had all the time in the world.

"All right, boy," I said. My voice was cracked and shaking. "Let's go."

The air felt heavy and ponderous, as if something kept passing through it and vanishing and leaving only a weight of sadness behind: the undertow of a greater, vaster, wholly invisible lake, pulling everything in its radius down to drown. That imaginary point where the line of water and sky finally met, I had found it. It was called death. This was a house of death. I could feel it, the dragging smothering-wet weight of it, in my skin and my stomach and every time I drew breath.

It felt right. It felt like something I'd always known about, and missed, the thing that had always been meant to fill the hollow spots inside me. All along. All my life.

The front doors were heavy, thick, dark wood, one of them cracked and almost swinging on the hinges. I eased the other one open, expecting it to creak long and loud like in the movies. It didn't make a sound. The black dog at my heels, I walked inside.

The walls were a startling bluish green, with a patina of fine grime; the linoleum underfoot, in patches, was all dirt. The air was heavy and sweet, the wrong sort of rotten-apple sweet, and every breath had the mildewy wet of a pool locker room, a shower stall. All sorts of hallways and doors, no lights, no furniture except a couple of broken chairs tossed in a corner. Splintery wooden doors with frosted glass windows, nothing marked. The first door led to a tiny empty room, some sort of office, the lone filing cabinet overturned and empty. Opening the second released a stench so harsh and overpowering I gasped and slammed it shut. My dog scratched and whined at that door and even as I took little heaving nauseous breaths I was laughing, remembering the neighbor's chihuahua who loved to stick his whole head in our compost pile and start snacking. It made me want to give this one treats, though I was good as certain it, he, never ate.

"Sorry," I whispered, as he reluctantly gave it up and trotted alongside me. "Maybe next time—"

Footsteps. No place to hide, so I froze in place; they didn't even see me, the little trio heading down another hallway transecting this one. Their shoes made the faintest squeaking sounds against the lino as they trudged along, their heads down, and vanished.

It's really true, then. Life in a dead house. I'd hoped I thought it up, more of my seeing-things hearing-things mishearing-things crazy. But somewhere inside, I always knew I hadn't.

Blackie let out another not-bark, a soft whuffing sound: They're gone now, keep moving. Better keep you trotting down that slaughterhouse chute. I headed for the intersecting hallway, going left where they'd crossed right. Old Nick's nails clicked softly against the flooring, the sound a steadying comfort.

The doors down this hallway were solid wood, not even a veiled, frosted hint at anything inside. Empty. Empty. Empty. Empty—

I had to close my eyes and blink hard for a moment because this room, the seventh, eighth maybe ninth, was the first with actual proper windows and it'd caught the full rising sun. Bigger than the others, bigger and bluer and full of makeshift cots just like the monastery back in Leyton, and the cots were full of people. Nobody stirred or turned their head as I walked in, no nurse or scientist or jail guard watched over them; I heard no sounds of breath, saw no telltale chest rise or fall. I approached the one nearest me, a woman with graying dark hair and a brow still knitted in arrested, waxen thought. I put shaking fingers to her lips, her nose and felt no exhaled breaths, slid them to the side of her neck—

And there was a pulse. Weak, maybe ebbing for good, but it leapt up beneath my fingers, then nothing, then as I was about to give up the ghost another tentative little throb. Again. Again. An agonizingly stretched-out rhythm. The slow frail beats of a slow frail heart.

Was this one of the lab's new projects, to try to bring back zombies of old? But zombies had no heartbeat, I remembered that quite distinctly from biology class. They ate, did they ever eat, but they excreted no waste, they used every bit of what they ingested and were more efficient at it than heaven allowed. ("So you're saying they're all full of shit," George Antich shouted from the back of the room, and Mr. Sutter laughed as hard as the rest of us.) They never drew actual, oxygenated breath.

So we were told.

I went to the other cots and some had a heartbeat, and some didn't, and one off in the corner, his skin gave under my touch in a way that made sickness crawl up my chest. Nothing. But he'd be full of life again soon enough, all sorts of different, opportunistic life merrily hatching and feeding away. Just you wait.

I headed for the door, absently patting the side of my leg, and then I heard a little whine and turned to see Napoleon sitting by the dead man, at the foot of the rickety filthy cot like he were keeping vigil. I patted my leg again, whistled. "Come on, boy."

Nothing but reproachful, piss-hole eyes staring back. I was getting impatient. "Rex? Fido? Champ? King? I *said*, get over here—"

He wouldn't move. The ferryman, he'd found his payment.

The room was growing lighter, the rising sun going from painfully intense tangerine to a softer, diffuse marmalade. Rover's eyes, as I squinted, didn't look sickly and jaundiced anymore; they were dual spots of that same strong, flame-shot color, flickering and changing as the sunlight changed. Sunspots. I went over and scratched him behind the ears and he half-closed his eyes in pleasure, like a real animal would.

"You're a good dog," I said. And I really meant it. I would miss him. I gave Chauncey one last pat and after making sure the hallway was empty, slipped out the door.

The hallways twisted and bent and buckled, the stink kept getting worse. Great patches of the floor were black with grime and there was a heap of dried-out . . . something, I wasn't going to get close enough to confirm they were actual turds. We never sank that low in Lepingville, we dug actual shit-pits before the ground froze, but that's lab types for you. Spoiled and lazy.

Wooden chairs and metal desks were piled high along the walls, I had to squeeze sideways past them a few times, but they gave me something to duck behind when I saw two more figures walking the opposite way, coming within yards of me and then abruptly turning and vanishing. They couldn't be my Scissor Men, for one they were both too short—but anyone who attacks you in the dead of night looks taller, stronger than the trees. Maybe the Scissors only brought back corpses, and then drifted back into the woods.

My feet, I could cut off my feet. Burning, aching, rawer than hell. I want Lisa. I want Lisa and Naomi to have got away. I won't think what Lisa's like right now, if Naomi didn't.

The hallway spilled into a wider corridor, two battered wooden doors sitting side by side. The first one was locked, all my rattling and tugging and a well-placed kick wouldn't make it budge. I tried the second. Maybe there'd be a window in the second. Something to shove open, break, for living air.

I didn't want to breathe in this fetidness for all eternity. That was Persephone's real despair, in the stories, I was sure of it. Not the forced marriage, not the specters of the dead, not underground darkness half the year for the rest of eternity—it was the *air*. Just like this. Bottle it, sell it as a perfumed warning, a word to the unwise.

The second door handle stuck, gave a little metallic gear-flutter, then opened with a soft *click* and there was sunlight, actual sunlight, from tiny rectangular windows too high in the wall to reach. A scratched metal desk in one corner, in another a rucked-up sea of blankets and flattened pillows bunched up together on the floor.

Lousy with mouse droppings, this room, and there was a huge spiderweb along the desk's edge, thick cottony whitish-gray like an athletic sock unstitched and stretched open. I pictured a mouse running unwitting toward the sticky strands, some mama mouse's blind hairless piglet babies, and made myself turn away.

A stack of notebooks sitting on the desk. A miniature filing cabinet next to the desk, warped and dented on the side; the bottom drawer was half-open, and peeking out was a little doll. A rag doll, like something Laura Ingalls might've played with before the undead forced her family out of their Kansas cabin, with a checked blue dress and bright red yarn for hair and a gray, grimy, resolutely sweet-smiling face. The whole drawer was a toy chest: picture books, a wooden top, a set of jacks, a kaleidoscope with a mouse-nibbled paper tube, toys a child might've played with a century ago or more. Taped above the desk, beneath the windows, on the closet door, all around the room were drawings, done on ripped-out notebook sheets or what looked like empty lab charts. The lakeshore, most of them, the Aquatorium, the shops along Lake Street, everywhere I'd passed getting here. One had groups of people dotting a beach, a bonfire of jagged orange lines in the middle: a beach picnic, after sunset, little white-coated figures holding marshmallows and hot dogs on sticks.

The tape on some of the pictures had given out, unable to stick to the greasy grime, but as I traversed the edge of the room, going from desk to closet to bedding to the tiny bank of windows, I could see that they laid out a pattern, told a story, marked the passage of time. The pictures nearest the filing cabinet were crude, clumsy, obviously the work of a small child. A child who'd learned proportion and a bit of perspective by the time we got to the desk, then shadowing and how to draw hands by the bedding, then sharper outlines and subtler facial expressions and by the time I got to the windows the skill on display was startling, the scrubby trees right above the dunes sketched out in black and white on a field of graph-hatched green but still so well, so painstakingly done, it really was those trees pinned down to life. Another picture, right next to it: A woman, carefully cross-hatched webbing all around her eyes but her expression youthful and exuberant, standing side by side with a younger, thatch-haired, unsmiling man. Both in lab coats.

Who'd lived here, in this room? For how long?

As I reached for the door handle I heard a sound from inside the closet, a rapid shallow intake of breath like an animal was inside. Is that you, King? A little test, to make sure I don't go licking in someone else's bowl? I'm pretty sure I passed. The sound became sharper, then forcibly stifled: a human being, hiding. Crying. Watching me through the crack in the door, as I made my little revolution of the room.

I went over and put a hand to the closet door, a steadying palm. "Who's there?" I said quietly.

No answer but another little breath.

"I can hear you," I said.

No answer. I turned the handle. I will not like what I see, I told myself, though nothing in this room or under that door smelled of death, I will not like what I—

I eased the door open and blinking into the closet's expansive darkness I saw more taped-up drawings, and a broken chair, and Natalie, her face contorted with misery, huddled up beside it.

I grabbed her and pulled her out of there rough and fast, like I was yanking a toddler away from a stove covered in boiling-over saucepans, and when I put arms out her tentative breaths became deep, furious sobs. I stroked her coalface hair, gone dusty and dull and sticking in dark threads to her cheeks, and made vague ridiculous murmuring sounds; she had a sour smell to her, the same chronically unwashed odor that I and Stephen and every other surviving human gave off and I welcomed it, that faint little milky stench as she raised arms to clutch me back, it was the smell of actual living things.

"What are you doing here," I whispered, too afraid to speak out loud. The shafts of sunlight filtering in made me squint and I turned eyes back toward the closet. "Did they pick you up, in the woods, after you and Maria—"

"She *left*," Natalie managed, and expelled a cascade of small sobs like sneezes before she could speak again. "We were going in circles in the woods and she went off the other way, and I was scared to follow and I kept calling at her to come back, and she never did, and then I couldn't find her at all and these men, they—"

"We're getting out of here," I said. Through those tiny windows, somehow, if need be. "We're going to get out of here."

Natalie cried harder. "They, they do things in here, they—there's dead bodies in—"

"I saw them. We're going to find a way back from here, and find what they've done with Stephen, and—" And cry, and scream, and know it's all deserved, here in my dry hollow plasterboard insides where no one can see. "There's barely anyone here, anyone alive. We're getting out."

"I found this room." She was laughing now, jerky spasmodic little noises, close to sick with fright. "They locked me in the C-Lab but I picked the lock, there was something dead on the floor but they never bothered fixing that lock, it had whitewash all over it but the Recovery Room was apple green. This pretty pale green with a little fish someone drew in black marker in one corner. I wanted the Recovery Room but then I found this. Can you believe it?"

*Natalie's dead,* Naomi said. They brought Natalie "home" too, the way they did Stephen. The way everyone in Paradise City despised them both, instinctively, all those good upright folk whose very cells recoiled from something they couldn't or wouldn't define. "How many of them are around here?" I said. "Do they make regular patrols? I saw at least four. Do they come down here?"

"I found *this room.* I can't believe it." She scrubbed her sleeve against her cheek and her face twisted up again. "They left it just like it was, my pictures, my toy box—"

"Do they patrol?" Natalie was telling me something I wasn't ready to hear, whose implications I wasn't ready to grasp and so I wouldn't hear it. "Those Scissor Men, the ones from the woods, are they outside?"

"I hid in the closet. Because I knew they'd come back here, to find me."

"Did you see when they brought you in?"

"I didn't recognize your voice. I thought you were one of them."

"Did you see anyone else?" I had her face in my hands now, part tenderness and part twitchy urge to squeeze hard and pop if she didn't stop babbling and help me. "Did you see anyone else from Paradise, anywhere here?"

"I—let's get out of here first, okay?" She pulled away from me, stood up with fists thrust deep in her jacket pockets, trembling horribly with the effort to keep calm. "You're lost, aren't you. I know my way back. I know it blind. They'll be down here soon."

Natalie took my arm, grasping tight, getting such a hold I almost stumbled. "I knew you'd come here for me, Amy," she said, as I tried to pull us toward the door. "I knew *you'd* come here. It's just I had to wait, I hate waiting, and I got scared."

"We have to go now." I was tugging back, trying to free my arm, but Natalie's fingers sunk in and clutched my sleeves like a cop seizing a pickpocket. "They'll be here soon. You said so yourself."

"You're lost. But now you're found. I know my way back."

"Good. Then we have to leave." I turned away, waggling my arm to try to get her to let go. "We have to get out."

"You're right. We do." I felt her swaying back and forth, trying to keep herself steady, not succumb to the instinct to run back into that closet and slam shut the loose rattling door. "We're getting out. We're getting out right now."

At the far end of my vision something flashed and gleamed, not like the sun, like glass or metal made painful-brilliant by the sun's reflection. Natalie's other hand came up and my neck was searing, a single thin clean ray like sunlight burning it clean through, and my groping hands felt wetness and I opened my mouth to scream but the damp was all in my throat now, bubbling-thick, I spat and choked and fell to the floor. She let me go. I fell.

The sunlight was too strong now, much too strong, it had burned the whole wall away and let the lake waters spill into the room. The tides flowed ceaseless into my mouth, and I drowned.

# NINETEEN

It's dark down here.

Darkness all around me, thudding sounds all in my ears. My limbs waver and flicker, boneless jelly-things in the dark icy water surrounding them, as easily broken as the spines of sea plants. My shoulder blades, the back of my head are stuck fast in the mud, the cold gelatinous murk on the floor of this great icy lake, this freezing sea. I can feel the suction pull of it holding my body in place, down at the bottom where I sank and drowned.

I drowned and I am dead. The thought of that means nothing.

Something flashes behind the lids of my closed eyes, spasmodic, a sudden memory. The glare of early sunlight against window glass, every heated yellow-orange spot a little pool where you could dip your fingers. The sheen of a sharp, metallic thing catching that light.

The suctioning mud at the lake bottom tugs hard at my hair, my elbows, the cloth of my jacket; then suddenly it eases, relaxes, and lets me go. I float upward, flapping uselessly in the current, and then it's as if I've taken the lake mud inside me, I breathe it and drink it and feel each limb growing full with it, nearly taut, air rushing into depleted balloons. There's mud all in my nostrils but I don't suffocate. The taste and smell of it is fungal, pungent, and as I rise through the depths I realize this dark muddy lake is no lake at all but a house, the house of my own body, mind, memory. I tunnel upward through the strata of myself, through everything hidden behind the thin pasteboard walls that I'd thought were all there was to me. I'm not hollow inside though, not anymore. The filthy mud, the hoarder's junk fills every crevice and seam, weighing me so far down I should be buried miles beneath.

I'm not buried. I'm surfacing.

I remember everything.

March, a few months ago. Winter sleet turned to freezing early-spring rain. Dave was long dead by then, in a blanket shroud in another house because the ground wouldn't budge for burial. It was thawing out now. Kristin lay on the couch in Dave's living room and she didn't move, didn't talk, didn't eat and then late that March, as I brought her what passed for breakfast, she slid her knees up close to her chin and made a hissing sound. She looked down at her own body like it had nothing to do with her, like it was misbehaving just to annoy her out of sleep, but by the time Ms. Acosta returned from foraging Kristin had rolled on her back and kept arching up with pain, great invisible fingers continually drawing her back and down into the drama of her own flesh.

It ate her up even before we started. She couldn't hear us as we hauled her up, tried to get her to walk between us, squat down for the delivery, the little skull was already poking out from between her legs like the hairy knuckle of some obscene, shoved-in finger and it all happened too fast, so fast. She bled like every period she hadn't had for nearly a year came on her all at once, deep dark red and gushing all down her thighs and soaking the sofa cushions, the carpet, but Ms. Acosta just kept saying, Push, Kristin, for Christ's sake just push, and there was nothing we could do.

I had Kristin's throat under my fingers trying to keep track of her pulse, that artery on the side of her neck, and I'd grabbed *Where There Is No Doctor* and natural childbirth books from all the library shelves, what was left of the libraries, I'd *studied* for this test, but in the end it all came to nothing. I flunked. The pulsations beneath my fingertips were like the wing flaps of a bird flying away: hard and vigorous leaving the ground, a sudden panicked, palpitating rush of speed to catch up with the flock and then, as it caught the current, slowing, slowing, no way to feel or hear it so far away. Gone. Kristin was gone. My head was all hazy but I saw a glint of metal, heard the snick of scissors.

Something slick and wet was in my arms. *My* arms. "Oh, Christ," I said. Very calm, like prayer. I wasn't praying. We were agnostics, my mother and I.

"Careful," Ms. Acosta said, her voice thick, distorted. She left the room and brought back a tablecloth, draping it over Kristin, and as the cornflower cloth took on new dark stains I turned away, I looked down at what Kristin had left me. A girl. Tiny, wrinkled, so red it looked raw and half-cooked at the same time and how could you tell healthy or sickly straight off, how did you even know? It cried loud, hard, that must mean good lungs, even though Kristin had stopped eating and there wasn't much to eat a lot of the time anyway that must mean it'd be all right. A girl. I need a girl's name.

"Susan," I said out loud, as we wrapped it up in a towel. Susan. When I named her, touched her, Ms. Acosta said nothing. She just looked at the little face, like a bit of paper scrunched up and hastily smoothed out again, and turned to me, thoughtful. Quiet. The cloud of gray hair around her face was thin and broken, ribbons of bare shell-colored scalp all woven through.

"You need to go out," she told me, her bird-whistle voice fluttering up and down as she took Susan from my grasp, as she lifted her away from me. "There's nothing here for a newborn to eat, try the other side of town where the hospital is. They might have formula left, something."

We'd already foraged in the hospital, a good dozen times. I imagined Susan sucking happily at the tube end of an IV bag, the kind with sugar water in them, the kind we found slashed open f or t heir c ontents a nd l ittering t he first floors we ever stepped inside. "There won't be anything," I said, touching the crazy dark thatch of hair smack atop the baby's head. Her dead dad's hair. "I looked for more food, last time we went for Dave, I couldn't—"

"So look again. Someone needs to check. I'll take care of all of this, and . . ." She looked around the room, at the blood on the sofa and the rug and smearing Susan's wrinkled sunken cheek, and shook her head hard like she often did to stave off crying. "Amy, just go."

I went. Because I thought it was real. Because I promised to take care of Kristin's baby. *You won't just leave my baby to fend for itself, will you?* No, Kristin, no I won't, I promised you, except right at the start right when it mattered I just handed her over, I gave her away without even the pretense of a fight, outside it's cold and dangerous and she'd just slow me down—

That's how faithfully I kept my promise. For a few seconds, until I thought it might slow me down.

For a shameful moment I'd actually wondered if we could somehow squeeze the milk from a dead woman's breasts, but now as I stumbled through the slushy rain puddles down Madison and Overmyer and Cypress I was only thinking, Why hadn't we done this weeks ago, when we had the chance, gathered supplies and stocked up blankets, baby clothes, formula—couldn't they eat chewed-up people food, newborns, like baby birds or wolves? "People" food, like newborns weren't people. Nothing at the hospital, I already knew there was nothing at the hospital.

Too much hospital to search, the baby would be hungry, Kristin's Susan, my Susan now, needed me to move fast. I nearly snapped an ankle on the ER parking lot's half-melted slick of ice, why hadn't I stuck closer to Dave's house, why did I still let Ms. Acosta give all the orders when it was only us left? Susan needed *me*, not her. Kristin made that very clear. She hated Ms. Acosta, hated her voice and touch. Susan needed me to hurry.

Off Forest Street, a house two blocks from the hospital, I found it: right there in the cabinets untouched by famine gangs, a *sealed* canister of formula, a huge one. I shouted out loud with happiness and ran, panting, nauseous with nerves, all the way back. We had water, bottled, to mix it with, a woodstove to heat it. We'd make it last.

I don't know how long I was gone, an hour or more, but when I got there Ms. Acosta was standing in the doorway waiting for me. No Susan in her arms. She looked beyond mere nausea, about to double over and spew, trembling and shivering in her layers of mismatched odiferous fleece like a dog staked in a freezing yard.

"I'm sorry, Amy." Her voice was as chalky and drained as her face. "I'm so sorry. It, she, just stopped breathing. Its lungs must've been weak. I tried, I kept trying, but there was nothing I could do."

She was breathing just fine, when I left. Susan was breathing and crying hard and that meant her lungs were just fine. I stood there, staring at Ms. Acosta, still clutching the canister of Healthy Start in my hands. She kept trying to look me in the face but she couldn't do it, her eyes kept jumping away and past my gaze like a camera on a shaky tripod. I set the formula down on the floor, next to the tall, heavy snow shovel we'd kept propped near the front door all winter.

"What happened," I said. Harsh, and flat.

"I just told you." There were tears in her eyes, brimming, unfeigned. But she still couldn't look at me.

"So let me see her." One of my sweaters, Dave's sweaters, the sleeve had twisted around my arm in a snarl of cheap acrylic and I tugged hard at it, wrenching, ready to rip it back into thread. "I helped her get born, I have a right to say good-bye. Let me see where you put her."

Ms. Acosta turned away. There was an old chest of drawers near the front hallway and she smoothed out the runner, kept moving Dave's wife's little china shepherdesses here and there and all over the wood like she was playing a game of Bo-Peep chess. My stomach had contracted to a thin, painful ribbon, snarled just like that sweater sleeve, and the space it should have occupied inside me was filling up fast with something else.

Something thick and hot, like steam, that got hotter and thicker as it traveled through my gut, my chest, headed for the veins.

"It *stopped breathing* because you did something to stop it. Didn't you?"

Her fingers curled around a purse-lipped shepherdess, all ruffles and flying ribbons and a tall maypole crook. I wanted the little smug-mouthed thing to come alive, there in her palm, so I could hurt it. "I know why it stopped. It 'just stopped' because you put your big ugly liver-spotted hand over its mouth, you squeezed her nostrils shut—"

"Stop it, Amy. Just stop it."

Her shoulders flinched, when I said it, like I'd kicked her in the back.

"Stop what? Stop saying what *actually happened*?" The hot squeezing thing inside me was sparking now, jumping, steam turning to molten metal. "You can't even look at me. You can't even look, because you lied to me and took her away and I listened to you and—"

"Amy." The shepherdesses were all in a line now, arranged by color of ribbon. Pink, baby blue, toothpaste green. "Stop."

There were tears slowly streaking down her cheeks, a hollowness in her eyes whose depths she'd never climb out of again. The hot thing, squeezing, sparking, let me feel no pity; it grew and expanded and propelled me toward her, I couldn't stop, it hauled me rough and fast like a little girl dragging a doll along the floor and I hit her, hard. She shouted, grabbed at my arms and we were struggling, hauling at each other and I was screaming, "What did you do with her! *What did you do!*"

"What I had to do!" She screamed right back, full in my face, her broken nails drawing blood. "So you wouldn't have to!"

"You killed her." I couldn't manage her cut-glass tears of

vague regret, horrible hypocritical tears, I was blubbering and choking like another baby past all comfort, Susan was dead, I'd given her away to death. "I promised Kristin over and over, I promised and that was *my* baby, Kristin gave her to me and you killed her—"

"Amy? Amy. Stop."

She did that thing I hated, that thing where someone puts their palms to your cheeks like they can mesmerize you by touch. "Look at yourself in a mirror sometime—I won't say look at *me*, all my hair falling out, but you're young, healthy as you can manage now, look at yourself." Each word was a stone thrown at my face. "Look what a skeleton you've become. Remember back in November, when your gums started bleeding? That's scurvy, that's why Dave kept making you eat the liver whenever he shot a deer, take all those vitamins we found. What happens when that formula runs out, when we can't feed a baby because we can barely feed ourselves? Rickets. Diarrhea. Edema, those skeleton babies with the swollen stomachs. Brain damage. How the hell do you think we'd manage, with a baby to worry about? How can we take care of her, when she gets sick? About as well as we did Dave? Or Kristin?" Shouting now, right in my face. "Is that what you want to have happen, again, after all this?"

She was saying it was really my fault, Dave dying. That's what she was doing. My fault I couldn't find more insulin, my fault we got a sudden freak thaw right when we *needed* snow and ice to help keep it cold. My fault I couldn't stanch Kristin's blood, all over the living room rug. My fault I handed Susan over to die. She was laughing at me, taunting me with how stupid I was, she pretended she was trying to explain things to me but really she was laughing inside.

"You're enjoying this," I whispered, and the person who said that was a stranger I'd never known lived inside me, slithering out my throat. "You're enjoying telling me just how much I fucked up—"

"Amy? You are not losing your mind *now*, not after we're almost through the winter—you want to end up like Kristin?" She was shouting again, pitiless. "You want to be helpless? Useless? A walking target? This is no damned time to talk crazy." She pulled away, trembling fingers stroking a shepherdess's lacy Marie Antoinette skirts. "There's gangs out there now, Amy, gangs of—things, those creatures that bit Dave, human beings too hungry to look at a baby and see a baby. Is that what you want to risk? No."

She shook her head, hard, almost baring her teeth. "You saw that during the sickness, we all did, I saw another little baby that got—it's done. It's done, and I've condemned myself to hell, but it happened fast and she's out of this world now and she's *safe*, she'll never suffer, and nobody will find her and decide to—nothing will find her. Nobody will find her."

She stared down at me, her mouth a straight thin colorless line, a gray-eyed gray ghost lit from within by the certainty that what she'd done was right. The sparking all through my nerves had become a steady flame, sucking down my every breath before I could take in any air so I felt light-headed, faint, and yet at the same time full of awful, growing strength.

"You heard me promise Kristin." I wasn't crying anymore, and something deeper inside me knew that wasn't good. "That I'd take care of her baby. That *I* would."

"Amy, in this world that's a promise you could never keep."

How dare you. How dare you tell me what I can and can't do, how dare you take it all away—I grabbed the shovel, the fire beneath my skin leaping up gleeful, greedy-hot, when she flinched and backed away. "Show me what you did with her." It was heavy, that shovel, thick metal with a solid wooden handle and nearly as tall as I was, and I felt strong, far too strong, as I raised it a few more inches from the floor. "Show me right now."

"Amy." She wasn't scared yet. She'd seen too much, before this, to be scared. Just wary. Sure I wouldn't do it. "Put that down and stop it."

You don't think I'll do it, do you? You can't even imagine it, like I couldn't possibly have imagined you'd take Kristin's child, the child she trusted to me, and—stupid, incompetent, that's what you thought of me. And now, stupid, incompetent and weak. I'll show you. I'll show you how weak I am.

"You won't show me. Because you can't even look, can you?" The shovel wasn't heavy anymore. It was a part of me, an extension of my arm. "I wasn't gone long enough for you to bury her. The ground isn't soft enough yet."

"Amy."

"The ground's not soft enough. Not to bury her deep, where the dogs won't get her." The shovel was light and words far too heavy, each one dropping slow from my lips like clumps of tar oozing from an oily puddle. "You hid her. You show me where she's gone."

"Amy?" She was breathing hard now, broken bits of dead-stem h air f alling i nto h er e yes. " Put t hat g oddamned s hovel down. I'll show you if you just put it down."

A lie all in your eyes. My mother used to say that, when I was little, I could never lie to her but she left me, she's gone. She was mine and she got taken away. "Show me right now. You show me exactly what you—"

"Amy! I swear to God, I'll—*stop it! Now! Amy!*"

She flung her arms out to try to grab the shovel, wrench it away. I don't know if I was hitting her before that, if that's what made me strike, but the shovel blade slammed into her arm, her face, her crumpled-up back and she was screaming things I couldn't hear, couldn't hear over the hiss, spit, rumble of tar bubbles all exploding with *you killed her, you killed her it was a baby Kristin's baby mine and you killed her.* She made a horrible groaning sound, huddled helpless and broken on the floor and all winter, I'd listened to her, all winter I'd done what she said and look where it got us, look at all of us dead, her bones were so frail and gave way so quickly and I couldn't stop, I couldn't stop. She let out another, sighing sound, like the water rush of the blood all inside her overflowing its banks, flooding her, drowning her, and then I was back in my own body. I was standing there, holding that shovel, and she was lying at my feet. What was left of her. What I'd left of her.

Oh, God. Not my God. Not ever, not anymore.

Wake up. Please wake up.

Bottles.

I brought back formula, that sealed formula canister, but it never even occurred to me to look for a bottle.

They w ould've b een r ight t here, i n t he h ouse o n F orest Street. L ined u p in t he s ame c abinet. I nside t he d ishwasher. Somewhere. Didn't think to look.

Didn't think at all.

. . .

There was blood on the walls. On the wall behind the sofa. On every part of the floor, the rug. Fresh spray of it, all over Kristin's tablecloth shroud. The shovel blade. My hands. My face, I felt wetness on it like rain. I dropped the shovel and animal sounds shuddered from inside me, horrible moaning noises like Ms. Acosta in death and what I've done, what I've done, what I've done. I was staggering around the perimeter of the room, almost sprinting, like a frantic captured thing stuck in a cage and I knocked over a chair as I ran, dusty old-lady lavender chair, and I tripped and went down with it and hoped I would hit my head but I was right there, wide awake, no oblivion after what I'd done. No rest. Never.

She didn't have a face anymore. Alicia Acosta, who got me through the winter in one piece, who went hungry so I and the pregnant woman could have food, I took away your face. It's leaking something now, not blood. I yanked at the tablecloth covering Kristin, pulled it away.

Ms. Acosta's body had twisted around somehow when I hit her so that her fleece and sweaters got torn open, her shirt; one limp hunger-shrunken breast thrust forward through the gaping cloth, nearly exposed. That lone breast spilling out, her tipped-back remains of a head were somehow so much more obscene than Kristin lying naked from the waist down in blood but I couldn't touch either of them, I let the tablecloth drop over Ms. Acosta's head and chest and then I was out the door, running.

Maplewood. Cypress. Sycamore. All that day I ran all over town, my head empty of everything but blood and fear, and then I collapsed in a front yard and lay there, shaking, clutching at the slush-coated stems of deadened winter grass. All night. Laughing, sobbing, shouting out incoherent bits of songs, my songs, other people's, nursery rhymes, gammon, spinach, wild stories I'd tell the cops when they found me. Except, no more cops, no civic security. National Guard, Emergency Environmental Hazard Hotline, FEMA, aunt or uncle, Dave, Kristin, Susan, Alicia. No home. No rest. No nothing. Forever.

I found the broken town security gates, and started walking.

Even then, even after everything that'd happened to us all, I still had to remind myself there weren't any more police. Nobody to arrest me, shoot me for security's sake. It didn't matter.

Something else was already following.

I lay there, at the bottom of that cold muddy lake, and then I floated slowly up, from the depths of that day in March I'd tried to shove aside, lock away, a broken dusty toy in the attic. But it was everything, that day, that moment when I stood there gripping that shovel bubbling and boiling over. I remember everything. I admit everything. I confess everything. I'm ready.

I'm not ready. I'm not. I'm so frightened I'm running around still inside my own head, overturning chairs, stumbling and falling over and over again into brokenness and blood. But I can't run anymore, not in death's own house. I have to be ready. Even my faithful black dog's deserted me. It's time.

I opened my eyes, and I woke up alive.

# TWENTY

My throat ached, a raw nauseous burn, as if I'd swallowed mouthfuls of rubbing alcohol—I could *smell* alcohol. Wafting up from under my chin, my own skin. I reached up, underneath, and traced a thin, bumpy little line starting just below one ear, following along the softness beneath the jawline and petering out, abruptly, on the other side.

Stitches.

I pushed up from my elbows, made myself sit. Something stiff and vaguely itchy was all over the front of my LCS jacket, a rusty bib-stain soaking the black cloth; I unzipped it, looked at my shirt beneath. Blood, my own blood. My neck, though, it'd been swabbed.

My stomach jolted with the sudden fear something had been cut out of me, my tongue, larynx—I actually reached into my mouth to feel my tongue was still there, nearly cut my fingers on my teeth. I coughed, thick and horribly congested like there were blood clots all through my throat, and spat out the words in a wet, painful croak:

"I'm—here."

A steady pulse, I felt it. Rapid with nerves. Soft heartbeat, just like always, right at the inner edge of one breast.

"Here, boy," I said, croaking still but already sounding more myself. "Come on, King. Come get me."

I stared at the door. Nothing. "Nick? Old Nick? Champ? Rex? I need you! Come get me!"

Of course he didn't come. I'd gotten cocky, thinking he was there to save me: He was there to guide me to the knife, encourage me down the chute. To make sure that when I did die, it was only at his master's appointed place and time. In his master's house.

But I wasn't dead. Someone killed me, and I wasn't dead. What happened, Prince? Was that part of the plan or not?

"Help," I called out. "I'm alive."

Nothing.

This room, it wasn't Natalie's room; it was completely empty, stripped bare. Empty except for the body lying in the far corner, beneath the windows: a man, lying facedown, a headful of tangled dark hair.

A lot of people have dark hair. Most of the human race has dark hair.

I turned him over and Stephen's face was slack and ashen, his skin cold and dry and grayish-white like some sort of jelly, a congealed fat. Eyes squeezed shut, mouth half-open in death. His throat was cut open ear-to-nearly-ear and stitched back together again, just like mine, if I were alive then he was alive too and I put fingers to his neck waiting. I waited. I kept waiting. I felt nothing. Hand to his chest. Fingers hovering at his nose and mouth, waiting to feel the light little sweep of expelled breath.

Gone. Drowned.

I pushed his jaw slowly shut, feeling the muscles already going stiff and inflexible. Took my time smoothing out the collar of his T-shirt where it'd come up in tangled folds from inside the jacket, tugged the hem down to cover his stomach, the small things you should do to assure nobody else you got killed is a storm-twisted stripped branch at the moment of death. He'd never wanted to leave Paradise City. That was all down to me. I cradled an arm around his head, so I could feel his hair under my hand, and cried so hard my broken throat seized up and spasmed and I doubled over, coughing, closing my eyes and fighting nausea as the threading in my flesh strained and tugged with the force of it. I was crumbling where I sat, every part of me sharp metal corroding; the saltwater streaming from me, brimming inside me, left pitted, potholed trails of rust.

Gone. I'd barely known him, a harsh thing inside me kept whispering, but it wasn't true, it didn't matter, I *had*. Nearly as many days as I'd known Lisa, in the end, and I loved Lisa and I'd never see her again because there was no way out of here, there isn't anything left, only the dead like me and Natalie (*She's dead*, Naomi warned us all, *Natalie's dead already*), killed for our crimes and brought back to watch over the true dead. All the dead were here somewhere, hiding in corners, I was sure of it, Stephen, Phoebe, Ms. Acosta, Bull's-eye Jason, my uncle and aunt—

I mopped the back of a hand over my eyes, hard enough to

bruise, furiously chasing every trace of tears. There was no way out of here and I'd brought myself here, I'd eaten my pomegranate seeds, way back in Dave's living room in Lepingville. It was my job now, Natalie's too I guessed, to look after all the dead-stayed-dead and I would do it. I'd clean every corner of this filthy aquarium tank, make it shine, no more stench or shit piles or corpses just tossed in corners with bloody tablecloths only half-covering their naked bodies, I'd fix it all, I'd fix it. That was my job now. Underworld custodian. Be proud of me, Dave. Be proud. I kissed Stephen and pressed my forehead to his, getting both of our faces wet, I had a job to do now, I had to say good-bye and go do it—

I didn't want to. I didn't want to.

I curled up on my side, pressing against that coldness like a cat seeking warmth, and his legs kicked out so sudden and hard I shouted, leapt backward, sprawled on the floor. Watching.

His mouth twitched, lips drawing back in a spastic grimace. Closing up again. Going fly-catching slack, like before I'd closed his mouth.

Hope and dread have exactly the same taste, a grainy, piss-sour porridge too thick to swallow down.

His body thrashed again, harder this time, feet scrabbling and donkey-kicking so they left clean tortoiseshell trails on that dirt-caked linoleum floor. Arms jerking up, back, limbs pushing against an unseen tide, like a man drowned and at the bottom of a lake slowly, impossibly, swimming to the surface. My throat was closing and I choked on piss-sour porridge, fighting the sickness of gulping it back, as I watched him, watched myself wake up. He arched up from the lino, feet and shoulder blades the only parts touching, and his hands flew to his chest, clutched and clawed like he was frantic to dig something out; then his arms went limp but his gray-sneakered feet jerked out violently, relaxed, convulsed again. Steady, rhythmic, mirroring the new-found beating of his heart.

He was grinning again, grinning wide, and his mouth was square and taut like a man about to shout, scream, curse the whole world, but his first breath wasn't a groan but a quiet sigh. Each one horribly audible at first, wheezing gasp iiiiiiiin, moaning expulsion oooouuuuuuut, then quieter again, so quiet, sound coalescing into movement as his chest began to rise. Fall. Rise. His feet lost their epileptic rhythm, resting still against the floor. His grayish-white skin changed color like the sky, going a faint, faded pink as the blood resumed its perpetual passe-partout through his body.

I had arms around him again, I'd been afraid he'd hurt him-self thrashing like that but I couldn't hold back, just hold on and wait. Come to the water's surface. To the air. Please. I couldn't say the words aloud because I was choking on the dread that I was wrong.

He stared at me like he didn't know who I was and then, like his own heart kicking him in the chest, I saw the sudden, star-tled strike of recognition. Memory. His mouth opened and his tongue ran along his teeth just like I'd done, like he was remind-ing himself how to speak.

"I thought you were dead," he said. "I thought—"

His voice croaked and creaked just like mine, as if he were still a boy and it were just starting to change. I pulled away to let him sit up and he winced, bent forward, every movement triggering a newfound cramp.

"Amy," he said. "I thought you were dead."

"I was," I said. Each word gelatinously thick and difficult, oozing slowly from my lips. "I was dead, and you were dead. Now we're—"

Now we're what? I don't know what. I don't want to think about what. Stephen looked at me, and he looked at my neck, and he reached out but his hand dropped down before it could touch. I'd stopped crying. He looked like he might start at any moment.

"I was praying you were normal," he said. "Ever since we first met." Still staring at my stitched-up skin, my cutthroat just like his. "I prayed you were normal. That you weren't like me."

He looked full into my face. His eyes were distraught, his smile a stubbornly futile barrier against terrible things.

"But if you were?" he said. "Then how could you have ever stayed with me?"

# TWENTY-ONE

"What's happened to me," I said.

He didn't answer.

"What's happened to me? And you?"

Stephen bit his lip. Sawed at a tender bruise-swollen corner piece, back and forth, until I could feel the rawness and abraded skin in my own mouth. "Sometimes it works," he said. "The procedures. A lot of times it doesn't. Sometimes it works, but then stops." He laughed in a raw, bitten-up way that almost scared me. "Some of us, it keeps working over and over again."

Stephen took my hand. He slid it down his chest, over the shirt front and right up against the skin, so that I felt something beneath the thin cloth, long and narrow and raised.

*Can I turn the lights off?* he'd asked.

"Over and over," I repeated.

He pulled his shirttails up. There was a line, a straight center parting, bisecting him up from the navel: a ropy, dirty-red surgical scar, thick with age and the accretions of reopening. Over and over. It parted in two when it reached his chest, one little wine-colored tributary coursing toward the left shoulder, one to the right. He pulled his shirt down and pushed back his hair. I couldn't see it at first, hiding in the juncture between the ear and scalp, but another thinner set of lines traversed the flesh there, tracing the contours of his skull as if the skin were a mere curtain flap all comers could push aside. Autopsy. Vivisection.

I actually put a hand to my own breast, behind my ear, feeling for it, but he shook his head. Unmarked. Yet.

"Did she do that?" I asked. "Did Natalie open you up, and—" She couldn't have, those were healed-over scars. The sun through the windows was high and strong, telling me I'd been lying here dead for hours, but she still wouldn't have had time. Still no time. "How did she? *Why* did she?"

"Amy. I'm sorry."

He grabbed me and was rocking me back and forth like I really had started crying but I was dry-eyed, vertiginous with confusion. Sitting curled against his sliced-up, sewn-up, scarred-up chest, feeling the faint steady pulsations of a heart stopped in tracks an entire night, it felt like the most natural thing I'd ever done in my life. And that made me scared.

"I could almost smell it on you," he said. A wretchedness all in him, like Lisa right after the tornado staring at our shopping cart in the trees. "Almost *see* it. But you'd never known me, and I'd never known you, and whenever Phoebe or whoever else would babble about this place you didn't seem to know—maybe you just didn't remember. I thought, maybe you really were here, all along, on another wing or another floor, and you just didn't remember it." He splayed a palm against my shoulder blades, each fingertip a tree root trying to take hold in hospitable ground. "It's so hard to remember anything."

I had my forehead pressed to the hollow of his neck, I'd rubbed it back and forth like a cat scent-marking someone's shin, and now I pulled back because I had to see his face, I had to see up-front what he was when that plaster wall inside him got kicked and blown down. He'd known what had happened here, all along, and barely said a word. "That night," I said. "When you stayed. That's why you wanted the lights off, so I wouldn't see your marks—"

"No," he said, and he laughed loud and flat like he'd done something terrible, so much more terrible than being afraid to show his whole truth. "You don't understand. It was so I wouldn't see any marks on you."

His washed-out, plain-John face, the mismatched nose and cheekbones and chin, every muscle in it was tense and tight waiting for me to—to what? Scream, run away? He saw my throat. He saw. "But you would've wanted to see," I said. "You would've *wanted* to. Because it'd mean that we were—the same." The same what, the same *what*. A word crawled drunkenly through the back of my head and I didn't want it there, trespassing unbidden over all my thoughts and all my life, get out, *get out*.

"I was dead," I said. "You were dead. Dead for hours. I wasn't breathing. My heart stopped. My body was cold, stiff. And now—I'm alive."

I gulped like someone catching their breath from mirth but I wasn't laughing, I wasn't. I was thinking of bottle-green hazard lights flashing all over Seventy-Third, of a redheaded woman fattened up in ash-gray protective gear and training flame at something noxious, sickening, not supposed to have mind or memory but it *knew* her, it knew—

"Zombies are extinct," I said. "The plague converted or killed them all. Every one of them. Except—we're not extinct." I gripped his shoulders in my hands. "Are we."

Stephen's eyes closed for a moment. He shook his head. "I don't know if that's what we are."

"We were *dead*, Stephen. Now we're alive. What the hell else do you call something that—"

"You don't get it, Amy, the experiments they did, they've fucked up my whole memory, remade all the—I didn't even remember Natalie. I must've known her, I had to know her, and I saw her every day in Paradise and I didn't remember." He was laughing again, hard enough I knew it hurt. "And she was counting on that, she must've been—counting on it."

I put a hand to his face, running fingers along the cheekbone, and he wheezed, coughed, tried very hard to stop laughing.

Zombies don't—didn't—breathe. They had no heartbeats. The fronts of both our shirts were stiff scarlet-claret-pink but zombies didn't have proper blood, they didn't bleed red. Those were basic, middle-school biological facts. So this can't be true. None of this can be true. I'm seeing what's not there all over again—but it was there, all the time, all that was intangible congealed into earth. My dog. That Angel of Death, leaving as many corpses as he chose in his wake.

"I killed someone," I said. "I killed someone, back home. I—I beat them to death. Not a baby, like, not a mercy killing, but a grown person, who wasn't sick. I'm a murderer. I killed someone. Is this our punishment?" I brushed ragged, unevenly chopped-off hair from his eyes. "Did you kill someone too?"

"I don't know." He had a hand on my back again, running it up and down like he could somehow soothe away all my crimes.

"I might have. Maybe that's why they brought me here. It's like I told you, Amy, I don't remember—"

The door was rattling. Clicking. Someone turning a key in a lock.

We were on our feet fast enough I swayed for a second, dizzy, and Stephen grabbed my arms, holding me steady. Trying to push me back behind him. I shook free and grabbed his hand in both of mine.

"Two guesses who that is," I said.

He shook his head. "I'd never even trust myself to try."

A decisive, clicking thud. A deadbolt, being opened. I heard a murmur of voices behind the door. More than one voice. My fingers went tighter.

"I wish I'd had a chance to hear some of your songs," Stephen said. Eyes steady on the door.

"I'll sing them," I said. I will. I'll sing them. I wish I'd sung them for Lisa too. They can't stop me. They. Except, maybe they can.

Zombies don't breathe air, they don't have the breath to sing. So what's true, can't be true. Except.

Her face was still wan and drained from all that crying but when Natalie slipped through the half-opened door she looked happy: sealskin-shiny hair, dark pink mouth, big brown eyes lit up soft and beatific. Running up to me like we were best friends, parted for months.

"You're alive," she said, and her voice was still a little shy, tentative, after everything she'd done. "You're both alive. I'm so happy. Isn't it wonderful?" She smiled at us, a real smile, like something beyond us all had granted sunshine and prayer. "Happy birthday."

She was happy for me, truly happy. No triumph, no gloating.

Zombies couldn't talk. *Oooooooooosss, oooooooossssss.* I could. That meant it couldn't be true.

"What have you done to us," I said, and my voice cracked and I despised it. "Explain."

"I have a surprise," Natalie said. "A wonderful surprise." She turned toward the door. "It's all right," she called, "you can come in!"

Nothing. Natalie's face distorted, sudden anger like a mouse-trap snapping shut. "Come *on*!"

The door opened a little wider. Natalie relaxed and smiled again, and Stephen tensed up, ready to spring. Waiting. The woman who walked in came slowly toward us, hesitant shaky steps like she was being pushed off a plank, and then she stopped in her tracks and swallowed with an audibly dry, breathless sound, brought a hand to her mouth.

Stephen, beside me, made a sound as well. A wordless excla-mation of surprise.

That woman's mouth was my mouth, the same shape and same thin lips and set above the very same small, squarish chin. Same hands, narrow like mine, with short thick-knuckled fin-gers. Same eyes. Same hair, still the same shade of red, except that gray was taking root and taking over like mint in a flower garden, like yellow grass-spots in a summer drought crowding out the green. Taller than me. I'd given up on that even back when I was twelve, I just knew I'd never get that extra half-foot of height. And I didn't.

"Oh, my God," she said. A sharp-edged sob. "My God. My God."

Did they destroy your memory too? *My God.* We don't be-lieve in all that, you and I. You know we don't, Mom.

# TWENTY-TWO

She ran toward me then like this really was a movie and I shoved her aside, I sent her skidding. She almost fell.

"You *left*," I said, with a venom even Ms. Acosta never heard. "You left me, you—"

"I'm sorry." My mother, Lucy Holliday, this half-gray stranger claiming her name, she was wiping her eyes before tears could reach her cheeks and I remembered from when I was small, after my father's funeral, her huddled in an armchair doing that when we were finally alone. "I'm sorry. I'm so sorry. I won't forgive myself, you can't forgive it, I don't—"

"You left me and you went off to die!" There was no one else in that room now but her and me, Stephen a shadow standing there with no idea what to do, Natalie a forgotten smudge on the wall. "You went to kill yourself and you left me there with *nothing* and now I'm the dead one! You see?" I jabbed at my own throat so hard it hurt, so hard I could've gone crying to my mother to make it better. "I'm dead! I'm dead and all you ever did was hang up the fucking phone, I was looking for you and you weren't there and I did something awful and you just hung up—it—"

"I thought you died. I wasn't thinking straight, Amy, I thought—the sickness, you don't know what it was like out here when it came through and we heard all about Lepingville, Morewood, I was sure you were dead—"

"You let *me* think you were dead!" Screaming now, I don't want quiet, I need to hurt something, I need to hurt myself. "You left me there by myself and everyone kept telling me you were dead, I pretended I believed them but you weren't dead, you *weren't* dead but you and all of them together, you let me think you were—"

"Amy." She was crying so hard and broken that everything in me ached to hug her, Mommy, stop that, please stop, but I held back shaking with the effort and it wasn't to punish her, it wasn't that at all. It was to punish me, me for letting myself start to believe they'd all been right. We won, Mom, I hate you for doing this to me but we won! We won. You're not dead. You never were.

"You're not dead," I said, and wanted to laugh but swallowed it down because with all the crying, laughing, I'd get sick right here on the floor. "You're not dead."

She shook her head. "I *am* dead, Amy. I am. I died before you were ever born. And then I went crazy, and I left you, and now they've done the same to you. Because I wasn't there to stop them. Because I—"

She stood there, her head down, quietly sobbing. I turned to Stephen but I could see he didn't know her, he was certain he'd never known her, and then I walked over and put my arms around her light and cautious as if she might snap in pieces. She cried that much harder, draining away with shame, and I picked up her dangling arms and fitted them around me, making them hold on, posing her like a soft-jointed doll. My mother isn't dead. I'm not dead. Her hair smelled all wrong, no more of her old cheap chamomile shampoo with a scent like dried mouthwash, but it was still hers. I stroked it, feeling how coarse and springy the gray was under the smoother, straighter red. So much gray. You just stopped being dead, Mom, don't get old.

"Please don't be sad," Natalie said, and it startled me because I'd forgotten she was there. She actually sounded like she meant it, like she was sad we couldn't be happy like her. "You don't understand. We're alive. Us, all of us, *we're* the living ones. Not those things outside here, that think they run the show. And humanity, real living humanity, we're going to bring it back."

I looked up at her and she back at me and she smiled, so glad, excited, like we were all at the start of something wonderful. "We're going to bring it back, Amy. *I'm* going to bring it back."

"The lab always worked at cross-purposes," Natalie said. "They were always fighting about what were the most important projects."

We were sitting on the floor now, Stephen and my mother and I, cross-legged with our backs against the wall. I had an arm around my mother and she had both of hers around me, and Stephen had my other hand. Shielding each other, ready to bolt as one, except the windows were too small and high up and

Natalie, something about her eyes made us not want to try for the door just yet. She kept plunking down wearily in front of us, leaping to her feet again in excitement, pacing up and down, down and up.

"I saw others," I said. "Did you kill them too? Are they really dead?"

"There was the stuff they let people know about, so they'd feel their tax dollars were going to important work. Public-minded work."

"What *work*?" Stephen's voice was cold, scornful, his fingers curled a round m ine t ense a nd t ight. " What w ork? T he l abs never *created* zombies—they were always around, thousands of years before this place was ever built. No scientist made them happen, no sickness—"

"They just were," I echoed. "And nobody's ever figured out why some people came back after death, and some stayed dead. Or why sometimes there were so few you could go all your life without seeing one, and other times they were everywhere. Pittsburgh. Detroit. Ypres. St. Petersburg. They never found any reason for those big outbreaks." I was enjoying this, perversely, reciting all this third-grader's who-doesn't-know-that back in the face of her *public-minded work*. "People complained about that, a lot, you know. Taxes funding places like this when the labs didn't find anything new, didn't accomplish shit—"

"Because of course," Natalie said, entirely unruffled, "if you didn't know about it, it mustn't have happened. Sorry, Amy, but if only what *you* know is what's true? Then God help us all."

She was back on the floor, fingers combing through a chunk of hair: Three thick strands, divided between fingers and thumb, and she reached up her other hand, started plaiting a decorative little braid. "Perception's as important as reality, that's what they always said around here. People liked hearing the labs had 'very promising' research results, how they were this close to eradicating the undead—they really did get close, you know, they were working on a sort of pesticide, something you could spray like they do for gypsy moths, mosquitoes. Of course, that was a big mistake." Natalie laughed, shaking her head, a vindictive little mother watching her child tumble off a tricycle. "That's what caused the mutations, you know. That pesticide. There were rumors someone meddled with it. Who knows. They sprayed it around the labs here and yeah, the zombies got sick, some of them died, but others lived and turned into what Billy and Mags are now, and then the *humans* all got sick and started dying and mutating and, you know, here we are. Last remnants of the Prairie Beach feeding plague." She shrugged. "You're right, though. All this happens, and still they never knew why some dead people revived and some didn't, genetic or environmental or what—"

"Perfectly easy way to make sure *nobody* ever came back." So weary, my mother sounded, as she held on to me. Like she couldn't believe it was me, like she couldn't trust her eyes and needed the solid tactile proof of bone and flesh. I felt the very same way. "Easy and proven. Cremation. Fire killed any undead, and a box of ashes can't revive. But people just didn't *want* to give up embalming and burial. Even with more and more bodies reviving and nobody knowing why. They believed the funeral homes, all that bullshit about how 'second-step embalming' would guarantee they stayed in the ground forever—and the labs needed to stay *just that close* to finding the big answer, without actually finding it. Lot of jobs depending on their not figuring it out." She glanced down at my jacket, her jacket, the LCS insignia with the mustard-yellow C slowly unraveling. "Their jobs. Their money. They could've just mandated cremation, and avoided all this."

"They had to string folks along," Natalie agreed. Her head was tilted toward her fingers, the fat, shiny little braid halfway complete. "For funding. Especially after the pesticide made things even worse. Perception was everything. But the real money, that went to the real research. The stuff nobody was supposed to know about."

"Us," Stephen said.

The word was flat and dull, a dirty coin dropped in a rusting slot. He gazed down at the floor, mouth held straight and grim, as though he were ashamed; as though he'd done all this, not had it done to him. I slid my fingers tighter around his and he gripped back almost hard enough to hurt.

"They didn't just want to keep people in the ground." Stephen rocked back and forth, forth and back as he spoke. Pulling his own memories together piece by scattered piece, shards stuck by force into the barest semblance of a vase. "They wanted to learn how to revive *certain* folks. Their own wives, husbands, children, parents, friends, each other—they wouldn't have to worry about cancer or car accidents or anything taking them before they wanted to go." Still rocking, tugging my hand in a gentle seesaw. "They wanted the power of life and death."

"Except not to create more undeads," said my mother. "Undeads are, were a whole different species, different brains, biology—the labs wanted to wake the dead, but keep them human. Keep them what they always were. Drop a stitch, unravel a little, start knitting the whole row again like you never stopped."

The Fates, from my old mythology book, with their scissors

to snick-snack off the long, short, infinitesimal thread of a human life. Scissor Women. The lab wanted a way to grab the two ends of each thread, tie a hasty knot, keep unspooling. I'd been made a fishing reel, the bait hook snapped off in Natalie's hands and sunk to the bottom of a dark, freezing lake; then she repaired the line. And wound me back up here again.

"Why me," I said. My mouth was dry.

"They tried and tried and tried." Natalie's voice was a bored singsong as she completed her little braid; her fingertips held it together, her other hand stroking up and down its bumpy, uneven twists. "Hundreds of test subjects. Maybe thousands. So many of the records got lost or destroyed during the plague. They'd bring people here, drugged, and kill them—with more drugs, like executions, it didn't hurt—and work on bringing them back—"

"How." I could've slid fingers around her neck and throttled but she was our only source of answers, my murderer, my reviver. "How did they bring them back. How did you bring us back."

"Drug addicts," my mother said. "Prostitutes." The corners of her mouth quirked in a rueful smile. "Homeless people. Criminals. Foster system children."

"Runaways," said Stephen. More bits and pieces, sharp and cutting, as if something here in this room, this building, had been waiting to hand them back. "The institutionalized. People nobody missed. The facilities got bribes, kickbacks for letting them take people. Supposedly. Assisted living, group homes, nursing homes—"

"Most of them died." Natalie let the braid go, combed it out again with her fingers. "Others, their brains post-revival were just . . . gone. Mush. They could maybe say a few words, follow orders but lights on, nobody's home. They'd dispose of those, fast, until they realized they'd created a whole group of workers they wouldn't have to pay."

That poor woman, Mike and Jason's gang fuck-toy. The deadness in her eyes, I'd thought it was from everything they'd done to her but maybe it was there before, maybe they saw it in her eyes and knew they could grab her without a struggle. She still tried to get away from them, though, there was still enough *her* in her to try to run away. My free hand clenched up, nails slicing at my palm.

"Naomi's Scissor Men," I said.

"I guess." Natalie shrugged. "They hang around here, they mostly do what they're told. They're not *that* scary."

Stephen raised his head, gazing at Natalie, and smiled. "Dozens of times," he said. "I don't know exactly how many, it ate holes in *my* brain too, but I know it was that many or more. But I could never figure out how they did it. How they brought me back. They were so careful never to let that penny drop. Tell me how we're all alive."

*"Homo novus."* Natalie was back on her feet, happy and excited, stretching like she'd just had a long, comforting nap. "The 'new man.' Human. Whatever. That's what they called us—"

"Us?" I said. "You're—"

"Of course I am, for God's sake." Sharp, impatient, like she were my kindergarten teacher and I'd just failed numbers and colors for the dozenth time. "You think I'd have wasted my time in Paradise, that dead freaks' *dump*, if I weren't looking for the rest of my family? However many of us were still alive? Scoured half of Gary those first months looking but—nothing." She plunked back down on the floor, arms wrapped tight around her knees. "I bet you believed all the rumors that those plague-dogs, those dead things who got the diseases, that they ran this place—"

"The exes," I said.

"Exes." Natalie thought that one over. "I like that. Yeah, some of them lived here for a while but they kept fighting, couldn't make things stick, a lot of them drifted into the woods and never came back. They're all just animals anyway, plague-dogs, exes. Dead animal carcasses walking around. All they want to do is fight and hunt. A few hung around, or made deals with me like that Billy, because they wanted something. They wanted the stuff I remember from before, the stuff the lab knew. They don't know they're doomed." Her voice cracked in a much older woman's laugh. "I couldn't help them if I wanted to. They're all doomed."

She leaned forward, smiling, as if all of us together shared in a wonderful joke the rest of the world couldn't fathom. "Everything you know," she whispered, "is wrong."

"You run this place," Stephen said.

He sounded every bit as disbelieving as I felt. That room, Natalie's room. Her drawings, I was sure of it, for how many years in this place? All her life? She knew Stephen, he didn't know her. All along. Even while I'd felt so horribly sorry for her.

"You really don't remember me at all, do you?" she asked him, and underneath the smiling triumph there was a flicker of something that almost, if you fixed your eyes just right, might have been wounded feelings. "We were both here at the very same time. Your mother, Amy, of course I'd heard all about Lucy, everyone had, but she was still way before my time, she was 'Sarah' back then—"

"I thought I got away." My mother shook her head, silent

mockery of her own delusions. "I actually thought I got away. I escaped, I—there was a guard here, he liked me. I used that. I escaped."

She raised her head, brushed strands of hair away from my forehead. I was still so angry at her leaving me behind but the touch of her fingers to my skin, it made the horrible feverish shovel-wielding thing inside me calm down and curl up to sleep. "Your father," she said.

"Dad worked here, before?"

She shook her head again. "Mike Holliday, that was your dad. The guard was your father."

My uncle and aunt, my dad's sister. The way they'd both look at me sometimes, like I were some drunken stranger at a party that only painful, martyred politeness kept them from throwing out. They knew. And she left me with them. "What did he know? I mean, my dad, about—"

"He knew what I was. Whose you were. He didn't care. He loved us. That I know. It's a long story." My mother glanced toward Natalie, and her eyes went hard. "And she's not going to hear it. It's none of her fucking business."

My dad was a mill worker. He died coming home, when I was five, when his car broke down on the Skyway and a gang of undeads dragged him away. I'd thought. I'd been told. Except that he knew things, maybe, he wasn't supposed to know. They never found his body. Which "they"?

"I was your age," my mother said to me. Her eyes were closed now against the sight of the room, the disjuncture of her own thoughts. "Around your age. I'd run away from home, from my father. Nobody looked for me. Squatting in those rotten old hazard houses here, maybe in East Chicago, with a bunch of other kids—I don't remember who or where. Like Stephen said, when you die and come back enough times you start losing the whole thread of—there was a man, in a car, he looked like he had money, and so I went with him. And I woke up in hell."

Natalie sighed. "That's so melodramatic, okay? You don't need to make it all sound so—"

"I think I was in jail," Stephen said. He slipped his hand from mine, rising to his feet. "Juvenile detention. For fighting. I got angry a lot. I was somewhere else, and I woke up here. We had rooms here, cells. Locked. That felt familiar. They wouldn't tell us why we were there, what they were doing to us. Like we were dumb animals, in cages, just waiting for—"

"They did use animals, to start, but it never worked—of course it wouldn't work, who ever heard of a zombie dog? Stupid to try. Anyway, it wasn't that bad." Natalie shrugged, impatient, this was all so very much not the point. "They did what they had to. None of us would be here if they hadn't."

"Injections, usually. But not always." Stephen tilted his head up to the windows, to the sheen of sunlight filtering through our mucky aquarium glass. "Hypothermia, sometimes. Afterward you were cut open, studied. Take samples of everything. See if your physiology was really still the same. How'd you do this to Amy, to all of us. Tell us how."

"There were—six of us, maybe, seven?" Natalie stood up too, fingers fluttering nervously. "After the plague, though, I thought I was the only one left."

"Killing each other in the hallways, here," Stephen said, and his lips curled back in the semblance of pleasure. "For meat. All the staff, the scientists. I got out, then. During the plague they caused."

"They never brought me back here," my mother said. "After I got out." She was combing her fingers through my hair now, the limp greasy ponytail halfway down my back, trying to work out the tangles. "I was stupid enough to think I'd lost them. But they knew. They knew all along where I was—they were watching me. Watching us, to see how I *integrated*, back with normal people. I integrated like shit is what I did, you saw, Amy." Her hand rested against my head, trembling. "They had plans for you. All along. I know they had plans for you."

"And you still left me. By myself. With people who knew I wasn't really theirs."

She pulled her hand away like she'd burned it. Like I'd burned it.

"I'd lost my mind," she said quietly. "After—that day. After I killed—I knew him, he stood there dead and rotten and his eyes, his voice, I knew them like my own and I went ahead and I killed him anyway. Just to prove I could do it. Just to prove I was on the side of the living." Her eyes, her voice, were faded and flat, worn down with a self-accusing misery that never ceased. "But I'm not one of them, not since the lab got hold of me, I'm a dead thing too and for like to kill like? Like I did that day? It's murder. He came back to find me, and I—and then I thought, but my daughter, she's a *living* thing. Leave her to the living. A corpse shouldn't care for a real live child. Go with the dead where you belong." Her hand came hovering close to my hair, my skin, needing to touch. "So I left you behind. It didn't take them long to find me. Bring me back here."

*Past time you came home,* they'd told Stephen. He'd turned his back on Natalie now, was watching me and my mother in silence. "So you were here all this time," I said.

"I wandered away, when the plague hit. Hid. Wandered back again. Nowhere else to go. I was sure you were dead." She touched my face, lingering on the wonder of our mutual flesh, half-conjoined, together in this rotten womb. She turned to Natalie. "I lived in the basements, hiding, I never lured anyone here, I haven't hurt *anyone*. What have you done to this place? What did you do to my daughter?"

"So I went to Paradise," Natalie continued, as if nobody else had spoken, "to see if more of us were left—and there was Stephen. Didn't even remember me, but he was nice, felt sorry for me with my whole poor-orphan act. Tried to *protect* me." She beamed. "He knew me, still. In some way. Deep down."

"And this is how you paid him back," I said.

Her eyes sparked. "He was valuable. The work here, the real work using our kind, it's valuable. I mean, Amy, my God, *you* were—I couldn't believe it when I met you, I'd seen your mom's picture in the files, you're a dead ringer, it had to be you. All those rumors she'd had a baby—do you have any idea what it means, that *homo novus* could come back to life, conceive a living child with another living human being? Do you even know? All those plague-dogs are sterile, but us"—her smile was proud, so proud, like she'd been behind all of it all along—"we're truly alive. Just like human beings, but better. You helped prove it."

Just *like* human beings. But not human, not really. Not deep inside. Stephen saw my face and he sat back down next to me, gripping my hands like he knew this feeling, that his whole life and everything he'd thought was true was retreating and receding like a hometown in the rearview mirror. A town I was hurtling away from down an empty, deserted highway, late at night, Don's car, no brakes. Of course he knew that feeling. Of course my mother did. And they didn't even have the memories of what they'd lost.

"And what have you proven," I asked.

Natalie shrugged. "That we can grow, age. That we're not

degenerate-rotten like zombies, or stuck in glue like the plague-dogs, we live, breathe, change—I've lived here all my life, since I was two or three. I'm the youngest one they ever brought back." Her face was suffused with half-embarrassed pride. "And I'm bringing all of us back. I'm finishing what they started."

She looked from me, to Stephen, to my mother, and smiled. "Daddy's d ead n ow," s he w hispered, " and I don't k now w hat became of Grandma. But now, I'll have a real family—but first, Amy, you have to tell me about the Friendly Man, the one who comes and goes. You have to tell me why he likes you better. Why he always comes for you, and he always leaves me behind."

A sound prickled at the edge of my consciousness, a subdued tinnitus I knew no one else could hear. It was the sound of an animal, a dog, scratching persistently at the room's heavy, impenetrable door.

"Daddy and Grandma," Stephen repeated. He held the words thoughtfully in his mouth, let them take on an edge of derision. "But you were here since you were little—they came to visit? Your real family?"

There was a flash of envy, resentful sadness in his eyes. Natalie was oblivious. "Tell me why he likes you better," she asked me, with desperate urgency. "I know he loves you best if you've killed someone, doesn't he. Well, I've killed things, I've killed rats and squirrels and one of those cats that used to hang around here, I meant to kill that Paradise girl I ran away with—"

"So what the hell stopped you?" I felt not anger but dull contempt at her excitement: A sullen child again, I was, stuck at the birthday party of a classmate I'd never liked. "Not nerves, obviously. Afraid Daddy would find out and ground you? Take away your bike?"

"Daddy's dead." Her features tensed with actual grief. "He wasn't my father for real but he took care of me and—he worked here. Daddy died in the plague. Grandma, I don't know what happened to Grandma, she disappeared when everyone got sick and I haven't found her. They ran the whole lab, you know, the whole thing. They supervised everyone, but I was their special project, the youngest one, they liked me—"

"The least squeaky guinea pig," Stephen said, and smiled when she flinched. "Tell us how you brought us back. How they did, over and over again."

"I thought you were dead, Amy," my mother said softly. "I thought the lab was gone, everyone who ran it was gone, if I'd had any idea they could still—"

"So why did you keep sending me those messages?" All my edges were dangerously thin, filed down to a translucence that could slice through anyone who came close. I wasn't human anymore, not human like other people are. Maybe I never had been, because my mother who conceived me, carried me never was. "Did you think it was cute? Did you like saying, Don't worry, I'll find you, just keep going, you just kept doing that even after all those men almost—and died right in front of—you called me a liar—"

I'd started crying again from plain confusion and Stephen was demanding *men, what men* and my mother was hugging me fiercely, the three of us were a huddled-up little flock of crows calling to each other and the prettiest little bird, the yellow finch trying so hard to show off her feathers, she was shut out. Even in the midst of misery that thought gave me an unholy satisfaction, scratched an itch inside me just like the sound of phantom-solid nails against a closed door.

"I never called you a liar." My mother glared up at Natalie, certain she'd found the true culprit. "I didn't send you messages, I wanted to, I wanted to so much but there wasn't any—"

"Yes, you did," Natalie said. "You must have." She bit her lip smiling. "Or someone did it for you."

That creature, the one who killed the men right before my eyes. The one who saved me. Shifting into the skins of dead people. The dead people I'd seen all over the road, following me and Lisa—my mother had been dead. They'd all been right, it turned out, all their nonsense about her dying. Because that creature, he only takes on the look of the dead. I drew back, studying her hard.

"You're really you," I said. "You're really—you're not *him*, again, in disguise."

She touched my hair again, so bewildered I could see she didn't know what the hell else to do, and that convinced me. "I—Amy, when I left I thought it was better to just leave. To go, and then everything fell apart—"

"It was the Friendly Man!" Natalie shouted, furious, triumphant. "He used to visit me too, when I was little, he can look like anyone who's died! Anyone he wants! Once when he came he looked like *me*, that was so strange. It was one of the bad nights, something went wrong and I almost stayed dead, and my dissection stitches got infected, bad, and I kept calling for Grandma and—"

She broke off, gulping, hands balled up by her sides. "He came to me. Ever since I was little, whenever I had to stay locked in my room with my drawings and I was lonely or when it hurt so I almost couldn't breathe. He said he loved me. He called me 'kiddo,' he kept saying, 'Courage, kiddo.' He told me I'd outlast everyone, everyone around me." Her eyes were shiny-wet and she blinked ferociously, almost squeezing them shut to hold it back. "And he was right."

Stephen turned to me. My mother. *Explain*.

"An Angel of Death," I told them. "A demon, maybe. I don't know. He can take the shape of anyone who died, sound like them—he's been following me, showing himself to me all along, except I didn't know what he was. He's followed me everywhere, since I left Lepingville."

He could sound like *me*. He could be walking around, looking and sounding just like me, somewhere else, just outside, right now. Because I'm dead too. The thought made me shivery and sick but Natalie was smiling, calm again, that Paradise moment of fear and loneliness she let slip vanished sudden as it arrived.

"We're all his," she said. "Everyone who's died, jumped in that big cold lake, he becomes part of us and we're part of him. He can look like us, sound like us. We're his special ones. But the people who killed someone else? Who *made* death with their own hands? They're the ones he loves best of all. He never leaves them."

The smile melted from her mouth. "Except, he hasn't come back yet for me."

Outside the door came scritch-scritching, stronger, longer, then an abrupt, attenuated *whuuuuufff!* so loud I almost jumped. Made myself keep still. This wasn't a confession I owed her, my own murderer.

"That's very interesting," I said. Bland and indifferent. He came back for me, my dog, he didn't leave me here alone after all. He was looking out for me. Or about to tear me into pieces, and even that, it was okay. Better than being left behind, forgotten.

"Tell me why he never came back for me." Natalie stood straight over me now and her foot prodded me in the thigh, urging me to get up, stop daydreaming and come recite for the class. "I knew you were family, even without looking like *her* I could tell right off. Just like Stephen could tell. The Friendly Man, he promised all the family would return here, everyone would—the birthplace!" She waved her arms, flinging them at the grime-smeared walls, the air so thick with decay it smelled like last autumn, an ordeal to breathe. "The family home. He promised we'd all come back here—"

"You're going to tell me how you brought us back." Stephen slid to his feet again, hands in his pockets, one corner of his mouth crooking up in a smile while the other was a stick-straight line of stone. "The medical records. The lab reports. Obviously you've got 'em, you went and—"

"*I'm* the lab report." Natalie scowled, baring her teeth. "I don't need records, good thing since they're all rotted trash or eaten up—they taught me, Daddy and Grandma, they didn't want me to be scared when they cut me up or injected me with stuff so they told me everything, how it worked, exactly what they did. They made me memorize everything, repeat it over and over until it was part of me. I'm smart. I didn't understand it at first. But now I do. You're proof, aren't you?" Her eyes flickered to his torn-up throat. "But either way, it's not all me. If you're meant to come back, I can make it happen—if you're meant to die, nothing I do can change it. Nothing anybody can do. But you're all here now. We're all here. Of all the test subjects, only us. That means something. It's got to."

My mother loosened her grasp on me and stood up. I followed suit. The scratching was louder now, the door handle rattling. It couldn't just be me who heard it. My mother, the noise was lending her strength.

"You won't keep us here by keeping secrets," she told Natalie, so calm, so quiet. "If that's your—"

"We're all supposed to be here, and stay here. We're family. That's what families *do!*" Natalie's voice rose to a shriek and then she subsided, startled at herself, gazing at me in desperation. "You were the only one of us who hadn't died at least once, hadn't dropped to the bottom of the lake. I had to do it. It was an initiation—"

"It was an *experiment.*" Stephen was hissing from between his teeth, quiet with purpose. "I can experiment too. I can do anything I have to do, to get you to talk—"

"Don't," my mother said quietly, putting a hand on his arm. Stephen shook it off.

"Phoebe and all the rest?" Natalie let out a curt little laugh. "The ones who thought I was somebody's poor orphan treated me like trash—except you didn't, Stephen, Amy didn't, you knew I was family. Daddy and Grandma, they protected me, almost nobody else here knew about me. Didn't matter how high their clearance was. I had my own secret rooms, so I'd be safe even when the plague hit." She tugged on a hank of hair, tugged hard like Lisa as if aching to tear it into threads. "All too busy bowing and scraping and sucking up to, what d'you call them, the exes? They're all dead, the exes, they're just rotting from the inside out now instead of—*you get away from that door!*"

I was reaching for the door handle but Natalie had her knife out again, and though she couldn't hurt Stephen or my mother without surprise on her side I still dropped my hand, took a few steps back toward her. So close outside it made me ache were snuffling noises, an animal's low pleading whine.

"It's okay, boy," I said, staring up at the windows suffused with daylight. "I'm here."

"Stop that," Natalie muttered, between gritted teeth. "Stop showing off."

"I'm here," I repeated, smiling. You cut me, kid, I cut you right back. That's how it always works.

"Who are you talking to?" my mother asked.

"You're staying here," Natalie said. "Not because I'm forcing you, because you have to. You'll never find out what you are otherwise, not without my telling you—"

"I can take care of that," Stephen said quietly.

Natalie's mouth quirked. "Yes you could, couldn't you? You'd love it. I bet Amy doesn't realize yet just how much you'd love it. In fact you'd love it so much you'd probably kill me before you got anything out of me—you know what Daddy used to say, before every new experiment? 'Measure twice, cut once.' You'd never bother with the measuring, you'd be having too much *fun* with the chop and slice—"

"You have to stop this now, Natalie," my mother said, and her calmness was like a smooth, cool stone, sinking peacefully to the bottom of a great freezing lake. "You need to tell us what you've done, and why. That's what families do, Natalie, families talk—"

"Like you talked to Amy?" Natalie snickered. "Like you didn't lie and lie, all the time you were—"

"Shut up," I whispered. "You shut your damned mouth about my mother."

The doorjamb was rattling now, low persistent *thud-thud-thud* as he tried to head-butt his way inside. I couldn't be the only one hearing it. They felt it too, the vibrations inside their bones, even thinking they didn't.

"No one they bring back is ever the same." My mother was advancing on Natalie now, slow, serene, barely bothering to notice the lethal little blade. Stephen approaching from the other side, silently backing her up. "Memory shifts, distorts, or just vanishes. Cognitive changes. Little bits of your personality, it's . . . you can actually feel things are disarranged, like someone broke into your bedroom, moved everything on the dresser just an inch to the left but you still can't quite *see* it—and you did that to my child." I could see the silent fury filling up every space inside my mother, for me, all for me. "You did that to her, because I lost my mind and left her to—you'll tell me what you've done. You owe her, if she's your 'sister,' to tell her."

"This is the only lab anywhere that's ever made dead humans live again at will. Do you realize that? They all tried, but this place, right here, this is the only one on *Earth*." Natalie was alight with the excitement of it, the pride. "This place, this spot. It's where the meteor hit, tens of thousands of years ago, that they think started all the changes, that made the dead revive. The secret's in the sands, the rocks, maybe even the water—all the beaches of the lake. All here, our home." The thought of that seemed to overwhelm her and she shook her head, brisk and swift, to bring herself back. "You have to stay. You have to stay because this is the place that made us all."

I took a step backward, closer to the rattling, shuddering door. "Come on, boy," I called. "Wanna go for a walk?"

Natalie's face went dark. "You were my special sacrifice," she spat. "You! I could tell you'd done something terrible, to get through the winter, the way you'd always act when Phoebe—you're one of his special children, the ones he loves best. When

I brought you here, gave you back to him, he was supposed to come." A tremor passed through her, shook her, subsided. "He left me, one day, and just never came back. Why didn't he come back? He was supposed to remember me, and come back like he promised, and I'd have all my family. Even without Daddy and Grandma, I'd have all of them."

The tremor returned. Gripped her harder. "The hell with him."

Muffled barking, outside the door. The tearing edge of a low growl. Stephen, my mother, they thought they couldn't hear it but I could see them distracted and glancing toward the door, suddenly uncertain what to do, as if they couldn't easily overpower a skinny little fourteen-year-old girl, knife or no knife. Maybe my dog had been Natalie's all along—no. I knew that wasn't true, I knew it because something inside me had shifted and moved that immovable bare inch after I raised up my hands to beat another human being to death, after I realized that though there were no witnesses the whole universe took notice. The very light of the world, inside my head, had changed. He was death's and he was for me. And Natalie, well, I didn't know why death wouldn't come for her. Maybe it didn't count, somehow, if you killed someone who could be brought back. Maybe Natalie was just trying too damned hard.

"He's not for you," I said, over the enraged animal frustration filling my ears, behind the door. "He's not for you. He's for me. I don't know why, but that's just how it is. Accept it, and tell me what you've done to us."

"He was mine first." Natalie's head whipped from Stephen to my mother, back again, every part of her tensed up waiting for them to spring. "He was mine *first*, before you ever met him, every time I hurt until I screamed he was there for me, I've done everything he could ever ask of me and he's supposed to come back—"

"Over and over, I came back. Are we still even human at all?" For just one quick moment Stephen's expression buckled, like an awning's last supporting rods snapping and veering back and forth in the wind. "Are we—immortal?"

Growling, banging, over and over, the slam of wooden door against metal doorframe and, like a hangnail tearing away from the skin, the exquisitely painful sensation of wood splintering.

"Immortality," Natalie said, and her face knotted up with laughter and disgust like the very thought was obscene. "That was never the idea. Never at all. Who'd want to be stuck just living and living and living, people around you saying the same crap over and over, pretending to change but making all the same mistakes as a hundred years before and a hundred before that, same jokes told a thousand times, every place already visited, everything you liked torn down or paved over, nothing to do, nothing to think— nothing. Who breaks their necks running after nothingness? Idiots, that's who."

The t hudding, t he t hudding o f t hat d oor a ll t hrough m y bones. My teeth banged and clicked without meaning to and it was like small persistent feet inside me kicking me, making me all juddery-sick, and Stephen and my mother both stared at the door not knowing why and came to stand beside me, I was that door, they had to be nearer it and me too.

"Were those your drawings?" I asked. "In the other room? Was that your doll?"

"Imagine aging as fast or slow as you wanted to." Natalie slashed the knife through the air, thick spongy fetid air like soft supermarket bread gone to mold. "You love being twenty-five?

You can be twenty-five for fifty years if you want—but when you get bored with it, then you can move on. Someone dies in an accident, gets cancer, people are always all, oh, she was so *young*, she had everything ahead of her? Think if they could bring you back, the very moment where you were before you were cut off. You can choose when, how, if you age. You can choose when you die, tomorrow or a thousand years from now. Someday. And why shouldn't we? Zombies got life again, they got it without rhyme or reason or doing anything to deserve it—why shouldn't human beings have that too? Why couldn't we climb out of the dirt too? That's what they were working on here, using us. You and I, all of us, that's what our lives amounted to."

She swallowed hard, her eyes shiny and full. "We meant something. Okay? It doesn't matter if the whole rest of the world forgot us, never wanted us, thought we were dog stuff on a shoe, they had no idea how much we actually meant—"

"So all of us, everywhere could just keep coming back and back and back," Stephen said. Glancing toward the door, to Natalie, to me, right back again. "Any time we die. Not just us."

"Not without help," said my mother. "Obviously."

"They w ere w orking o n i t." B oth N atalie's h ands c urled around the knife handle, holding tight. She gazed at her fingers like something surprising, precious. "They were halfway there, and they needed us, and Grandma made sure I knew everything I needed to about their work so if something happened, something big, I wouldn't need them—we're the half-measures, the unfinished experiments. But I'm going to make us whole."

Splinter. Crunch. The sound was all through me but the door was still whole, impenetrable, he wouldn't show himself. I couldn't stand it.

"Am I human?" I asked, and my splintering stomach clutched

up wishing never to hear the answer. "Am I undead? What did you make of—what did they make of us?"

"People go on and on about God, God and heaven and damnation—" Natalie shook her head. "It's all death. Life's all just slow death, decay, rolling down this huge, endless slope with nothingness at the bottom—that's what Daddy used to say. That's what Grandma would say. They said it was horrible, and wrong, how death cast a shadow over living time. The only master of everything that ever lived, is death."

She smiled, as lit up and young as she really was—not yet decaying like every human past their earliest youth, not yet rolling slowly downhill, still full of light and happiness and promise. "But we're changing that. Us, the half-measures, the throwaways. Together. We're enslaving death. He's going to work for us. He was our master, the only one, for all mankind's existence—"

A wet, crunching squeal outside, like the pain of something bitten through its soft fatty flesh straight to its bones. Pain, and outrage.

"And now," she said, touching her hand to Stephen's neck, pulling it away. "Now, he's our servant."

"You can't do that," I said. And it was like something else was speaking, through me. Warning her.

Natalie looked at me. She knew. It was all part of her too. Part of all of us. She stared back in defiance, in hate, of me and of something far beyond me.

"Just watch us," she whispered. "You just watch."

An invisible booted foot slammed into the doorframe again, again, shaking the door and my body and the tremors reached far beyond me through every wall and floor, the soft stair-step sweep of the lakeshore and every dry scraping grass and tree, through the sky and water and eaten-up half-ruined memory and the dark hollow places in everything. The door flew wide open, banging against the greasy blue-green wall, and something huge and dark and solid with life rushed past me, knocked my mother to the floor and fell on Natalie, slavering, famished.

The wetness of blood was on me like rain.

# TWENTY-THREE

A girl screaming, high little-girl panicked sound, and the shrill, skittering howl of an animal in pain. Blood everywhere and Natalie was waxen white doll hands and feet under a suffocating pile of black fur, fingers folded round a knife slicked red; she slashed wild and clumsy at anything in reach as my black dog, my dog grown so horribly huge from when he'd trotted at my heels just hours ago, snapped its teeth left of her head, right, biting down on air as they wrestled on the floor. Stephen tried to tackle it from behind, wrench it off Natalie like Lisa had dragged the Leyton dog away from me, but it threw him off and he hit the floor skidding, palms razed, my mother crawling over and throwing herself on me, certain we were next.

"Is that what you were calling to?" she cried. "Is that what's been following you?"

I couldn't explain, I couldn't. Natalie slashed with her knife, shouting, my dog snapped teeth inches from Stephen's throat and I screamed, Get away, my God just get away from it, and he was staggering backward bleeding not from dog bites but from Natalie's knife. It bled now, my dog, it was whining with pain like the Leyton dog not understanding why it was being hurt, why this was happening when it was only doing what its master told it to—

"Enough, boy!" I shouted, absurdly. "That's enough now! Stop!"

To my amazement he pulled back, positioning himself, his unnatural gargantuan weight, between Natalie and the rest of us. Breathing hard, face white with exhaustion and untouchable fury, she ran at him and he lunged, jaws no longer seeking mere air, and as they rolled on the floor again there was so much blood I closed my eyes to memory, back in Dave's living room staggering from sofa to chair to what have I done, what have I done—someone was pulling me to my feet, Stephen and my mother were pushing me toward the door.

"We've got to get out of here," Stephen managed, still breathless, angry peeled-pink rawness striating his palms, "we have to get out—"

"You're not going anywhere!" Natalie screamed. She had a thin blood-streaked arm wrapped around my dog's muzzle, muffled growls escaping; his teeth flashed as his jaw half-opened, half-closed, as though he were repeating her words. "You're staying, you're staying here with me—"

He wrenched free and threw her on her back. She slid on her heels, knife lost and arms thrown protectively over her face, and I couldn't watch her die. I was between Stephen and my mother, grabbing their hands, running out the door.

A sound rang in my ears, my black dog's incessant barking and whining. Not from the attack, not from pain. Because I was leaving, and he was lonely. I was leaving him all alone. I'm sorry, boy. I'm truly so sorry.

"I don't—know—where we are," I said, as the door slammed behind us. Gulping for air, clutching hard at my throat that throbbed now like all the sutures might burst open.

From the room we'd left behind came thuds and crashing, muffled screams, alternating with an ominous, unreal silence. Stephen craned his head down the hallway and cursed in frustration. "I don't remember. I don't fucking *remember* how to—"

"Left," my mother whispered, pulling us down the hallway. "I think left. The gurneys always came through this way."

We stumbled over uneven crumbling lino slicked with grime, gasping at the stench of shit and the overpowering milk-sour of decay; with head-snapping abruptness my mother pulled us left, right, left, straight ahead, doubling backward whenever memory failed her. We reached a tiny atrium like the hub of a wheel, the walls lined in glass-protected black-and-white drawings like something from an anatomy book and hallway spokes poking out from four different directions. A compass room. My mother came to a halt, staring down each hallway disoriented and lost, while Stephen ventured a little ways down each one in turn.

"Yellow," he said suddenly, pointing to the north and south hallways: Unlike east and west these had little bright yellow tiles scattered along the flooring, like bits of plaque in an artery. "I went someplace with those yellow tiles to get out of here, I remember that." He actually grinned in relief, the relief of finally remembering something necessary. "Yellow tiles. There aren't that many in the whole—"

I ran down the south hallway. The glass covering those drawings was perfectly clean, not one streak of dust, which meant people came down here to clean it which meant we had to hurry—all solid wooden doors, down south. I turned and ran right past Stephen and my mother down the north hallway. Some solid, some with frosted glass windows like I'd seen when I first walked inside. Windows of any sort meant fewer secrets, not as deep into the lab.

"This way!" I shouted, and they followed me north, having no better guess.

My throat hurt so much I clutched it in real fear the stitches might split wide open, that I'd drain out like a field-dressed animal on the floor. The hallway became wider and lighter and then came an actual embankment of clear glass, windows we could reach and break through to get to the sloping weed-choked lawns they showed right outside—and then feet were clattering from the opposite direction, at the end of the hall. They let out a yell when they saw us, running for us in angry triumph, and I spun around in such panic I almost knocked my mother to the floor. She stumbled, pushed me ahead of her as we ran back away from the light.

"You're not going anywhere!" An ex's voice, every syllable slicing and striking at the ears. One of the ones who'd grabbed us in the forest, who'd hit Stephen in the face when he tried to get away. "This is your home, you're staying home where you belong or we'll—"

"Fuck you," Stephen snarled, and as they came closer he pushed me and my mother down a stub of a hallway, toward a single metal door leading to a stairwell.

"Lower depths," he said, truly breathless now. "There's a way out here, there's a tunnel, evacuation—route—into the trees—"

We clattered down the stairs, around a corner and he doubled over coughing, gasping, spots of blood welling up on his neck. The basement door flew open with a hollow slam, shouts penetrating the air like loose icicles thudding into soft snow; as Stephen straightened up, gray-faced, and pushed ahead I saw recognition in my mother's eyes, soft glint of a memory all those sudden deaths and slight returns hadn't taken away. The basement hallway veered sharp and graceful to the left but she pulled us right, yanking Stephen's arm when he hesitated, and then we were in a tiny, stifling supply closet, crouching beneath a shelf crammed with leaking bottles that stank of bleach.

"Coming closer," my mother gasped, actually laughing as she pressed against the closet's flimsy back wall, seeking—seeking what? Thin like plywood, that wall, the shelf not flush with it but built inches forward, and Stephen and I got the idea quick, squeezing in fingertips to help her. "They wouldn't know about this here, goddamned opportunists, only wandered in here after the plague, they must be, otherwise this'd be the first place they'd—left! Pull to the *left*!"

The false wall slid a few inches, buckled forward instead of to the side like it'd warped out of its frame. Footsteps coming. My mother hauled and pushed and swore in frustration, and then Stephen shoved it back a bit farther. Shouting now. Shouting for us. Closer. Panicked, I tugged at the wall's splintering edge with all my strength until I heard a creaking snap; little wooden needles stabbed my fingers, my palms but it was wide enough now for a person to squeeze through. We pushed through the empty space behind. A mop and pair of brooms thudded through the opening like they wanted to come too, then we were standing in a windowless, whitewashed concrete cell with a long, curving ramp leading upward, upward into the dark. Stephen stared in amazement.

"I don't know this place," he muttered, and turned to my mother with a look verging on respect: If she knew about this, surely somewhere deep inside she knew everything that might keep us alive. The look of an unwilling, conscripted soldier, dragged to safety from no-man's-land by one of the supposed enemy. "I never did—"

"People—back there," I managed, my chest watery and burning like a great blister, the flesh of my palms torn up. "Rooms of them, hearts beating, they're like us, we have to—"

Voices so close, just outside, they'd check the supply closet, find our hidden door. No time, no time. Exhausted and aching, we dragged ourselves up the dirty whitewash of the ramp, farther, higher.

They'll find us, I thought, as we ran. They'll find us. Too late. But it got so quiet the farther we went up the rabbit hole, twisting, turning, walls and ceiling so close and everything so dark my breath seized up claustrophobic but then, suddenly, a tiny flight of steps. A double trapdoor up above, outside light leaking around the frame, and we reached up and pushed and clean cool air rushed in, we were in the light. My fingers seized the thin cords of flower stems, the dry muck of dead leaf-clumps, crawling-snake tree roots as we crawled out, together, away from the fetidness and the rot. My mother slammed the trapdoor shut and we sat there for long seconds recovering our breaths, unable to move; then we were staggering filthy, disoriented, into the deeper shade of the woods.

. . .

"I should have—" Stephen coughed, gasped, threw a hand out to a tree to support himself. "Her knife. When it dropped."

"No time." My mother threw herself to the ground with a sigh, back resting against the thick, gnarled bark of that same old oak. "I have to stop. Sorry. My God."

"Where are we?" he asked. So sure she could tell us, right down to latitude-longitude.

"Somewhere up on that ridge above the lab. Don't know just where. I don't remember."

Far enough, anyway, for now. I sat down next to her, even though I was afraid if I stopped moving the exhaustion would leap on top of me, eat me up. I put my head against her shoulder and she took me to her, rocking back and forth with a casual ease like we'd never been parted. I pulled Stephen's head into my lap and he wrapped an arm around my legs, holding on. The air, I'd get enough of the cool sweet cleansing outside air.

"My throat," I said. Hoarse and croaking like some tree frog just hopped from a branch. "I was swallowing blood, I drowned in it. I shouldn't be able to talk—"

"It's only a skin wound now," Stephen said, muffled against the cloth of my dirt-stiff jeans. Weary with the contemplation of it. "The muscles and blood vessels, everything beneath it, they've already healed. So we'll just pull the fucking things out, when we can." A smothered laugh. "Just like always."

My mother touched a finger to the wounds on my neck, and said nothing.

"Gary," I said to her. "This place. You'd always told me you grew up here—"

"And I did. This place. That's no lie."

Why was I asking this now, of all times? But I hadn't ever felt as though I were from anywhere, really: All my—our—

Lepingville life had been like squatting in a stranger's empty untended home, and if she knew the path out of death's house she might know more, might know where she—we—first came from. Where we really belonged.

"And before that?" I asked.

"Maybe East Chicago, like I said. I don't know. I don't know." Eyes half-closed now, head pressed hard against the bark. "I told you, I've forgotten so much. Where I lived, when my birthday was, what my parents looked like. Only sensations, intuitions, when I try to think back, or—remember when we'd make breakfast for dinner, Friday pancakes and bacon? I'd eat it and think, This meant something to me, once, before. These tastes, sitting here, this pale yellow paint in the kitchen. Except I don't know if it was really a memory, or just something I'd always wanted and never had."

Every Friday night, when her shifts let her come home for Friday dinner. Pancakes and bacon. She splurged sometimes on real maple syrup, but honestly we both liked the artificial, extra-sugary cheap stuff better. "But you don't know," I said, "what *actually* happened."

Stephen shifted against my knee. "Déjà vu all over again."

"I remember," my mother said, "absolutely everything about the two of us."

I reached out and tucked her hair behind her ear: still messy, still just short of curly, the gray bits with that broken-off springy quality I remembered from working a comb through Ms. Acosta's hair, her smiling at how carefully I did it so it never tugged or hurt. Because I hadn't wanted to hurt her.

"I killed someone," I said. It's getting so easy now, to say it. "Ms. Acosta, remember her, Mom? From school? That day she ran after me when you—she survived the plague too, she didn't get sick. I killed her. I wasn't defending myself. It's just, she—she did something, she thought she was doing what she had to, but she lied to me and I got so angry and—and she died."

My mother nodded and the hollow sorrow in her didn't mutate into shock or revulsion. Because she blamed *herself*, her absence for—that wasn't right, not right at all. It was my fault. "I hit her. I killed her. She had no face anymore and the blood was everywhere." My voice shook and I swallowed, waited. "Because I was angry. It's just that when I came back to the house, she lied to me, is the thing, she sent me out of the house so she could—are we dead? Are we some new kind of undead?"

"I don't know," my mother said. "I truly don't, Amy, I don't know why we're here, I don't know how they succeeded with us when they failed so badly with—nearly everyone else. There's a mass grave near here, Amy, I'm glad I can't remember just where. All the mistakes buried and gone. I saw—" She shook her head hard. "I don't know if you can call me human. I'm sorry."

"Just don't fucking call me *homo novus*," said Stephen. He straightened up, slow and wincing like an arthritic old man, and got back on his feet, offered us both a hand. "I *know* I never heard anything so stupid before, she must've made it up."

"Are we human." I grabbed Stephen's hand, pulled myself up, tried to pin my mother down with my eyes like that could change the answer. "Are we living. Are we—"

"Do you still do your music?" she asked.

"I lost my notebook." Walking now, all three of us, zigzagging through the woods with eyes out for company. "With all the songs. My guitar. I still remember a lot of them. What are we?"

"I told you I didn't know. I told you. I know what I have to think I am." She turned to me, fingers spearing a dead leaf stuck to my hair. "Whatever they did to you it's over, Amy, it didn't take the rest of your life away. You remember me, you—" Her face distorted suddenly, smoothed and settled just as quick, and I saw that one terrible hidden fear of hers subside. "You're human. You're a human being. That I know."

What was it Stephen said, back in the gardens of Paradise? The pure rottenness of judging humanity by memory? That creature my mother killed, so long ago now, he'd remembered something about her. He remembered what they were to each other. I stumbled, nearly fell over a thick undulating tree root, and hands reached out to hold me steady.

"What I know," I said, "is that I'm crazy. And evil. That's what I know about myself."

"You're no such thing," my mother said. We were in a dank, sheltered clearing now, the tree trunks huddling close together as if for warmth and the ground a dusty coffee-brown with dead leaves, only the weakest sunlight pushing through. "We're no such thing."

"What the fuck would you know about *anything* I am?"

The words snapped out of me like a coiled-up snake, surprised from hibernation, striking with all the venom it had. Tears blurred the ground, dead coffee leaves all at the bottom of a puddle, and when she hugged me I grabbed hold, squeezed and sank fingers in almost hoping she'd hurt.

"I could learn," she said. Quietly pleading, from somewhere above my head. "Again. We could both learn. It was never safe, when you were growing up, to tell you what really—I'm sorry, young man, what's your name again? I've always been shit with names. That much I don't think they caused."

Stephen was standing near the edge of the clearing, awkward and embarrassed. "Stephen Henry. Supposedly. Last name, middle name, Henry, I don't know. That's what got written down everywhere."

My mother released me, held out a hand to him. "I was Sarah before, I don't know my last name. That person is dead. I'm Lucy Holliday now. I always liked the name Lucy. Welcome to the family."

Stephen glanced at me, uncertainty in his eyes. Then he clasped her fingers, briefly, gazing at the ground.

"I need to know," I said, "if I'm human or not. If I'm actually here or not. I've never been sure." Death's "special" children. Were we all, always, never like the others? Marked from birth? "Ever since I was little, I've never been sure."

My mother gazed past the close-knit trees, toward the direction of the lake.

"Welcome to the family," she told me.

There was a rush of footsteps, snapping branches and we turned and ran.

This is what a deer feels like, this is what a fox feels like as it's hurtling through the underbrush, madness in human form thundering after it. The air seared my raw throat as I leapt over another tree root arching thrillingly high from the ground, slid and skidded on the leaves. A mere four of them behind us but that was enough, more than enough, so close I could hear their harsh torn-up breaths and they weren't getting me again, they weren't getting—Stephen shouted something, a garbled little roar, then my mother had my bleeding fingers in hers and they were coming at us from the other side, surrounded.

Stephen got a fist square in a Scissor face and the man's grunt of pure shock made me cough up a laugh, and then something heavy was on my back and my hand was torn away from my mother's, I was pitched full-face in the leaves with the breath knocked out of me, a knee stabbing into the small of my back. Inchoate shouts of rage all around me, the roar of what felt like dozens of voices at once, and I wouldn't ever stop screaming, I wouldn't go quiet. One of my hands was pinned behind me, the other sinking fast into the decaying layer-cake of the leaves. Those huge lolloping tree roots would let me hold on, save me, my fingers were white-knuckled clutching the bark but he had that arm now and was twisting hard enough to break, the pain shaking me loose, fingers unfurling—

From behind me came a howl of pain and I was free, lying in quiet agony against the leaves. I rolled onto my side, tears welling up when a dead branch stabbed one of my palms, and saw my ambusher sprawled breathless on the forest floor. Mags's candy-apple hair spilled in a great snarl past her shoulders, shins caked in dirt and her flowered green dress smeared with blood; she'd tossed aside my Scissor Man like a spent cigarette, he actually cowered and tried to scoot away from her in a great rustle of mucky leaves. Stephen and my mother were still wrestling with the others, they had Stephen by an arm and a leg but he was punching, kicking, his face distorted in rage, my mother's arms were bent back as she screamed and screamed. I crawled toward her, tried to run, and then someone else had me so light and quick as if fights like this were nothing, as if humans were all fragile-winged things lighting on his palm just to be trapped in his fingers and crushed. His big wide bare feet were sickly pale, spotted in sticky leaf-tattoos, his breath against my back consumptively rasping and deep.

"Our deal's off!" he shouted to the others, the gear-grind of his voice rolling right over all our frail little squeaks of protest. "You understand me? No more guinea pigs! No more meat deliveries until we get what we want!"

"What *you* want?" The Scissor Man Stephen punched had bled from the mouth, bled and healed so quickly I wanted to rip the skin open all over again, but his eyes were lively and sparking with derision. "This ain't about what you want, maggot trap, it never was! You just keep feeding 'em up and handing 'em over because you won't get a fucking thing out of us if we can't test—"

"Fuck your tests!" Billy wrenched an arm up behind my back, so high I almost screamed again. "Fuck your tests and your experiments and your dicking around, lolling on the throne doing fuck-all but wasting fresh meat—you promised us! You said you could reverse all this! You said you could turn it all around! We want our old lives back! We want to die!"

"Get your hands off my daughter!" my mother shouted. "She's not what you want, I'm the—"

Choking noises, as they shoved her face back into the leaves. Stephen doubled over as a fist sank into his stomach, gasping.

"We won't bring you back this time," the Scissor Man muttered. "We don't need your ass. We've got plenty others." He looked up at me, smiling past me right into Billy's face. "That one you've got there, we actually need. Put it down—"

Mags kicked the Scissor Man still lying on the ground, again, again, grinned in glee as he moaned and doubled up. The others had their hands full, panting as my mother rabbit-thrashed at the leaves and Stephen tried to grab the knife they held to his throat. "You heard him," Mags said, her tongue crushing glass. "Give us what we want, or you don't get shit."

Mags had my legs now, they were carrying me off between them just like yesterday, only yesterday. "Stephen!" I shouted. *"Mom!"*

"Shut it, you little bitch," Billy muttered, jerking my arm so hard my vision almost went and I prayed, godless prayer, for it to stay in the socket. "You open your goddamned mouth when I tell you to, and then you don't open it ever again."

Back on my feet again, barely, each of them gripping an arm and my sneakers dirt-dragging with every step. I saw the brown-and-white flash, the startled polished-stone eye of a deer bounding away as we approached, saw Mags gaze after it with a sudden, sorrowful longing past any sort of bodily hunger. Then they pushed me farther into the trees.

# TWENTY-FOUR

"You show up, you and that bitch Lisa, and everything gets fucked." Billy's voice dropped lower with simmering rage. "Jessie's fucking hoo-family she didn't kill when she had a chance, destroyed everything, that sister of hers and *you* gallivanting around turning everything to shit with your—"

"I never wanted to be there!" Wasting what energy I had left yelling, tearing and ripping at my own fiery-raw throat, but anger turned me reckless. "I never wanted part of your shithole, Lisa didn't, Don made us come with him—"

Billy snorted. "Yeah, Don, that goddamned frail-fucker? If I ever see his ass again, he's dead. I'll find a way to kill him."

"We'll never see Don's ass again, Father William," Mags said, hauling at my elbow. "His or his little bitch's, they couldn't clear out fast enough after—"

"Your Lisa? Your fucking Lisa?" Billy, oblivious, jerked at my other arm so hard I cried out, gulped back nausea. "They rioted on me, all the little frails, and she helped them! I fed and clothed their asses, me and Mags, and they try to burn the place to the ground! All of it! And she *helped* them!"

"No, I can't believe it," I shouted back, breathing shallow and sure I'd throw up from all their wrenching at me, "why would anyone do something like that after you kidnapped them, and put guards up everywhere to try to keep them in, and killed Kevin—"

"She helped them! She actually went and—"

"Fine, so she fucking helped them, she and the other little saints." Mags had already shrugged it all off, burdens of queendom thrown aside like some heavy moth-eaten coat. "Wintertime comes around again, let them riot over that, they'll be begging for us to come back and—quit dragging your goddamned feet!"

"Let go of me!" I screamed, and she hit me across the mouth. My head snapped back and I tasted blood and help me, Lisa, Mom, Stephen, somebody, I'm about to get my throat torn open again and this time it'll stick—we'd stopped now, another dark little clearing lousy with clumps of mushrooms and sickly white ruffles of fungus all over the trees. Billy threw me against a sticky tree trunk and leaned over me breathing in ragged swallows of air, pupils down to pinpoints despite the dim light and pale blue irises flat and glassy as a doll's. My shoulders curled up, trying to pull away, but Mags was breathing down my neck from the other side and there was nowhere to go.

"She helped them set *fire* to the place," he whispered, and like a quick flame jumping on a gas burner there lit in his eyes something beyond the deposed king's anger: an atavistic animal fear, smoldering perpetual inside. "Kitchen burnt down, whole row of houses, all in a night—Don found you by accident, you know that? It was all nothing but a goddamned accident." He had my face in his hands now like he could kiss me, like he could crush my cheekbones and squeeze me for pulp. "Wouldn't have known what we had until that bitch Phoebe started yapping, you and that Stephen, there was supposed to be something special about you—"

"Me and the whole kitchen crew," I said, and the insanity in me, in him, was leaking out of both of us ready to blaze in fury and consume everything I'd known of the world. "All of us, right? Except you missed one, you missed Natalie. You missed the most important one of all."

My words meant nothing to him, to Mags, even if they'd been listening. "You were supposed to help us," Mags snarled, grabbing my shoulder and shoving it against the slimed-up bark. "I don't know how, but—you and that boy, something in you would show them how to turn all this around and let us die." She turned and spat at the lab, the lake, the bent-up old-man beachfront trees. "Be patient, be patient, we're *working* on it, all we ever got—fuck patient, fuck secrets." Another shove. "You tell me what it is about you, what'll change it all back. You spit it out now."

"I don't know!" Her hands twisted hard enough to snap bones, I really was going to throw up— "I don't know why I'm even here! They killed me, I died, but I came back!" I tilted my chin up, the evidence right there, the itching trickle of blood oozing from behind my ear down to the collarbone. "I came back like you did! Just like you! I don't know how it happened, I can't change anything, I—"

"You *fucked* with us!" Billy screamed, and twisted some more at my arm so the pain made me start crying in earnest. "You and that little shit Stephen, you don't fuck with me, you don't fuck with *her*! Nobody and nothing fucks with us ever again!"

He touched his forehead so perversely gentle to mine that I started shaking, it would hurt, whatever they were about to do would hurt until I cried and screamed to die. "You start talking. You start talking and don't stop until you spit out everything you know or Mags here'll start with your fingers. You don't fucking need those. One, by one."

That man in the street, that man so hunger-crazed from the plague he put his own hand in his mouth, bit down in a mass of blood until— "I don't know! *I don't know!*"

Mags took my hand, grasped the index finger, started to twist and bend it back. I screamed and screamed and then something made Billy thud against me, knock foreheads and pull away with a grunt of surprise. He was staggering backward against an assault of kicking feet and bared animal teeth and Lisa, it was Lisa come running from the trees, a singed stench clinging to her skin and clothes and she threw herself on him. They rolled together on the damp-dry ground, their eyes wild, and my ears filled with the hollow smack of fist against flesh and bone. Mags hadn't let go of my hand, I'd *force* her to let go.

"Run, Amy!" Lisa was screaming, gasping at another blow to her face, kicking Billy so hard he growled. *"Run!"*

There was nowhere to run I wouldn't end up back where I started, all alone. Mags twisted at my fingers like nothing had interrupted us, so calm, and knowing I'd die for it I grabbed a knot of taffy-colored hair, sank my free hand in and pulled. We were rolling on the ground now too and her fist met my eye, I'd go blind, I'd suffocate under her soft rollicking fleshly ex-weight.

I'd hurt her, I'd hurt *her*. My head spun, my fingers throbbed, my shoulder ached, my torn-up hands stung and burned, I'd hurt her badly as that, ten times worse—I got a knee into Mags's stomach, my head snapped back again under her fist and silvery slivers of light swam from behind my lids, not stars but little fish. A blow to my bad arm, making it shudder and vibrate. My ribs. My stomach. I choked trying not to retch and my hands were scrabbling for a hold in that soft pale flesh that couldn't scar or bruise, that had no memory in it at all. She punched again and I made a high, scared and scary sound, a rabbit in the jaws of a cat, all I could grab hold of was folds of filthy green flowered cloth like grandma upholstery, that goddamned spill of matted grease-locked hair—

"I won't tell you anything!" I screamed. My fingers flailed, trying to press down against her eyes—they didn't want to bend, my swollen-jointed fingers, it hurt so much to bend them and that was her fault, all of this, all her fault. "I'm never saying a fucking thing!"

She had my shoulders now, pushing with both hands, it hurt so much I wanted to pass out. Her gray eyes were wide and serene. "Then I'll tear your tongue out," she whispered, and I knew she wasn't joking, that smile reminiscent like she'd done it before. "You can write it with a stick in the dirt, you filthy piece of rotten meat—"

I was weak, weak and stupid and about to die, it hurts, it hurts so much, I don't want it to hurt. Little frail, about to be gutted, killed, eaten, killed again, killed forever. Mags settled her weight against me, enjoying the show.

"I haven't had a really good hoo-kill in years," she said. "Not a good feeding one, not since before Billy and I got sick. You came along just the right time." Hand to the side of my head, yanking my chin up and back. "That's one thing they can't take away."

A good hoo-kill. *Hoo. Oooooosssss.* You're dead, you *talk* dead, you shouldn't even be here. I shouldn't be. I'm dead. I *died*. I died like you died. There were riots in the grocery stores and I kicked a man's head so hard something crunched and broke, I didn't mean to do it but then came the second time, the deliberate time, I'm you, Mags, Billy, I am *you*. You're all I am and all I'll ever be. Mags's cushiony, columnar fingers explored the sutures on my throat, a mocking little tap dance from one side of my neck to the next. She laughed, doubly happy.

"I knew it," she said. "Little lab rat."

Then she dug her fingers in, to rip them all open.

I don't know what happened next. I'll never know. Every part of me was screaming-hurt and drained dry and her nails were sliding in to tear me all up, but inside me something caught hold. It caught fire. It didn't matter anymore how much I hurt. My arms shook and something hot and scorching brought a different sort of tears to my eyes and I pulled so easy from Mags's clutches, I wrenched my head away like her iron-band hands were nothing. I took her by surprise, I so loved taking her by surprise. I sank teeth into her arm, hanging on, head shaking to bite down deeper and she roared in rage.

"Rotten little bitch!" she screamed, a hand in my hair slamming my head against the leaves, the tree roots again, again. I didn't even feel it. My body's just a dead skinned hide draped over what's actually me and you can't get to it, wet stickiness dripping in my hair now that must be my own blood, it didn't matter. You can't kill me, bitch, I'm *dead*.

"I won't tell you anything." Laughing still, my arms and legs flying up to hit, kick, scrabble heels back down in the soft forest ground like I was built for this place, born-reborn to it. "Nothing, not a—" She got my jaw again, my teeth slamming together under the impact so it echoed through my skull. "Not a thing, nothing!"

"Then you're nothing," she whispered, with the sighing softness of breath, the last breath, leaving a body for good. "You're nothing. And this is all over."

Her hands were around my throat. Throttling. About to snap.

My nails caught on soft powdery-smooth flesh that tore open, that spilled a wetness far too thick over my hands, and with her fingers still circling my neck I twisted, kicked. My feet thudded and something bent and cracked beneath them, I heard a shocked scream that wasn't me, my teeth found flesh again and a taste foul and necrotic coursed into my mouth, this isn't me doing this, that dark lake water is rushing over my head again but I'm breathing it in as air, flying through it, sailing over dark coursing tributaries like the veins buried in my own body—

A pulsating thud, all in my ears. What a child like Kristin's child hears in the womb, its mother's heartbeat, dwarfing and drowning out its own.

I was standing over her. I had no memory of rising up but I was standing over her, over Mags where she lay on the ground, and the rushing searing drowning thing inside me, hot enough to melt glass, cooled and congealed into dark, spiky, shining shards. Hard glassy bristles, like the fur of a great black dog. My own breath, sobbing and ragged in my ears. Over and over again.

The taste coating, sticking to my mouth was so foul I bent over and spat, again and again. My hands were winey-syrupy, a purplish tarry stuff ground into the nails and smeared over my palms and I tried scrubbing them on the tree bark, flinched at the pain, stared at Mags where she lay still and quiet on the ground. Her face, the eyes wide-open startled, scored with lines down the cheek like my own fingernails. Throat a torn, tarry mess. Her gut. Ripped open, kicked open, a great soup of decay where vital organs should've been soaking her flowered green dress, coursing down her soft pale springy-firm thighs, saturating the leaves and tree roots and ground.

The smell. You can't imagine the smell, oozing from all inside her. Kill it, Mom. Kill it. Set it on fire.

I staggered backward, waiting for her invulnerable undying ex's body to close up, knit together. It just lay there, limp and depleted, a wineskin burst open. I was dizzy and my slammed-around head kept doing a kaleidoscope tilt and then there were sounds behind me, Billy and Lisa had smelled it too, heard it too and they let each other go. We both had black eyes, Lisa and I: Mine swelling up, squeezing my vision down to the slit in a window blind, hers already yellowing and fading as the blood sank back into subsiding flesh. Billy, torn up, fucked up, heaving breaths like he'd run a race. All of us, staring down at Mags not believing what we saw.

Billy kicked at the leaves, like they were road barriers blocking his way, and came so slowly closer, waiting for her to wake up. His pale blue eyes were round and wide, the whites on full display, taking it all in and not seeing what they saw.

"Not funny," he said, as he stood over her. "Not fucking funny, Margaret May, get the hell up."

She didn't move.

"Mags," he said quietly.

The ground beneath my feet danced, circled, like it was taunting me, playing tag. I staggered again and almost fell and Lisa caught me, hung on, made murmuring sounds of would-be comfort that had no words, no end, no point. Billy was kneeling in the stinking saturated leaves, a hand touching Mags's snarled auburn hair.

"Mags. Get up. Wake up. Mags." Order. Bargain. Plea. "Mags."

Lisa kept an arm wrapped tight around me, a hand to her mouth.

"Mags," Billy said again. All quiet.

Then a sound came out of him that pulled all the energy from the tree roots, the ground, the air, a howling anguish punching holes in the sky. He seized her shoulders, shook her rotten remains like he could jostle the life back into her, and he turned to me, his hands—both our hands—smeared with horrific stinking ooze, his eyes shiny and face feverish with wild impossible hope.

"Kill me," he said, and as he laughed his pale round rabbit eyes brimmed and spilled over. "Can't kill myself. We both tried, she and I. Tried and tried. You don't know how fucking many times. So kill me."

I just stood there, the swaying ground and trees finally straightening up, trying to understand how she could be lying there unmoving, unhealed, dead. Billy stroked her hair, passed a hand over her eyelids to close them, then screamed to me and the tree roots and the air, "Kill ME!"

What do I do? I don't know what to do, I don't know what I *did*. It has to be a trick. It has to. Lisa was still murmuring, whispering, the nervous drone of some meditative mosquito. Billy laughing again, stony, hollow, as his face grew damp like rain.

"You wanna die?" he whispered, and all the hollowed-out despair in him flared up, searing, like a dead tree catching a discarded cigarette's flame. "You wanna get outta this tramp-around, tread-around life and have any peace and quiet, ever? Any rest? You ain't gonna." Each syllable snapped and flared up as it left his mouth, more dead branches for the fire. "You'll live forever, nothing but endless fucking *living* and breathing and stumbling around the trees, no point, no purpose, no nothing, everyone you care about gone and you don't get to follow, you just keep going on and on and on and—that's what you can have! You can have it!" Screaming, an air-rich roar of flame consuming the clearing, acres of trees, every last thing in its path. *"You can have it!* You'll have it! And you'll curse every worthless fucking second that you're—"

He pressed his face to Mags's forehead, choking, sobbing. The stench of her, strong and sharp and porridge-thick, still spilling out on every part of the ground, the leaves, the rug, the wall behind the sofa, the tablecloth of a mutual shroud. I wrenched away from Lisa and I ran.

I stumbled in the direction Stephen, my mother had gone but I didn't get very far. Lisa was right behind me, she half-tackled me just the slightest bit gentler than Mags and then I was sobbing against her shoulder. That goddamned sound again, that there-there noise she kept dress rehearsing, her kind couldn't even do that much without Brillo-scrubbing a human's ears.

"Shut up," I whispered. A good soft sound. "Shut up, shut up, shut up—"

"I looked for you all night," Lisa said, and kept rocking me back and forth with a quiet ferocity. "I heard one of them screaming you got away and that's my girl, that's—I went back to Paradise, I thought maybe you'd gone back, and some of the buildings were already on fire. The commissary." Her fingers touched the edge of my eye, now swollen almost shut. Her own face, she might never have been hit at all. "Kevin, Billy doing that, it was the last straw. I don't know what'll happen to them, everyone left, I've got Naomi, she's here with me, but—"

"How did I do that?" I coughed, almost doubled over. "Mags. How did I do that. It's impossible. How."

"I don't know," she said. "I don't know."

She touched my hands, still sticky with what had happened. My mouth. "Your teeth," she said, with a distant sort of wonder. "They're like—they're so sharp now. They've changed." She made a sound that wasn't quite a laugh. "They're like mine."

My teeth. I touched them myself, ran a tongue along their edges: still square like human teeth, the slight up-and-down unevenness I'd always had. I put a fingertip to them, examining each in turn. When I took my hand away that finger was bleeding.

"What does that mean," I said.

She shook her head. "I don't know."

"The lab." I put bleeding fingers to my swollen eye, felt a jolt of pain when I touched it and my hand flew back down to my side. Everything hurt, my eye, my mouth, my throat, my hands, my whole body, but something told me I should've been hurting more. Adrenaline. That's all. "Lisa, the lab, when Natalie disappeared, it—"

"I know."

"They're taking people for it, human beings, they're still taking them right now, it's filthy and there's not even electricity but they've been doing things that—"

"Amy." Her face was somber. "Just trust me, I know better than you could possibly imagine."

*Patient Zero*, Phoebe said. Poor crazy backstabbing dead Phoebe I wasted so much energy hating. Something about Lisa's brother. He couldn't be the "Daddy" of Natalie's dreams, could—

why couldn't he be. Why couldn't anyone. Lisa's hand traced my jawline, tears in her eyes as she touched my throat.

"Oh, God, Jim," she murmured, all to herself. "What the hell did you really do in that place, all those years. What'd you do to all of us."

I pulled away. "So what did he do?"

She shook her head. I knew I'd never get an answer.

A wailing sound emanated from the trees, rising, falling, and I walked quietly back in because I wasn't running away from what I did, not a second time. Billy lay on the leaves next to Mag's torn-up, how-the-hell-did-I-tear-her-up body, his eyes squeezed shut and sobs convulsing him, like they were working their way up from his feet and out his mouth; he didn't see me, he didn't see anything around him. Phoebe had that same look, after Kevin died: a wild dizzy sickness, like they were both trapped on tiny boats spinning and drifting crazy onto a hostile, lethal sea. I saw what he did to Phoebe, I shouldn't have any pity.

How could I not have pity? We were one and the same, Billy and I. Killers together. This wasn't the second time, this was the *third* and I didn't even know how I'd—I got out of there fast, I turned and fled like I'd sworn I wouldn't and Lisa was standing there, waiting. She pulled something from her pocket, a squashed candy bar with a singed-smelling wrapper.

"Eat," she said, shoving it at me without ceremony. I ate, every mouthful a big clump of stale peanuts stuck together with caramel like rubber cement.

"I didn't mean to kill her," I said. Maybe that was actually true. My lips were coated with melted sugar, they came unstuck when I talked like an old envelope flap. The candy was dry and hard and it hurt like hell to swallow. "I didn't know—how could she die? How?"

Lisa just shook her head. When she saw the fear in my eyes she smiled, ran a hand over my cheek.

"I've had nightmares since I got sick about never dying," she said. "Never. Being trapped here forever. So if I'm wrong, if something out there could actually kill me—fine. I'm ready. It's only Naomi and my sister I'm worried about." She watched the chunks of peanuts disappear down my throat. "And you."

I grabbed Lisa's hand, and she almost jumped. I could see it on her face, her face that couldn't hide her feelings for shit: My grip was far too strong, stronger than it'd ever been since she knew me. Sugar rush, Lisa, that's all, right? "Tell me. Tell me how I did it. Tell me or I'll—"

"Amy!" My mother's voice, calling out scared, and despite everything something in me leapt up so high and easy hearing it, like a stag bounding toward a cool river. "Amy!"

"Here!" I shouted, and took off running, Lisa behind me, in the direction of her voice. "Over here!"

The trees here at the wood's edge were a mere curtain scrim over the high uncut grass of the lab's back lawn, the lab itself, just a few hundred yards up the hill. I saw two people there waiting for me, *alive*, and I laughed with an edge of true hysteria and then I stumbled over something and almost fell, and I looked down.

It was a foot. A human foot, unevenly severed, still in its black lace-up shoe and with a toothpick edge of bone sticking from the torn-away bit of shin.

The stench was an impenetrable fog rushing into pores, nostrils, mouths: the same smell that poured from Mags's body, when I somehow killed her. There were bodies strewn between us and one of them was the black lace-up's owner, he lay there broken and in pieces and some of the pieces were missing. He bled red but the others around him, they were full of an indiscriminate stew of winey-black rot, their bodies tureens of bone cracked open along the sides. The Scissor Men, the ex-humans, who had pursued us believing like we believed that nothing could bring them down.

My mother stood there next to Stephen, ashen-faced. She gripped something in her fist, like a clump of hair, but holding it had stained her fingers red. Her face, her clothes, covered in tarry blackness just like mine. Stephen, his shirtfront and hair matted in winey rot, squatted near one of the bodies. He looked up at me, eyes full of defiance and fear, and swallowed down some of the same stuff smeared all over his mouth, cheeks, neck. A mouthful of blood.

I came forward and took my mother's hand. Gently uncurled the fingers, one by one, and she let the bloody torn-off thing she'd been holding fall to the ground. *Your teeth, they're so sharp now. Like mine.*

"Mom, this is Lisa," I said. "I met her on the road. She looked out for me for a while. She and Stephen already met. Lisa, this is Lucy. My mother."

Lisa nodded, looked suddenly almost shy and awkward as she glanced at us all together.

"Are you okay?" she asked my mother.

My mother thought that one over. "We can all pretend we are, together," she mused, locks of salt-and-paprika hair falling over her face. "It'd help pass the time."

Lisa nodded again. A good answer, I could see her thinking. A good answer.

"I'll be right back," she said. "I have to go get—don't go off anywhere, Amy. Or any of you. Christ, I told her to stay by the lilacs no matter what, if she's wandered off I swear I'll—"

She ran off, threading through the birches. Stephen reached up with his sleeve covering his hand, wiped what traces he could from his mouth.

"Are we dead," I asked, again. "Living dead. Dead living—"

"I don't know," my mother said. "I don't know."

"Do we—can we—eat human flesh." The question was a hard suet lump in my throat and I forced it out, like coughing up something swallowed the wrong way.

Stephen put his hands in his pockets, stared at the ground with his face knotted up.

"There's something in my head now," he said, "when I get scared enough. I don't know if it was there, before, it's like I said, I have a terrible time remembering a lot of things—" He shook his head. "I can do . . . things like this. And it's like I don't even know I've done them, until they've happened."

He glanced over at my mother and I saw the gratitude of knowing it wasn't only him, of knowing that someone else had been forced or bred or made exactly this way. He looked at me and I saw him waiting for me to turn my back, resigned and waiting. I reached up and touched his hair.

"Mags is dead," I said. "I killed her."

His eyes widened. "That's not even poss—"

"And this is? What you did?"

He had no answer for that.

"I didn't even know I'd done it," I said. "Until it happened."

My mother took me in her arms, gave me a short, sharp shock of a hug. Stephen kissed me. When I looked up again Lisa was standing there watching us, arms wrapped around her body in the old way like she could somehow push this wrong skin of hers into a good fit. Beside her, leaves and dirt clods sticking to her hair and her eyes bleary with sleep, was Naomi. Here with Lisa all along, hiding, seeing and remembering God knew what.

My mother looked from Naomi to the bodies and back again with alarm, but Naomi's eyes studying it all were big and dark and so very matter-of-fact, so used to the supposedly unthinkable. We had all seen all of it, before. *There are Scissor Men, there are.* Had she seen Mags's body, Billy huddled crushed and broken beside it? She'd called them Mommy and Daddy, once. I nodded at Naomi, woman to woman, and she nodded back.

"This is Naomi," Lisa said to my mother, curling a palm around the top of Naomi's head. "My daughter."

Naomi's expression didn't change, but she leaned into the touch. My mother managed a smile.

"That day back in Lepingville," I said to her. "The day I snuck out to watch you on the intrusion call, and—"

"Yes," my mother said. "I remember."

"Was that my father?" I laughed. I couldn't help it. "Or my dad? It was, wasn't it. Which one was it?"

*Ooooooossss.* Holding out his hand. Her hands, curling that much tighter around the flamethrower. She looked back at me.

"They never found your dad's body," she said. "I had nothing to bury, nothing to burn. Then—" She closed her eyes hard for a moment. "—and then, there he was. A body to burn. And that's what I did."

That screaming when he died again, ceaseless screaming, the noise like a scalpel teasing agony from bleeding skin. Right in front of me. Ms. Acosta, lying there on the floor, one pale, nearly bared breast and fingers half-curled in panic her last remnant of intact flesh. There she was. And that's what I did.

"We have to get out of here," I said.

She nodded and we headed side by side toward the patches

of pink laboratory brick, the swaths of thick open grass. Everyone followed, Naomi bringing up the rear with Lisa and clutching at a long, curling, dead strip of tree bark like a teddy bear as she walked.

The wind was picking up, the grass around our shins bowing and flattening and the tiny gnarled trees at the top of the dune-face doing an easy little list back, forth, back. We made our slow wounded way through the grass and toward the narrow white gravel road, waiting to be seen. Waiting to see who'd see us.

But nobody came out of the lab, ever. Instead we heard footsteps behind us, tracing the path we'd just deserted, and Stephen slid a protective arm along my shoulders as we all turned around. She was breathing hard, bruised, great smears of drying blood splayed like handprints over her cheeks and arms and sealskin hair, but she was bright-eyed, smiling. She still had her knife.

"I saw them," she said, buoyant with pleasure. "The Scissor Men. You got them *all*. The ones who thought nothing could ever touch them." Her eyes on Lisa were derisive, gleeful with triumph, and she laughed. "That's what your kind thought, isn't it? That you were better than all of us? Well, guess what, things are different now. The ones who came back—the exes? *We're* the only thing that can kill them. God, Amy, your eye looks terrible. Sorry."

"Give me my fucking dog back," I said. "I know he's not dead, however much of his blood you've got on you. That's not how it works."

Natalie snorted. "I told you, you don't need Death now. You killed what they all thought could never die—and it was dying all along. Rotten, liquid, all on the inside." Her eyes flickered contemptuously to Lisa again, back to me. "You should be dead right now, all of you. You aren't. The master is the servant. That's the whole point. We're already halfway there."

I studied her up and down, down and up, like the tougher girls at school used to do right before a fight. "Give me my dog."

"God, you're boring," she hissed. "I can't, okay? He just vanished, we were in there and he could've bitten my face off and then, it was like he was black sand or something, under my hands. He dissolved."

Death had deserted her again, it still didn't want her. I could almost have felt sorry for her, if things had been different. Stephen smiled as he stared at her, a thin mocking smile like he was thinking just the same thing.

"You still haven't told us," he said. "How we're 'almost halfway there.' Or how we can kill what isn't meant to be killed. I never knew we could do that, I never *could* do that before and God knows I tried—"

"Come back with me," she whispered. A hand on my arm, all naked, unfeigned appeal. "Come on. Okay? Not *them*"—her eyes flickered to Naomi and Lisa—"just, you guys. We belong here, this really is our home and I can't clean it up all by myself—"

"You already killed me once," I said, and the thought of that ridiculous statement being true made me want to dissolve into giggles there on the gravel. "You're not getting another chance."

Her expression hardened. "And if I hadn't you'd be dead right now. You'd never have been able to fight any of them, you know that! Why are you so angry? I don't have to tell you what Daddy and Grandma told me, it was a secret! I'm not supposed to tell anyone! It was all just in case something happened to them, if you stay with me you'll see it for yourself!"

She was pleading now, actual desperation, like the Natalie I'd thought I'd known back in Paradise City. Like the person she really was somewhere inside, might have remained for her entire life, if this place had never had her. How could anyone live with themselves, knowing that? Realizing they'd never know just what they really were? The ringing chorus inside us both, in us all, human and inhuman and impossible to sort out each from each, it made me even dizzier and I turned my head away. My mother put a hand to the back of my head.

"You're making too big a deal out of this," Natalie said. "We're all human beings here, we're not monsters—you want to know how it all works? Then you have to stay. The story's right *here*. In the sands. This is the only place on Earth, the only one where Death doesn't have a boot on humanity's neck—you'd be dead if it weren't for me!" Shouting at my mother now, angry like a toddler sensing their promised candy treat slipping away. "You'd all be dead!"

"You disgust me," I said. "Everything about you disgusts me."

"You're no different than me," she hissed. Her face was flushed, tears of genuine hurt in her eyes. "I don't know why he loves you better, why you get pets and presents and—we're both the same, both of us are the same. Inside, you're no different than me."

I reached out a hand, touched her thick tangled black hair. She blinked back the wetness in surprise.

"You're right," I said. "I'm not. But that's exactly the problem, isn't it."

My fingers lingered, memorizing the color so dark it had that faintest sheen of icy blue, the texture silken and thick even when long uncombed: one good thing nobody had been able to take away from her, here or in Paradise or anywhere else. One good thing to take with me wherever I was going. Then my hand dropped and I turned my back on the lab and her, stepping off the cheerful gamboling white stone road.

"Where are you going?" she demanded. "You can't just wander around the sands and find anything, you know how many people tried that? You won't find anything by yourself!"

Some of the beaches had little whitewashed wooden stairways leading down to the dunes, I'd seen pictures, but here was just a slim sandy pathway tucked between two thick, tufted outcroppings of beach grass, up at the top of the hill. I took a handful of tufts for support, winced in surprise at how sharp they felt against my cut-up palm, slid my feet like a skater down the ridge.

"You have to come back!" Natalie shouted. "You have to!"

Standing up here you could see the whole long sweep of the beach: rucked-up dry beige sand like frosting clumsily spread on a cake, then the wet stuff at the shoreline a darker sugar-brown, smoothed out by the tides, studded with the dried fruits of stones. The trees up on the ridge, when you took just a few steps closer to the water, already looked distant and lonely like they were somewhere far removed.

"Watch your feet," someone said softly behind me. My mother, probably talking to Naomi. I kept going, ignoring the grit in my shoes, the sand easy underfoot as we traveled down.

"Come back!" Natalie was screaming, as far away and untouchable as the trees. "Come back!"

Seagulls strutted along the sands, absorbed in whatever it is seagulls do all day, wheeled briskly away at the human approach. Nothing but old bones here sticking out of the sand, there'd been all those wild rumors near the end that lake sands and the waters cured the plague; you heard stories, crazy stories, about people burrowing in near the shoreline, like sand crabs trying to escape a predator's shadow. The sky was hard and painfully clear, the remains of Chicago a bluish shadow out on the horizon just across the lake.

"Come back! Please come back!" Fear, and thwarted rage, and begging. "I don't want to be here all alone! Please! It's so lonely by myself, I don't want to be alone!"

She was too far away now, I could barely hear her. A seagull marched past me, with that comically furious, head-bobbing bird's concentration; I turned at the last minute, walking along the damp tide line studying the brown-sugar sand, the stones of a dozen-some muted colors like dust-caked stained glass, splintered bones picked clean months past. The gull kept straight on toward the water.

# TWENTY-FIVE

"Don't," my mother said, running up to me quickly as I bent down. "All you'll do is get sand in your eye."

She was right, of course. I put down the wet, cool handful I'd vaguely thought to slop over my bruised eye and gazed out toward the water, the faint bluish shadow of a dead steel mill—dead long before the plague, operations shifted to China, though I'd seen decades-old pictures of its thick white smoke wafting over the shore—still sitting at the far end of the sands. Naomi came up beside me, bark strip abandoned for a lake stone.

"If you put it to your ear," she said, holding it out to me, "it sings. Just like a shell."

I put it to my ear, and heard nothing but the thick, contented silence of a tiny slab of rock. That was a sermon I saw advertised once, on the marquee of that little church near our house: THE STONES WILL SING. LUKE 19:40. Red graffiti sprayed on the side of their white cinderblock building, calling them heretics, Satanists, necrophiles, kept bleeding through the hasty cover of paint. I handed the stone back to Naomi and she slipped it in her pocket, staring at me like I'd know what to do next.

"Don't look at me." I shrugged.

Stephen picked up a stone, raised his arm to hurl it at the water, but something in Naomi's face made him drop it back to the sand.

"It's headed out there anyway," he pointed out. "Just like it came in with the tides—"

"They're all headed out," Naomi agreed. Happy, suddenly, like someone finally understood. "But not yet. Right now, we still need them."

The air is so different, out here by the water: so still and yet the noise of every murmur, footstep, birdsong carries so clear, like the sounding of a great glass chime. The feather-flaps of the gulls, as they marched around the sand not giving a damn we were there, they were deafening. "I wish I still had my guitar," I said. "It was a cheap shitty guitar, but still. It got lost along with everything else."

"Just as long as it wasn't a recorder." Stephen made a rueful face. "Did you have to do that ever in music class, keep tooting like an idiot into some stupid little fucking plastic—"

"You *do* remember something!" I stopped right there in my tracks, I was so pleased. "See? A real memory. We had to do that in third grade, I had this lunatic teacher who made us play 'Greensleeves' and 'Madman Across the Water' until they were coming out our—"

Stephen shook his head, gazed at the sand.

"Actually, I've just seen it in pictures," he said. "Kids doing that. That's it."

Like I'd only seen the beach in pictures, before this, but it turned out to be true after all. He remembered something, one specific thing. I was sure of it. I'd believe in it for him, that memory, even if he couldn't bring himself to think it was really his.

New songs. How about a murder ballad? In just under a year I've killed three people, two of them before I ever had the excuse of what Natalie did to me. Just under a year. Stephen, his face pale and drawn and his eyes so weary, his mouth coated in blood. *There's something in my head now, when I get scared enough.* I already had that in me when I killed Ms. Acosta, I didn't need scientific intervention. Rage was my one horrible, worthless excuse. *Do we eat human flesh now? Could we?* What a ridiculous question. Anyone could, anywhere. Last winter. People could do so many things, so many awful things, if that was all that stood between them and death. Humankind dreaded its king, its emperor, just that much.

So maybe, Natalie was right. Maybe any king, any ruler inspiring that much fear and dread, applauding such chaos, clasping those of us who caused it so close, deserved nothing better than to be deposed, assassinated—

"Naomi!" Lisa called.

Naomi was running, all flying dark hair and spindle-limbs and bits of driftwood in her fists. They came up to meet her, Lisa and my mother, faces sagging with an exhaustion sleep couldn't hope to repair; we all stood there, together, where the dry sand rolled over and surrendered to the wet, as cautious and reserved as the mutual strangers we all were.

"Where are we going?" I asked.

"East," Lisa said. "Cowles Shores, over the county line. My sister—I think Jessie sees things, sometimes, that other people don't. Knows things she doesn't talk about. At least not with me."

She gave me a look then, Lisa did. She and my mother. *Amy, who are you talking to?* I just gazed back, acknowledging nothing. Another crazy person then, this sister, just like me. Somehow I wasn't surprised. Except my own craziness, every bit of it, somehow it was all turning from haze to flesh. And nobody could explain how.

"She sees things," Lisa repeated. "And never talks about them. When we were all sick, she somehow figured out how to save us, how to—" She turned to me, almost laughing. "She's out in Cowles Shores now, she's turned into a hermit. A hermit crab, burrowed in the sand. She never was great with people. Things . . . follow her. Just like they do you." She swallowed, thrust her hands into her pockets. "What happened, last fall, the lab might've helped start it but it's so much bigger than anything Jim—than anyone ever planned. I can feel it. Like how heavy the air gets, how you can see the sky all weighted down, right before the thunder starts. This is beyond anything Natalie can understand, or control—we have to figure this out together. Somehow." She wrenched at the strands of hair fringing an ear, so hard I saw my mother wince. "I thought we had forever, to figure it all out. We don't. And we have to."

Stephen touched fingers to his throat, grabbed at a loose loop of suture, pulled at it before I could stop him like Lisa had pulled on her hair. It didn't bleed. Naomi had wandered off again, digging sand ditches with her feet.

"And what exactly do we do," he said, "if we figure it all out?"

Lisa shook her head. "I don't have the slightest idea. But . . . the bigger thing, out there, maybe if we try to work it out then it'll toss us a sop. Tell us what it's up to, what it really wants." She glanced at me. "Tell one of us, anyway."

My mother held a long black stick in her hand, balancing it against her fingertips, tracing thin raggedy lines along the sand. "Is it like this everywhere?" She dug an idle, wandering circle, bulging at one end like an unevenly filled balloon. "Does anyone know?"

"Why isn't anyone following us?" Stephen asked. "Those can't be the only ones who work here, the ones we—"

"Because they know we'll come back," my mother said. She obliterated the circle with her foot and traced a parabola, sun rays or spikes arching from its sides. "Because if the secret's in the sands, like Natalie said—the secret of us, whatever that is—then we won't go very far." She stared down at her picture. "We never did anyway, did we? Even after we got away, we stayed here. Even against all common sense something in us didn't dare leave this place, its orbit, for good. Maybe there's a reason for that. Maybe we'll even figure it out."

What are we, what the hell are we now? How can anyone else possibly tell us?

My mother drew stars in the sand. "Whatever we find out," she said, "we can't blame Natalie for everything. I know what they did to me." She looked up at Stephen. "You know what they did to you. Imagine that happening over and over again, all your life, since you were a tiny child and nobody would help you. Nobody. You'd lose your mind, you couldn't help it, you'd—"

"And who says that wasn't our lives too?" Stephen demanded, that coldness creeping back into his voice. "Who says? God knows, we wouldn't remember it."

They stared at each other, quiet, my mother's cheeks and jaw tightening into a precise curve of tension like fingers drawing shut. Then Stephen tilted his head and squinted into the sun, up at the trees on the dune ridge. "Billy won't just sit there for-ever," he said. "We should go."

Naomi came trotting up, like she'd had an ear cocked to our conversation all along. As she surely had. Lisa led us along the shoreline, away from the lab and toward the faraway shadow of the dead steel mill; we walked in silence, my throbbing eye, ach-ing legs, burning chest and feet and sand-itching throat bringing up the rear. Naomi ran ahead, slowed down, dropped back to Lisa's side like the pendulum of a rundown clock.

Stephen was wrong, I thought. Billy had to leave Mags some-time, if only to eat, he had to—but he still might decide to stay beside her, forever. And I'd done that to him. Lisa's face, when she spoke of her daughter, the expanse of unhealed grief in her eyes wide as the sky above us and as mercilessly indifferent. Billy, the realization I'd left him completely alone in the world, just as he'd done to Phoebe in his turn, making him split that inner sky open with his screaming. That rotten thing in the Lepingville woods, pleading with my mother to—no. Human emotions, those were, no other creature alive, dead-alive, can feel them! That's what they told us, that's how it is. That's how it works!

Right?

That's how I know I'm still human. Isn't it? So just like Billy, then. Just like that dead man walking. Just like, just like.

Mommy, what's a "human" anyway?

Something wet and cold touched my hand and I started, actu-ally looked up like a fool half-expecting spatters of rain. The sky was a straight sweep of hard china blue, just a lone creamy smear of cloud-white near the horizon. I looked down, and smiled as it nuzzled my shin.

"A puppy!" Naomi shouted. She danced around it, delighted,

but he only had eyes for me. I reached down, smiling at the touch of rough fur, the smooth, close-cornered planes of a real, living animal's skull. He was covered in angry scratches and cuts, blood scabbing up his fur, but he was already starting to heal. I scritched behind his ears and he wagged his tail.

"Where'd it come from?" my mother demanded. She, Stephen, Lisa, all staring at me so disconcerted, like I'd kept this a secret from them all along. "Amy? Is that what you were calling to, through the door back in—"

"What do you think of Nick, for a name?" I asked them. "Like Old Nick. Or is that stupid?"

Stephen watched my fingers as I stroked the dog's back, wary, waiting for it to rear up and try to tear my hand off at the wrist. Nick's tail thudded against the soft gritty sand. "Amy, are you sure it's not here to—"

"Or Nick Drake. The folk singer? He had a song, 'Black-Eyed Dog.' I know, yellow-eyed dog, but close enough. The fur and all." You didn't even strictly need a guitar, for folk music, just your voice. That I still had. "That's his name. Old Nick Drake."

Dislike in Stephen's face as he stared at Nick, shading into resignation: *Well, fine then, but I'm not feeding it.* My mother reached out, gently petted Nick's head, lingering on the solidity of fur and bone as if to assure herself he were really there. I wasn't entirely sure myself.

"Come on then, Nick," she said. "Time for a walk."

We walked along side by side, behind the others, watching lake waters spill over the sands in a subdued, languorous rush; marveling that somehow, for some reason that might not bear examining, we were actually here to see it at all.

.   .   .

We'd looped the long way around the lab grounds, their bit of the forest perimeter, and now we were on the farthest edge; cut straight through and we could find Lake Street again, pick up the ghost highway of U.S. 12, head straight east without ever leaving the heart of the Dunes.

Miles to go. I caught my toe on a rock and Stephen grabbed my arm, pulled me back before I could sprain something. My eye was killing me, the skin around it tick-swollen tight and too tender to touch.

"Is there such a thing as an ice pack you don't need to refrigerate?" I asked him. "If there is and you find it, I'll love you forever—"

"There'll be something, in the old pharmacy. Some aspirin, at least." Stephen looped his arm through mine, ignoring Nick entirely. "Unless Paradise already got it all—do you think the old grandmother's still out there?"

I blinked, or rather winked in confusion. "What grandmother?"

"Remember Natalie said 'Daddy' was dead, 'Grandma' was missing, and they're the ones who ran the lab, whatever big earthshaking project we all are—" His eyes flickered to my mother. "Missing doesn't mean anything, these days. She could still be out there, Grandma. Making her own plans. Making her way back."

Dead doesn't mean anything either, these days. If it ever really did.

"If she's coming back," I said, "we'll be long gone anyway." Unless we meet her along the road. Unless, in the guise of that death angel, I'd already long since met her. "We'll—"

"Lisa," Naomi said, breathless, "Miss Lucy—look." She pointed back down the clearing. "Someone's following us."

The stranger trailing us was close enough I could make out he was a man, too far away to let me see his face. Tall, his shoulders high and poised as a dancer's under a long black coat, he stood with hands in his pockets, a thin ray of sunlight snaking through the treetops to illuminate a head of blond, or silver, or pure white hair. Dark trousers. Feet wide and pale and bare just like Billy's, but he was far too gaunt to be Billy. Every time I tried concentrating on his face, it was like something blurred and contracted in my good eye and all I saw of his nose, mouth, chin were the vaguest of outlines, like one of Natalie's drawings left half-completed.

"I don't know him," my mother murmured.

Stephen shook his head in agreement. But would they even know if they did? It wasn't just me, though, seeing him there. Not this time. It was all of us.

"Do you want something?" Stephen called out. Disdainful, indifferent, with a thread of nervous anger. "Whatever it is, we haven't got it. Go find your own people, we don't want you."

He just stood there, watching us. He shifted his hands from his pockets, long thin mushroom-white hands that he clasped before him, and something about the sight of those fingers so slowly, precisely folding together, like the thick petals of some sickly flower curling up and closing on the stem, made a twitching revulsion seize my skin. I took a step backward, not minding the tree roots, my eyes still on him. He took a step forward, just the one.

"Watch out, Amy," Lisa muttered.

I stepped forward again. He stepped back. Forward. Back. Never an inch closer, not retreating, that same ribbon-length of space always between us and himself. Advance. Retreat. The mountain, always looming jagged and cold in the distance, was hell-bent on not coming to Mohammed.

Nick put his ears back and growled, the low, rumbling sound you hear right before the sky tears open and more lightning courses down to split a dead tree in two. The man just stood there, as I knew he would. Everyone kept looking at me, like I'd have any idea what to do.

"Ignore him," I said, and even I didn't understand the sudden urgency in my own voice. "Ignore him. Let's just go."

We went. The few times I looked over my shoulder he was still there, never catching up.

"It's just another Scissor Man," Stephen said. He swiveled his head around and glowered. "Let them track us wherever they want. Right? They're just wasting their time. They want to say hi, we'll give them a little surprise."

Naomi gripped Lisa's hand as we angled around a copse of serene silvery birches, and when Lisa picked her up she didn't wriggle or whine. My mother poked her beach branch in a staccato against the dirt. "Is it the man you saw before?" she asked me, her voice a low murmur. "The . . . ghost, the creature, you said followed you here?"

I shrugged. "It could be. He can look like nearly anyone, anyone who's died. Even you."

Even me.

Something small and furry shot through the trees with a great snapping of twigs. Nick perked up instantly, ready to cut loose and run, and when I muttered *stay*—no idea if he even knew what that meant—he took off running anyway for a few yards, glanced around bewildered like he'd already forgotten what he sought, padded reluctantly back to my side as I broke from the group and waded through the underbrush. The trees were growing sparser now, the sunlight stronger; Lake Street,

U.S. 12 were barely a half-mile off. Nick held off to mark another tree while I rubbed at the stabbing ache in my shins.

"Amy?" my mother called, sharp with anxiety.

"I'm coming!" I shouted. "Hang on!"

Still not used to being around people, so many people. It was still better this way. Nick could testify, there was no trusting the decisions I made all alone.

I crouched down to tighten my shoelaces, and when I straightened up again the other one, the ghost, the shape-shucking thing who'd followed me here was standing right in front of me: neatly gray combed hair, little wire-frame glasses, a face so bland and ordinary you could stand inches away and still never describe him. Jeans, sneakers, a wrinkled blue shirt. No black coat, no bare feet.

Nick bounded back through the trees, chasing after the others. Leaving the two of us all alone. The gray-haired man looked at me, and he smiled.

"Who are you?" I said. But I knew who he was. Even never having seen this face, this particular dead man's face before.

His smile widened. "Even those who don't know me all that well," he offered, "they say I'm pretty friendly to strangers. A friendly man. Do you agree?"

I turned my head, looked behind me. The man in black was still there, stopped stock-still with his hands folded before him waiting for me to move. That's the rule in chess: Black goes second. I didn't remember anything else about the game, other than that the king was worthless and I could never make sense of the knights' little jumping Ls. I turned back to the gray-haired man. Explain. But you never have, and never will.

"No," he said, and nodded, quite courteously, at the man in

black. "That's not me. As you can see." He sighed a little, the reluctantly delighted bearer of bad news. "Actually, I'm afraid that he's something worse than I am, something much worse—but, you know, you'll just have to deal with that yourself." His eyes, gray as his hair, lit up with mirth. "You can do it. You're a big girl now."

"Amy!" Footsteps crunched over twigs and squelched through the leaves, my mother coming to look for me. "Are you okay?"

"Lake Street's just over yonder," the gray-haired man said. His arm pointed, perfectly straight, through the thinned-out cottonwoods and oaks. "I advise you keep going. Just keep going, and I'll find all of you."

"Are you all right?" Stephen poked his head into the clearing. "That dog ran back without you, and—Amy? What's wrong?"

He'd vanished, the gray-haired man, so quickly Stephen hadn't even seen him. So quickly, I hadn't either. Stephen's eyes narrowed as he looked behind me and I knew the thing in black, the Something Much Worse, hadn't gone anywhere, wasn't going anywhere without me. But I was used to that, well used to it. Just ask Nick.

All my crazy, all that time, it turned out it was really the farthest thing from crazy; either that, or the whole world had gone crazy too. Either way, it meant everything I'd feared, I'd hoped I just imagined—this whole new world, this place of hollow towns and empty roads and immortality bleeding and dying on the ground, everything I'd thought must surely be a dream that someday, if I were very good, might up and fly away—it wasn't. It was the truth. I'd just have to deal with it, we'd all have to deal with it, or die. If we were ever even allowed to die. No choice. You're a big girl now.

All the people around me who've died, and now I can't imagine how we're all here, living. Breathing. Naomi and Lisa. Stephen, my mother, me: more than human, less than human, never really human at all. The man, creature, thing following us, who can't possibly be real. We shouldn't be here. I shouldn't.

"I'm okay," I told Stephen, my mother, Lisa, Naomi as they crowded around me, as Nick sniffed suspiciously at my legs. "I just stopped to tie my shoes."

We took up the path again, ambling upward and downward and then steadily up through the remaining trees. A winter-pitted Honda still sat in a tiny service station's parking lot, cheek by jowl with the forest's far edge; Lake Street opened up wide and empty at the curb.

My thoughts kept twisting, turning in ever-widening circles. My feet, at least, knew where they were going; just a few miles removed lay U.S. 12, and the long road east.

Read on for a taster of another book by
Joan Frances Turner:

# Dust

Nine years ago, I was alive. Nine years ago, Jessica Anne Porter was fifteen and lived in a nice house in the very well-guarded town of Lepingville, an hour out of Chicago, and got okay grades and wanted to do something someday with animal rights. Her hair was auburn dyed something brighter, I forget what. I don't see bright colors well anymore. She had a mother, father, a sister in her first year of college, a brother in his last—neither of them could wait to get out of the house, they barely spoke to her parents. And her parents barely spoke to each other. Then one day they were in a rare good mood and took her out to dinner, and then there was the Toyota ride home.

Dad took the back roads home, the scenic tour. You weren't supposed to do that, you were supposed to stay on the main highway with the blindingly sulfurous roadside lights (the "environmental hazards," as we called them, you never put it more directly than that, supposedly hated bright light) and the toll booths. Each booth had a FUNDING COMMUNITY SAFETY sign so you wouldn't throw a tantrum as you forked over your money, a sentry bearing an emergency flamethrower. See? Safety. Suck on that, you suburban cheapskates. The small, cramped booths could serve as safe houses in a pinch, if a "hazard" somehow surprised you on the road. They had to let you in, that was the law. But my dad had paid four tolls in eighteen miles just to get to the restaurant and my mom complained the road lights gave her headaches and it was a pretty night and for once nobody was screaming at each other so why not take the old road, the long way home? Rest your eyes. Have a bit of peace and quiet.

It was two miles from the county line, where the former industrial park gave way to beachy dune grass and rows of half-built condos sat empty along the roadside, silhouetted in weirdly dim, soft white road lights. The old-fashioned kind. This was after they finally passed the moratorium on residential building in rural areas, the one the developers held up as long as they could, until the "hazards" somehow got into that gated community near the Taltree Preserve; whose woods, fields and ex-farmlands these are, even they then managed to figure out. Nothing hazardous that night, though, just the dark sky and the low fuzzy whiteness and everything peaceful and sleepy until suddenly there were two blinding headlights bearing down on us from the wrong side of the road, howling brakes and screaming and then, like the lost breath from a hard stomach punch, everything gathered into a fist and struck, and then stopped.

I remember a pickup truck, yellow, gone faded saffron under the road lights. And a woman's voice, not my mother's, moaning over and over like some nauseated prayer while I lay on the pavement dying, *Oh Christ, oh God, oh Christ oh Christ oh Christ oh my God* and I thought, Lady, it's a little late for that now isn't it? Her voice was washed out, staticky with the buzz of a million angry flies eating her up, and the buzzing became louder and louder and there were new flashing lights, red ones, but it was too late, I was all eaten up, and I closed my eyes and fell asleep for a long time.

Then, days or weeks or months after the funeral, I woke up.

In old horror movies where someone gets buried alive, there's always that moment where they blink into the darkness, pat and grope around the coffin walls and let out that big oxygen-wasting scream as the screen goes black. Me, though, I knew I was dead, really dead and not put away by mistake, and another giant fist was gripping my brain and nerves and shoving away shock, surprise, bewilderment, only letting me think one thing: *Out*. And I knew, with absolute certainty, that I would break free. I didn't seem to need air anymore, so I could take my time.

I tried putting my hands out just like in the movies, to feel the force and weight I was fighting—six feet under, that's a lot of piled-up dirt—and that's how I found out my right arm was shot to pieces. The left could rattle the box a bit, but not enough. I raised my legs, each movement a good long achy stretch after the best nap in the world, and pressed my palm, knees, feet against the white satiny padding overhead. Felt a rattle. Pressed harder. Heard a creak.

Then I kicked.

The first blow tore through the satin lining and slammed into the wood without a moment's pain; the second splintered it, cracked it, and I kicked and kneed and punched until I hit shards of timber and musty air and then, so hard my whole body rattled, a solid concrete ceiling overhead. A grave liner, Teresa explained to me later, another box for my box, but I felt real panic at the sight and had to make myself keep kicking, harder, harder, and that awful concrete became fine white dust that gave way to an avalanche of dirt. I was gulping down mouthfuls of mud and I was sad for my shirt, they'd buried me in my favorite T-shirt that read ANIMALS ARE NOT OURS TO EAT, WEAR, OR EXPERIMENT ON and now it was plastered mute with damp black dirt, but I kept swimming one-handed, kicking, tunneling upward through a crumbling sea. The moist tides of soil were endless, then I felt something finer and powdery-dry and my good hand found thin cords of grassroots, poked through the green carpet-weave and ripped a long jagged slit open to the air. The *air*—I didn't need it, maybe, but as I lay there drained and exhausted and felt it cool on my dirt-caked back I almost cried.

The sunset was a needle-thrust in my eyes. I crouched in my own grave hole, retching up pebbles and earth, and gasped at the smells of the world: the turned soil, the broken grass stems I clutched in my fist, graveside flowers old and new, the trees and plants and the thousands of people and animals that'd left scents behind traversing the cemetery grounds. My own dead, dirty stink, and it still didn't shock me, I was too distracted by the other million fits and starts of odor flooding my nostrils— this was how to experience the world, this note of mushrooms sprouting in damp grass, this trace of old rubber from a sneaker sole, compared to this banquet eyes and ears told you nothing! My head pounded, painlessly, like a great throbbing vein: the hard pulsations of my new brain, my undead brain, but I didn't know that yet. I reached up, like someone would be there to lift me, and touched something rough and cold. A tombstone, my tombstone: AUGUST 14, 2001. I died on August 14, 2001, but what day was it now? Where was I now? Where would I go, where will I sleep, do I *have* to sleep—

I smelled it before I saw it, darting quick and confused across the grass. Rabbit. Fresh, living rabbit.

Every other scent and smell in the world instantly vanished. Hunger rattled my skull and shook my bones—pork chops, hamburgers, steaks rare and bloody, everything that would have made me vomit when I was alive but I had to have them now, I had to have them raw and oozing juice and if I didn't get that rabbit, if I didn't kill it and devour it *now*, I had nothing to live for at all. I staggered to my feet and stood there trembling, legs stiff and exhausted, but before I could even try to run for my food something bloated and rotten in the shape of a man, his dark suit jacket torn and spilling fat little white grubs, crawled on all fours from the pile of dirt that had been his grave. The grave next to mine. The rabbit had halted too soon, crouching frozen with fear by our collective tombstone, and as I watched it spasm and kick against death, as I watched my father sink long teeth into its skull and spit out soft tufts of brown fur, I was small again and only wanted to scream and cry, Daddy, why did you take my toy?

Something crawled from behind a yew tree, feverish and fast. A woman in the rags of my mother's favorite blue sweater fell on him, grabbing the rabbit's meaty hindquarters for herself, and held on tight and chewed no matter how hard he punched and kicked, so hard she sobbed between bites: Whap, cry, swallow, whap, cry, swallow.

But, Daddy, that's *my* toy.

They rolled on the ground, snarling with rage.

And you. What are *you* doing in my mom's favorite sweater?

But they'd dropped the rabbit carcass, fighting that hard, and I was so hungry and it was so good and I knew the answers to my questions, I already knew.

A garter snake slithered over my mother's foot and they both went crazy, grabbing fistfuls of grass where it had shot out of reach. Arguing again, fighting forever, only with sounds now and no words—screeching violins, deafening pounding drums. I was gone already, walking away. I never saw them again.

I scraped a deep, gouging ridge in my back, crawling through a gap I'd torn in the cemetery fence, and felt only a paper cut. A pinprick. I ran my tongue along my teeth and almost screamed; the fence's barbed wire was nothing, but my teeth had all grown long and blade-edged and when I pulled my hand from my mouth, there was something thick and syrupy from the new cut on my tongue and fingers, almost like blood but black. Coffin liquor, Florian told me later, my own putrefaction flowing through my veins. My hand was swollen and livid, the veins and arteries gone dark.

I could barely walk. I staggered, tried crawling like my mom had but with the bad arm that wasn't any better. CALUMET COUNTY MEMORIAL PARK, read the sign; that told me I was in the middle of nowhere, if you insist on burying instead of burning they make you do it far away from everything and don't come crying to us if the funeral procession gets attacked, but where this particular nowhere was I had no idea. Other than me and that garter snake, no sign of life. I crawled and stumbled and crawled again, pushing through grass, gravel, leaves and underbrush. Snapping branches scared me, a single car speeding by terrified me; it'd find me and run me down if it got a chance. I didn't feel like a monster but I knew I looked like one. I cried from fear, wept from hunger, black syrupy tears splattering my muddy shirt.

I kept walking, deep into the countryside, no company but the animals I was too scared to stop and hunt. What the hell was

I looking for? My throbbing skull started pounding in earnest, yielding to real pain, and my ears were flooded with a sudden off-kilter symphony of screeches, buzzes, trumpet squawks, strings sliced shrilly in half. The buzzing like flies, that sound I remembered from dying. I shook my head to get rid of it, like real flies stuck in my head, and it grew louder and sharper and became muffled disjointed words:

*—another one—grave—Joe—see—*

I started shaking. Never mind what had happened to me and my parents, never mind the guard posts along the highways and every Lepingville entrance and exit, never mind all the school safety drills and town committee handouts about the others, the "hazards," the reasons you either burn like a Good Responsible Person or you get buried behind barbed wire in No Humans' Land—never mind all that because it couldn't be true, *I* couldn't be true—

*—circles—follow—*

Circles, d izzy a nd h unger-sick a round t he s ame c lump o f trees, and I couldn't find those voices or escape them but I tried to follow them not knowing why: hot-hotter-COLD—turn left—warmer-warmer-COLD—not so far left—so hungry-hotter-COLD—straight ahead—too quiet—turn around. My guts twisted hot-hotter—ON FIRE with emptiness, no more meat, no nothing. Voices faded, returned in tinny crashes of music, then vanished. I was on the worst ice-cream truck chase in the history of the world, but if I kept going the voices would find me, they'd tell me where to go and feed me and take me in—but then I took a wrong turn and it was cold-colder-absolute zero, every sound gone. The clouds overhead seemed to burst and collapse like bubbles, inky night pouring in as I stood there covered in mud and black blood. All alone.

I doubled over, threw my head back and screamed. Franken-stein's monster, roaring, and it felt so good that I crouched in the leaves and shouted louder, ripping myself inside out with hunger and fear. Something small and furry shot past me, terrified of the sounds I was making, and I could have chased it but my head pounded and throbbed and everything before my eyes melted, sliding off my plane of vision as I succumbed to the vertigo. A spoon heated seething red scraped my gut away piece by piece, slow starvation cauterizing my insides, and I pounded my forehead, my good fist, against the ground and wailed.

I don't know how long I lay there. Silence, my horrible crying met with utter silence, and then I felt what I thought was an insect brushing my face. No, not an insect—soft swollen fingers. A stench pressed in on all sides, I was fresh and sweet in com-parison, but I was too tired to move and it couldn't mean any-thing. I was all alone.

The fingers touched my ruined right arm, lifted it. It fell back with a soft thud. *Chit-chit*, I heard, a strange wet-dry click like someone chewing a mouthful of popcorn kernels. I pulled myself upright, and looked.

The whole right side of his face was smashed in, concave forehead and crushed cheekbone and one eye bugging precari-ously from a broken socket. He was purplish-black, and dirty white: Maggots seethed from every pore and crawled across him in excited wriggly piles, blowflies waving and blooming and wilt-ing, the bits of bone they'd scraped clean glinting like tiny mo-saic tiles. Scraps of jeans and a leather jacket clung to the sticky seething mess of his flesh. He was big, big-shouldered, a good foot taller; *chit-chitter*, he went, even standing still.

Behind him were more stinking, seething masses shaped like

people, their skin in the thin moonlight every color bruises go: some barely rotten at all, one shriveled and bony as an unwrapped mummy, one so bloated and gas-blackened it scared me. Standing right behind Bug Man was a half-skeleton with wild dark hair and silver rings clinking on her finger bones, eyes bulging nearly out of her head as she sized me up, grinned and let out a loud, belching guffaw. They all groaned with laughter. Their teeth looked the way mine felt, long and jagged and dull gray like tarnished blades.

I can't explain it. You can be a monster yourself and still scream, puke, faint seeing what you are staring back at you, but none of it seemed monstrous. It was pretty, almost, the weirdest kind of pretty, seeing how they were all young or old in their own inhuman way, how slowly and methodically the bugs took care of everything, how clean bones and pulsating brains were underneath the skin. How natural it all was. But then those teeth, so dull and dirty but a glint at the tips, if you looked closely, the flash of a needle that could crunch through bones and penetrate to the marrow. Under their laughter a thrumming sound, not quite musical but not quite mere noise, and the longer I stared the more the shapeless sounds took on outlines, defined themselves, by whom I was looking at: That one there, with the bleary laugh, a trumpet; the one with the thin sad face, banjo; the black-haired scarecrow with the rings, shrill strings. Bug Man's noise was louder and stronger than the rest, so I mistook him for the leader. Electric guitar, that would blast you flat to the ground if you got too close.

I reached out and touched his face. *Chit-chit*, said the bugs. He grunted, almost belched the crude shape of words, a caveman with a rotted tongue—but soon as all that *hrruh-hrruh-*

*mmmuhhhhh* shot through my head it became waves of sound, transformed radio waves, and then words precise and clear as pieces of glass glittering on the beach.

"I'm Joe," he said. "Happy birthday."

The others mumbled something in turn but I couldn't hear them properly just yet, only their noises that were almost but not quite trumpets and banjos and strings. The smell of fresh flesh wafted over me, and Joe the Bug Man stepped aside as someone in a ragged black fedora emerged from the trees, something swinging from his hand, and dropped a warm furry just-dead thing right at my feet. A possum, its neck neatly snapped.

My stomach gurgled and Fedora Man snorted, walking away. Dark drops fell on the carcass, *plink-plonk*, and Joe laughed, reached out to wipe the black drool from my mouth. "Go on. Eat."

I ate and ate and couldn't stop. Rich raw meat. Warm blood. Leftovers from God's refrigerator. When I looked up again, putting down the bones I'd been chewing to twigs to get at the marrow, they were all standing over me. The dark-haired one with the rings smiled.

"I'm Teresa," she said. Jerked her head toward a soft, bloated gaseous mass with a lone lamplike eye and ragged remnants of red hair. "That's Lillian. Remember her name, even if you don't remember mine."

Lillian, the chieftainess, though of course I didn't know that yet. Teresa was her second in command back then, already planning, scheming. They both watched me crunch another bone down to splinters, then Teresa smiled.

"Good girl," she said. "Now, time to earn your food."

Her fists caught me in the jaw, chest, gut, and when they all piled on me at once, my gang induction, all that meat came rocketing straight up again. Dry bony feet kicked me, squelching rotting ones, and Joe sat there watching it all happen. I crawled through a gap in the fists and feet, even one-armed it was better than tottering on legs that would never work properly again, and I rose up and punched Joe hard in the gut and he gasped, laughed harder, and hit me back more viciously than all the others. I hung on. Bones cracked, his and mine. They only pulled me off when we were both dizzy and spitting out mouthfuls of bilious dark blood, and even one-armed I'd passed my test so well that Teresa, then Lillian, beat me up again so I'd remember who was in charge. I couldn't move for three days. They brought me rabbit, squirrel, the dog-ends of deer. They'd been needing someone new who could really fight, they said, and didn't hide their surprise that the someone was me.

But there wasn't anyone to fight, not in the middle of nowhere in a former county park with only squirrels and deer and each other for company. They were the first gang for me, the only gang, and so I didn't question why we all stayed out here when other gangs routinely marauded in the poorer, unguarded human areas, the ones whose property taxes just couldn't float guard teams and electrified fences and infrared video security, it's like they all *want* to be attacked, too bad, so sad, why don't they all just quit their goddamned whining and move somewhere else?

"You broke six of my ribs," Joe told me, when I could stand and walk again; he said it nose-to-nose clenching my good arm hard enough to snap but there was admiration in his eyes, that little hiss in his voice that someone gets when you're not at all what they expected, when they realize they're not gonna get what they want without a fight and they like it. That singular sound of: *Damn, woman.* "Six. You stomped me like a fucking cardboard box."

"I'm hungry," I told him, and there wasn't any whining in my voice, no please-feed-me, just a hard flat-out demand for what I required. He liked demands, I could tell already. Hearing them, issuing them. "I'm always hungry."

"You're supposed to be."

He pulled me aside from the group, from everyone smirking at us both. Florian, the walking skeleton with the watery blue eyes, he was the only other one of them I liked. "It's time you learn to hunt," Joe said. "I'll show you how. Lillian's a shit hunter, don't let her tell you anything. You'll be good at it. Put some of that crazy to use."

Plenty to hunt. Plenty to hunt far outside our attenuated neck of the woods. Plenty of low-hanging two-legged fruit rotting on the vine in Gary and East Chicago and South Chicago and parts of Hammond and Whiting, plenty of what I kept being told, over and over again, secondhand, have heard, they say, everybody knows, is the only real meat. But turns out, I didn't want brains, I didn't need hoos; meat was meat, any fresh kill would do, and it did for all of us, for all their talk.

"So just what the hell are we looking for?" I asked Joe on our first watch patrol together at the wood's very edge, sitting side by side against a tree trunk, not watching anything but the wind kicking up the dry dead stalks of a neighboring cornfield gone to weeds. "There's nobody here. There's never anybody, Ben said, nothing but feral cats and every now and then a crazy-ass bum—"

"Do they still go around saying you can shoot us?" Joe interrupted, squinting into the painfully blue sky. High noon, the whole rest of the gang deep asleep. "Guns don't work. Not pistols, not machine guns, not automatic rifles, never be afraid of any little hoo who comes at you waving a gun—"

"So Sam said." I'd started liking Sam too, not half so worn out and dusty as Florian but with so much wearier, sadder eyes. "But they don't say that anymore. Didn't."

"Fire. That's it. Or a good stomp to the head, till your skull's kicked in." He folded his arms, a little humorous glint in his eye. "Like a flattened cardboard box. Otherwise you'll just crumble to dust, whenever it's your time. Stomping, or fire. Ever seen a crazy hoo-vigilante wandering around the woods with a flame-thrower, thinking he's gonna toast our collective asses once and for all?"

"So what would we do then?" They don't go for controlled rural burns anymore, once they realized all that does is send the surviving "hazards" crowding closer and closer to hoo-territory. Gotta eat. Of course, hell with what the government does or doesn't do, all it takes is one crazy redneck with a book of matches. It's just been sheer luck. "By the time we see him, already too late."

"What do we do then?" Joe chuckled, still gazing up at the sky. "Mostly we die. But at least we die knowing who got us, and we don't die alone." He raked one leather-jacketed shoulder against the tree bark, working away at the ceaseless bug-itch of his own rotten skin. "Died alone once. I'm not doing it again." He turned to look at me, narrow dark eyes staring from a seething feeding sea. "Never. Ever."

I stared back, watching the perpetual movement of his skin as the maggots and flies crawled around and into every niche of flesh, made the worn creased jacket sleeves wriggle all of their own accord. Dead? Bursting with life, literally, all the life you could possibly want, that d-word applied to any of us was so ludicrous and willfully oblivious and just plain bigoted and how old and aged was Joe, anyway? Not by hoo-measure, but by our own lights? He'd said he died sometime in the fifties but couldn't remember just when. I'd forget too, he said, in time.

"I don't want to die alone either," I said. "Again."

Joe just laughed and shook his head. "Not a larva on her yet, and she's already hand-wringing—you have any idea how many decades Florian's got on you? Sam? You're a goddamned baby. You're so young."

"And you're not so damned old either," I said. Asked. Worried. "However much you brag." Silence. "Right?"

His eyes were adrift and lost in his own face, that whole ocean of insect life; I had to look that much harder at him to read his expressions, gauge his mood. Keep my attention on him constantly. If it had been me I'd have been creeped out, someone staring at me all the time like that, watching every last thing I do. Joe, he didn't mind.

"I'm not so old," he said, softly. Then he grinned. "And I can't drop even if I wanted to, now I've got a goddamned diaper-shitting baby to feed—"

I hit him, and he laughed again and louder and we wrestled until I shrieked for my arm, not my good arm, goddammit. The sky was pure cloudless blue that whole afternoon and the sun pressed in hard on dark-loving undead eyes but it was still beautiful, the sky, the woods, even that ratty old cornfield, all ours.

What the hell were we looking for? He never did answer that question. Him or anyone else.

They were the first gang, the only gang for me. Lingering out here in the middle of nowhere, years and years, shy kids at the perimeter of the playground, hiding and skulking when there was not a thing to hide from, there had to be a reason for that, it had to be some sort of deliberate strategy, I thought. It couldn't be that some of them stayed out here because it was easy. Because they really had been big noises in faster, stronger, more aggressive gangs, but they'd washed out or been thrown out or left thinking they'd be king hoo-killers all on their own, crowned and canonized, and it never happened.

Because they were old, some of them, older and dustier than they liked to say. Because they were young, and hiding was easier. Because they just didn't care for killing, not really, not once the hunger that never really left you got put in its place up on the shelf for another few hours, and that was a shameful thing even fleetingly to think so they just kept very quiet.

And then there was me. And now that I knew I could fight and that it wasn't hard to hunt I could have left any time, kept to myself for years or decades and avoided all the trouble that came after. I stayed because of Joe—his smile, the loud pounding music in his head, the way he hit right back and looked at me afterward with shrewdness, new respect, and then something more. Every time. What would repulse any sane human, the bugs, the smell, the casual brutality, the gleeful killing, meant less than nothing to me now. Even knowing then and later that I should have collected my strength and wits, turned around and left for good, no looking back. I stayed because of him.

Like I said, I was fifteen.

# HUNGRY FOR FRESH

## BLOOD ?

Then come and join us at
**www.facebook.com/BerkleyUK**,
where we're dedicated to keeping you
fully up to date on all of our SF, fantasy
and supernatural fiction releases.

- Author Q&As
- Exclusive cover reveals
- Exclusive competitions
- Advance readers' copies
- Guest blogs from our authors
- Excellent reading recommendations

BERKLEY UK
PENGUIN

And we'd love to hear from you, email
us at **berkleyuk@uk.penguingroup.com**